Praise for Mons Kallentoft

"The latest hot Swedish import."

—*Entertainment Weekly*

"A splendid representative of the Swedish crime novel, in all its elegance and eeriness."

—*Booklist,* starred review of *Midwinter Blood*

"The highest suspense."

—Camilla Lackberg, internationally bestselling author of *The Ice Child*

"Kallentoft is gifted. . . . He has a knack for characterization and describing the slow burn of police work."

—*The Age* (Australia)

"Kallentoft writes vividly and harshly."

—*The Washington Times*

"Edgy."

—*Library Journal*

"One of the best-realized female heroines I've read by a male writer."

—*The Guardian* (UK) on the Malin Fors series

"One of those books that will keep you up throughout the night. . . . Make room on your shelf—and calendar—for this one."

—Bookreporter.com on *Autumn Killing*

"Evocative, atmospheric, ingenious."

—*Kirkus Reviews* on *Summer Death*

"A sizzling, heart-pounding murder mystery and a masterful work of literary fiction with a compelling female character at its center."

—*The Paramus Post* on *Summer Death*

"Gritty. . . . Utterly convincing."

—*Publishers Weekly*, starred review of *Summer Death*

ALSO BY MONS KALLENTOFT

Midwinter Blood

Summer Death

Autumn Killing

Spring Remains

ALSO BY MARKUS LUTTEMAN

El Choco

Exposed

Patrik Sjöberg (coauthor)

Per Holknekt 1960–2014: A Biography (coauthor)

Blood Moon

ZACK

A Thriller

Mons Kallentoft

and

Markus Lutteman

Translated by Neil Smith

EMILY BESTLER BOOKS

WASHINGTON SQUARE PRESS

NEW YORK LONDON TORONTO SYDNEY NEW DELHI

WASHINGTON
SQUARE PRESS

An Imprint of Simon & Schuster, Inc.
1230 Avenue of the Americas
New York, NY 10020

First Emily Bestler Books/Washington Square Press trade paperback edition January 2018

EMILY BESTLER BOOKS / WASHINGTON SQUARE PRESS and colophon are trademarks of Simon & Schuster, Inc.

For information about special discounts for bulk purchases, please contact Simon & Schuster Special Sales at 1-866-506-1949 or business@simonandschuster.com.

The Simon & Schuster Speakers Bureau can bring authors to your live event. For more information, or to book an event, contact the Simon & Schuster Speakers Bureau at 1-866-248-3049 or visit our website at www.simonspeakers.com.

Interior design by Kyoko Watanabe

Manufactured in the United States of America

10 9 8 7 6 5 4 3 2 1

Library of Congress Cataloging-in-Publication Data

Names: Kallentoft, Mons, 1968– author. | Lutteman, Markus, author. | Smith,Neil, 1964– translator.
Title: Zack : a thriller / by Mons Kallentoft and Markus Lutteman ; translated by Neil Smith. Other titles: Zack. English. Description: First Washington Square Press paperback edition. | New York : Emily Bestler Books / Atria, 2018.
Identifiers: LCCN 2017012581 (print) | LCCN 2017026999 (ebook) | ISBN 9781476788159 (Ebook) | ISBN 9781476788135 (trade pbk. original)
Subjects: LCSH: Police—Sweden—Stockholm—Fiction. | Murder—Investigation—Fiction. | GSAFD: Mystery fiction. Classification: LCC PT9877.21.A48 (ebook) | LCC PT9877.21.A48 Z3313 2018 (print) | DDC 839.73/8—dc23
LC record available at https://lccn.loc.gov/2017012581

ISBN 978-1-4767-8813-5
ISBN 978-1-4767-8815-9 (ebook)

Who will fetch the man-eating mares?
Who will slay Diomedes, the Thracian king?
Who will rescue the innocent?
Our hero, our hero, our hero.

Prologue

1999

THE TWELVE-YEAR-OLD boy is lying on his back in the wild grass, breathing heavily.

The August night is dark and warm.

The iron-tainted smell of fresh blood mixes with the flowers in the meadow, and he looks at the vast sky with big, wide-awake eyes.

The whole sky seems to be full of shimmering dots. Even within celestial bodies like Ursa Major, Cassiopeia, and Orion, there are masses of other smaller stars fighting for space. There's a long stripe across the sky where the stars are so tightly concentrated that they form a white fog.

The Milky Way.

The boy's middle-school teacher once said that the sun is just an insignificant dot on the edge of the Milky Way galaxy. And if the sun was just an insignificant dot, what did that make the Earth? A grain of sand, barely worth even noticing.

It had been difficult to take in. It was like nothing you ever did mattered.

Now, as the boy lies in the meadow staring up at incomprehensible infinity, he wishes that were the case. That nothing really mattered. That what happened this evening could just disappear into the galaxy's vast maelstrom of things that don't matter.

The other person is lying just a few yards away in the tall grass. The boy doesn't dare turn his head and look.

He coughs, feeling the pain in his ribs. The damp is starting to seep through his T-shirt, and he is suddenly aware of the loud chirruping of the crickets. He doesn't like the sound. It's like they're telling tales:

"He's here! We can see him!"

The boy knows he can't lie here any longer. He needs to move. But he's so incredibly tired.

He can feel his body being pressed into the ground, as if the world were accelerating. The stars are getting closer. The white streak of the Milky Way is growing clearer, as are the hideous faces hidden in the dark gaps in the space dust.

Just take me away from here. Out into space. Out into the vastness of forgetting.

PART I

About how the forgotten are destroyed,

How hungry jaws open,

And how those still living scream in the underworld.

1

STOCKHOLM 2014

THE HEAT in the old shipyard is almost unbearable.

Spilled oil sticks to people's shoes on the crowded dance floor, and the air is almost too humid for sweat to escape.

There are no windows, no one knows that the morning sun has started to light up the shabby brick walls. There is no closing time here, no last orders at the bar. The organizer keeps going for as long as he thinks it's worth it—or until the police show up. It's an ordinary Sunday night in the middle of June, but Stockholm's nocturnal angels are beating their wings like never before.

The DJ slowly builds up the intensity and the speed of the bass gets faster. The dance floor responds with a cheer and the temperature inside the old assembly hall rises still higher.

A young man close to the center of the dance floor has stripped his top off. He's dancing with the self-confidence of someone who doesn't care what anyone else thinks. Some of his blond hair is stuck to the sweat on his forehead, and as he brushes it away the gesture is watched by a number of women. They scan his face, then move lower to his smooth athletic, naked torso. And like what they see.

Two women make repeated attempts to get eye contact with him. They're in their twenties, one has a straight blond bob, the other long dark hair. They're both wearing tight dresses that stop at the top of their thighs.

They're whispering to each other, describing the way he looks as though he were a god, with his full lips and straight, prominent nose. Like the hero in some old-fashioned book for girls, or an ancient Greek drama. He glances briefly back at them. Nothing more. All he wants to do right now is dance. Surrender his body to the rhythmic looping music and free his soul from all thought and feeling.

He takes a swig from the bottle of beer clutched in his hand, looks around. Suddenly his face cracks into a broad smile and his eyes light up. He takes a few steps forward and stumbles over a cable, but regains his balance and heads toward the dark-haired woman. For a few brief seconds she seems to be wondering what to say to him, then she gets pushed aside by a thickset man in a black vest forcing his way past her from behind. The two men raise their right arms in the air and their palms meet in a powerful slap. They embrace, and the thickset man says something into the blond man's ear. He nods in response and they push their way off the dance floor.

THE MEN'S rooms stink of piss from the rusty trough of the urinal, and the tiled walls are covered with tags and stickers advertising underground clubs and obscure websites.

The door closes behind them and the noise is muffled to such an extent that they no longer have to shout in each other's ears. The bare-chested man grabs hold of his friend's huge shoulders and gives him a gentle shake.

"Fuck, Abdula, it's good to see you! I was starting to think you were never going to show up."

"Oh, you know, had some things to do."

"At this time of day?"

Zack looks at his watch. Three thirty-five.

"You're working late."

Abdula smiles.

"Whatever it takes to get good stuff for my friend."

He opens the door to one of the three cubicles and makes a theatrically low bow.

"After you, Monsieur Herry."

The toilet lid is covered with little scratches from razor blades and other sharp objects. Abdula empties a small transparent bag and chops the contents up with a Visa card from Nordea Bank. Zack can't help looking at the card as the cocaine is cut.

"KHAN, ABDULAH," it says below the sixteen digits.

He knows that his friend actually spells his name differently, but the Tax Office managed to get both names wrong when the Kahn family arrived in Sweden in 1993. Years later Abdula tried to get them to correct their mistake, which they were prepared to do—for several thousand kronor. Abdula chose to carry on having his name misspelled.

"There you go. Dig in!" he says, passing a thick pink straw to Zack.

Zack looks at his friend in surprise.

"What the fuck's this? Have you started snorting coke with straws from McDonald's?"

"Not McDonald's. Theirs are too long and thin. This one's from the new milk-shake place at Hornstull. They're a bit too long, so I cut them in half. Then they're the perfect size."

"Yeah, but what the fuck, why use straws at all? Pink ones, at that?! What happened to the chrome tube you had in that gorgeous little case?" Zack asks, with sarcastic stress on the word *gorgeous*.

"The cops, you know. If you've got something like that in your pocket, they go ballistic at once, even if you're completely clean."

"Yeah, yeah. Give it here, then," Zack says, snatching the straw.

He lowers his nose to it and inhales sharply as he moves the straw along the line.

They sit on the cramped cubicle floor next to the toilet for a while, just looking at each other as they wait for the cocaine to kick in.

Thoughts become focused again. Vision gets clearer. Everything's fine. Everything's great. The world has sharply chiseled edges.

Zack looks into Abdula's eyes. He knows plenty of people, but only has one real friend. And they've been through a hell of a lot together. Years of madness, hardship, and constant struggle. And love, brotherly love.

I'd take a bullet for you, Zack thinks.

He feels his chest lurch at the thought. Abdula meets his gaze and it's as if he can read his friend's mind. He nods gently back at him.

BACK ON the dance floor. There's hardly any oxygen left in the hot, sticky air. The boundary between agony and ecstasy is slowly dissolving.

The monotonous beat is driving Zack crazy. Crazy in a good way. His chest is dripping with sweat and his blond hair is getting curlier in the humid air. Two girls are dancing right next to them. The blonde and the brunette. Shoulder bumping against shoulder. Thigh against thigh. The music is pumping. Another visit to the toilet. Four people squeezed into the cubicle. The Visa card like a woodpecker on the toilet lid. The girls giggle. Take the first lines. Their low-cut tops hide virtually nothing as they bend over. They toss their heads back, their hair flying, and instinctively put their hands to their nostrils. Straighten up. Bodies pressed tightly in the cramped space. Lips meeting. Tongues.

"DID HE use his tongue when he kissed you?"

The three Asian women are giggling in delight on the shabby sofa in the living room of the apartment out in one of the mass-housing projects in Hallonbergen. The Mekong whiskey has had the usual effect. The atmosphere is considerably lighter now.

"What a question! I'm not saying," says the young woman kneeling on a cushion on the other side of the coffee table, but her shy smile gives her away.

"But, Mi Mi, you're only eighteen," the oldest woman in the room says, pretending to be upset, and the other two women giggle again.

"Unless perhaps you were only seventeen when it happened?"

"No, I'd had my birthday. It was in October. October sixteen," she says, losing herself in the memory.

Four tea lights are floating in a dish of water on the table, spreading a shimmering glow over the terracotta-colored wallpaper. The room smells vaguely of coriander, chili, rice, and dried fish after the evening meal.

The rice whiskey on the table is starting to run out, as is the two-quart bottle of Coca-Cola. The last bag of chips is empty.

The women are tired, their bodies ache. They ought to get some sleep, but it's good to sit up late and just relax for a while. They talk almost exclusively about life back home, about the ongoing floods that have struck so many villages in their old home district, about the children living with grandparents.

But it hurts, talking about their children and families. They never feel farther from home than when they do that. It's nice to focus on an eighteen-year-old girl's romantic concerns instead.

Forty-three-year-old Daw Mya leans forward and refills her glass. A bit of Mekong at the bottom, then plenty of Coke. She turns to Mi Mi.

"Any more for the queen of tongue kissing?"

Mi Mi blushes and the others giggle loudly once again. She remembers the evening by the river. The way Yan Naing's body seemed simultaneously hard and soft. Warm as the night around them. His lips and tongue even warmer, as moist as the rain on the first days of the monsoon.

THE WOMEN'S laughter spreads through the summer night from the open living-room window. A lone man is marching with firm strides along the path below. He looks up briefly toward the window before taking a shortcut through the playground toward the door.

A broken swing is spinning slowly on its one remaining chain. On the rotting wooden frame of the sandbox there are fragments of green glass from a broken bottle.

The apartment block is large and unwelcoming, like a concrete bunker. One of a row of identical buildings. Beige brick façades, dark gray balconies. Satellite dishes everywhere.

The elevator is out of order, but he would have taken the stairs even if it had been working. Doesn't want to make more noise than necessary.

Somewhere a dog is barking. A bag of trash outside a door on the third floor spreads a smell of rotten fish through the stairwell. He goes up one more floor and stops outside a door on which someone has sprayed the words DEATH TO ALL NIGGERS in black paint. There's nothing else on it. No number, no name, just the gluey remnants of a torn-off nameplate on the mailbox.

He pushes the handle down cautiously, expecting it to be locked, but the door swings open.

The living room is hidden from the hall, but the women's chatter can be heard clearly through the doorway to his right. He sees flickering light on the wall, then a gilded Buddha on a shelf, surrounded by four tea lights in lilac candleholders.

Mi Mi stiffens when she sees the strange man step into the room with a pistol in his hand. She wants to scream but can't, and when she realizes that it's too late—that everything ends here—a rapid sequence of memories flashes through her head. Splashing and laughter as she swims in the Gyaing River with her cousin Myat Noe, her first trip to the big market in Pa-an, the rain on the day of her exams, Grandma's wrinkled hands in her hair, Yan Naing's hands on her body, and his friendly, hungry eyes, the look she wants to remember forever. And then the light of the street lamps flickering past the gap in the tarpaulin covering the back of the truck after she had said her tearful farewells to her family in the camp.

Farewell to Yan Naing.

It's so cramped and uncomfortable lying there with all those strangers. The lights flicker past faster and faster.

IN THE end the flickering light of the stroboscope gets to be too much. The lightness induced by the cocaine has faded and Zack can feel everything getting too close, bodies, sweat, desire. He says a quick good-bye to Abdula, then swerves elegantly through the dancing crowd and practically runs down the heavy old wooden staircase toward the big metal door. A bouncer with steroid-pumped biceps pulls it closed behind him and the noise finally shrinks to a muffled thud, and he suddenly finds himself in the middle of a dreamlike summer's morning.

Daylight, sunshine, birdsong.

He takes deep breaths of the fresh summer air, astonished at how beautiful the morning is and how alive the world feels. Then he starts to walk toward the city. A cool breeze from the sea caresses his face and bare chest, making the hairs on his arms stand up. Then he remembers that his top is still hanging on a railing back inside.

He hesitates for a moment. Should he go back and get it, force his way back into that boiling cauldron of sweat?

He looks up at the enormous building he has just left and suddenly feels very small. Huge, solid, and industrial, it looms above him in an almost eerily oppressive way. A remnant of a former age that refuses to surrender its pride. That refuses to recognize that there's no need for heavy industrial complexes at this latitude.

The large lettering on the wall has almost peeled off, but the outline is still legible.

HERALDUS.

Zack wonders why the powerful industrial conglomerate has left the building to stand derelict and decaying. As a memorial to a bygone era, perhaps? Or a monument to a failure that mustn't be forgotten? Maybe it was just an illustration of the company's fabled ability to change direction rapidly: okay, there's no more money to be had here. Let's pull down the shutters and move on to the next gold mine.

The muffled thud of the bass is making some windows toward the top of the building rattle. He wonders if the company's management knows that the old shipyard has been transformed into a sweaty underground club.

He turns around again and carries on toward the city. His T-shirt can stay where it is.

Thin strands of steam rise from the tarmac as it heats up in the morning sunlight. The water lies motionless beyond the reeds. On the other side of the inlet there are huge houses, row upon row of them. Luxurious new buildings with panoramic windows facing the water. Old stone buildings that look like manor houses, with heavy pillars holding up the roofs above their doorways. Overblown white motorboats moored at private jetties.

Who lives like that? he thinks. Rock stars? Hockey players who've moved back home from Canada?

No, probably people with real power. Rich families with generations of greed and ruthlessness behind them. The sort who would have done business with the Nazis, like the Wallenbergs.

Damn.

Eight minutes later he's sitting in the back of a taxi, resting his forehead wearily against the window. The sound of the tires on the tarmac is soporific.

A couple of police cars go past in the opposite direction. A succession of unimaginative apartment blocks flickers past, as tightly packed as those bodies on the dance floor. Like the buildings where he grew up. Places that seemed to be built for gray anonymity. For people who don't belong.

People who just have to be stored somewhere.

People kept in the dark.

Like him and his dad.

He had been six years old when they moved out to Bredäng from Kungsholmen in the city center. He remembers how his dad had done his best to make the whole thing sound exciting, telling him that they were going to live right at the top of a big building, and would be able to see for miles.

"Even the stars will seem closer," he had said. "And you're going to have so many new friends."

Zack had been beaten up out in the yard on the second day. He lied and said he'd been hit on the nose by a football. Then he had asked:

"Dad, why did we move here?" even though he already knew the answer.

Because Mom was dead.

He remembers how his dad had tried to explain. Talking about money. Zack didn't understand it all at the time, but enough of it. They had a lot less money now, and that meant they could no longer live in the center of the city.

Only people who were rich were allowed to live there.

The concrete is replaced by vegetation again, woodland on both sides of the road now, the water visible through the trees on the right. Out onto Highway 222, so empty at this time of day it feels almost unreal. Into Kvarnholmen, looping around Henriksdalsringen's monumental apartment blocks up on their hill. Across the bridge to Södermalm. Past the quay where the Finland ferries lie ready to receive their next cargo of passengers eager to enjoy the fake luxury and the opportunity to be unfaithful to their partners. Past the junction at Slussen, then along Skeppsbron in Gamla Stan. Shimmering water everywhere. The view toward the island of Skeppsholmen, its buildings clambering out of the rocks, is like a strange mirage from another time.

The taxi has the streets to itself and the city center goes past in a flash. Into the smart district now, Östermalm. Heavy stone buildings, old money, power passed down through the generations. Zack's stomach clenches slightly, the way it always does when he's here.

The taxi swings into a cul-de-sac close to Humlegården and stops outside a smart white four-story building from the turn of the century, with stone walls and a black iron gate. Zack hands over some crumpled hundred-kronor notes to the driver and jumps out. The black metal gate swings open without a sound. He closes it behind him, follows the path across the neat lawn, and opens the heavy oak door. It never ceases to amaze him that there is no coded lock on the building.

"That's because there are mostly diplomatic offices here," she always replies. "It would make things too complicated."

But still. What a paradise for the homeless. Especially in the winter.

Occasionally he toys with the idea of spreading a rumor, so that the suited men with their briefcases have to climb over sleeping drunks and zigzag between pools of vomit and piss when they go to work each morning. It would do them good.

He opens the gate of the old Asea elevator and sits down on the green leather seat as he is carried up to the sixth floor right at the top of the building. There are only two doors up there. One leads to the attic. He rings the doorbell on the other one.

A woman of about thirty, with tousled hair, steel-rimmed glasses, and a thin, black silk dressing gown opens the door.

Mera Leosson.

Her sharp cheekbones stand out clearly against the whitewashed walls of the hall, and she tilts her head slightly as she studies his face with a confident eye.

She walks up to him and gives him an intense kiss that she concludes with a little bite of his lower lip. Then she takes his hand and leads him through the spacious white hall, where works of art by Americans like Richard Aldrich, Justin Lieberman, and Gerald Davis fight for attention. Zack likes Davis's mad tableaux, mirrors for all the desires that can exist inside a person. And he knows how proud Mera is of the paintings.

They go through the large sitting room with its tasteful mixture of eighteenth-century furniture and modern Danish design, with more contemporary art on the walls, and into the bedroom with its vast, bespoke, handmade bed that cost roughly twice what Zack earns in a year.

Mera takes her glasses off, opens her dressing gown, and pushes him backward onto the bed.

HER HEAD hits the floor with a bang. Half of Mi Mi's face is gone and the woman next to her can no longer scream because her mouth is full of fragments of brain tissue.

The man pulls the trigger again. The silencer makes the shot sound more like someone hitting a punching bag than a bullet firing, and he feels the pistol jerk as another woman flies backward when the bullet hits her high in the chest.

Two of the women are lying on the floor now. A third has ended up halfway off the sofa with her legs at an odd angle.

Only one left now.

The oldest hag.

Does she even know how filthy she is?

And the noise she's making! Bitches shouldn't make a fuss. Women are always like that, all women, chattering and babbling, wanting attention, and sometimes you have to let them have it, even if you're only pretending.

But not here.

Not now.

The filth is going to be swept away here, and silence will reign.

She carries on screaming a load of words he doesn't understand, looks at him, and clasps her hands together, shaking them in front of her as if in ecstatic prayer.

Like that's going to help.

SHE'S LYING on her back as he traces his way over her with his tongue, with all of his fingers, and her skin is warm and moist with sweat.

He closes his eyes. Uses his other senses, feels her tiniest muscles cramping, and he likes the fact that he can bring her to this, that she can take him to this place, this moment, that belongs to them alone.

He rolls her over onto her stomach.

Kisses the back of her neck.

Spreads her legs.

Pushes deep into her heat.

But that's too gentle for her.

She thrusts herself back. Bouncing herself off him. Harder. Then harder still.

Until it hurts.

But Mera wants it like that. Wants it to hurt, until everything becomes a glowing, fluid now with no real boundaries.

She screams out loud as the first wave washes over her. Zack is supporting himself on his arms, his hands and fingers splayed out on the silk sheet. He pushes her down. Thrusting hard. He's getting close now as well.

Their bodies slap against each other.

He shuts his eyes.

No.

Not again. He doesn't want to see those images in his mind, not now.

He can see her fair hair and black-and-white face in the photographs as she's lying on the ground. The gaping black opening just under the tip of her chin.

The bloody knife lunging through the air, the last bullet whining, drooling wolves' jaws hunting through the darkness. Everything explodes.

Then it's over.

But it's never over. The darkness is never over. The light that was once there, in his mom's blond hair, no longer exists.

He can see a smiling woman looking up at him with clear eyes.

He lies down beside her. Breathes out.

She twines one of her long legs around him and whispers in his ear:

"Zack Herry. Zack Herry. Zack Herry."

2

THE HUGE, concrete monstrosity on Kungsholmsgatan stares down at Zack reproachfully.

A vast building, in various shades of gray. Almost scornfully ugly. As if it had been designed by a sadistic architect, with the express purpose of tormenting future passersby with its imposing ugliness.

Like a prison, he thinks. Not just for the people locked up inside, but for everyone.

People get shut away in there, imprisoned in their careers. Their profession becomes a drug. They hate it, but they can't get out of it. They've got nowhere else to go.

The fabric of the tight hooded jacket strains as he runs his hands through his hair. Mera's top. White with a pink pattern, and at least three sizes too small. He's guessing that it broadcasts the fact that he's had a quickie from quite some distance.

But who cares?

He yawns so widely that his jawbone creaks, as he pushes through the door to the headquarters of the Norrmalm police. The cool summer air is instantly replaced by something stagnant and rotten. Monday air. Behind the bulletproof glass at the other end of the lobby a row of police officers sit side by side. A woman in her forties says good morning and smiles at him with warmth in her eyes, and looks embarrassed when he smiles back. But in the men's eyes there's nothing but coldness. Zack is younger than them, but he's already progressed considerably further.

He holds his magnetic card to the door and steps inside the air lock. The linoleum floor is worn, the plaster tiles on the ceiling stained. An environment tainted by indifference and a chronic lack of money.

In the cramped, windowless changing room he squeezes out of the hooded jacket. He notices the label, Juicy Couture, before hanging it up in his battered blue locker. He has no idea what it cost, but guesses that it was expensive. Mera doesn't have many items of clothing that cost less than a thousand kronor.

She earns almost four times as much as him. But she still makes out that her salary is nowhere near what it should be. She's aiming high, wants more of everything.

Her father, Allan Bergenskjöld, runs one of the big supermarkets, ICA Maxi, out in Nacka, and earns millions every year.

He's proud of her, and Zack knows he would probably never have been accepted as her boyfriend if it hadn't been for the two men from Alby who, high on Xanor, tried to rob the store one spring evening two years ago.

Zack and his colleague Benny Christiansen had just left the scene of a traffic accident nearby when they got a call about shots being fired inside ICA Maxi.

The first thing they saw when they entered the premises was a young employee lying on the floor by the meat counter, shot in the shoulder.

Then they heard a pain-filled scream from the office.

Zack had quickly crept closer.

Heard agitated voices from within.

"Open the safe, you old fucker. Otherwise we break the next finger!"

Zack had seen the tall, slim Allan Bergenskjöld kneeling in front of a wall safe.

He had begun to enter the six-digit code with trembling hands as the robbers waited impatiently behind him. Two men in balaclava helmets. One with a Glock in his hand.

"For fuck's sake, get a move on!"

Zack started with the man with the pistol. Kicked him so hard in the side of the head that he crashed into a bookcase full of accounts files and collapsed in a heap.

The second man turned around, astonished, as the heavy sole of Zack's left boot hit him in the mouth.

He landed on the coffee-stained carpet in front of Allan Bergenskjöld. He started yelling and tried to get to his feet, but Zack hit him in the face, laid him out facedown, and cuffed him.

Allan Bergenskjöld had sat quietly, watching with fascination as Zack calmly and methodically searched the robber. He barely seemed to have noticed that Benny had come in and handcuffed the man who was lying unconscious among the files.

At the fancy dinner Allan Bergenskjöld later held to thank Zack out at his huge villa in Djursholm—"a glass of wine and a bite to eat," as he put it—Zack had been partnered with Mera for dinner.

He had felt a certain resistance to her at first. Too rich, too well dressed, too cool.

Too different to him.

And yet somehow not.

He himself is capable of a coolness that frightens him, the origins of which he can't help wondering about.

He had taken it for granted that she lived well off her father's money. But as the evening progressed he had been forced to rethink his opinion of her.

She did, admittedly, live in an apartment in a building owned by Allan Bergenskjöld, but she had built up her career on her own. Mera refused to follow in her father's footsteps, and had even adopted her mother's maiden name to avoid accusations of using her father's name to open doors for her. She was strong and independent, and kept challenging Zack with her sharp mind.

They had met again the following evening, and almost a week passed before Zack returned to his own flat. He smiles at the memory as he pulls on a white V-neck cotton top from his locker, where it was hanging between a leather jacket and pair of Acne jeans.

He slings the jacket over his shoulder.

Mera gave it to him on his twenty-seventh birthday, and he is very fond of it. Fitted, black, fashionably scruffy. He had never heard of the brand, Rick Owens. Then he found out by accident that it had cost twenty-two thousand kronor, and didn't dare wear it for several weeks. Now he rarely wears anything else, on or off duty. The jacket is just the right size to conceal his holster.

HE GETS into the elevator and presses the button for the sixth floor. He leans against the wall of the elevator and closes his eyes. He feels a passing wave of nausea as it stops. He holds his passcard against another magnetic lock. Above the box there is a discreet white sign with black lettering.

SPECIAL CRIMES UNIT.

The open-plan office spreads out in front of him. The ventilation is better here than in reception, the ceiling is higher and the computer screens newer. The desktops, matte-varnished pale birch, can be raised and lowered. New black office chairs with comfortable backs made of woven leather. Windows with a view of green treetops instead of a paved inner courtyard.

Zack sees Niklas Svensson from behind as he disappears around the corner. Otherwise the office is empty. He goes over to the coffeemaker and makes his selection. First espresso. Then ordinary black coffee, extra strong. All in the same mug.

He hopes it helps.

In the meeting room the core team is already in place. Niklas Svensson, Deniz Akin, Sirpa Hemälainen, and Rudolf Gräns. They're all sitting in their usual places around the oval table, but for some reason Zack thinks they're looking at him in an odd way.

As if they know what he was doing last night.

"Good morning," he says curtly, and sits down next to Deniz.

SHE GLANCES up from her phone with a look that suggests that it seems to be anything but a good morning for him.

"Everything okay, Zack?" she asks, looking at him for several seconds before evidently concluding that things are more or less okay and continuing to scroll through some news headlines.

"Fine," he says, glancing at the others.

Sirpa is staring at her phone as well, while Rudolf and Niklas are quietly discussing some big police operation last night.

"Eight patrols, and the rapid response unit," Niklas says. "Almost like the good old days of proper raves."

"So where was it, exactly?" Rudolf asks, adjusting his dark glasses.

"In some old warehouse. Owned by Heraldus, evidently. Likely to be a big fuss in the media, I'd guess," Niklas says.

Zack remembers the peeling lettering on the old shipyard building and feels his anxiety move down his spine like cracks in winter ice.

Fuck. There'd been a raid at the club he'd been at? It must have happened right after he left. They couldn't have stayed open much longer than that, surely? But why? Things had been pretty well behaved last night. Someone must have talked, unless there was an undercover cop there?

Someone who would have seen him. And now everyone knows.

"They brought in fifteen people. Most of them have already been released, apparently," Niklas says.

Abdula? Did they get him? How much could he have had on him? Fuck. Fuck, fuck, fuck.

Zack feels like getting up and running out of the room to call his friend. But that wouldn't be good. Not now, not here, and not from this cell.

He tries to take a few calm deep breaths, to slow his pulse down. He turns to Niklas.

"When did this happen?" he asks in as neutral a voice as he can manage.

"Last night," Niklas says. "Or, rather, this morning. At five o'clock, if I heard right."

Niklas looks at Zack for a second or so too long.

"You get out and about a bit, Zack. Do you know about this place?"

Out and about. Just the sort of thing a respectable family man from Näsbyparken would say. Someone whose only recurrent worry is getting to preschool in time. Someone who hasn't even been to a pub in the past five years.

He forces himself to laugh politely.

"Well, illegal raves aren't really my thing. The bartenders at places like that tend to be pretty shit. Unless you have a taste for warm lager or high-energy drinks mixed with smuggled spirits."

Sirpa joins the conversation:

"I thought you might actually have been there last night. It looks to me like you're a bit short on sleep right now."

Sirpa, the computer genius. Straight to the point, as usual. Zack usually loves her unvarnished black humor, but right now it just makes him feel uncomfortable. *Is it that fucking obvious?* he wonders. Or has she heard something?

He smiles at her.

"I was lying in bed thinking of you, you know that."

"Poor you, having such terrible nightmares," she retorts, making everyone round the table laugh. Even Zack.

Douglas Juste comes into the room. The soles of his Carmina shoes hit the floor hard.

"Good morning!"

The formal note in Douglas's voice annoys Zack. The exaggerated politeness, as if he were saying hello to distant acquaintances rather than people he knows well.

Zack has never met anyone who so obviously inhabits the role of boss the way Douglas does. He could have been in charge of any publically listed conglomerate. Tall and energetic. Always freshly shaven. Always well dressed. His hair still free of gray at the age of forty-nine.

But Douglas can afford it. He comes from old money. Industrial money. His great-grandfather helped found a number of engineering companies in the Mälar Valley. Several of them are still going successfully, with factories in Lithuania, Poland, China, and Kenya.

Zack has never heard a decent explanation as to why Douglas is sitting in Police Headquarters rather than in some fancy director's office. "He wanted to go his own way," someone once said. "Rebelled against his father," was another suggestion.

One day I'll ask him myself, Zack thinks. Because there's something broken in there. Douglas is the kind of man who smiles with his mouth but not the rest of his face. A man whose prestigious relationships always go wrong.

But he worked with Mom before she died. And he always speaks well of her.

Douglas sits down at the end of the table closest to the door, runs his hand through his wavy blond hair, and adjusts his papers as he does the obligatory little cough that always precedes his opening phrase.

"I've been given unofficial assurances that our unit isn't going to be affected by the restructuring of National Crime. Not unexpected, admittedly, but still good to hear."

Douglas starts almost every meeting with a piece of news from above, preferably something that shows that he has a seat at the table during informal discussions at the very highest level.

"Yes, these constant reorganizations," Douglas sighs, and is rewarded with some murmurs of agreement.

Who gives a shit? Zack thinks. His head feels like it's about to explode with exhaustion and his thoughts are with Abdula, who could well be in custody.

What happened out at the shipyard? Did anyone recognize me?

He needs to forget about that for the time being. He has

to concentrate on Douglas as he moves on to the next item on the agenda.

"The verdicts on the weapons smugglers from Västerås have been delivered. You all remember them, I take it?"

The others nod. It was one of the unit's first cases. It had started when a total of fourteen very realistic replica Kalashnikovs had been found in various raids in different parts of the country within a short space of time. The police feared that a process of mass distribution of automatic weapons was under way, and the Special Crimes Unit had been given the task of locating the source and stemming the flow.

Zack and his colleagues eventually managed to trace the weapons back to an illegal factory in the countryside of northwest Pakistan. They also found a container with 173 automatic guns in Gothenburg harbor, and arrested the three individuals suspected of being primarily responsible for their import.

Zack had saved the lives of four Gothenburg police officers during the operation, and was given a medal for his efforts. He also ended up with a price on his head from an Islamic hate site, and since then his identity has been protected.

"As usual, the sentences are ridiculously short," Douglas goes on. "Six months, one year, and three years. That's not punishment, that's more like a pause for breath."

"Come on, what the hell? We won!" Deniz says. "We got the bastards. And now they're off the streets for a while and the smuggling route has been broken."

Deniz Akin, the complete opposite of Douglas Juste. Scruffy, blunt, and brutal. Nothing can stop her from getting ahead, away from where she comes from.

Zack looks at her. He and Deniz work together most of

the time, and he likes having her as his partner, even if he'd prefer to work alone. But he can't deny that they work well together. Trust each other, the way people can only do when they've faced danger together.

Deniz is thirty-five, and he thinks she's beautiful, with her long dark hair and that large tattoo on her upper right arm. A condor in flight above a large wave.

Sometimes Zack wonders if he should point out how unlikely an image that is. Condors fly many thousands of feet up in the Andes Mountains, not over the sea. But he likes her too much. Besides, if Deniz was a condor, she wouldn't care that she was supposed to stick to mountains. She'd break free and head down to the sea anyway.

Maybe that's what she had in mind when she got the tattoo?

Zack will never forget the rainy night during a fruitless stakeout last autumn when Deniz first opened up to him and told him a bit about her background.

About her escape from Kurdistan.

She was only twelve years old when she saw something she wasn't meant to see. Something she can never forget, no matter how much she might want to.

Deniz's best friend, Jasmina, was supposed to be marrying a cousin, which had all been arranged a long time before. But Jasmina had fallen in love with a boy from the next village, and rumor had it that the pair of them had been meeting in an abandoned barn.

The official cause of death was self-immolation. Jasmina had been unable to bear the shame, and had set fire to herself.

But Deniz knew the truth. She had been hiding behind some rocks, and watched as Jasmina's four brothers stood in a circle around her. She had seen them pour gasoline on her clothes, and had seen them light the match.

She fled that same night. She put her little brother on her back and ran.

It would have been quicker to go alone, but she wanted to save five-year-old Sarkawt as well. She didn't want him to grow up into the sort of young man who got a congratulatory slap on the back from the older men if he killed his own sister.

In the mountains they had been hunted by wolves. It had sounded as if the wild animals' howling had come from all directions at once as the echoes bounced between the dark mountainsides. They had taken refuge in a cave, pressing through a narrow crack that the wolves couldn't get through. They had sat there in the darkness all day and all night, while the wolves padded about outside, licking their lips hungrily.

She took to stealing things for the first time. Food and money. She got lifts with traveling salesmen, had to flee again, and eventually made contact with some well-disposed smugglers who were on their way to Greece. She had given them all the money she had, and they had been carried over six hundred miles on bumpy country roads.

It had been pitch-black when they reached the border. She carried Sarkawt on her back again as she crept through a minefield after the smugglers, and she had shielded his eyes to stop him seeing the swollen corpses of drowned migrants as they waded across the ice-cold river Evros at dawn.

Then the smugglers left them, and she found herself abandoned on Greek territory. No money, no food, and with a very hungry little boy clutching her hand.

Deniz has seen the very worst side of life, and knows that

it can literally be about eating or being eaten. Fighting or dying.

Zack wonders how she would react if she knew his secrets.

But perhaps she knows more than he thinks?

Keeping an eye on him, making sure he doesn't go too far.

Is that what's going on?

Douglas goes on talking about sentences and punishments, and mentions a few other criminals who are about to be released, two members of the Red and White Crew who are suspected of being behind an unsolved mutilation in Hall Prison.

"After serving an unreasonably lengthy sentence in the brutal Swedish justice system, these two deeply remorseful citizens will now do everything in their power to find their place as law-abiding members of Swedish society," Douglas says in a voice dripping with irony.

Zack is no longer listening. His eyes are stinging and his mind is working at top speed.

How long would Abdula have to serve if they caught him?

And what about me?

Deniz's impudent voice breaks into the conversation again, and something in her tone makes Zack drop his thoughts of Abdula and think about Mera instead. Her face earlier that morning, in the hall of her penthouse.

So different from Deniz, yet with certain similarities. They're both hardworking career women with sharp minds and sharper elbows. But while Deniz works with reality, Mera works with fiction, more or less. She's a PR consultant with her own business. She invents stories for companies to make people want to buy their products. *Corporate storytelling*. Making them empathize with yogurt.

Zack finds her ruthlessness sexy.

He can see her standing naked in front of him. Feel the warmth as he runs his fingers over her skin, her sweet scent as he breathes close to her, her taste. The way she likes it when he gets his handcuffs out. More than he does, actually.

"Bit shaky today, Zack?"

Douglas rouses him from his musings. He nods toward Zack's trembling right hand as it rests on the pale tabletop.

Zack hasn't even noticed it. Out of reflex he moves his hand to his thigh, out of sight of the others.

"No problem. I didn't sleep too well last night, that's all. The bedroom was too damn hot . . ." he says.

But Douglas doesn't look away. There's sympathy in his eyes, a sort of paternal look that irritates Zack. But it isn't just him. The whole damn table is looking at him, stripping him with their eyes.

What do they think of him? What do they know?

What if we get called in to work on the illegal club? But they're the Special Crimes Unit, so they shouldn't be involved. Unless some particularly ugly fish got caught in the net last night.

He looks at Sirpa. She'll manage to find out the names of every last bastard who was there if she's asked to. She'll find her way behind encryptions and fire walls to gather information. What will she do if she finds Zack's name in obscure places in the nocturnal jungle where off-duty police officers really shouldn't be?

And then there's Rudolf, the elder statesman, who seems to be staring at him through his big, black sunglasses, and Zack is suddenly worried the old man can read his mind.

The wall behind Rudolf seems to be slowly bulging into the room, and Zack gets a feeling that the wall behind is pressing toward him.

What the hell's going on?

He suddenly gets up from his chair, almost knocking his coffee over with one hand, excuses himself, and hurries out of the room.

He yanks open the door to the restroom and shuts and locks it behind him.

For a while he just sits there in the comforting, silent darkness. He leans against the wall, exhausted, but jumps when the hand dryer roars into action and blasts hot air on his right arm.

He fumbles for the light switch. The sharp glare makes him hold up his hand instinctively and jerk backward.

He takes a lurching step toward the washbasin, rests his hands on the cool surface, and sees pink and red spots dance before his eyes as he looks down at the gleaming porcelain. The dryer finally falls silent. He takes two deep breaths and then looks up at his reflection.

Not a pretty sight.

It's as if all pigmentation fled his skin during the early hours of the morning, and he seems to have aged a year for every hour he actually slept. He turns his head to see more of the whites of his eyes. They're almost pink today. His eye-drops have been fighting a hopeless battle against the effects of a lack of sleep.

He shuts his eyes again. Turns the tap on and rinses his face a few times. He takes another deep breath, leans closer to the mirror, and looks himself right in the eye.

Zack.

Pull yourself together.

Remember who you are.

For a moment he sees his face in a different mirror, in a different men's room, only a few hours ago. He hears the girls giggling, sees Abdula smiling behind his shoulder, feels the sting in his nose.

No. Look at yourself.

Detective Inspector Zack Herry. That's who you are. No one else.

Nothing else.

When he opens the door to the meeting room the conversation falls silent instantly. Everyone is looking at him.

They've been talking about me, he thinks. *About what I was doing last night.*

So say so, he thinks. *Don't just sit there.*

But he can't see any accusation in his boss's eyes. Only concern and sympathy.

Douglas turns to the others again.

"Well, as I was just saying. National Crime will be moving out of the second floor, and . . ."

Zack stops listening. Looks around at all the brilliant detectives in the room.

What the fuck am I doing here? he thinks.

He closes his eyes again and tries to focus.

We're a diverse bunch. And I'm the best among us.

But the words don't ring true.

A rapid knock on the door makes Zack jump so violently that Douglas gives him a questioning glance.

Internal Investigations, Zack thinks.

They've come to get me. It's over. Thank you and good-bye, coke-snorting cop.

Douglas's assistant sticks her head into the room and says in her warm, soft voice:

"There's a Mr. Westberg on the phone. He says it's extremely urgent."

Douglas pulls an irritated face.

"I can't talk right now, tell him I'll call back in fifteen minutes."

The assistant closes the door and Douglas clears his throat again.

"Well. Seeing as just for once we don't have an ongoing case to discuss, I suggest we take the opportunity to clear some of the backlog of paperwork."

He checks his list.

"Deniz, the aliens unit have been onto me regarding that old report about the Albanians. And, Niklas, you've got that report to finish about the Tindra kidnapping?'

They both nod and let out a quiet sigh.

Zack breathes out. The illegal club is going to be some other department's headache. But he still needs to find out what the raid was all about. And he has to get hold of a list of who was arrested.

"Rudolf, have you got anything you'd like to add?" Douglas wonders.

They almost always conclude like this. With Rudolf given the opportunity to add some comment or make a suggestion before they get up and leave the room.

Everyone falls silent and turns toward the sixty-three-year-old man in the sunglasses and loose, crumpled suit. He's sitting opposite Zack, leaning back in his chair with his hands clasped together in his lap.

"Thanks very much," he says in a calm, amiable voice, "but I haven't got anything of note to add. No doubt like the rest of my colleagues, I am busy considering the wise words about crime and punishment aired by the chair of today's meeting."

Zack glances at Douglas, smiling inside. A pinprick wrapped in cotton wool.

Typical Rudolf.

Rudolf suffered a minor stroke ten years ago and was left blind. Permanently condemned to a life of darkness.

His colleagues in the regional crime unit were extremely upset. But just as they were trying to think of a suitable leaving gift for their much-loved detective superintendent, Rudolf himself called to tell them he was planning to return to work the following week.

His bosses exchanged condescending glances. What did they want with a stumbling blind man in regional crime? Other police officers who got injured, had breakdowns, or otherwise ended up useless could always be put to work filing or sorting out case notes, but what could they do with Rudolf? A man who could no longer even see his own hands?

"I want to do my job, just as I've always done," he said. "There's nothing wrong with my hearing, nor with my brain. I'll need help from other people's eyes, that's true, but there are one or two detectives in this building who could use a bit of help from my brain in return."

The protests quickly died away.

Rudolf had always been good at deduction, but it was as if he could see connections even more clearly now that he could no longer use his eyes. As if he were better able to think outside normal parameters. Sometimes it seemed to Zack that he had an almost uncanny knack of identifying the way perpetrators thought and predicting their next move. As time went by, he was given the nickname "the Oracle."

When Zack and Rudolf started working in the same team Zack often forgot that his older colleague couldn't see. Sometimes he would ask Rudolf to come and look at a photograph or read something, and he felt like an idiot every time he realized his mistake.

But Rudolf never reacted badly. It was almost as if he appreciated the fact that Zack didn't get hung up on his disability.

Zack often wonders what Rudolf can see in his internal theater.

What can you see right now?

Are you looking at me, or are you staring into the very deepest darkness?

3

SUKAYANA PRIKON steps off the escalator, walks through the door, and feels the enclosed air of the shopping center hit her.

She feels stressed, just like the people walking in the opposite direction. But theirs is a different stress.

Not like hers.

Forty-five minutes have passed since she found Mi Mi's text message:

> Help us he kill all

She's tried calling ten times since then. She's tried the others as well. Their phones ring, but no one answers.

The text was sent at 2:47, and Sukayana Prikon curses herself for the hundredth time for having her cell switched off last night.

But why wouldn't it have been? It's always switched off at night, after all. She has to be able to get some sleep without those dirty men calling and disturbing her.

Almost every morning when she switches her phone back on there's someone who's left a message.

"I'm so horny, can't you get someone for me?" they slur in their 3 a.m. messages.

As if she ran some sort of escort agency.

Why don't they answer?

The shopping center has been designed to form a little square. To her left there's a bronze sculpture of five horses, and behind them an escalator to the floor above.

Was that the quickest way to get there? She can't remember, it's been so long since she was last here.

She half runs out to the bus station instead, breathing in the pleasant scent of herbs being unloaded from a van by a market trader. A little farther away a man with a white beard is hanging up a display of colorful kaftans.

She goes around the corner of the shopping center and follows the path up a steep slope. Beautiful greenery to her left, uninspiring apartment blocks up to her right.

She walks through the rows of identical buildings. Beige brick façades, gray walkways. She sees the number she's looking for above a doorway and runs across the shabby little play area.

A cold wind meets her as she walks into the shadow of the building, and she shivers uneasily. Her stomach clenches, and when she opens the front door her hands feel strangely stiff.

The elevator door is blocked by yellow-and-black striped tape and a sign with the words OUT OF ORDER on it. Her body feels heavy as she walks up the stairs, and by the time she reaches the fourth floor she's out of breath and her brow is sweating.

She stops outside the door of the flat and digs about in her handbag for the key, but just as she gets hold of the key ring she stops.

Help us

he kill all

She can hear something inside the flat.

Music.

Why?

They would never have forgotten to switch off the television or stereo before leaving for the massage parlor. Electricity costs money, and they're never wasteful.

She doesn't want to open the door.

But inserts the key and turns it.

Opens the door cautiously.

"Hello?"

No answer, just silence.

There's a faint smell of food in the flat, and for a moment she's sitting at home with her parents, watching Mom crush spices with her ancient mortar and pestle.

And she can smell something else. Something that reminds her of the market in Klong Toey.

A smell of iron. Like the smell of the stalls selling freshly butchered meat.

"Hello? Daw Mya? Mi Mi?"

A heavy weight settles in her stomach. She takes a cautious step into the hall and closes the door behind her. It clicks shut automatically, and she panics and quickly unlocks it again and leaves it ajar. Doesn't want to be locked in here.

The music falls silent and is replaced by a chirpy voice that she recognizes from one of the morning talk shows on television. Peter Jihde, maybe? She walks slowly into the living room.

It takes a moment for her brain to understand that the one-eyed lump of flesh sticking out of the silk pajamas is all that's left of a human face.

Then she sees the other three bodies. So bloody. So mutilated.

And it's as if she can no longer breathe, as if a huge fist has wrenched the air from her lungs and is pressing her down.

She falls to her knees. Whimpers and rocks her body

back and forth. Her hands clasp together in prayer and she can feel the spirits of the dead drifting around her, like an unquiet chill. Like the wind in the shadow of the building.

She wants to run.

Away.

Down the stairs.

Home.

But who can escape their fate? Who can do what she has done without one day being made to pay?

She takes out her cell.

Calls 112.

Then she leaves the flat behind her.

4

THEY TAKE the stairs two at a time. Aware that every second can make all the difference. Sixteen steps in each flight. Then a new floor. A quick turn to the right. Sixteen more steps.

This morning's tiredness has blown away. He hates the fact that the elevator is broken. But loves having to make an effort, feel his jeans strain around his thighs, the way the stairs are drawing every last bit of strength from his muscles.

Deniz is right behind him. He can hear her slightly labored breathing. She's in good shape, but not as good as him.

Third flight now.

There's a loud buzz of voices in several languages and Zack looks up to see a dozen or so people crowded onto the landing above them. A woman in a black hijab with pink beads around her eyes is weeping loudly, and is being comforted by a man with a thick black mustache, who's dressed in a sweater and neatly pressed brown woolen trousers.

The flight of steps leading to the last floor has been cordoned off.

Good. Quick work, Zack thinks. An overweight uniformed officer in his fifties is standing guard on the other side of the blue-and-white striped tape. Zack can see he's doing a good job. He's keeping his cool in spite of all the waving arms and shouted questions. He smiles amiably and keeps patiently repeating that he doesn't know what's happened, and that he can't let anyone through.

Zack and Deniz push their way through the crowd and hold their badges up to their colleague behind the cordon.

"Hi, Zack Herry, Special Crimes Unit. My colleague, Deniz Akin."

The policeman nods to them and lifts the cordon slightly.

"Go right ahead," he says. "But it's not a pretty sight."

THE DOOR to the flat is open and Zack and Deniz almost collide with two paramedics on their way out. Zack and Deniz say hello to them as they pull on protective blue shoe-covers.

They walk into the living room. Zack stops just inside the door.

Oh, God.

Holy fucking God.

If he does exist, he certainly isn't here.

Deniz pushes aside the arm he has instinctively raised to shield her. She goes over to one of the bodies and squats down to examine the injuries, but Zack remains standing in the doorway.

He can't make any sense of what he's seeing. As if he were looking at a surreal installation by an artist on the brink of a mental breakdown. An artist who loves red, and who's used several quarts of the color for this particular piece. As if the most grotesque of Francis Bacon's paintings has become reality.

The room is bathed in sunlight, which only exacerbates the sense of unreality. The bodies are lying at unnatural angles with their trousers pulled down and their genitals destroyed, and the room reeks of excrement and blood and urine.

Of death.

Of grass.

Damp grass and blood.

Black stars, and beyond them even blacker darkness.

Deeds that can never be undone.

No. Not now. Not here.

Zack shuts his eyes tight. He quickly puts a lid on his inner thoughts and looks around the room instead. The furnishing is minimal. Impersonal. No pictures on the walls, just a small pine shelf with some tea lights and a small brass Buddha. An apartment furnished by people who are only planning to live here for a short time.

There's a laptop computer on a simple birch veneer desk. A black Compaq that looks antiquated. On the screen a Skype invitation is flashing, with a picture of a smiling Thai family. An older woman, two children, a girl and a boy around ten years old, twins, perhaps.

Zack feels like going over and closing the lid, doesn't want the family on the screen to have to look out into this room. But he doesn't. Forensics can do that.

He hears a deep cough from Deniz and turns around. She stands up with her hand over her mouth. He can feel his own nausea from that morning coming back. He shivers. The shudder moves through his whole body and the hairs on his arms stand up.

Two forensics officers enter the flat carrying their cases. Zack doesn't recognize them.

"Where's Koltberg?" he asks.

Samuel Koltberg is regarded as the most talented forensics officer in Stockholm, and has therefore become closely linked with the Special Crimes Unit.

"On holiday in Mallorca. I think he's supposed to be flying home today," one of the technicians replies.

Good, Zack thinks. At least we don't have to deal with him today.

He looks over at the computer again, at the happily smiling girl, and the even more cheerful boy.

Is that your mom lying there?

ZACK LEAVES the living room and looks around the apartment. Two rooms plus the kitchen. There's a neatly made double bed in the bedroom, some white wardrobes, a chest of drawers made of pale wood, and two mattresses leaning against the wall.

He goes out onto the balcony and looks down at the grounds. His adrenaline is starting to give way to tiredness, and all he wants to do is lean his head against the cool railing and shut his eyes for a while. More police have arrived and are cordoning off an expanded area covering ten square yards around the entrance. Crowds of curious onlookers have gathered beyond the blue-and-white tape, and a little farther away a broken swing sways forlornly in the weak breeze.

A blue Volvo XC60 pulls into the yard. It stops a short distance from the cordon and Douglas gets out and adjusts his hair. He glances up at Zack and gives him a slight nod. Zack raises his hand and returns the greeting.

A mother walks into the play area with her daughter. A young blond woman, with an equally blond little girl.

Mother and daughter. Alive.

The girl rushes over to one of the swings and soon picks up speed with an energetic pendulum movement. Her mother glances anxiously toward the crowd, but the girl is bubbling with laughter, entirely unaware of what has happened to their neighbors.

More cars arrive. Men and women with cameras and notebooks jump out. Zack recognizes two of them from *Aftonbladet.*

Zack wonders when the media were last in Hallonbergen. In the aftermath of another murder? Or maybe a wave of break-ins. But they never bother to report on ordinary life here.

"Hey, Zack!"

He looks down but can't see the person calling.

"Zack, over here!"

A young man in a blue shirt and jacket is leaning out from a balcony on the same floor that Zack's on, but in the next stairwell. Fredrik Bylund from *Expressen.* A tenacious bastard. Spins his crime stories beyond recognition, but actually okay to deal with. Once he managed to provide them with some invaluable information for a case they were working on. Zack even managed to persuade him against publishing a story on one occasion. An extremely rare occurrence.

"Has this got anything to do with organized crime?" Fredrik Bylund shouts.

Zack thinks for a moment. Chooses his words carefully to avoid crazy quotations in the headlines.

"At this stage we're keeping an open mind," he says, aware that it makes him sound like one of Mera's PR trainees.

"So you're not ruling it out?"

A typical journalist's question, the answer to which can be spun any way at all.

"We're not ruling anything out."

Zack knows he hasn't given Bylund a thing, but he can still see the headline in front of him:

POLICE: ORGANIZED CRIME COULD BE BEHIND BLOODBATH

A red van from TV4 with an aerial on its roof rolls into the yard. It parks with one wheel up on the grass, more or less blocking in the ambulance that's parked in front of it. Three people jump out. A man in a patterned shirt runs over to the cordon while a bald cameraman begins setting up his tripod outside it in preparation for a live broadcast. The third person, a female reporter with long blond hair, is holding her cell mobile between her shoulder and her cheek as she scribbles down prompts for her piece to camera.

"Is it true that you've got four dead bodies in there?" Bylund calls.

Zack nods.

"All women?"

Zack nods again. That information will be public knowledge within an hour anyway.

"I need to go back in and do some work."

"Hang on, just a few more questions. How were they killed?"

Zack ignores Bylund and closes the door behind him. Deniz is wearing plastic gloves, and is kneeling down as she searches through the chest of drawers. She sticks her hand in and pulls out a white tube, which she inspects carefully.

"What's that?" Zack asks.

"Genital lubricant," Deniz says. "Helps keep things moisturized."

"So?" Zack says.

"Nothing, really, it's just that there's a whole box of it. There must be at least twenty tubes here. And there are several other disposable tubes of ointment for itching and genital infections."

"Maybe there was a sale at the drugstore?"

"A tube like this lasts ages. Either all four women had boyfriends they slept with ten times a day, or . . ."

"Or they were prostitutes," Zack concludes. "Which means we're dealing with pimps and johns and undeclared income."

"Exactly what I was thinking," Deniz says. "But we can't put too much store in that yet. There are no clothes in the wardrobes that suggest they were selling sex," she says. "Ordinary clothes, nothing particularly provocative."

She opens more drawers.

Stops abruptly. Frowns.

"But my suspicions have just got stronger," she says.

She beckons Zack over. He looks down in the drawer. A bumper box of condoms. Profile. Thin. Grande. Mixpack.

Douglas enters the room.

"How's it going?" he says.

"Have you been in the living room?" Zack asks.

"Yes. Very unpleasant sight. What do you think?"

Deniz shows him the contents of the chest of drawers, and explains her theory. Douglas nods.

"I'll make sure the prostitution unit gets brought in straightaway. Have you found any purses or ID papers?"

"Not yet. Judging by their appearance and taste in whiskey, I'd say they're from Thailand," Zack says. "And the fact that there are four of them living in an unfurnished flat suggests that they haven't been here very long."

"Or are here illegally," Douglas says.

"Human trafficking?" Deniz asks.

"One of many things we're going to have to look into. We've got to try to find out who raised the alarm. The caller asked to stay anonymous, which means we can't get hold of the number."

"What? But we've got four murders to solve," Deniz says.

"They'll fall back on confidentiality legislation. But naturally we'll put in a request for both the number and the recording of the call, and we'll probably get them in the end, but it might take some time. All we've got to go on for the time being is that the caller was female."

"So we don't know why she didn't stay until the police arrived?" Zack asks.

"No. And that's obviously very odd behavior."

"The call could have been made by the killer," Deniz says.

"Female mass murderers are extremely rare," Douglas says. "And people who raise the alarm about things they've done usually stay and wait for the police. But you might be right. Unless she's got other reasons for wanting to keep out of our way."

Keep out of the way.

Did you manage to do that last night, Abdula?

Zack excuses himself and goes out onto the balcony again. He looks for Bylund, but he's gone, so he gets out his private pay-as-you-go cell and calls Abdula.

In the background the little girl is still swinging up toward the sky.

Her mom is smiling at her, and seems to have forgotten the commotion around them now.

I used to swing like that, Zack thinks, as the phone rings at the other end. Farther and farther up toward the sky, away from everything for a few brief moments. Lurching up into the atmosphere, away from Dad's coughing and sores and hands fumbling for medicine bottles.

"Hello?" a familiar voice says.

Zack closes the balcony door behind him.

"Zack here. Just wanted to make sure you weren't picked up," he whispers.

"No, but all hell broke loose there after you left. Shame. I wouldn't have had any trouble getting one of those girls to go home with me."

"Do you know what they were looking for? Some sort of undercover operation?"

"You're the cop, not me. They started lining up loads of people against the wall, but I didn't feel like hanging around for that."

Zack smiles. There always seem to be emergency exits in Abdula's life. As if he really were as invincible as he's always tried to make out.

"So everything's fine, then?"

"Everything's always fine. You know that."

Zack laughs.

"I've got to go. Speak later."

"Take it easy out there with the good guys."

Zack feels a bit calmer as he puts the phone back in his pocket. Abdula's free, and the raid doesn't seem to have been anything out of the ordinary, the sort of thing that uses up a lot of resources but only ever leads to a few insignificant fines for narcotics offenses.

But he could have been there when they stormed in. How would he have got out of that? Maybe he could have snuck out with Abdula.

They've done so many crazy things together. Like when Zack was accepted to the Police Academy and Abdula made him spray his tag across the entrance to Police Headquarters to prove they would still be friends.

The tag has been washed away.

But the friendship endures.

Stronger than ever.

He watches the paramedics emerge from the door carrying a stretcher. The body is covered by health service blankets, but when one of the paramedics climbs into the ambulance an arm falls out and sways in the air.

The arm is slight and skinny. The palm is turned outward, facing Zack. As if the woman under the blanket were asking someone to take her hand in theirs. As if she wants someone to help her up.

Up from the stretcher.

Back to life.

To her family, somewhere far away.

Or back to the time when she was a little girl, swinging up to the sky.

5

DENIZ IS sitting on the bed.

Looks around the room. Sees the tawdriness of it all. Can smell the violence from the next room.

She shuts her eyes.

Thinks how she hates men.

Sometimes.

But feelings like that don't lead anywhere.

She opens her eyes again.

Zack. She can see him out on the balcony. His muscular frame, curly blond hair. He's okay.

The sight in the next room. The blood, the shattered bodies. Who could have wished the women so much harm?

She knows what men can do to women, what fathers can do to their own daughters, and, above all, what brothers can do to their sisters. If you're going to survive in this world, you have to meet force with force, and realize that it's you or me.

Sometimes you can't back down.

Not in the face of this sort of brutality.

The forensics officers' cameras click away in the living room. Quiet voices discuss the possible angles of the killer's shots.

"I need coffee," Zack says when he comes in from the balcony.

"Let's see if we can sneak out of a back door somewhere," Deniz replies.

"I'll come with you," Douglas says.

The sun feels merciless as they open the basement door and emerge at the back of the building. No journalists there. They're all hanging around outside the cordon around the front.

They follow the path down to the shopping center, find a branch of Coffee House by George next to an Oriental supermarket, and get espressos to take out. On their way out of the café they see a reporter interviewing a woman with a stroller outside the entrance to the subway station.

"Looks like they've already started on the side story: *A suburb living in terror*," Douglas says. "They need to find a few locals who say it doesn't feel safe living here, and that they're going to be keeping their children indoors from now on."

They sit down on a low stone wall in the shade of a large oak on the way back up to the apartment blocks.

Douglas's phone rings and he excuses himself and walks away from them.

Deniz and Zack immediately start talking about what they saw in the apartment. How the murderer wasn't content merely to kill the women, but also shot them in their genitals.

"You have to be perverted to do something like that," Deniz says.

"We could be dealing with a crazy client. A sadistic sex maniac," Zack says.

The children on the computer.

Children with no mother now.

He senses Douglas's hand on his shoulder, and its paternal warmth feels good. A weight holding him down to earth. But there's something wrong, it's as if Douglas is leaning on him, and not the other way around.

Douglas sits down beside them again.

He's usually quick to take the initiative in conversations like this, but on this occasion he's more reserved. Nothing like the self-assured boss who pushed his way through the crowd of reporters when he arrived at the scene, parting them like a sea.

It's as if his mind is elsewhere.

Has he finished with another woman? Has someone scratched the Warhol painting in his Östermalm home? Was that what the phone call was about?

I'm too hard on him, Zack goes on to think. He's basically okay.

Then Douglas finds his focus again.

"So, they seem to have been prostitutes. Which means we might be dealing with trafficking. There's money to be made, bringing in women from Asia and putting them to work."

"Who could be involved in that, then?" Deniz asks.

"I'm not particularly clued up on it," Douglas says. "But some of the biker gangs are supposed to be involved in running Thai massage parlors."

Zack searches his memories of the apartment and finds himself thinking about the graffiti on the door.

DEATH TO ALL NIGGERS.

"Could it be a white hate crime? Right-wing extremists?"

"Not impossible," Deniz says. "I checked a few of their websites for another case recently, and there isn't exactly a shortage of inflammatory articles about the 'import' of Thai women. But God knows if one of them would be capable of something like this. They usually stick to spreading their hatred online."

"Ever heard of Anders Behring Breivik?" Zack says.

Deniz changes tack:

"We need to get hold of the woman who made the call."

"We will," Douglas says, standing up from the wall. "We'd better start pulling at a few of these threads. I'll call Sirpa. And we'll have to bring in Östman as well."

Zack and Deniz look at each other. Tommy Östman, a criminal profiler, isn't officially employed within the unit, but gets called in when necessary. He used to be renowned throughout Police Headquarters as a real charmer, the sort who was the life and soul of any party. But in the end he was spending most of his evenings partying, and his family had had enough.

These days he's a sober alcoholic, with no trace of his earlier charm, and a man who seems to have found new and questionable ways of holding his dopamine levels stable.

But the profiles he produces have ended the livelihoods of numerous career criminals, and have led to plenty of violent thugs being taken off the streets.

THE APARTMENT looks like a laboratory when they return. Measuring devices, test tubes, plastic bags containing hair and fabrics, and, in the middle of the living room, a portable sample kit connected to a MacBook Pro.

The black Compaq laptop is gone.

Thank goodness.

A man in a white coat is leaning nonchalantly over the shoulder of a woman tapping at the MacBook's keyboard.

"Any results yet?" he asks impatiently.

Koltberg.

Damn, Zack thinks. He must have come straight from the airport.

Koltberg turns around when he hears the voices of the three detectives in the hall. He stalks over to Zack. His coat is hanging open and Zack has time to notice that Sam is wearing the red necktie of power with a blue shirt today, before the complaints begin.

"Well, this is just great, isn't it? One of the bodies disappeared before I even got here. How did you think I was going to examine it? By teleport, maybe?"

The forty-three-year-old coroner raises his eyebrows toward his receding hairline and adopts an exaggeratedly affronted expression.

Zack feels like punching him in the face. *You arrogant fucking bastard.*

He knows Koltberg thinks he's an inexperienced upstart who hasn't got where he is on his own merits but because of his mother's reputation. And it doesn't seem to make any difference what Zack does to prove the opposite, Koltberg simply can't accept a twenty-seven-year-old as an equal.

What the fuck gives Koltberg the right to an opinion? Zack wonders. After all, he grew up in a wealthy doctor's family, with a summer cottage out in the archipelago and a mom who could afford to be a housewife.

What the fuck does he know about anything?

Zack has a sudden flashback.

He's ten years old and is standing in the kitchen of their apartment in Bredäng. He takes a break from the washing up to look down into the yard. His friends are playing football and laughing, but he's shut inside the stifling heat on the eighth floor. His dad is lying on the sofa after a bad relapse, and has a big, red, butterfly-shaped rash across his cheeks. Zack spends all day cooking, cleaning, and doing the washing, but his dad never says thank you. He barely says anything at all. He's just sad, and complains about the pain in his joints.

The doctors call the illness lupus, and Zack has just been told by a social worker that his dad will never get better.

He looks down at the football, which seems to float back and forth across the yard. His friends are puppets, governed by some unknown force.

He grabs hold of the cheap stone windowsill, pressing his hands against it until his knuckles turn white, and looks up at the gray sky and tries to imagine the endless expanse of air he knows is up there behind the clouds. Then he hears his dad cough, then say:

"Bring me my inhaler, I need it now."

What the fuck does Koltberg know?

"Did you have a good time in Mallorca?" Zack says to him. "You look nice and relaxed."

Koltberg loses his train of thought. He seems to be considering a vicious retort, but doesn't have time to reload before Douglas appears at Zack's side.

"There's no murder weapon at the scene," Koltberg says to Douglas instead, in a considerably calmer voice.

"Anything else?"

"One of the women was holding a cell phone. A Nokia, not exactly flavor of the month these days. Whatever. She made a call at two forty-five last night. Two minutes later she sent this text."

He holds the phone up to Zack and Douglas.

Help us
he kill all

"My preliminary conclusion is that she died immediately after that."

"Who did she contact?" Douglas asks.

"The number's listed under the name *Sukayana*, and she called it several times yesterday morning. I made a note of the name and number."

He holds a note out to Douglas, who glances quickly at the number and then hands it on to Zack.

"Can you check this out with Sirpa?"

Zack takes the note and goes into the bedroom, calling Sirpa as he walks.

The tubes of lubricant are gone. As are the condoms. Sometimes Forensics is very quick.

Sirpa answers after the first ring. Half a minute later she's found the answer to Zack's question.

"There's only one Sukayana in the whole of Sweden. Sukayana Prikon, registered as living on Gaveliusgatan. She owns the Sawatdii massage parlor on Södermalm."

"So, Thai massage," Zack says. "Anything else?"

"Bound to be. But you'll have to give me a bit of time."

They hang up and Zack returns to the others and repeats what Sirpa told him.

"If Sukayana Prikon was these women's boss, then the whole thing starts to look like pimping," Deniz says. "Maybe trafficking as well. And if that's the case, then it's hardly surprising that she didn't want to stay here and wait for the police."

"I don't get it, though," Zack says. "It looks like she received the text at two forty-seven, but didn't sound the alarm until six hours later. Would she have had her cell switched off?"

THE JOURNALISTS swarm around them as they leave the crime scene to go to Sawatdii, Sukayana Prikon's massage parlor. There is a clatter of cameras, several people shout questions at the same time, and a number of iPhones set to record are thrust into their faces.

It's almost noon and the sun is oppressively hot. Its intense rays are attacking the suburb, seeming to want to put everyone in their place.

Zack and Deniz force their way through the reporters.

Ignore their questions.

"You drive," Zack says, and they're soon sitting in the car, rolling slowly past the play area.

The mother is still there with her daughter on the swing.

As if their lives are an endless pendulum motion rather than a line with a beginning and an end.

6

"LET'S GO in," Deniz says, eager to find out what they might discover behind the white crocheted curtain hanging behind the neon-pink OPEN sign in the window of the door.

"Hang on a moment," Zack says.

They're standing on the pavement outside the Thai massage parlor at Lindvallsplan, near Hornstull. Where the murdered women probably worked. It's located on the ground floor of a 1970s building with a yellow stone façade and windows that look like they could fall out of their brown aluminum frames at any moment, transforming into deadly projectiles on their way down to the pavement.

Above the doorframe a frayed, sun-bleached Thai flag is flapping gently in the warm breeze.

Glittery letters spelling out SAWATDII TRADITIONAL THAI MASSAGE have been stuck on the window.

Cheap sign, cheap name, Zack thinks.

Three large photographs show blond, fair-skinned women lying on massage tables being treated by young Oriental women with dazzling white smiles. The women's bodies are covered by white towels, and the masseuses are dressed smartly. Short-sleeved shirts and burgundy trousers, no sexier than the uniforms worn by staff at Södermalm Hospital not far away. On a shelf below the pictures there's a selection of exclusive massage oils and moisturizing creams.

"This is all fake," Zack says.

"How can you tell?"

"I did a bit of googling in the car. Traditional Thai massage is done on the floor, and without any oil at all. And the clients keep their clothes on."

"This couldn't just be a Swedish version, and they're doing some kind of mash-up massage?"

"Maybe. But the most important thing is what's missing. There's no statue of Buddha in the window."

"So?"

"In Thailand that means: we sell everything."

"And you found that out on Google as well?"

"No."

Shuffling footsteps behind Zack make him turn around. A bearded man, reeking of body odor, stops, and holds out a dirt-stained hand.

"You haven't got a few kronor to spare for the bus, have you, son?"

Zack feels like telling him to get lost, but he digs in his jeans pocket and finds some coins to give the homeless guy. Sometimes he offers them a hot dog or burger. No one should have to starve. He rarely gives them money, because they only spend it on alcohol, but the day's events have left him feeling shaken.

The man thanks him and shuffles on past Zack, then catches sight of Deniz. He stops and turns back to Zack.

"What the fuck, you're taking your girlfriend to the whorehouse?"

Deniz turns calmly toward the homeless man, leans forward, and whispers right next to his ear, almost sensually:

"You've got two choices. Either you carry on walking right now, or I rip your balls off. Here and now."

He stares at her for a few seconds, speechless. Then he turns and moves off toward the subway station as quickly as his shaky legs will carry him.

Whorehouse? Zack thinks. Is it really that obvious?

He pushes the massage parlor's door handle.

The lobby is small, the air heavy with liniment and incense. The pale yellow walls are decorated with posters of Thai beaches and the strains of some Southeast Asian string instrument are coming from hidden speakers.

A thin Thai woman is sitting behind the reception desk reading some sheets of letter-size paper. She's wearing a white blouse and a thin red summer jacket, and looks to be in her sixties.

"Hello," Zack and Deniz say almost simultaneously.

The woman looks up at them and stiffens. Something about their posture or the way they said hello has given them away.

She quickly gets up from her chair, but one arm is still hidden by the counter and Zack has time to think that she's got a weapon. He crouches down instinctively and puts his hand to the holster inside his jacket, but by that time the woman has already opened the white door behind her and disappeared.

How can such an old woman move so fast? Zack wonders, rushing after her.

He finds himself in a dark blue corridor lined with curtained doors, and just catches sight of one of the woman's gym shoes disappearing through an open door at the far end.

He runs after her and emerges into a large, rectangular courtyard containing a number of trees.

Where is she?

A door slams shut to his right.

There. He hurries across the tarmac and pulls the handle. Locked. A coded lock. Shit.

He quickly evaluates the door. It opens inward, and doesn't look that solid.

He backs up a few steps, takes aim, and throws himself at the door as hard as he can. It gives way and he tumbles into a stairwell, landing on his knees, and when he puts his arms out to stop himself he feels pain shoot through his right shoulder as if he's been stabbed.

He listens for footsteps but can't hear anything. If she'd gone up he'd be able to hear her. So, down the stairs and out.

"Zack!"

Deniz's voice from the courtyard. But there's no time to wait for her to catch up.

"She's running. I'm going after her!" he cries as he gets to his feet and starts to run. There are five steps down to the hall leading to the front door. He takes them in one bound and shoves the heavy door open with both hands. The pain in his shoulder is intense, it feels like someone's trying to pull the joint apart. There's something seriously wrong with it.

Serves you right for being so fucking clumsy.

A different street.

He loses his bearings for a moment.

Looks right. No sign of the woman.

Looks left. The water beyond Bergsunds Strand is shimmering in the sunlight fifty yards away.

Where is she?

Then he sees her appear from behind some trees a hundred and fifty yards ahead of him. Running along a cycle path beside the water with light, easy strides. He must have misjudged her age. No sixty-year-old runs like that. Her legs are moving in a way that makes it look like they don't belong to the rest of her body.

Zack runs down Bergsgatan, crosses Bergsunds Strand, and reaches the cycle path just as the woman disappears into the shadows beneath the Liljeholmen Bridge.

The energy that was coursing through him when he ran up the stairs out in Hallonbergen is all gone, and his steps are heavy.

He can feel the effects of the night in him. His body is longing for more cocaine.

For more sleep.

The sun is baking his hair and back, and he feels like tearing off his jacket and top. He's already out of breath, and curses his nocturnal adventures.

People in sunglasses crowding the pavement terrace of the bar next to the bridge cheer him on, raising their glasses of golden beer to him.

Shut the fuck up!

He gets a few brief seconds of cool as he runs through the shadow under the bridge and emerges into Tantolunden. The large park is heaving with people. Families with strollers, groups of friends with disposable barbeques, office workers in shirtsleeves who've left off early.

He scans the area as he runs on. He thinks he can see her off to the left, but he's wrong, it's a young girl chasing after a Frisbee.

He puts his foot down on a large lump of wood, stumbles and loses his balance, regains it, and staggers on as a group of angry skittle players yell at him from behind.

"Watch where you're going!"

"Damn idiot. He knocked the kingpin over."

He catches sight of her again. She appears in his field of

vision between two outsized stroller parasols. She's changed direction, is running south now, toward the green hill covered with allotments.

Several people have stopped to watch the woman running. Then they see him. A well-built man, six feet three inches tall, chasing a skinny little Asian woman. A mugger?

Someone gets their cell phone out. Not to call the police, but to record the chase.

Zack leaps over a picnic blanket and zigzags past a circle of teenagers throwing a basketball between themselves.

The distance is shrinking. Seventy-five yards. Fifty.

The trees are getting closer. He has to catch her before she makes it into the maze of little paths winding between the bushes and allotment cottages. Twenty yards now. The world has shrunk to a tunnel. Every sense except sight has been disconnected. The chase is the only thing that matters.

Ten yards.

Five.

He throws himself forward, feet first, and knocks her to the ground like a defender brutally tackling an opponent in a football match. She screams and falls headfirst into a family picnic. Juice, rosé wine, and pasta salad spill across the Burberry blanket and designer picnic basket with its plates, cutlery, glasses, and bottles.

A toddler starts crying. Her mother screams. A man in a linen jacket snatches the child away but says nothing.

The woman rolls across the grass, away from the wreckage of the picnic, and Zack manages to grab one of her ankles.

Zack sits astride the woman. And puts his knee down on a packet of vanilla wafers.

He's surrounded by people shouting and yelling, but he

has switched off, can't hear anything. He grabs the woman's flailing arms and presses her down into the grass.

That smell is there again.

The smell of grass.

He hates that smell.

Zack is knocked aside before he has time to register the fact that someone has kicked him hard in the ribs. He loses his breath and suddenly feels a number of heavy hands on his back and shoulders.

Two male voices:

"Leave her alone, you bastard!"

"Kajsa, call the police. Quick!"

Zack is still clutching one sleeve of the woman's jacket, but other hands are trying to loosen his fingers, and he can feel the woman trying to pull free of her jacket.

A heavy man sits down on his back and he yelps:

"I *am* the police!"

But the men don't seem to hear him.

Zack is still clutching onto the jacket, but it feels light now. Far too light. He pulls it toward him. Empty.

His first instinct is to lash out and hurt the man. But he stops himself. These people are innocent. Picnicking fathers. They don't deserve to be hurt.

"I'm a police officer," he shouts again. "Get off! I'm a police officer!"

The man sitting on top of him is unsure.

"What do you mean, police? Where's your ID?"

"If you move a bit, I can get it out."

A voice from behind:

"The bastard's bluffing. Don't let go of him."

Soon I'm going to hurt you really badly after all.

I know how to.

And I'm fucking good at it.

Almost too good. As if some higher power were guiding my hands, my body, my thoughts, helping me keep my cool, even though I might be in mortal danger. It's like some sort of almost superhuman courage takeover.

"Let him get his ID out," someone else says. "But keep hold of him."

The man on his back gets up, but stands with his feet on either side of Zack, with his hands on his shoulders. Zack gets up onto his knees and reaches for his ID. He opens the left-hand side of his jacket in an intentionally expansive gesture so that his holster and service pistol are clearly visible.

"Shit, he's telling the truth."

Zack looks around as he holds out his ID, trying to see where the woman is.

She's vanished again.

"Listen, well . . . Shit, sorry, pal," the man who was sitting on Zack's back says. He's wearing a black Mötley Crüe T-shirt that's stretched uncomfortably tight across his stomach. He looks like he's in his forties. "We thought . . . well, you know . . ."

The others are standing around him in a circle. Completely silent. Worried. Have they committed a crime? Violence against a public official, perhaps? Or aiding a fugitive?

Zack manages to suppress his anger.

"Don't worry," he says, looking at the three men who were holding him. "You thought you were stopping an idiot who was chasing an innocent woman. More people should do that."

Then Zack catches sight of her.

She's just stepped out onto the path fifty yards away. She looks back toward the allotments, evidently assuming that Zack has gone in there after her. When she can't see him she slows down slightly and turns off toward the mini-golf course.

Zack waits until she's got her back to him, then hurries after her. He's badly bruised and is having trouble taking deep breaths. There's a stabbing pain in his ribs and his shoulder is burning. It feels like he's treading water, but he's gaining on her fast.

She doesn't see him until it's too late. There's no time for her to accelerate quickly enough and he catches up with her next to a hot-dog stall down by the water. There are loads of people here too. Everyone in the food line is staring. Zack changes tactic and decides against bringing her to the ground. Instead he takes a firm grip of her upper left arm and makes her slow down. Eventually she stops, still facing away from him. Her breathing is heavy and hoarse. Her shoulders are rising and falling quickly. Zack begins to draw her aside gently, away from prying eyes. He tries to identify a quieter spot. Maybe up by the allotments? He swings around and starts walking toward the vegetation.

It seems like the woman has given up, and Zack relaxes. They enter a narrow path, and walk around some large mock-orange bushes in bloom. They've just passed four pensioners on a bench when the woman suddenly does a quick jujitsu maneuver with her arm and Zack's hand ends up at a very painful angle. Then she pulls free and draws a stiletto, the thin blade becoming a shimmering snake as she raises it toward him.

A white-haired woman on the bench screams, and out of the corner of his eye Zack sees people stop and stare.

I should have been prepared.

She's holding the knife in front of her. Moving slowly around him in a circle. An alert look in her eyes.

Zack holds up his ID, both to her and everyone around them. He has no desire to find himself lying beneath another overweight busybody.

The woman ignores the ID. She's staring intently at Zack's face, still circling him with the knife raised. Zack sees that the distance between them isn't shrinking.

The pistol isn't an option under the circumstances. Too many people in the vicinity. He goes on holding his police ID in front of him and waits for the right moment.

His years of martial arts training come into their own now. When other people would be at their most anxious, he is as focused as he can be.

Calm. In spite of being tired and out of breath, and in spite of the threat.

"I'm a police officer," he repeats. "See for yourself."

She takes her eyes off him and looks at his ID, and the battle is won. With a movement so fast that the woman doesn't have time to react, Zack whips out his telescopic baton and jerks it open.

A Bonowi EKA Camlock, the police's new model. Zack likes it. It can be opened easily with two fingers, or a quick snap of the wrist. Like now.

The lightweight black steel shoots out of the handle with a metallic click and the baton hits the woman's wrist with a dull thud.

The knife blade flashes in the sunlight as it spins through the air. Before it lands on the dust of the path Zack has already locked the woman's right arm behind her back.

They head slowly away from the water. Zack walks behind her, still holding her arm locked behind her back. He pushes her arm higher up, leans forward, and says in a low voice:

"What the hell was the point of all that?"

"I'm not saying anything," the woman replies, in perfect Swedish.

7

THE MASSAGE parlor's neon sign is switched off and the door locked. On a sagging blue sofa in the lobby the woman who ran so fast sits with her legs crossed, tugging absent-mindedly at the multicolored wristbands on her left arm. The flickering light of the television on the wall casts shadows on her face and Zack once again detects the smell of liniment—he could do with rubbing a couple of pounds into his shoulder.

He and Deniz have pulled over a couple of chairs and have started the interrogation, but their questions are being met with silence.

"Come on," Zack says. "I'm going to find out anyway, it will just take a bit longer. Are you Sukayana Prikon?"

The woman goes on studying her wristbands. She's no longer scared. Just stubborn.

Zack is surprised by her coolness. Four of her employees have been brutally murdered, but she's just sitting there like a teenager forced to listen as her parents preach at her.

A way of blocking emotions, he thinks. Unless she's more hardened than most people. Not many people would pull a knife on another person, no matter what the circumstances.

Zack wonders what she could have been through earlier in her life, what it was that's made her so thick-skinned.

"Okay, let's try this instead," he eventually says, and takes out his police cell and the note Douglas gave him. He keys in the number and the woman's phone starts to ring in her red handbag.

"So we know who you are. Sukayana. At least that's what your murdered staff called you."

She lets out an audible sigh, looks up from her hands, and stares into the wall with cold black eyes. What lies behind that gaze?

Nothing?

"Yes, that's me," she says.

"Well then, Sukayana. Tell us about the women. Who they were, what their names were, where they were from," Zack says.

"From Thailand, like me. Good girls, all of them. Reliable, clever. Popular with clients. The only thing they had trouble with was punctuality, but that had started to get better."

"And their names?"

Sukayana hesitates for a moment, then replies:

"Prataporn Sirawhat, Pehn Shinanaroi, Armorn Rattanakosin, and Pakpho Rikritwata."

Zack takes a spiral-bound notepad and ballpoint pen from his inside pocket and hands them to her.

"Can you write the names down?"

She writes quickly, in neat, clear handwriting.

Zack can see the mutilated women in his mind's eye. The blood, the brain tissue. Which one was which?

"We'd like you to identify them for us. Later."

She looks him in the eye, and for the first time there's someone behind her gaze.

"Why did you run when we arrived?" Deniz asks.

"I panicked. I thought that lunatic was coming for me."

Zack nods. A natural reaction.

He's still sweaty from the chase. He's never felt under such scrutiny as when he led Sukayana Prikon back through Tantolunden toward the massage parlor. He was prepared for more attacks by middle-aged dads, but instead Deniz ran to join him and people began to realize what was going on.

The walk to Lindvallsplan was uneventful, until they encountered a man with a large Alsatian. When the dog began to bark at a small terrier, the woman started to panic. She tugged and jerked to get free, and when that didn't work she crouched behind Zack and Deniz and screamed at them to protect her.

It was as if the dog and its bared teeth had woken hidden memories.

When she eventually calmed down and Deniz asked how she was, she simply said:

"I just don't like dogs."

"Was it you who found the women in the flat?" Zack asks her.

Sukayana Prikon shakes her head.

"One of them sent you a text message. To the number I just called. 'Help us. He kill all.' A few hours later you called her number several times. And when she didn't answer you traveled out to their flat. That's right, isn't it?"

She shakes her head again, but she can't hide her fear. And her pupils are unnaturally small.

"Didn't it worry you when you received the text?" Deniz asks.

Sukayana Prikon doesn't answer.

"Who could he be? The man in the text, the one who killed them all?"

"I've got no idea."

"What were you doing last night, Sukayana?" Zack asks.

"I was at home asleep. I work twelve hours a day. At night I sleep."

"Is there anyone who can confirm where you were?"

"No."

Her tone is hard, resistant.

"We're going to need to know more about your business activities if we're going to find the perpetrator," Deniz says.

"There's not much to say. It's a perfectly ordinary massage parlor."

"Do you run the parlor on your own?"

"Yes."

"You don't have any partners?"

"No."

Quick answers, Zack thinks. Too quick?

"Who are your clients?"

"All sorts. Businessmen, cleaners, students. Lots of regulars."

"And it's just massage?" Zack says. "No . . ."

"Sexual services, you mean? Just because it's a Thai parlor? We don't do anything like that."

"We found large quantities of lubricant and condoms in the flat out in Hallonbergen. That suggests prostitution," Deniz says.

"It suggests they had a life outside the parlor. If you can see past your prejudices."

Sukayana Prikon is about to say something else, but stops herself. Zack thinks he can see something else in her eyes, a resignation bordering on grief behind her hard exterior, and she gives him a look that says: So, young man, what does someone like you know about this world?

The theme tune of the afternoon news comes on the television and Zack looks up at the screen. 4:00 p.m. Is it already that late?

Sukayana Prikon shifts position on the sofa, folds her arms, and fixes her eyes on Zack. In an almost derisive tone she says:

"What do you actually think? These poor women, why wouldn't they jerk off a Swede for five hundred kronor? They can earn the average annual Thai salary in a week here in Sweden."

"So they were prostitutes, then?" Deniz asks.

"I didn't say that. When they were here they provided Thai massage. What they got up to in their spare time is none of my business, is it?" Sukayana Prikon replies.

Zack wonders whom she's protecting. Herself, or the murdered women? Their pimps?

Or their clients. The flabby Svenssons who exploit young women when they're at their most vulnerable.

A quick fuck after work, then home to their wives and children.

But who am I to moralize?

The television is showing a report from a shopping center on the edge of the city. The CEO of a property company is commenting on claims that the firm is charging tenants extortionate rents.

"That's simply not true. Our rents are at a level that's very reasonable for the market, and in this context it's important to remember that . . ."

Sukayana Prikon looks up at the television. Snorts at the CEO.

"In my homeland they're all like him: corrupt."

She reaches for the remote and switches the television off.

Deniz changes tack:

"Sukayana, who might have wanted to murder your employees?"

"I've got no idea. Like I said, they were nice. Minded their own business, and were careful not to cause any problems."

"So there was no client who'd got angry with them, or behaved in a strange way?" Zack asks.

Who lost his temper because he wasn't allowed to treat them however he wanted?

"No. Not that I've seen."

"Do you have a register of clients?"

"Why do you want to know?"

"Right now we're not ruling anything out in our search for potential perpetrators, and anyone who's come into contact with the four women recently is of interest, not least your clients."

"I've got some names and addresses among the invoices, but no more than that. Most of them pay cash, and I never write down their names."

"But you must have some sort of accounts?"

"Of course. But there I usually only write down first names."

"We'd like to see them anyway," Deniz says. "And we need to contact the victims' families. How can we get hold of them?"

Sukayana leans back in the sofa and looks like she's thinking.

"I don't think any of them had relatives here in Sweden. You're probably going to have to try to find them in Thailand."

"How did you come into contact with the women?" Zack asks.

More silence. Deeper this time without the buzz of the television.

"This is a murder investigation, and the common denominator between the victims is you. We're not going to give up until we get answers. You can talk to us, or you can spend all night sitting in a gloomy interview room."

Sukayana Prikon looks at her wristbands again.

Deniz goes on in a gentler voice than Zack:

"We're not corrupt, not like that guy in a suit on the news. We're actually very good at our job, but we can't solve this without your help."

"There's a company," Sukayana Prikon says after a brief pause. "Recruitment Solutions Ltd. They help me to find good workers from Thailand."

"Have you got their number?"

"I'll see."

She digs through her handbag and pulls out a cell phone with a sparkling pink cover.

"No, I haven't got it. I usually check their website when I call them."

Zack is studying Sukayana Prikon's movements. He's still having trouble matching her age with her quickness and agility, and can't help wondering about her desperate behavior in Tantolunden.

I thought that lunatic was coming for me.

He would have done the same thing in her situation.

But what if the desperation had a different cause, what if she had actually hired someone to kill the women? He's having trouble thinking she could have done it herself.

But why would she want them dead? They worked for her, after all. To stop them talking, maybe, or to avoid prosecution for procuring?

The phone calls she made that morning to the dead women's cell phones seem to suggest that she didn't know they were dead, though.

Zack's mind keeps working. Perhaps something had happened, something that made them want to leave? Or take revenge?

Zack realizes that he's got stuck on the prostitution angle. That's the sort of thing he criticizes older, more jaded colleagues for, detectives who have made up their minds about the way things are before the investigation has even started, and therefore end up missing or discounting vital information.

He can't let himself get like that.

"That was a very neat maneuver you pulled when you got free of me," he says instead. "Have you had jujitsu training?"

She smiles at the compliment.

"In the past. My grandfather taught me when I was little."

"Here in Stockholm?"

"No, I was born in Thailand. I came here when I was thirteen."

"Why?"

"Same reason as most other people. In the hope of a better life in a wealthier country."

She says this in a tone of voice that lets Zack understand that reality didn't quite live up to expectations.

"We're going to have to take a few things away from here with us," he tells her. "Your computer and phone, among other things. I'd also like you to find your financial records, files, and year-end accounts."

"But you can't do that. This is my whole livelihood."

"Yes, we can. According to chapter twenty-six of the penal code."

"But how am I going to . . . ?"

Zack interrupts her.

"But we're *not* going to take you in, even though you tried to escape and threatened a police officer with a knife. We understand that you were frightened."

Zack looks at Deniz. She nods. She agrees with him.

"We'll need to talk to you again, though. Soon. So make sure we can find you."

Sukayana Prikon opens her mouth to protest, then shuts it again and remains silent.

She gives Zack her cell.

"I appreciate that this will cause you problems," he says, "and I promise to let you have it back tomorrow. Okay?"

She nods.

Like a grandmother reluctantly agreeing to do what a stubborn grandchild wants.

"Now, show me where you keep your files."

Zack turns to Deniz.

"Can you call for another car? We're going to need a bit of help."

Fifteen minutes later they're standing out on the street. The heat is still oppressive. The smell of an early barbeque drifts down from a nearby balcony.

Zack puts on his Ray-Ban Aviators, texts Sirpa, and asks her to check out Recruitment Solutions Ltd.

Sukayana Prikon is standing in the door, glowering at the newly arrived police officers who are carrying out a box of files.

Zack gently massages his shoulder and wonders if letting her go free is a mistake. She has no alibi. And even if she didn't have anything to do with the murders, she may herself be in danger. Whoever killed her girls might also be after her. In which case she'd be safer in custody.

But the police don't lock people up to protect them, he thinks. And Sukayana Prikon seems to be the sort of person who can look after herself.

8

SIRPA HEMÄLAINEN rubs her aching left knee with one hand as she quickly scrolls through the search results with the other.

One site appears on the list several times: *thai-massage.nu*, some sort of forum where readers comment and give marks to various massage parlors in Sweden. But so far she's only found hints about prostitution at Sawatdii, nothing definite.

"Your *whole* body gets looked after here . . ."

". . . not frightened to take a firm grip of any problems."

"Every muscle relaxed except one. And in the end that relaxed as well."

On *Flashback*, people were more explicit about "the slant-eyed whores at Hornstull" and the "Thai tarts at Sawatdii," but Sirpa has checked out the rumors on *Flashback* enough times in the past to take everything written there with a grain of salt.

She takes a short break to rub both knees at the same time. She stretches her legs and kicks the air for a while. It hurts, but in a good way. Like when the blood starts flowing again through frozen fingertips.

She reaches for her half-full cup of coffee, takes a small sip, and pulls a face. Cold.

She checks the time on the computer screen. Three hours without a break.

Come on now, Sirpa. You know what the doctor said. Get up and walk every hour. Ideally more often than that.

She stands up from her secluded corner behind the two twenty-four-inch screens and looks out across the open-plan office. Completely empty. The others are still out in the field.

As for herself, she hasn't been out in the field since November 7, 1998.

The accident still haunts her at night. Not as much as it used to, but each time it's as if she's forced to experience the whole thing all over again. The concrete blocks racing toward them. Her colleague Stig yelling: "Fuuuck!"

More terrifying in the dream than reality, the emotion clearer each time, as if memory were a diamond cutter that could highlight the worst instead of the most beautiful.

It wasn't even icy that day. It was the brakes. They just stopped working, without any warning.

Stig died in the accident. Leaving a wife and two young children.

And her knees were wrecked.

Seventeen months later her husband met someone else. Sirpa knows that work is the only thing that has stopped her becoming a chain-smoking, embittered old cow, always going on about how much pain she's in.

These days she smiles when she sees herself in the mirror in the morning, and her colleagues are pleased to see her when she arrives at work. She's the sort of person who makes other people laugh.

The sort of person who solves crimes. Who finds things no one else can.

Sirpa could make a good living as a consultant, traveling around and giving lectures about Internet security. But she's happy just looking after a few online courses. She wants to work at the sharp end. Such as here, in the Special Crimes Unit. Where she can make a real difference. Ericsson will have to try to protect their secrets on their own without her help.

She keeps typing, searching through the morass at the bottom of the Internet, feeling as though she's drowning in rancid grease. She feels like going to the bathroom for a wash, but soap and water don't have any effect on this sort of dirt.

She wades through stagnant swamps that reek of ingrained prejudice and built-up hatred. She works through forum after forum. Saves interesting links and fragments of text in a separate document. Highlights anything she'll have to take a closer look at.

Hatred of Thai women seems to be a specific subculture among right-wing extremists. Sirpa can feel herself getting more and more depressed as she skims the posts.

> These copulating yellow women are spreading across the world like a slant-eyed plague. We've got to take a stand against it. We've got to spread the word and build barriers. Soon it will be too late. **In the nation's interest**

> Let's treat these whores to a taste of their own medicine! Gang rape is the only language Thai cunts understand. **The Swede**

> I KNOW that the so-called "massage institutes" are disguised whorehouses, because I've found out the truth for myself. It was at the Sawatdii parlor on Södermalm in Stockholm. I asked what sort of massage they offered, and they said that everything could be arranged. I decided to see if it really was as bad as that, so I went in and paid 300

> kronor for a "happy ending" handjob. I reported the incident to the police, but nothing's happened. I bet the police are customers. What's this foreign filth doing to our society? They ought to be shot, deported, put in camps. Who knows what diseases they're spreading? **Gustav Vasa**

"Gustav Vasa, my ass," Sirpa mutters to herself as she types quickly to search for other posts by the same alias on other forums.

She finds plenty. Most of all on the site *whatwomenwant .se*, some sort of forum for scoring porn films. She reads some of Gustav Vasa's comments.

> I want to see warning signs when there are yellow bitches in films. All of us fighting against needless interracial breeding might get upset by nasty surprises like that. The fact that the woman in question was treated pretty roughly by the four men and that the scene concluded with a double penetration of her back passage might be counted in its favor under the circumstances.

She moves on. Opens a WordPress blog called "Gustav Vasa," and reads with mounting interest.

It's a site promoting extreme right-wing opinions. Reprinting articles from *Avpixla*. Publishing posts on how immigration is ripping the heart out of Swedish culture.

So, Gustav Vasa. You're both a pervert and a right-wing extremist. You're worth a closer look.

She searches for the name of the owner of the domain name and finds it without any trouble.

Now let's find out who you really are, she thinks.

This is the part she enjoys. Finding the true identities behind the pseudonyms. Checking their family backgrounds, court convictions, and tax records. She knows from experience that plenty of the people who complain about "benefit-stealing quota-fillers" owe a lot of tax and are keen exploiters of Swedish society's various financial safety nets.

But not Gustav Vasa. He seems to be pretty comfortably off.

She carries on her search in more databases, and finds one result for his ID number in an abandoned preliminary investigation into an alleged rape.

Her revulsion grows with every word she reads.

She saves the file in a folder on her desktop and carries on looking. She discovers that he is involved in an ongoing civil case, and is suddenly convinced that he's the person they're looking for.

"Are you making progress, Sirpa?"

Svensson and Gräns are walking toward her between the desks.

"Hate, hate, hate," she replies. "But if we're looking for a crazy client I think I've found a rather interesting candidate."

"Let's hear it," Niklas says, leaning inquisitively over her screen and looking at the black-and-white passport photograph.

"His name's Peter Karlson. Thirty-six years old. It's his birthday today, believe it or not. He's development manager at D'Inc, an IT company based in one of the Hötorget skyscrapers. In the evenings he praises sadistic porn films and spews racist bile on a fanatical nationalist blog with over forty thousand unique visitors each week."

"Is that a lot?" Niklas asks.

"Quite a lot. More than a lot of local newspapers can boast."

Sirpa pulls up a chair for Rudolf and invites him to sit down.

"But here's the really interesting thing," she goes on. "In September last year he was accused of rape, both vaginal and anal, by a young woman he'd arranged to meet from a dating site. The allegations couldn't be proved, but it's very clear that the head of the preliminary investigation wasn't exactly delighted to have to let him go. He's also the plaintiff in an ongoing civil case, concerning an unpaid bill for massage treatment. Guess where?"

"You're kidding. Sawatdii?"

"Exactly. He's contesting the invoice on the grounds that the masseuse couldn't do her job. The case is still going on."

Niklas lets out a whistle of approval.

"But that's not all. Peter Karlson also has a bronze medal for pistol shooting at the junior Swedish championships."

"Does he have a gun at the moment?"

"Nothing registered."

"That racist blog, does it have any particular focus?" Rudolf asks.

"Yes, quite an interesting one under the circumstances. I'll play you one of the posts."

She opens the blog, highlights the text, then switches on the MacBook's voice-over function. An artificial voice reads out the highlighted text:

> The Muslims' desperation to rape our Swedish women is both a serious and widespread problem, but we mustn't forget all the other aliens causing trouble for society.
>
> Take tax-dodging Asians, for instance. They exploit our goodwill and suck as much money out of the welfare state

as they can. They take all they can without giving anything back. They steal money that should have gone to schools and care of the elderly and send it to their cousins in Thailand and Vietnam.

Their crimes aren't as visible as the more violent Muslims', but the effects of them swindling billions will have devastating consequences both for coming generations and the people who built this country.

They must be stopped.

Rudolf adjusts his sunglasses and says:

"So here we've got a man who has an unresolved dispute with one of the murdered women, who doesn't like Asians, is a good shot and a sexual pervert by nature."

Niklas looks at the time.

"Half past five. Do you think he might still be at work?"

"It's worth a try. People who earn that sort of money don't usually go home at four o'clock."

"Okay, let's go."

Rudolf stands up and buttons his jacket as he considers the words the computer just read out.

Has there always been so much hate? Maybe the hate itself has always been constant, just not as visible. What's new about the digital world, he thinks, is that we can see each other's unfiltered thoughts.

Is humanity really ready for the kind of psychological challenge inherent in constantly being able to give voice to its very worst sides? Like an endless traffic jam in which everyone is blowing their car horn.

9

IN THE sluggish rush-hour traffic Zack and Deniz are crossing the Western Bridge on their way back to Police Headquarters when Zack's phone rings.

It's Sirpa.

"We've found a pretty clear suspect," she says, and gives him Peter Karlson's background.

"Where is he?" Zack asks.

"The Oracle and Niklas are already on their way. I just wanted you to know. But I've found something else as well which points in a different direction. About Recruitment Solutions Ltd."

Zack never ceases to be amazed at how fast Sirpa is. It hasn't been more than a quarter of an hour since he called Douglas and gave him an outline of their interview with Sukayana Prikon. That means Sirpa first heard the name just five minutes ago.

"What have you found?"

"There's an interesting connection to the criminal biker gang 'Brotherhood of No Mercy.' The club's president, Sonny Järvinen, is on the board of Recruitment Solutions."

Zack recognizes the name. Sonny Järvinen makes regular appearances in the media, most recently in connection to revelations that members of the club had defrauded National Health Insurance of millions in sickness benefits.

He recalls laughing when he read it. Those damned bikers. They call themselves "one percenters," and claim to stand outside normal society, but when it comes to sickness benefits they've got nothing against being part of a tax-financed system. Which proves what they really are: troublemakers who crawl home to Mommy when the money runs out.

"Can you check where their clubhouse is? They've moved, haven't they?" he asks.

"Already done," Sirpa says. "Have you got paper and pen?"

"No, but a damn good memory."

A few seconds later Zack ends the call and says to Deniz:

"Sirpa's found both a crazy john and a biker gang with connections to Sawatdii."

"What do we start with?"

"Niklas and Rudolf are dealing with the crazy guy. You and I are heading to the clubhouse in Bromma."

The traffic on the Traneberg Bridge is even worse than the Western Bridge. The speedometer barely registers any movement at all.

The sun makes the water of Ulvsundasjön look like a thin silk shawl caught in a gentle breeze, and Zack gazes enviously down at three men in kayaks far below. The water looks soft and gentle as the kayaks' pointed noses pierce the surface.

Then he thinks of the body they found tucked between some rocks near the water in Minneberg the previous autumn. At first they thought the skinny man had been tortured. Several bones in his body were broken and he looked like he'd been subjected to several hard blows to the face with a blunt object.

That turned out to be wrong.

He'd jumped from the bridge and got smashed up when he hit the water.

Not so soft and gentle that time.

And it had given Koltberg an opportunity to smirk at them.

"What do you know about the Brotherhood of No Mercy?" Deniz asks.

"They're a bunch of upstarts who've managed to earn the respect of the Hells Angels and other biker gangs in the past two or three years. That means they're seriously violent. Two unsolved murders this spring alone point to them, but there hasn't been enough evidence to press charges."

"Okay, so Sukayana uses a company run by criminals to get women for her massage parlor. She'd hardly do that if it wasn't about prostitution. And now something's gone so badly wrong that all those women had to be killed. But what?"

"I think it's about more than just wanting to get rid of them. They could have done that in a far easier way—burying them out in the forest, anything, really. My feeling is that someone's making some kind of point with this."

"You mean their competitors?"

"Maybe. Someone who wanted to take a share of the market from the Brotherhood and found a very brutal way of doing it."

They pass Alvik and carry on toward the airport and out-of-town shopping outlets, where people hunt for short-term happiness in the form of bargains. Then they turn into the Ulvsunda housing project. Their surroundings instantly become uglier and dirtier. Shabby buildings, high fences, cracks in the tarmac.

"Stop here," Zack says, pointing. "There it is."

Deniz pulls over to the edge of the pavement. Some thirty yards ahead of them a large concrete wall rises up, topped by spirals of barbed wire. Inside the wall they can see an old industrial building made of corrugated metal.

"Shall we go and see if Sonny Järvinen would like to give us a guided tour of his fortress?" Zack says.

"I bet he's got loads of fluffy throw pillows on the sofa, and 'Carpe diem' written on the wall above it," Deniz says.

They ring on the entryphone by the rusty iron gate. A tin sign bearing the club's logo is fastened at eye level. Two stylized bearded men with their arms around each other's shoulders. Angular black faces against a red background.

Zack notices for the first time that the men's arms have grown together. The same old myth about inseparable brothers. A myth that falls apart the moment anyone gets fed up with being pushed around or decides to put their own family first.

They ring again. No answer.

"Time to call for reinforcements?" Deniz asks.

"Do you think that's necessary? We only want to talk to him, after all."

Zack looks along the wall. It's about thirteen feet high. A security camera is pointing down at them, but it looks dead. Are they blind inside there?

He thinks of Rudolf Gräns. No one is truly blind. Perhaps they don't need cameras to feel the presence of strangers.

But it's so quiet. So desolate. As if every business on the entire estate has quickly shut up shop, leaving them in a ghost town.

Zack looks at Deniz. She's on high alert, just like him. This is when she's at her best, he thinks.

He really doesn't like this silence. Waiting for backup would be the sensible option.

Besides, it looks like Rudolf and Niklas are on their way to pick up a suspect. Maybe this is just a dead end.

"Let's go in," he says, regardless.

He puts a foot on one of the hinges of the gate and nimbly climbs up. The pain in his shoulder is almost gone now.

The fingers of his left hand take hold of the gap between the top of the gate and the wall. He puts his other foot in a small hole in the concrete and grabs hold of the top of the wall with his hands. He tenses his muscles and heaves himself up to look through the barbed wire. Two shiny Harley-Davidsons are parked carelessly in front of the building, but he can't see any sign of movement. Not a sound.

The tarmacked yard is tidier than he had been expecting. A short distance away are two large charcoal grills, a long bench, some round plastic tables, and several stacks of white plastic chairs. Against the wall is a bench press. Weights of various sizes are hung on iron poles fixed to the wall.

Close to the gate there are three-foot-high pallets of Rockwool insulation in red-and-white packs, and farther away, three feet or so from the wall, are some even taller stacks of rough timber.

Building work under way, Zack thinks, as a dog starts to bark inside the building.

If there's anyone here, Zack thinks, they know something's going on now.

Next to the insulation there are a number of black garbage bags, some tied shut, others full to bursting with empty beer cans. There are wasps and plenty of flies buzzing round the bags.

A smell of fermenting beer reaches his nostrils on the faint breeze, but also something else. Something rotten.

What's in those bags?

His skin crawls as he imagines what might be hidden beneath the black plastic.

Human remains.

More dead women.

Is that smell coming from their rotting flesh?

The dog barks louder.

His heart is beating violently inside his leather jacket.

Still no sign of movement in the yard.

Even the main building seems empty. The windows of the office block are dark, and there's no movement behind the blinds on the upper floor.

Zack pulls himself up and crouches on top of the wall. The barbed wire fastens in his jacket and jeans, but he manages to stand on the spiral of wire with one foot as he carefully frees himself from the sharp barbs.

His eyes sweep the yard and buildings again.

Then the dog falls silent.

A trickle of sweat runs down between Zack's shoulder blades, but nothing happens.

He looks around one last time, then stands up, puts both feet on the barbed wire, and jumps down onto the tarmac on the other side.

There's a metallic rustling as the compressed barbed wire springs back into shape, but Zack lands softly and silently. He immediately runs over to the main building, resisting the urge to stop and investigate the stinking sacks. Keeping his back to the wall, he looks around before edging closer to the corner of the building. A black van is parked by a loading bay.

There must be someone here. But where are they?

His breathing gets faster.

His head feels as lucid as it does after three lines of cocaine. Fear and threat make the present moment clear. People meditate for years to get this feeling, he thinks.

He leaves the shadow of the building and walks almost silently over to the gate in the wall.

He presses a button with a symbol of a key on it and hears the bolt in the lock click.

The gate opens and Deniz is about to say something when her eyes fix on a point above Zack's shoulder.

"On the roof! Take cover!"

The bullet hits the gate with a metallic clang. They run forward and throw themselves behind the packs of insulation. Zack shoots back, and through the thunder of guns going off and the dog barking he hears Deniz call for backup.

There are muffled thuds as two bullets hit the insulation, and it occurs to Zack that he ought to be getting frightened. But he never gets scared in situations like this.

Zack curses the fact that they left their bulletproof vests in the car. If the bikers have weapons of a slightly larger caliber they'll easily be able to shoot through the insulation.

A bullet hits one of the garbage bags with a squelch. Fragments of the black plastic are torn away, revealing a bloody piece of meat.

Human remains?

Another shot goes off, but the sound is different, more muted.

A rifle.

"Fuck. There's at least two of them," Zack says. "Can you see anyone?"

"I can't see a damn thing," Deniz says. "We've got to get out of here."

The stench from the garbage bags is unbearable now.

Zack yells as loudly as he can:

"We're police officers! Put your weapons down!"

A bullet hits the wall behind them and Zack feels his cheek burn as sharp fragments of mortar spray in all directions.

I can't die in this fucking dump.

I can't fail my promise to Mom.

Another shot is fired and he hears Deniz scream in pain as the sound of the dog's barking echoes across the yard.

10

THE ENTRANCE to the fifth of the Hötorget skyscrapers is covered from floor to ceiling with polished black marble. No one can avoid the underlying message: there's money here.

Niklas and Rudolf step into an elevator with shiny white walls behind its gold-colored doors. The buttons are chrome, each one surrounded by a discreet circle of blue light. A soft female voice addresses them from a hidden speaker:

"Which floor, please?"

"Sixteen," Rudolf replies.

"Sixteen," the voice repeats, and the elevator begins to move, silently and gently.

Rudolf and Niklas can't help laughing.

"Marvelous that scientists have chosen to devote their resources to making life easier for us old folk who can't see so well," Rudolf says. "Bit different to Police Headquarters."

The reception area on the sixteenth floor has an oiled wooden floor. A few anemic tubular metal chairs are arranged in front of a white Corian reception desk. The air is pleasantly cool, neither dry nor damp, perfect for people and computers alike.

Niklas gently guides Rudolf with one arm as they walk across the reception area.

A young blond woman with her hair in a French twist sits

behind the desk. D'Inc's logo is lit up in large green italics on the white wall behind her.

"How can I help you?" she asks, adjusting her black jacket. Niklas recognizes it from Maison Martin Margiela's guest collection for H&M: his wife, Helena, bought one just like it.

Perhaps the people here aren't as cool as they're trying to make out, he thinks. Or else Helena's cooler than I thought.

The woman's smile is so poised and professionally polite that Niklas is reminded of the hubots, the human robots in the television series *Real Humans*. They aren't that different from his neighbors out in Näsbypark.

"We're looking for Peter Karlson."

"Do you have an appointment?"

The receptionist tilts her head at precisely the right angle. Her teeth are white as chalk, and perfectly straight.

"No," he replies.

The woman looks at them skeptically, particularly the old man with the dated sunglasses. She looks as if she thinks everything about him is wrong. His creased, ill-fitting jacket, cheap trousers, hesitant gait. He doesn't belong in the friction-free world she's striving for.

"Peter's extremely busy, so if you haven't made an appointment I'm afraid I'm not going to be able to help you. But perhaps I could give him a message?"

Niklas pulls out his ID.

"We're police officers."

The woman's hubot smile stiffens into a grimace.

"Wait here, please. Do have a seat."

They've just had time to sit down when the receptionist comes back. Her voice is politely friendly again.

"Would you mind waiting a few minutes? Peter just needs

to finish a call. Perhaps you'd like a cup of coffee in the meantime?"

"Thanks, but no, thanks," Rudolf replies.

Niklas notes that she's staring at him again as if she's trying to reconcile herself to the fact that this handicapped old man is going to have to be on the premises for a while longer.

Rudolf turns his face toward her, as if he can actually see her.

"We won't clutter the place up for long. You don't have to worry."

The woman looks surprised and blinks nervously a few times. Then she excuses herself and retreats behind the reception desk.

A frosted-glass office door opens and Peter Karlson emerges with the determined stride of someone who believes that time is money. His smart suit is dark blue, but his speckled green tie doesn't match it, and his brown shoes look rather scuffed. His short brown hair is combed in a side parting, and his straight, dark eyebrows accentuate his blue eyes. He has thin lips, and there's a barely perceptible dimple in his chin. He looks better than Niklas was expecting. Nothing like a deranged Neanderthal from the darkest corners of the Internet.

"I don't really understand how I can help you, gentlemen, but why don't we go into my office?"

They enter Karlson's office and the center of Stockholm spreads out before Niklas's eyes.

If only Rudolf could see this.

The black-and-white paving of Sergels Torg, the glass front of Kulturhuset, the people inside it like fish in an aquarium. The two blocks of the parliament building, the heavy bulk of the Royal Palace, and the boats on Riddarfjärden.

Niklas lets his eyes roam across the famous landmarks. Skansen, Hammarbybacken, the old Tax Office skyscraper. The view goes on forever from up here.

They sit down on white leather armchairs. Niklas skips the introductory pleasantries.

"As part of an ongoing criminal investigation, online comments made under the pseudonym of Gustav Vasa have turned out to be of interest. Seeing as you're the man behind that alias and the blog of the same name, we'd like to ask you some questions."

Karlson's surprise at having his alias unmasked is only visible for a fraction of a second. He starts, but then his arrogant façade is back in place again and he leans back slowly in his chair.

"What do you want to know?"

"Where you were last night, for instance."

"A number of witnesses can confirm that I was in Edsviken last night. It was a very pleasant party, actually. A gathering of urbane north Europeans socializing politely and exchanging experiences and thoughts about the future. The sort of party everyone likes, wouldn't you say?"

"How long were you there?"

"I went home shortly after midnight."

"Is there anyone who can confirm that's what you did?"

"No, I live alone. What's this actually about?"

"The opinions that you express on your blog . . ." Niklas begins.

". . . aren't my own," Peter Karlson interjects. "Of course not. You saw that for yourselves. 'Gustav Vasa.' He's a fabricated character I sometimes play with. Like a sort of role play, you could say."

Peter Karlson looks at his Breitling watch.

"I have to say, it's rather tragic that you should harbor ridiculous suspicions that I might be involved in any sort of criminal activity."

"No one has suggested anything like that," Rudolf responds calmly.

"Really? You march in here and insinuate that something I write for my own amusement might be connected to a crime. That's on the verge of harassment, actually. What are you investigating, anyway?"

Rudolf leans forward and asks curiously:

"What harm have women from Thailand ever done you?"

"I have nothing against them at all," Peter Karlson replies, giving an innocent shrug of his shoulders. "Nothing at all. As long as they adhere to Swedish laws and regulations, they're welcome to live here if they want to."

"But on the Internet you wrote that they should be shot?" Niklas says.

"Like I said, those are the views of a fictitious character. I allow him to be something of a polar opposite to myself."

"And you wrote that you paid for sex with them."

Peter Karlson leans closer to Niklas.

"Haven't you ever fantasized about shooting and killing someone? Or having sex with someone other than your wife?"

"You like hurting women, is that right? You did carry out that rape you were reported for, didn't you?" Niklas asks.

Peter Karlson smiles.

It strikes Niklas that Karlson's face is just like his office. Highly polished, blemish free, and utterly devoid of any genuine warmth. Does he have what it takes to shoot four women and then sit here and mock two police officers? Quite possibly.

He looks into those ice-blue eyes and sees in them a psychopath who could well believe himself capable of committing the perfect crime. Who believes he could remove all the evidence. And, from what Koltberg has said, it looks like the murderer did a pretty good job of that.

"It was very good of you to make the sort of sacrifice that you did at the Sawatdii massage parlor," Rudolf says gently.

Peter Karlson looks at him with distaste.

"Perhaps you're a little hard of hearing. The post I wrote online was fictitious. I've never been to a massage parlor."

"Did you feel dirty afterward, or was it actually rather nice?" Rudolf goes on, taking off his sunglasses and rubbing his eyes.

Peter Karlson's tight lips crack into a malicious smile.

"Now I get it. You think I've got something to do with those murders out in Hallonbergen. Those Thai women you found this morning. I saw it on the *Dagens Nyheter* website. You're completely mad."

"Do you still have any pistols from when you used to shoot for sport?" Niklas asks.

Peter Karlson simply shakes his head.

"Perhaps you think it's more exciting to shoot live targets than boring old cutouts? Particularly if the targets are foreigners who are sucking all the money they can out of Swedish society. The sort who demand payment in full for their poorly executed services," Rudolf says.

"I think this meeting is over now. Let me show you out."

Rudolf and Niklas stand up, and Peter Karlson moves quickly to hold the door open. He mockingly offers to lead Rudolf out.

"After all, we don't want you knocking anything over, do we?"

He puts his arm on Rudolf's shoulder. Rudolf lets it stay there. Feels the weight, the warmth, feels the other man's presence course through him.

In his mind's eye he can see Peter Karlson sitting on a massage table in a cramped room smelling of cheap oil. His trousers are pulled down to his ankles, and a slender hand is moving up and down as he leans his head back and groans.

Peter Karlson calls the elevator for them and waits until they've stepped into it.

"Oh yes, there was one more thing," Rudolf says, turning around.

"Really, what?" Peter Karlson says irritably.

The elevator doors are closing.

"Happy birthday."

11

MORE BULLETS smash into the wall behind Zack and Deniz, but they've managed to move from behind the packs of Rockwool to the big stack of timber a few yards away. The planks are tightly packed, and the stack is at least three feet across. No bullets are going to get through that.

Deniz's face is contorted and she's clenching her teeth tightly. She's clutching her neck with one hand, and when she takes it away her fingers are bright red.

"Fucking hell!" she says.

"Let me see," Zack says.

He leans over and inspects the wound. A flash of memory goes through his mind. He sees another neck, another wound. A wound that means everything.

He screws his eyes shut and forces himself back to the present. A trickle of blood has already run under Deniz's top, making irregular stains on the fabric.

"It's not deep, but it's bleeding a lot," Zack says.

He tears off a long strip of his own top, then a smaller piece that he rolls into a ball and presses against the wound.

"Here, hold this."

He ties the longer piece of fabric around her neck, making sure that the ball of cloth is pressed tight against the wound.

"Say if it gets too tight. It seems a bit unnecessary to strangle you to death in order to stop the bleeding."

"It's okay," she says, and shoots him a look of gratitude. Then she squeezes his hand.

"Thanks, I'll be fine," and Zack thinks that he'd take a bullet for her, and that she'd do the same for him.

A heavy silence has settled on the yard again. Even the dog has stopped barking. It's almost worse than listening to the gunfire. They sit there on high alert, expecting to see the barrels of rifles poke around the timber at any moment.

"We're police officers!" Zack shouts again. "Put your weapons down!"

He takes off his Rick Owens jacket, puts it on the end of his pistol, and carefully raises it above the planks.

He wonders how Mera would react if she could see this.

Bam, bam, bam.

Someone fires three shots in rapid succession. The jacket jerks and Zack almost loses his grip on it.

Okay, they're still on the roof. They don't give a damn who we are. And they know how to aim. Fuck.

He feels himself getting angry. He's not thinking of staying there much longer, forced into a corner with an injured colleague in need of treatment.

"Can you still shoot?" he asks Deniz.

She nods.

"Okay, cover me when I give the word."

He'd rather stay with her, but knows he has to move.

Zack pulls his jacket on again, creeps as close to the edge of the planks as he dares, and gets ready.

"Now!" he yells.

Deniz fires shot after shot, and Zack sprints over to a fire escape that leads up to the roof.

He doesn't know if they've seen him or not, and makes

his way up as cautiously as he can. Maybe he can take them by surprise.

He's holding his Sig Sauer out in front of him. Looking upward the whole time, ready to fire at the slightest movement.

Further shots echo from the roof and Zack hurries up the last few steps. They won't hear him now anyway.

He sticks his head up above the edge. It doesn't even occur to him that he might get hit.

Five yards away, staring at the pile of wood, lie two men with big beards and black sleeveless tunics. The man closest to him is incredibly fat, and is clutching a double-barreled elk rifle in his hands. The second man is partially hidden by his huge comrade, but Zack knows he's armed with at least a pistol.

Zack's just about to set foot on the roof when the bearded man with the rifle pulls his gun back to reload it. He snaps the barrel open and digs laboriously in his left pocket for more cartridges.

And looks right at Zack.

"He's on the roof! Shoot the bastard!"

The man with the pistol gets quickly to his knees behind his colleague's vast bulk, but before he even has time to aim Zack is flying through the air toward him, and kicks him so hard in his muscular lower arm that the gun sails several yards through the air.

Zack lands with his elbow right in the stomach of the fat man with the rifle.

Punches him hard on the nose so that his head hits the felted roof with an unpleasant crunching sound.

His body relaxes and he lies motionless.

From the corner of his eye Zack sees the other man's foot heading at full speed toward his chest.

Zack parries the kick with his arms and a quick swerve of the hips. The man loses his balance and Zack smashes his clenched fist up into the man's crotch.

Their roles are reversed now.

The biker is on his knees and Zack on his feet. The man tries to stand, still clutching his crotch with one hand, but he doesn't have time to straighten up. The sole of Zack's shoe hits him in the mouth, and he flies back and lands heavily on his spine.

Zack feels the blood rushing through his veins.

He doesn't waste any time.

He rolls the man with the pistol onto his stomach and twists one of his arms up behind his back. The man groans and starts to struggle, but then Zack pushes his arm up even farther.

"You shot my colleague, you bastard. So shut the fuck up."

He forces the man's arm up so brutally that there's a cracking sound. The man screams and Zack pulls his handcuffs from his belt and locks the man's arms behind his back.

"Lie still otherwise I'll rub your fucking face on the roofing felt."

But the man couldn't move even if he wanted to.

Zack pulls some cable ties from the inside pocket of his jacket. The man doesn't protest when Zack crosses his legs and pulls one of the ties tightly around his ankles.

Zack moves on to the big, unconscious man, rolls him over onto his stomach as well, and ties his hands behind his back.

He looks like an ancient turtle.

Zack is about to start on the man's legs when he hears a screeching sound from the building below him, as if a sticking window were being forced open.

"Don't shoot, don't shoot!" someone down there yells. "It was a mistake. You're cops, aren't you?"

"Which we said loudly and clearly a number of times," Zack says in a loud voice.

Silence.

What's happening with Deniz?

Then a hopeless lie:

"We didn't hear that in here."

There's a refreshing breeze up on the roof, but the wind brings with it the awful smell of the garbage bags.

"Deniz!" Zack calls.

"Here," she replies. "I've got them covered. There's three of them."

Zack stands on the edge of the roof, with his pistol pointing downward.

"Come out now. With your hands above your heads. One at a time."

Thirty seconds pass. Then three bearded bikers emerge from the building with their hands above their heads. Two are seriously big guys, the third considerably shorter and thinner. A man with rat-colored hair in a ponytail and a furrowed brow. Zack recognizes him at once: Sonny Järvinen.

"Is there anyone left inside the building?" Zack says, feeling his anger growing.

You just tried to shoot us.

You bastards.

"No, just us," Sonny Järvinen replies calmly, smiling toward Zack.

"The slightest movement and we'll fire. My colleague and I have both got our weapons aimed at you."

Finally police sirens can be heard in the distance. A helicopter approaches. It circles low over the club before disappearing again. Zack remains on the roof until the first reinforcements have entered the yard. He calls some of his colleagues up onto the roof, then rushes down the fire escape.

He feels like racing over to Sonny Järvinen and smashing his pistol into his skull, but resists.

Goes over to the black garbage bags instead.

They really do smell of dead bodies.

The bikers watch him open the first bag, but their expressions don't change. It's impossible to tell if they've got something to hide.

The smell of decay is so strong that he starts to retch.

"It's venison," Sonny Järvinen shouts. "Our freezer broke when we were at a meeting in Copenhagen."

"Shut up," Zack says, and looks down into the bag.

Joints of meat, freezer bags.

Hundreds of wriggling white maggots.

"Okay, I believe you."

He moves away from the bags and wonders who the bikers had really been expecting. Presumably not two plainclothes detectives.

But maybe someone who's pissed off because the Brotherhood has murdered four prostitutes?

Is that what this is all about, or is it something else entirely? He doesn't know yet, and is far too angry for his brain to work properly.

The three men from inside the building have been lined up against the inside of the wall. They're searched and cuffed. The other two are on their way down the fire escape, surrounded by police officers. The fire escape shakes with each step the fat man takes.

One uniformed officer leads a large dog out from the

building. It looks like a mix of Rottweiler, Alsatian, and something else, the sort of creature a gangster with an interest in dogs could be imagined to breed.

"Any guns?" Zack asks one of his colleagues from the rapid response unit.

"No."

"Okay, check the building. I know they were armed three minutes ago. They can't have had time to hide the guns very well."

"We were all unarmed," Sonny Järvinen calls from over by the wall. "It would be interesting to hear how you're thinking of proving the opposite."

Zack rushes over to Järvinen. Grabs hold of his vest and pulls him toward him so his face is close to Zack's.

Guarded eyes.

"We appreciate that you were just sitting in there playing on your Xbox," Zack says, "but we'll take a little look anyway. And from now on you speak when I tell you to. Okay?"

Sonny Järvinen grins when Zack lets go of him.

Zack looks at Deniz. She's sitting on a pile of planks and looks very pale. The strip of cloth around her neck is stained with blood, and the front of her top is almost entirely red.

He goes over to her.

"Do you know if there's an ambulance on the way?"

"No, I'm okay for a while yet."

"You need to get to a hospital."

She flashes him a glare.

"I'll go soon. Okay?"

The gang members are put in the police van. The fat man takes up the whole of the front row of seats, and the van's suspension sinks under his weight.

"Leave Järvinen here," Zack says. "We'll take care of him."

Zack and Deniz sit with him on the plastic chairs in the yard as their colleagues search the building.

Sonny Järvinen is wearing a black T-shirt under his club vest, and Zack can't help being surprised by how skinny his arms are. At the same time he realizes what that means: this is a man who rules with his head.

The gang leader has bags under his green eyes, but the look in them is alert and intelligent.

"You must have been seriously jumpy to start shooting just like that," Zack says.

Sonny Järvinen gives a light shrug.

"You know how it is when you get unexpected visitors."

"Who were you expecting?" Zack asks.

"None of your fucking business," Sonny Järvinen says, spitting on the ground in front of him.

Zack gets up from his chair. He can't hold back any longer, and slaps Sonny Järvinen across the face with his palm open, sending his chair flying and landing him on his back.

"Zack, for God's sake!" Deniz yells.

"Now we're going to take a little drive down to the station," Zack says as he helps Sonny Järvinen up. "Just you and us."

THEY LEAVE the industrial zone and drive past the huge stores by Bromma Airport. In the almost full parking lot the evening sun is painting the cars in bright colors.

On Ulvsundavägen, just after they've passed Lillsjön, Zack turns off onto a narrow gravel track that leads to a forgotten patch of woodland squeezed in between the nondescript villas.

He switches the engine off.

Lets silence spread through the car. The feeling that now

it's just us and you, Sonny. Now we can do whatever we like with you.

Zack turns toward Sonny Järvinen. He's sitting in the backseat next to Deniz, who is still wearing her bloody top, with a small bandage around her neck. She's refused to go to the hospital.

Sonny is the butcher, the victim. Or vice versa.

He fixes his eyes on Järvinen, who looks away instinctively.

"Damn it, look at me!"

And the bikers' leader meets his gaze.

"Here's how it is," Zack says. "You're going to tell us what we want to know. Otherwise I'm going to pull you out of this car and shoot you in the back, and then Deniz and I will make it look like you tried to escape."

"You'd never do something like that," Sonny Järvinen sneers.

"You tried to shoot us. An eye for an eye," Deniz says.

Sonny Järvinen looks from one to the other. Decides that they're probably serious.

Nods slowly.

"The Thai women," Zack says. "You set them to work as prostitutes, and take a cut of the money. We know that. Did the women threaten to give you away, is that why you killed them?"

Sonny Järvinen's expression doesn't change at all.

"We didn't kill them," he says. "But it doesn't matter what I say, does it? You seem to have your theory all worked out."

"Let me start from a different angle: two of your men are going to get locked away for the attempted murder of two police officers. They won't be able to guard the club building for quite a few years. And it was completely unnecessary, you know that. But it wasn't us you were waiting for. Was it?"

"You never know who might show up," Sonny Järvinen says. "We weren't expecting anyone special today."

You're lying, Zack thinks. Everything about you screams that you're lying.

"I want you to talk a bit about how you recruit staff from Thailand," Deniz says.

"What do you want to know?"

"Where do you find the girls?"

"Which girls?"

Zack leans over and grabs Sonny Järvinen by one ear, and twists it hard. The man's scream echoes around the car.

"No stupid fucking games, okay? Four women have been murdered."

Zack lets go, and Järvinen starts talking:

"It's not hard to entice women from Thailand to come and work in Sweden. Salaries are many times higher, they get one or two days off a week, and paid holidays. They'll do anything for the chance to come here. I try to find good workplaces for them. And likewise, to help Swedish companies get good workers. Cleaners, kitchen staff, masseuses, you name it. In return for my work, I get an arrangement fee, all aboveboard, paid to Recruitment Solutions Ltd, which is owned by the club. It's a perfectly legitimate business. You're welcome to take a look at the accounts," he says, not without a degree of pride.

A woman walks past the car with walking poles.

Disappears into the forest.

Zack is astonished at how these biker gangs are run. They don't hesitate to commit the most brutal of crimes in order to gain an illegal income for themselves and the club, but at the same time they're almost bursting with pride whenever they manage to earn money legally.

"How do the women find out about you?" Zack asks.

"Via our local contacts in Phuket and Bangkok. Have you been to Phuket?" Sonny asks.

"This isn't a tourist quiz, okay?" Deniz hisses. "What were you doing last night?"

"We had a club party in the yard. There are loads of witnesses."

Who'd say anything for your sake, Zack thinks.

Considering all the beer cans in the garbage and the rings under Sonny's eyes, it's a perfectly plausible explanation.

The day after, Zack thinks. Just like me.

"Do you work with the Sawatdii massage parlor at Hornstull?" Deniz asks.

"That dump? Fuck, no. They can't even be bothered to provide the real thing."

Interesting, Zack thinks. Sukayana Prikon says she gets hold of her employees through Sonny Järvinen's company, but Sonny Järvinen denies it point-blank.

Someone's lying, and it's not even a good lie.

The answer will be documented in the company accounts, assuming they haven't been doing business on the side.

Has something gone wrong with their collaboration with Sukayana Prikon? Has she neglected to pay the arrangement fee, or give the Brotherhood their cut of the prostitution money? Did the women in the massage parlor threaten to give the game away? Or did the murdered women belong to a competitor to the Brotherhood, and now they're scared of reprisals?

"The real thing?" Deniz says.

"Forget it."

"No, I want you to explain."

Sonny Järvinen stares ahead of him before saying:

"I just mean that maybe not everything is what it seems to be. Take a look at the employees' wages. They're supposed to be on real slave contracts."

"Who supplies Sawatdii with staff?" she asks.

Sonny Järvinen gives a theatrical shrug that Zack interprets as yet another lie.

"No idea, actually. I just think it's disgraceful, the way they're exploited like that."

"Good of you to be so concerned about vulnerable women," Deniz says acidly, fixing her eyes on him. "Because you people would never do anything like that, would you? Exploit women?"

And we're back where we started, Zack thinks, as he hears Sonny say:

"We're not involved in . . ."

Zack sees Deniz's hand fly up. The blow hits Järvinen hard on the cheek. He cries out, and Zack yells back:

"You set Thai women up as prostitutes, and take most of the money. We know that. One more time: Did the women threaten to report you, is that why you killed them? Weren't they paying you your share? Well? You killed them, didn't you?"

Sonny Järvinen says nothing.

Stubbornness in his eyes.

Are you thinking about the women you had murdered? Zack thinks.

Or are you wondering how to get your revenge? Maybe Sukayana was telling the truth about working with you after all.

We should have brought her in. Pushed her harder about who controls her business behind the scenes.

But that will have to wait until tomorrow.

"Go on, then, shoot me," Sonny Järvinen says. "That's not the worst that can happen."

"What do you mean by that?"

"I'm not saying anything else."

"Who are you so frightened of that you're prepared to start shooting wildly in all directions?" Zack asks.

Sonny Järvinen gets a very unpleasant look in his eyes, and he leans forward, closer to Zack.

"We're not frightened of anyone. You need to get that seriously fucking straight. Why would anyone want to fuck with us?"

"Maybe someone doesn't like the fact that you killed four of their women?"

Sonny Järvinen turns and looks out of the window, and this time he remains silent.

12

ZACK CATCHES sight of her the moment he opens the front door.

No, he thinks, not now.

He's too tired, too hung over, suffering too much withdrawal.

He's got too much to deal with.

He wouldn't even be able to handle Mera.

But there she sits, Ester.

A skinny eleven-year-old girl with perfectly straight light ginger hair that just reaches her shoulders. She's wearing a blue-and-white striped summer dress, and is sitting on the stairs leaning against the wall, with her knees pulled up and an open book in her arms.

She lights up when she sees him. A weary glow in her almost cobalt-blue eyes changes to something alert and hopeful, and dimples appear in her cheeks below her short, pointed nose.

"Hi, Zack."

"Hello, Ester."

All he really wants to do is slump on the sofa and do nothing. Be on his own. Against his will he starts thinking of an excuse, but then he sees that she's a bundle of expectation.

He feels ashamed.

This isn't about me now.

She stands up and greets him with a big hug. He can feel her warmth as she wraps both arms around him and leans her cheek against his chest. He hugs her back with one arm while he gets the keys out of his jeans pocket with the other.

"Do you want to come in for a bit?"

"I'd love to."

She bends over and picks up the book and a red folder that was next to her on the floor.

Ester Nilsson lives in a small two-room apartment on the second floor with her mother, Veronica, a fifty-three-year-old on sickness benefits who suffers from long-term depression and holds her soul together with the help of various psychiatric drugs.

We're very similar, you and I, Ester, he often thinks when they're together. The child who has to shoulder far too much responsibility, longing for the parent who disappeared, and forced to look after the one who is still there. You're never angry, and nor was I. I used to watch the boys playing football down in the yard. But I never got angry. I used to dream.

Hid my anger inside me.

No one should have to be that alone.

Like you are.

Like I was.

He unlocks the door, kicks off his shoes, and hangs his jacket on a hook. The holes made by the bullets are clearly visible in the expensive leather. They seem to belong there, though. Rick Owens would probably have put them there himself if only he'd thought of it.

Two window envelopes and a copy of the free newspaper the *Heart of Kungsholmen* are lying on the doormat. He leaves them there.

Sometimes he finds drawings from Ester among the mail

on the floor. Usually exciting fairy-tale images involving trolls and witches. She's good, Zack thinks, especially when she uses pencils and felt-tips. Then she manages to draw shadows and more natural nuances of color. Her subjects are almost always unpleasant, with danger lurking among the trees or under the water.

On one occasion, about two years ago, he came home and found a very colorful drawing on the hall floor. The picture was dominated by a large red heart, and inside it Ester had written his name in beautiful, shaded dark blue letters:

Zacharias.

He had picked up the drawing.

Read his own name over and over again.

Smelled it.

He had taped the picture to his fridge, and there it remained until a month ago, when Ester asked him to take it down because it was so embarrassing.

It's dusty in the gloom of the flat, and the air is stale.

Zack rolls up the blind and opens the side window as far as it will go. It's turned eight o'clock and the traffic on the street immediately below the window has thinned out.

To start with he had trouble shutting out the noise of the traffic, particularly in the mornings and afternoons. He didn't only have to get used to the cars and buses on Kungsholms Strand, but also the Klara highway and the eight railway lines on the other side of the water.

He tugs his holster off and tosses it on the bed. As usual, he's forgotten to lock his pistol in the weapons store at Police Headquarters. He must be due his second official warning for that.

Who cares? he thinks as he walks to the fridge and takes out a Coke.

"Do you want one?" he asks Ester.

"No, I'm only allowed to drink that on Saturday, you know that."

Zack sinks onto the sofa. Ester sits down close beside him, so that they're touching, and it's nice to be near someone else, someone who doesn't want to shoot him, or have more from him than just a bit of closeness.

He takes deep gulps of the chilled drink and Ester watches him as if he were stupid.

"Do you know there are nine teaspoons of sugar in a can like that?"

"Only nine?" Zack says. "That makes it almost a health drink."

He nudges her gently in the side with his elbow.

"Oh, stop it," she says, trying not to smile.

She opens the folder.

"Can you test me on my English homework?"

"Is this for that summer course you're doing?"

"Yes."

"I thought you were doing math?"

"It's math and English."

Zack knows that Ester wants to get onto the new specialist math course at Engelbrekt School when she starts year seven. And for that she needs to pass the entrance test. But she'll be fine.

He can see her presenting her PhD at the Royal Institute of Technology in fifteen or twenty years' time. Smartly dressed and so brilliant that her debating partners lose their thread. On that day he will sit in the audience in his best clothes and congratulate her with the biggest bouquet of flowers that has ever been seen in a Swedish lecture hall.

"Okay, where's this homework, then?" he says.

She pulls a sheet of letter-size paper out of a plastic sleeve and hands it to him. It's a list of forty words. Difficult words, in Zack's opinion, and many of them relating to mathematics. Circumference, ruler, calculator, cubic foot estimate.

Ester runs through all the vocabulary without hesitating once. As usual.

Zack passes the sheet of paper back to her.

"What was that book you were reading out on the stairs?" he asks.

"*The Count of Monte Cristo*."

"I read that when I was your age. Actually, I was probably a bit older. Are you enjoying it?"

"Haven't decided. It's a bit old-fashioned, but I like that Edmond never gives up, and that he manages to escape from prison. But I haven't got to that bit yet."

Ester looks down at the cover and Zack in turn looks at Ester. You're a little Edmond Dantès, he thinks. Innocent, but sentenced to a dreadful life. But maybe you'll find your own treasure in the end.

You've got to.

No question.

Zack dreams about her sometimes. Her disembodied smiling face against a white background.

He looks at the time. Eight thirty-five p.m.

"When do you have to be home?"

"Mom's already asleep."

She never quite manages to conceal her shame when she talks about her mother. Zack knows how she feels, and he takes care never to ask how things are at home, or how her mom is. Ester comes down to see him for some fresh air, not to be given the third degree.

He got sick because you were so difficult.

One of the teachers at Bredäng School told him that once.

About Dad.

And he believed it at the time. And felt ashamed in a way he doesn't ever want Ester to have to feel.

"Would you like to watch a film?"

She lights up.

"Which one?"

"Shall we watch our favorite?"

"Yes, let's!"

Zack hunts through his films and puts Chaplin's *The Great Dictator* in the Blu-ray player.

Then he clears a messy heap of magazines off the coffee table: the *Economist*, *Vanity Fair*, *Fighter* magazine, and *Filter*.

He puts his feet up on the table and Ester does the same.

They spend the first forty-five minutes laughing at Hynkel the dictator's ridiculous behavior. Then Ester falls asleep with her head on his arm.

He lets her stay like that until the film is over, then he carries her out of the apartment and up the stairs, unlocking the door with the key she carries around her neck. The flat smells of old food, and large dust balls blow across the floor when he opens the door.

He carefully lays Ester down on her bed and tucks her in. The cute faces of One Direction stare up at him from the duvet cover. Zack knows that Ester doesn't actually like the boy band, but her mom gave it to her, and she doesn't mind pretending to like them in order to make her happy.

Veronica is lying on the sofa in the living room, snoring. Zack shakes her gently and she lifts her head sleepily and looks at him with a confused expression on her face. Her breath smells almost as bad as the garbage bags out at the bikers' clubhouse.

"It's me, Zack. I've just brought Ester up. She's in bed asleep now."

Veronica's eyes become slightly clearer.

"You're so kind, Zack," she says in a slurred voice, then falls asleep again the instant her head hits the sofa cushion.

He goes back downstairs to his own apartment again. It feels empty without Ester. Bare and abandoned.

Anyone could be living there. There's really nothing that says anything about who he is.

An Ikea sofa, an Ikea bed, an Ikea television table. A small bar table with two tall chairs in the kitchen alcove—also from Ikea.

That's all. No pictures, no pot plants, no curtains.

The only thing that stands out is the old oak chest of drawers in the corner, the one he used to have in his bedroom as a boy out in Bredäng.

On top of the chest is a framed photograph of a handsome man in a suit, with his arm around a young woman in a police uniform.

His parents.

From the all-too-brief good old days.

They were good, weren't they?

You were happy then, weren't you?

His mom is smiling and looks happy, and the wind is lifting her blond hair, making it look like rays of sunlight against the sea in the background.

Dad looks strong. Healthy.

The best bodyguard in Stockholm.

Zack tries to imagine what it was like, but can only remember how it ended.

Dad's cries out in the hallway, waking him at night.

The fear as he clutched his teddy bear, got out of bed, and cautiously opened his door.

The telephone handset swinging on the end of its cord. Dad curled up on the floor in a fetal position.

He sees himself in his soft tiger pajamas, laying his teddy bear next to his father before going back to bed and pulling the covers over his head. Lying alone in a darkness that slowly fills with his own exhaled air. And somehow he realizes that Mom won't be coming home tonight, possibly never again, and he puts his hands over his ears and screws his eyes shut as tightly as he can to make the bad thing disappear.

What does never mean to a five-year-old?

What did the word mean to me then?

A black, nameless feeling.

A feeling that he still hasn't found a name for.

He looks away from the photograph and sits down on the sofa again. He picks up a copy of *Filter* from the floor and begins leafing idly through it, but gives up after just a few pages.

He calls Abdula instead, needs to hear exactly what happened at the club, but the call goes straight to voicemail. He sends a text:

Want to meet up?

Abdula answers almost instantly.

Can't tonight. Tomorrow?

Ok. Laters.

Zack has a slight headache, and can feel a very familiar anxiety and restlessness creeping through his body.

He hardly ever takes drugs after seeing Ester. It feels nothing but grubby and unpleasant in a way that it never quite does on other occasions.

He shuts his eyes and listens to the soporific sound of the traffic, but his mind is bursting with unresolved thoughts and images. He sees the murdered women in his mind's eye. Sukayana Prikon's stiletto flashing in the sunlight. Hears Deniz scream and sees the blood on her neck. Feels his body respond to the memory as his pulse rate increases.

This won't do.

Zack goes out into the hall and opens the cupboard door. A black plastic sack inside topples over, spilling paperback books onto the floor. Alice Munro, Oscar Wilde, Cormac McCarthy.

Fucking hell.

He puts them back in the sack and shoves it hard against the wall. Then he reaches in and pulls out his black biker's leathers.

His red-and-black Suzuki Hayabusa is down in the garage, chained securely to the wall.

His most cherished possession.

It cost him almost half his inheritance from his dad. The rest went on the deposit for the flat.

The inheritance.

A father's unexpected surprise for his son.

He had left four hundred thousand kronor in a safe deposit box.

Money that could have given them both a better life while Dad was still alive. They wouldn't have had to count every krona.

But presumably the money was Dad's way of saying thank you. Thank you, my son, for looking after me.

Zack starts the motorbike and heads out into the late summer evening. He drives south, through the greenery of Rålambshovsparken and up onto the Western Bridge, and looks out across the shimmering water of Riddarfjärden. The flashy buildings along Norr Mälarstrand are behind him, almost an even smarter address than Mera's on Östermalm.

At Hornstull he bears right and crosses the Liljeholmen bridge, then turns off onto Hägerstensvägen just before he reaches the E20 highway.

He decelerates and drives slowly through the affluent suburban streets of Hägersten. Smells the leafy gardens, full of apple trees. There seems to be no end to the villas. Row after row of them. None of them worth less than five million. Expensive cars parked in the driveways, the water just a stone's throw away.

And then it happens, where Mälarhöjdsvägen ends and he turns left into Ålgrytevägen: he crosses an invisible boundary.

Everything changes. Mälarhöjden becomes Bredäng. Attractive 1920s villas are replaced by gray mass housing. Beautiful becomes ugly. Affluent becomes poor.

Zack pulls over and stops in front of one of the vast apartment blocks.

Gröna stugans väg—"Green Cottage Road." The most misleading street name in the whole of Sweden. There's nothing that isn't gray.

The eighth floor of nine. No balcony. A view of a gray parking lot and the next huge, gray building.

This was where they had ended up, Dad and him.

This was where he stood among the banana boxes that

first evening, looking out over his new neighborhood. The leaves had fallen, and the surroundings were so drained of color that he could easily have been living in a black-and-white film.

It was all raw and cold. Strange smells in the stairwell. Names on the doors that he couldn't pronounce.

He remembers being aware of his heart beating in his chest more clearly than ever before. He stood on tiptoe and rested his cheek against the glass, trying to see home to Kungsholmen, but all he could see was woodland and more buildings. When Dad came into the kitchen and asked if everything was okay, he quickly wiped his tears on his sleeve and replied:

"Sure."

Zack chains the motorbike to a lamppost and walks along the path to the underground station.

Rows of gray apartment blocks thrust up to his left. Barbed wire fencing around dismal industrial premises to his right. And, closer to the station, gray walls on either side of the narrow path.

He turns around just before the fast-food kiosk and walks back up toward the blocks. Hears an underground train approaching and looks through the fence toward the tunnel that's been blasted through the rock.

That was where he saw them when he had been helping Dad with the shopping and was running back with three bags from the supermarket more than twenty years ago.

Three against one.

The leader had a deep voice and a downy mustache, and he was standing down by the rails at the end of the tunnel, holding out above the tracks a dark-haired boy who only looked a year or so older than Zack.

Zack didn't understand how they dared to be down there at all.

"You're not so tough now, are you, you little coon!"

Two more boys stood alongside laughing. One skinny with cropped hair, the other pudgy with a trucker's cap on back to front.

They looked slightly older than the leader, maybe eleven or twelve.

"You're fucking right there, Seb," the boy with the cap said.

The rails started to hum, and Zack almost stopped breathing. Were they going to hold the boy like that when the train came? His head would be crushed!

Zack let go of the shopping bags and ran back down to the kiosk, where two men in their twenties were waiting for their food. They looked tough, had long hair and black T-shirts with band logos on them. Hard-rockers. Zack would never have dared talk to them normally, but any doubts left him in a flash. As if he had grown, become someone different.

"Help! You've got to help. There are three boys holding another one out above the railway track over there! Quick!"

"What the . . . ? Show us!"

Zack ran ahead of them, and when he got there he could see the light from the train approaching in the tunnel.

One of the rockers jumped over the fence and roared:

"Let the kid go, you fucking idiot, or I'll kill you!"

Then he ran down to the tracks.

Seb looked terrified. He shoved the boy onto the tracks and quickly scrambled up the rocks on the other side together with his friends.

The train emerged from the tunnel and the rocker managed to yank the dark-haired boy off the tracks at the last second.

"Thanks," he said when the shriek of the train's brakes had finally died away.

"Don't thank me, thank that lad up there. He was the one who noticed what was going on."

"Which one?"

The boy looked up curiously toward Zack, but Zack quickly bent down and picked up his shopping bags. Milk was trickling from one of them. He hurried home on shaky legs, and when his dad was putting the milk-soaked food away in the kitchen Zack said he had fallen over on the way home.

HE WALKS back up to Gröna Stugans Väg, starts his motorbike, and carries on south along Bredängsvägen.

Away to the west some thin veils of cloud are being colored pink in the darkening sky. Zack thinks they look like birds drifting off into the heavens.

Away from Bredäng.

Toward freedom.

Out on the E20 he opens the throttle and enjoys the sensation of the world turning into a multicolored tunnel.

13

SUKAYANA PRIKON rubs her neck as she walks home along Högbergsgatan. She lifts her head up and to the side to loosen her stiff muscles, and sees a strange cloud formation off to the west. It looks unpleasant. Like a big dragon with its wings stretched out, circling around up there looking for prey.

For someone like her.

She quickens her pace. Angry with herself for letting her imagination run away with her.

As if reality weren't frightening enough as it is.

The lump in her stomach is refusing to shift.

So many questions.

So much anxiety.

So much blood.

A rustling sound makes her turn around. Is there someone there?

She holds her breath and listens.

Looks around in all directions.

The old buildings from the turn of the last century seem almost deserted, only a few windows are lit up, and there's no one else in sight. The air is mild, and the darkness of night is incapable of entirely suppressing the summer light.

There's another rustle, and a hedgehog peers out from some bushes over by one of the buildings.

She breathes out, turns around, and carries on walking.

She thinks about Mi Mi. So young. Practically a child.

And Daw Mya, who had two children waiting for her back home.

The whole time she keeps seeing terrible images. The blood. The flesh. The dead eye staring back at her.

It's her fault.

But she didn't have a choice.

Who could have resisted the threats she had received?

Her neck aches. The muscles are as taut as the strings on a violin.

She's been sitting in an Internet café for several hours, deleting emails from her Outlook account.

"In this business you never save anything digitally," they had told her. Yet they themselves still used email to conduct business.

She hopes she got there ahead of the police's forensics officers. Maybe they haven't started to examine her computer yet.

She thinks about the two police officers who came to see her. They'd never be able to understand.

And she's worried about her phone. She never thought they'd take that.

But there are other things worth being much more scared about.

She hopes the young policeman will keep his promise and bring her phone back tomorrow, but she doesn't believe he will. People in positions of authority are much better at taking than giving.

She wonders what the punishment for procuring is.

But they'll help her. Of course they will, won't they?

The bad people.

The ones she really doesn't want anything to do with.

She ought to run. Just abandon everything and leave. She's got some money saved up. It would last her a year or so.

But after that?

Starting again at the age of sixty-one. Impossible.

She turns right into Götgatan and sees the old Tax Office tower rise up in front of her. She's read somewhere that the Swedes are the most taxed people in the world. But society seems to work the way it should. She can't understand it. Her own accounts would never be sustainable if she didn't keep a share of the money off the books.

What does everyone else do? Are they all doing the same?

She's been through the accounts ledger that the police missed and tried to massage the figures with the help of forged invoices and fake receipts. But the business still looks barely profitable. Its real income is made from its other activities. The ones that never appear in the accounts.

She turns off into Åsögatan, mostly out of habit. Usually she likes the peace and quiet there. Such a contrast to the hustle and bustle of Götgatan.

But this evening the buildings are too dark and gray.

Vaguely threatening.

She cuts through a side street to Skånegatan instead. Much more life there, a comforting hubbub from the pavement terraces of the bars and restaurants.

Sukayana Prikon carries on until she reaches the dense vegetation of Vitabergs Park, and finds herself thinking of the chase through Tantolunden earlier that day.

It was a vain attempt to get away.

No one can escape their fate.

But what harm had Mi Mi and the others done?

She sees the eye staring at her from the ravaged face.

She can't think anymore. She has to sleep. Tomorrow will be better. It must be.

She takes several deep breaths. Tries to buck herself up.

She's going to get through this, just like she managed to get through her marriage to a Swedish man. He used to hit her, but she hit back.

She walks down the slope behind the park's large open-air stage and emerges onto Gaveliusgatan. Almost home now. She's longing for the softness of her bed.

A sound makes her jump.

A car door opening right next to her.

She sees the sliding door of a van glide open and arms reach out toward her. A stinking rag is pressed over her nose and mouth as someone grabs hold of her from behind.

She is picked up off the ground and drifts into an unreal white fog.

14

THE DENSE night sky outside the apartment window is full of tiny pricks of light. As if all the stars want to show off at the same time in Zack's dream. Cassiopeia, the Big Dipper, Orion, Hydra, and Leo.

He rolls over in bed and murmurs something inaudible.

The clock on the chest of drawers says 3:34, and in his internal world the myriad stars of the heavens are transforming into the frosty image of a woman's face.

She beckons him with a soft, whispering voice, like the wind speaking:

"Zack, Zack, come to me."

Once more he longs to travel up to the stars, up to the whispering voice. He's on his way now, can feel the gravitational force of the Earth slowly loosen its grip. Up, up.

Away.

But the woman's face is changing. The stars are swirling around, changing places, until a contorted face with black eyes and bestial teeth stares down at Zack.

He wants to get out of the dream now.

But it won't let go, and carries him higher and higher up, and the being waiting for him is made of pure evil.

Zack wants to turn around but he can't. Slowly he approaches the female figure's face, which is staring at him with distaste.

"Get lost, you disgusting little creature."

But then she changes again. Her features relax, and she sounds worried as she looks down at him beseechingly:

"This is wrong, darling."

She shuts her eyes, turns her face away, and sobs hysterically before disappearing into a black, screaming darkness.

THE ACRID stench of excrement is the first thing Sukayana Prikon notices as she slowly comes back to life. A disgusting smell made not by human beings, but animals.

Dogs?

She snaps awake.

Has to get away, up, out, because she's somewhere she shouldn't be.

Wherever it is she's lying, it's dark, and when she tries to get up she immediately hits her head. She wants to sit up, but it's impossible. She feels around her.

Rough wood.

On all sides.

Is it a coffin? Have they buried me alive?

She tries kicking her legs, and realizes she can't move them freely.

There's something chafing against her thighs. As if her legs were sticking out of the coffin.

What is this? Where am I?

"Hello?" she cries. "Is there anyone there?"

But there's nothing but silence on all sides of her.

She tries to think. She remembers the van door opening and the foul-smelling rag being pressed over her face.

She's been kidnapped.

But where have they taken her?

She kicks her legs again. Feels the rough wooden floor

scrape her skin, and there's that same acrid smell again.

The darkness and silence are a violent, thunderous wave now. Everything is wrong. Terribly wrong. The darkness, the stench, and the coffin.

Must get up. Out.

Must get away.

She doesn't understand.

What are they going to do to her legs?

Blood courses through her body and her heartbeat is pounding so hard in her temples that it hurts. She has to get free.

Now, now, now.

She pushes hard against the walls, tries to twist in both directions, but she can't move at all.

She thinks about torture methods she's read about. The sort where they hit the soles of your feet with batons until the pain spreads through your whole body.

Or are they going to pour boiling water on her legs? More and more, until the skin comes loose? She's heard of that too.

Is that what they're thinking of doing? But why? What has she done wrong? She's been conscientious in her work. Always paid on time. Kept her staff in good order.

It's not her fault they're dead.

But she's talked to the police. She's let them look through her computer and accounts. Is that what she's being punished for?

But what could she have done? This isn't like Thailand, where you can pay the police to look the other way.

She searches for cracks that she could try to prize open, but the only things that break are her nails.

She feels like howling now, but she's too scared of what might happen.

Is this the end?

No tears, Sukayana.

She's going to get out of the coffin.

Now, try!

She strains her back against the wood.

Roars.

But only inside.

She falls still when she hears the sound of voices nearby, several male voices talking quietly.

Then she hears the first growl.

The scream gushes out of her, she can't help it. She screams and screams, and she pushes upward so hard that her skin breaks. She kicks wildly in all directions, but gets nowhere.

Instead the box itself starts to move. It's swinging back and forth, and her legs can no longer reach the ground. The men give each other orders, and she can feel herself being moved sideways. Then the movement stops abruptly, and she sways to and fro in the air.

The growling is clearer now. An animal is whimpering loudly very close to her, and another is barking some distance away.

The box is lowered.

Down toward the terrible sounds.

She doesn't understand.

Doesn't want to understand.

The box hits the floor and she can feel cold concrete and scratchy straw against her legs.

The men's voices above her now. She thinks she recognizes one of them, and realizes what that means.

She hears the sound of the animals' claws on the concrete floor and soon feels their hot breath against the bare skin of her legs.

Sniffing.

Exploring.

The men are laughing now.

And Sukayana screams and screams.

THE DISTANT screams sound like terrifying whispers through the damp walls. Whispers that cut straight to your marrow.

The girls cry quietly and hug each other. Stroke each other's hair and backs with fingers whose tips are scabbed and raw after hours of fruitless efforts to dig their way out through the hard earth floor.

A car engine starts. Doors are slammed shut.

Steps approaching.

Whom are they going to fetch now?

Who's going to disappear forever?

Than Than Oo?

The child in her belly, due to come out soon, will it ever have a chance to live?

And what about her? She's only fourteen years old.

Gruff voices outside the door now. The sound of a key being inserted in the padlock.

A bolt is slid back and their cell is bathed in light from a single torch.

And now it's their turn to scream.

ZACK STARES up at the ceiling, wide awake, breathing heavily. He's kicked the covers off and his naked body is wet with sweat.

He's scared. The dream has scared him more than anything he's experienced when he's awake. It's a fear that creeps out into every pore, making him feel nauseous. As if he's seen something no person should see. As if he's just peered in through one of the gates of hell.

He switches on the bedside lamp, picks up a screwdriver from the floor, and stumbles over to the corner of the room. He carefully prizes off a length of skirting board and lifts the corner of the yellow plastic flooring.

Under the mat is a wooden floor. Zack sticks the screwdriver into a gap and carefully levers it up. The wooden lid creaks, but eventually he pulls it free and sticks his hand into the hidden compartment.

He takes out the thick, black leather folder. A name tag has been inserted into a small plastic sleeve in one corner.

Anna Herry.

He sits on the floor with his back against the bed, and in the pale light of the bedside lamp he carefully leafs through the documents, newspaper clippings, and photographs.

On top are some yellowed pages from *Expressen* and *Aftonbladet*. He unfolds one of them.

NEWSFLASH: POLICEWOMAN KILLED IN KNIFE ATTACK

A large black-and-white picture of Tysta Marigången. A black tunnel where the anxious glow of bare neon lights reflects like silver from the filthy windows of abandoned shops. The police cordon hangs limply, waiting. Beneath that picture a smaller one, of a black puddle on the paved floor.

Your blood, Mom.

The life that ran out of you.

Zack looks at the large picture. The chill in its gray tones, a place that seems devoid of all empathy.

It must have been cold as she lay there in the passageway. So lonely.

Were you scared, Mom?

Or did it happen quickly?

Did you have time to think of me?

Zack pulls the police photograph of the crime scene out of an envelope in the folder. The pool of blood is almost a yard in diameter.

He carries on looking. More photographs of the passageway, from different angles.

Then pictures from the postmortem.

Zack pauses over the first close-up. His mom's slender, beautiful neck, traced with fine blue veins. And then the deep cut across it. Like a plowed furrow through her almost transparent white skin.

He moves on to the next photograph. It's taken from the same angle, but shows her whole face. Her eyelids are closed but her mouth is open. He's never been able to read her face in this picture. She doesn't seem to be suffering, but there's nothing peaceful about her. There's something intangible about the set of her mouth. As if Mona Lisa's mouth were open and she was trying to say something.

What did you want to say, Mom?

There are eight pictures of her on the postmortem table. Some whole-body shots. His mother, completely naked in that cold room. Zack's seen the photographs a thousand times. Even so, his hands are trembling as he holds them, and he wishes he could look away, make the truth a lie.

But instead he stares at them for a long time, trying to see something he hasn't seen before. For the first time he thinks she looks young, and realizes that he's only three years younger than she was when she died.

Soon I'll be older than my own mother.

It's an impossible thought.

He remembers one afternoon when just the two of them were at home, and it felt like they had all the time in the world.

A moment with no horizon.

He was sitting in her lap, asking her about so many things. About the Earth and the heavens, about cars and airplanes. She was his mom, she knew everything, could do everything.

If he ever had a small child in his lap, would the child think the same about him? Would he seem as patient and inexhaustible in the child's eyes?

Is that what Ester sees in him?

No.

He doesn't think he can do any of the things his mom was good at. Or, to be more accurate, the things he assumed she was good at. He doesn't remember that much. But he remembers her voice. And he remembers her embrace.

The way she would hug him hard, hard, hard.

But never too hard.

Did you, Mom?

He puts the pictures back in the envelope and takes out the file containing the records of the investigation. On the front of the preliminary investigation report is the stamp he hates:

CASE DROPPED

Zack knows the story by heart. She was working on her first case as a homicide detective. A surgeon had died in what looked at first to be an accident. A gas pipe had come away from the stove while he was asleep, and he never woke up again.

But both the stove manufacturer and the police's own forensics experts reached the same conclusion: the pipe could never have come loose without help.

Anna Herry conducted a long series of interviews with the victim's colleagues and people close to him. Late one afternoon she called home and told Roy she needed to do a few hours overtime. She sounded stressed, almost upset.

"I think I'm on to something," she said.

She left Police Headquarters sometime between 11:30 and midnight, but she never came home.

A huge amount of police resources was deployed, as it always is when an officer has been murdered. But the murder of Anna Herry seemed to have aroused stronger emotions than usual, and when Zack spoke to her former bosses many years later he finally understood why.

Anna Herry had been one of the few female homicide detectives in the early nineties, an important marker in a male-dominated profession with a problematic macho image. She was clearly highly intelligent, and could hold her own against the men. She was also very good-looking and knew how to deal with journalists.

The combination of these factors meant that she had been on her way to becoming a symbol for the future of the police force. A door opener for other women, and an eye-opener for more conservative colleagues and politicians.

Then she was murdered. Brutally murdered, in a seedy place and by an obviously ruthless killer. It was like an attack against the entire force.

Her killer had to be caught.

But he wasn't caught.

A number of men were taken in for questioning. One of them was even remanded in custody, suspected on good grounds of having committed the murder. But the case wasn't strong enough. The prosecutor couldn't even prove that the man had been in the center of Stockholm on the night of the murder.

Eighteen months after the killing, the investigation was

put on the back burner, and a couple of years after that it was dropped.

Zack remembers his father swearing quietly to himself when he read the written notification, then, with a great effort, crumpling the paper up between his stiff, aching fingers and tossing it in the garbage.

Later that evening, when Roy was watching the news on television, Zack crept into the kitchen and pulled out the ball of paper. He straightened it out as best he could, and that night he sat with his pocket flashlight and tried to spell his way through the difficult words.

He was only seven years old at the time, and didn't understand everything it said. But what he did understand was enough: the police were going to stop looking for his mom's killer.

That night he decided he was going to join the police.

He took a drawing pin off the bulletin board in his room, sat down on the blue carpet, and pricked out a drop of blood.

Then he pressed his hand to the crumpled sheet of paper and said his promise out loud to himself:

"I, Zacharias Herry, swear that I will never give up until I've found the person who killed my mom."

It ended up being rather a large bloodstain. He remembers thinking that it looked good. As if it was really serious.

He can see himself as a seven-year-old.

A small figure in pajamas, aware of the cruelty of the world at far too young an age. Who, somewhere deep in his childish soul, realizes that it's fundamentally up to the individual to create his own truth and make his own fate.

He takes the crumpled, yellowed sheet of paper out of a plastic sleeve in the folder and looks at it.

The blood print has long since turned black. It looks so small, he thinks. The same color as the pool of his mom's blood in Tysta Marigången.

One day I'm going to find your killer, Mom.

Often it feels like everything is far too late, that all possible avenues have already been explored. But he knows that isn't the case. He knows that a murderer always leaves a trail, and he knows that the chances of getting a suspect convicted are greater now than when the investigation was conducted.

Zack leafs through some sheets of paper that haven't yet turned yellow.

His own interviews with the original detectives. Nine sheets of letter-size paper.

He reads a few quotes:

"We never even came close."

"Sorry, Zack. It was impossible to identify a real suspect. That arrest was just playing to the gallery. Believe me, that man was innocent."

He looks through his own photographs of Tysta Marigången. There's an international accountancy firm there now, the sort that helps rich people hide their money away in tax havens. But the place is just as dark and run down. Just as unpleasant in the eyes of the general public as it always has been.

He feels like heading out into the night now.

Looking for forgetfulness and the thud of heavy bass.

But the clock on the bedside table is saying it's already 4:30. So he takes two 5-milligram Stesolid tablets from his secret stash under the floor.

He swallows them down with water and regrets it immediately.

What on earth is he doing?

Taking pills to help him sleep.

When did he actually start doing that?

He tries to think.

Six months ago, maybe. When the dreams started to get really bad.

When he found himself waking up screaming almost every night. When he started to see things during the day as well.

When every spot of blood became his mother's blood. When every starlit night forced him onto his back out in that meadow.

Night after night.

Just as bad as it had been in real life.

Worse, even.

He always knew in advance how it would end, but could still never do anything different.

It wasn't intentional.

But you did it, Zack.

He hadn't dreamed about it for several years. He loved his new job. He was doing his best. Doing good things. Getting praised for what he did. Helping the good guys. Catching the bad guys. Demonstrating a courage that few people could muster.

He'd stopped obsessing about the past.

But now it's as if those first few years in the police had merely been a warm-up, and only now is everything getting serious. As if all his cases so far were simply exercises, and now he has to prove himself properly.

He put up with the dreams for a few weeks, then he asked Abdula to get him some tranquilizers. That wasn't enough. His sheets were still soaked with sweat every time he found himself sitting up in bed, hyperventilating.

He started taking stronger drugs. And slept better. Got himself some breathing space.

And it was only a temporary measure, after all.

A fuck of a long while for something temporary, don't you think?

Who gives a shit?

It'll work out.

Everything works out in the end.

He falls asleep in a comforting narcotic haze.

But then comes the darkness within the darkness.

He's being chased by unknown beasts of prey. Their jaws are snapping at his neck. Then he dreams that he walks up to one of the shot women and sees his mom's face. Sam Koltberg is laughing loudly in his blue doctor's coat as he cuts away at her crotch. But the windows of the mortuary are open. Zack throws himself out into the night and finds the dead Thai women again. They're the most beautiful of all the stars in the black vault of the heavens.

PART II

About the men close to the edge of heaven,

About lust, violence, and boys becoming men,

And how the jagged teeth of night snap at anything human.

15

A MURMUR of chatter from twenty or so weary police officers greets Zack as he opens the door to the lecture hall. Douglas is standing onstage, connecting the wires from the projector to his laptop.

Zack takes a seat toward the back, where the sloping ash-wood roof drops sharply toward the pale green, fabric-covered walls. The whole of the Special Crimes Unit is there, as well as a number of uniforms. The air is already stuffy and full of testosterone, even though almost half of the assembled officers are women.

He knows Douglas likes to gather together as many of his colleagues as possible at an early stage of an investigation, to make sure the right information gets disseminated.

Zack can see the neatly coiffed back of Sam Koltberg's head in the first row. Off to the side he catches sight of Tommy Östman.

Zack yawns.

All he wants is to get back out into the field and carry on working the case, but he knows he's got to put up with this run-through before he can get going.

Fortunately he feels much brighter today than yesterday. His body has recovered, despite another night of broken sleep, and the pain in his shoulder has gone.

Douglas clears his throat, welcomes them all, and gives a

brief summary of the previous day's events and the state of the investigation.

He points the little remote at his computer and passport photographs of the four women appear on the white screen.

"The passports of the murdered women have been found tucked away at the bottom of a drawer in the apartment, and, as you can see here, they're all Thai citizens. The names match the ones Zack and Deniz found out, but—strangely enough—we haven't had any matches in official records in Thailand. Our contact in Bangkok has managed to find a woman with the same name and ID number as one of the victims, but she's running a clothes shop in Surat Thani and is very much alive. So we must assume that the passports are fakes—albeit very good fakes—and that the dead women could be anyone. We've sent the information to our colleagues in Thailand, so we'll have to see what they can come up with."

"Why were they using fake passports?"

The voice is gruff, and comes from a thickset policeman in the second row.

"Several reasons. If the women obtained the passports themselves, it could be that they were trying to protect their families. If they were picked up abroad, their relatives back home wouldn't be questioned about it. There's a lot of evidence to suggest that they were prostitutes—we've found medical certificates stating that they didn't have HIV or any other venereal diseases, for instance. It's not unusual for people paying for sex to want to see that sort of certificate.

"If a so-called recruitment agency organized the passports, the intention may have been to stop the women's relatives finding them, and make it harder for the police if anything went wrong. As it obviously has."

Not even the genuine article, Zack thinks. Wasn't that

what Sonny Järvinen had said? Did he mean that they came from a different country? Cambodia, perhaps. That looked like it would soon be as popular a destination for sex tourism as Thailand.

Sukayana Prikon must have been lying to us, giving us false names. Unless she didn't know any better? We need to talk to her again.

"Any more questions so far?" Douglas asks. "Okay. Tommy, your turn."

The tall, ungainly figure of the profiler, Tommy Östman, steps awkwardly up onto the stage. His face is thin, with deep wrinkles around his mouth, and his beige corduroy suit has shiny patches on the knees and elbows.

"I've produced a perpetrator profile based on the information we've got, but so far unfortunately that's just what was found at the crime scene."

He coughs from deep in his lungs and Zack can't help wondering if the signs will always be there, if Östman will look and sound like an old alcoholic until his dying day.

None of his colleagues was probably ever expecting to see him sober again. But somehow he managed to pull himself together. He went back to college in Uppsala and a few years later made an unexpected return as a profiler.

Quite an achievement, Zack thinks. So why is he always so bitter and miserable? After all, he's more or less conquered Mount Everest.

Possibly because he hasn't managed to defeat all his demons. Because he still gambles way too much, legally and illegally. The wages department now pays his rent and electricity bill before paying his salary into his bank account, and his official cell has a block on it to prevent him calling the most common betting companies.

Östman coughs again and goes on:

"In all likelihood, these offenses were committed by a man."

His hoarse voice, which in other contexts can sound weak and uncertain, becomes firmer as he talks about the possible perpetrator.

"We're dealing with a single male, as suggested by the text message, 'He kill all,' and I'm convinced that this is the case. A cold, calculating man. A man used to moving in criminal circles. Used to violence. Angry with women. Possibly a loner with warped ideas and ideals. Probably not someone who belongs to any organized group, like a biker gang. Unless this was a commission, and someone wants us to think it was the work of a madman," he says.

The next man up at the podium is Sam Koltberg. Today dressed in a gray jacket, white shirt, and a blue tie with three crowns on it.

As if he were some sort of fucking king, Zack thinks.

Koltberg looks around the room and manages to flash Zack a contemptuous glare before he starts to speak:

"The crime scene was basically clean. No fingerprints or other physical evidence of the perpetrator or perpetrators. We've sent samples to the National Forensics Lab for analysis, but obviously the results will only be of interest when we've got a suspect we can compare them with, or if we get a match in the database. There's a mixture of blood on the floor and some of the furniture, but we've been able to confirm that it all came from the women."

Koltberg asks Douglas to bring up some pictures of the crime scene. The first is an overview that makes some of the officers instinctively turn their heads away.

"Three of the women were shot twice, the fourth three

times. In each case they were shot in the chest or face before being shot in the crotch. At least three of the women were already dead by the time the perpetrator fired the second shot. We're less sure of the fourth case, because the body had already been taken away to the mortuary by the time we arrived at the scene."

Zack can't help thinking that Koltberg is looking at him again.

Does he still think it was my fault that the paramedics took that woman away? he wonders. Or is it the way I dress that upsets him? If it is, fine. Sooner jeans and a T-shirt than a ridiculous tie.

"The bullets came from a nine-millimeter Beretta, one of the commonest guns in the world, and a popular pistol here in Sweden. They're also smuggled in from the Balkans in large numbers, which means that the quantity of unregistered weapons is believed to be high."

Koltberg steps down and Douglas takes over again.

"We've questioned a potential suspect who fits the profile pretty well," Douglas says, and gives a brief summary of Peter Karlson's background and the interview with him on Monday evening.

"Right now he doesn't have an alibi for the time of the murders, so we need to take a closer look at him today."

"But the fact that he fell out with the massage parlor over an invoice—is that really a credible motive for a multiple homicide?" the gruff policeman says again with a slight chuckle.

"I agree that it might sound like a weak motive, but in this instance that invoice could just have been the catalyst, the straw that broke the camel's back.

"Niklas, do you want to add anything?"

Niklas stands up and adjusts his jacket.

"Peter Karlson is a hatemonger of the intellectual variety. A fanatic who probably has the capacity and the contacts to build up a well-funded Aryan resistance movement in the business community. I got a feeling that the meeting he mentioned out in Edsviken could have been about that very subject. He also seems to have decided to direct his hatred primarily at Asians. Which is why I think he's of interest to us, both as a potential lone perpetrator, or as part of something larger."

"Obviously, you're going to carry on looking into him today," Douglas says, clicking to bring up a picture of Sonny Järvinen on the screen.

"And then we've got the biker gang, the Brotherhood of No Mercy. It's long been known that the club controls a large number of massage parlors in the Stockholm region, and our working theory is that the undeclared earnings from prostitution have made the business a target for organized crime.

"There are two hundred massage parlors in Stockholm alone, and they bring in an average of fifteen thousand kronor a day in declared earnings. The true figure is probably many times that, especially if we're talking about more than just massages, so it's a business big enough to be worth fighting over. But what we don't know is what percentage of the parlors are linked to organized crime."

"Is the Sawatdii parlor run by this biker gang, then?" a female officer in the third row asks.

"According to Sawatdii's manager, Sukayana Prikon, they've helped her recruit staff, but Sonny Järvinen, the gang leader, denies this. We're going to be looking through the accounts of both the massage parlor and the recruitment company run by the bikers today, in the hope of finding confirmation of the connection. We're also going to question her further today, not least to find out the women's true identities. We have to find some way of contacting their relatives."

Zack hopes he'll be allowed to conduct the interview. He'd relish the opportunity to question her a bit harder about her links to the biker gang, as well as the fake passports. And he might be able to return her phone to her, as a sign of goodwill.

Douglas invites Deniz to give an account of the unexpected shootout at the biker's clubhouse. She gets to her feet and Zack sees that she's covered up the bandage around her neck with a multicolored scarf. It looks good. The others listen carefully—it's not every day that their colleagues find themselves in a gunfight.

"There's no doubt that the bikers were ready for a fight when we arrived," she says. "That doesn't necessarily mean they've got anything to do with the murders, but at the very least it's an interesting coincidence. The question is: Who or what were they expecting?"

She runs through the underlying motives that could indicate the involvement of the Brotherhood in the murders. Then she sits back down and Douglas goes on:

"Questioning the bikers hasn't thrown up anything useful, but that's hardly unexpected. These individuals know how to keep their mouths shut. But they seem nervous, so something might be going on. Two of them have been released on the advice of the prosecutor, two have been remanded in custody, charged with the attempted murder of Zack and Deniz, and their leader, Sonny Järvinen, is in custody for incitement to murder. The custody hearings are going to be held tomorrow, but we'll have another go at them today. Järvinen, anyway. We'll have to see what that gives us."

Sirpa is sitting a few rows in front of Zack. He watches her stand up with an effort and raise her hand to speak.

"Sirpa," Douglas says.

"I started to put together a database of customers based on the information in Sukayana Prikon's computer last night. We've also added the names we found in her cell phone, and in those belonging to the murdered women."

"We?" Douglas asks.

"Yes, it took a bit of time, but I had the help of an alert and talented trainee," she says, nodding with a smile to a young woman with her dark hair in a ponytail. The trainee blushes and glances nervously around the room.

"Either way, we've got a list of just over fifty names, numbers, and anonymous email addresses, so obviously we'll be trying to identify them all as quickly as possible."

Douglas nods his approval.

"Good work. I'll see to it that you get any names that might crop up when the accounts and most recent invoices have been examined."

Zack lets out a large yawn and stretches. The room has got very warm, and he can feel his lower back sweating. Meetings like this drain him of energy.

Douglas delegates work to the group leaders. The owners of the most lucrative massage parlors are to be questioned for information, and old tip-offs about prostitution from the public will be dusted off and looked at again.

"Okay, people. Out into the real world with you."

16

THE MOTHER pushing the twin buggy is in a hurry. There's never enough time to get everything done, and this particular Tuesday morning seems worse than ever.

Wrestling the boys into the car.

"Need a pee!"

Out again, and suddenly they're running late.

Their doctor's appointment was two minutes ago.

But at least the sun is shining.

She half-jogs from the parking lot toward the main entrance of the Södermalm Hospital, the one with the projecting white roof and red benches. She doesn't see the car before it bounces over the curb of the pavement and brakes hard just a yard or so in front of her buggy. One of the back doors opens and something is pushed out. Very gradually, as if time has slowed down, the body tumbles toward the tarmac and hits the ground right in front of the stroller.

The car drives off at high speed.

The three-year-old boys start screaming, and when their mother sees what the children have seen, she starts screaming as well. Two men come running over to help, but pull back instantly.

"Oh, fucking hell!" one of the men says.

His legs feel like they're about to give way, but he grabs

hold of a street sign and clings on as the vomit gushes from his mouth.

It's a woman's body. She's lying on the tarmac, not quite on her side, wearing nothing but a white undershirt and underpants. Her thin clothes are flecked with blood and excrement, but that isn't what's making the woman and children scream and the man throw up.

It's what's missing.

Her legs.

It looks like someone's torn them from her body by force, or carved them off with a blunt instrument. Stringy remnants of sinew and muscle dangle from what's left of her thighs. Thick leather belts have been strapped tight around the stumps to stop the bleeding, and from the left thigh a stubby white bone protrudes a few inches.

The mother quickly turns the stroller away from the body so abruptly that the boys start screaming even louder.

"Do something, do something!" she shrieks at the men standing there staring at the mutilated woman.

One of them pulls out his phone and starts to dial 112 with trembling fingers. Then he remembers where he is and runs back in through the swinging doors instead.

The older man walks tentatively up to the woman, as if he were approaching a firework that hadn't yet gone off.

An acrid stench he's never smelled before.

Never wants to smell again.

Blood, flesh, and excrement. A few flies are already buzzing around the wounds.

Then he hears her groan and sees her move her head slightly.

"Dear God, she's alive," he mutters to himself.

He kneels down stiffly beside her head, but doesn't know what to do. He gently strokes her hair and says:

"There, now, it's going to be okay. You'll see. The doctors are on their way."

More people have gathered around the woman. They can't stop staring at the mutilated body, as if they were witnessing some macabre play, and a man in a suit who's just come out of the hospital stops midstride.

"Out of the way!"

He is suddenly shoved in the back and stumbles aside as two women and a man, all in white coats, come rushing out with a gurney.

The first white coat is an anesthetist, Marianne Edberg, a wiry, gray-haired woman in her sixties. She immediately puts two fingers to the woman's neck and brushes the hair away from her face. The mutilated woman seems to be roughly the same age as her.

Who dumped you here? she thinks. Who could be monstrous enough to inflict this sort of damage on another human being?

She looks down at the woman's thighs, or rather what's left of them. She's seen a lot of things, but nothing remotely like this.

A nurse comes out with a blue emergency bicycle loaded with medical equipment.

"What do you need?" she says.

"She's got a pulse. It's weak, but she's breathing," Marianne Edberg says.

With practiced movements they lift the woman onto the gurney. Two small pools of blood have formed on the tarmac under the stumps of her legs.

They fix an oxygen mask over her nose and mouth, run toward the elevator, and press the button for the first level below the ground floor.

"This is going to be tight," Marianne Edberg says as the door slides open and she sees the emergency room ahead of her.

17

DOUGLAS'S PHONE starts to vibrate in his jacket pocket just as the last police officers are leaving the lecture hall. He looks at the screen. Number withheld. Probably some spotty call-center salesman, but it could be from another official body. He takes the call.

"Juste . . . Yes, that's me. When? Can we come over? Thanks, I'll send two of my officers at once."

He runs out into the corridor and shouts:

"Zack! Deniz!"

They're about to step into the elevator when they hear his voice.

"You've got to get to Södermalm Hospital. A woman who's had her legs cut off has just been brought in. Thai appearance, according to the doctor. And they say it doesn't look like an accident."

Zack and Deniz see the concern in his eyes. They look at each other.

Another young woman from a massage parlor?

Or Sukayana Prikon?

FIFTEEN MINUTES later Deniz parks the car outside the white canopied entrance of the hospital. Zack drums his fingers on the dashboard. On the way he's been repeating the same phrase to himself, over and over again.

"It can't be Sukayana. It can't be her."

The emergency room is full of people, most of them sitting quietly and waiting patiently for their turn.

The yellow walls of the waiting room seem to have a soothing effect.

A middle-aged woman in a lilac-spotted fleece is standing at the reception desk discussing something with the nurse on the other side of the glass. Zack and Deniz show their ID and push in front of her.

"We're police officers. It's urgent," Zack says.

The woman in the fleece looks annoyed, but can't think of anything to say.

Zack tells the nurse why they're there.

She looks up at him, and stares at his face. She blushes, but quickly pulls herself together as she recognizes the seriousness in his voice.

"Just a moment, I'll check."

Zack and Deniz look around the waiting room. A few elderly people, a teenage girl with her arm in plaster, several children with runny noses. No one who seems seriously injured.

The nurse returns. She's trying to stay focused, but can't help smiling shyly at Zack. "The patient's no longer down here. She's being operated on in the OR now."

"Where's that?"

"The hybrid operating room, a special unit in the operating department. You can't see her at the moment, but you can talk to the doctor who saw her when she was brought in."

"Thanks."

"Follow me."

IN A windowless office with pale yellow walls Zack and Deniz introduce themselves to Marianne Edberg. She's sitting behind a beech-veneer desk and Zack can't help noticing the skepticism in her eyes as she looks at him. A twenty-seven-year-old wearing a T-shirt and leather jacket isn't what she was expecting.

He's starting to get fed up with looks like that. What does he have to do to be accepted?

Deniz in her turquoise top, patterned scarf, and dark gray jacket seems to meet with approval, though.

"Have you managed to identify the woman yet?" she asks as they sit down on the visitors' chairs.

"No. Our first priority is to save her life, not to . . ."

The doctor stops herself, as if she's realized how sharp she sounded. She puts a hand to her forehead and takes a deep breath before going on:

"You must forgive me if I sound upset, but I'm so angry that someone could just dump a seriously injured woman on the pavement like that. Like she was an animal."

"And we want to catch whoever did that," Deniz says. "Did you or any of your colleagues see who brought her here?"

"No, by the time we got the alert she was already there. All on her own."

"But there must have been other witnesses?"

"Of course. But I haven't had a moment to think about that. I got the alarm, ran outside, and there she was. And then nothing else mattered."

"Do you know if any of the people who saw what happened left their contact details?"

"Check with the staff on the reception desk down at the

main entrance. I'd guess that's where they would have gone to sound the alarm."

We need to get hold of that car as soon as possible, Zack thinks. Find the madmen who did this. Someone must have noticed the registration number or seen more of what happened. And if the injured woman does turn out to be Sukayana Prikon, the car would also be an important piece of the puzzle in their murder investigation.

"Let's split up," Deniz tells Zack. "You find out who the injured woman is, and I'll go down to reception and see what information they've got."

"Okay, I'll come and find you there."

Zack turns back to Marianne Edberg.

"Is there any way I could take a look inside the operating theater? We really do need to identify the victim, and there's a good chance I'd recognize her if I could just see her face."

"You can take a look through the window. I'll show you the way, then we can talk as we go."

They head down a long, deserted corridor, where someone has seen fit to stick a pink, rose-patterned border along the middle of the pale blue wall. A faint smell of surgical spirit and disinfectant fills the air, and Zack inhales memories of fragile lives and inoperable illnesses. He often went to the hospital with his dad, and used to visit him in Danderyd when he was receiving dangerously high doses of cortisone.

But he can't think about that now.

"What injuries has she got?" he asks.

"Both legs were cut off high up her thighs," Marianne Edberg says. "And it looks like she was attacked by dogs."

"Dogs?"

"Or some sort of large carnivore. Both the bite marks and the way the flesh was torn from the bone point in that direction. I go hunting myself, and I've seen similar injuries inflicted by predators before. We also had to wash a lot of excrement off her body, and it smelled considerably worse than just human excrement."

So you're a hunter, Zack thinks. That seems like a paradox. Saving lives at work, then donning a camouflage jacket and extinguishing life elsewhere in your free time.

"So you're saying she was attacked by a mad dog? Or some other predator, a wolf, or something?"

"It's most likely that it was a dog that did it, or several dogs. As far as I'm aware, wild wolves have never attacked anyone in Sweden, even if there are plenty of sightings in the Stockholm area these days."

"Is any of the excrement still there?" Zack asks, seeing in his mind's eye the mixed-breed dog out at the Brotherhood of No Mercy's clubhouse. He's also wondering if Peter Karlson has a dog.

"No, we had to wash her because of the risk of infection. But I did save a sample. I thought it could be useful to you."

"Good thinking," Zack says.

He falls silent for a few moments, thinking over what the doctor has told him about the injuries.

"Could they have attacked her afterward?" he asks.

"How do you mean?"

"Could anyone have cut her legs off, and then left her for whatever those animals were?"

Marianne Edberg raises her eyebrows, as if she were only just beginning to appreciate what the woman might have been subjected to.

"It's possible," she says.

They enter the X-ray department and walk into the room where patients are sedated before operations. Unless the situation is critical, as it was this time, in which case the gurney is wheeled straight into the hybrid operating theater.

Marianne Edberg points toward a round window in a door.

"She's in there."

Zack looks through the window. The operating room is large and airy. Gleaming metal, shining white walls and floor. A large X-ray machine hangs from the ceiling, along with two active television monitors and operating lamps with LED lights. Below them stand six people in protective masks, working on the woman. Some are dressed in green, others in blue. There are leads running into her body from the anesthetic apparatus on one side of the table and a bag of blood on a drip stand on the other. Further tubes and cables lead off to other machines Zack can't see.

The woman is largely concealed by a green sheet, but her gaping wounds are exposed, with thin tubes inserted into the bleeding stumps.

One of the staff in blue moves away to fetch an instrument, giving Zack a chance to see the patient's face.

He feels like screaming and slamming his hand against the wall.

But he manages to stop himself.

"Fuck," he whispers, so quietly that Marianne Edberg barely hears.

Why didn't we take her in? Why didn't we offer her some sort of protection?

He runs his hands through his hair, shuts his eyes, and tries to gather his thoughts.

"So you do recognize her, then?" Marianne Edberg says.

"Her name is Sukayana Prikon. I talked to her yesterday in connection with a murder investigation."

Marianne Edberg raises her eyebrows.

"Is she suspected of murder?"

"No, she's just of interest to our investigation. But we believe she's got important information for us."

Marianne Edberg considers this, and nods silently.

Zack looks into the operating theater again. Watches the doctors trying to save what's left of her legs.

He tries to take a deep breath, but the air only seems to get halfway into his lungs.

I could have arrested her for attacking me with that knife. Or for procurement. Maybe we had enough to bring her in for that.

He looks at the stumps of her legs again and feels his own knees wobble.

"When do you think we'll be able to question her?"

"She's lost a lot of blood, and her injuries are extremely serious. And her CRP values are through the roof, which means she's fighting some sort of infection as well. We don't know what yet. If she survives, it'll be a while before she's up to being questioned."

"We're going to have to put a guard on her."

"I understand," Marianne Edberg says with a look of resignation. "I'm afraid it's getting more and more common to see police officers on our wards."

And if that gun-carrying biker gang is involved in this mess, Zack thinks, there's not much chance of that ending anytime soon.

DENIZ IS sitting on a bench rubbing the bandage under her scarf when Zack arrives in the entrance hall.

"It was Sukayana," he says before she has time to ask the question. "It looks like her legs have been eaten by dogs."

"Dogs?"

"Or something. Some sort of predator, anyway. And there's no guarantee that she's going to survive."

Deniz looks angry. Says:

"Sonny Järvinen and his acolytes seem to like macho dogs."

Zack nods.

"How did you get on?" he asks.

"They haven't got a thing. Nothing. All they know is that a car stopped and left her on the ground. But no one reported a registration number or make of car, not even the fucking color. And at least five people saw it."

"Did you get any of their names or phone numbers?"

"Do you think those idiots behind the desk took any details? 'Oh, we didn't think of that,'" Deniz says, in a mocking imitation of their voices.

On the way out to the car Zack almost steps in a pile of vomit outside the hospital. And there's a fresh parking ticket on the windshield. He tears it in two and throws it on the ground.

They sit in silence for a long while on their way back to Police Headquarters on Kungsholmen. Zack can't shake off the image of Sukayana Prikon in the operating theater, the way there was nothing where her legs should have been, the skin of her face all but lifeless.

They stop at a red light by the entrance to the subway station at Fridhemsplan, its blue-and-white sign beckoning people into the subway, while the ice-cream kiosk next to the newsstand is doing brisk business.

People pass by as if it were a perfectly ordinary summer's day, as if they lived in a world without evil, without any problems.

Zack feels like opening the window and telling them about Sukayana Prikon.

About the Thai women, if that's what they were.

About all the women like them.

About all the victims of trafficking, hundreds of thousands of them.

What were you mixed up in, Sukayana Prikon?

He can see the fleshy stumps of her legs in front of him.

His private phone buzzes. He ignores it.

"Suppose Sukayana Prikon hasn't been doing business with Recruitment Solutions Ltd, and that we're not going to find anything in the accounts," he says to Deniz. "If that's the case, why would she have tried to lead us in that direction?"

"Because she wanted to put us on the wrong track?"

"But why? And would the Brotherhood have set dogs on her as revenge for that?"

"No, but what if she knows something else? Who the Brotherhood's competitors are, for instance. Who they were expecting when they started shooting at us? Maybe she was trying to lead us in a specific direction."

"Such as?"

"I don't know. Toward other people who are involved, perhaps—people we don't know about. The Brotherhood's rivals."

Zack's phone buzzes again and again, and at the next red light he takes it out and starts reading.

Good tackle, mate.

Krille

Nice work, tough guy!

Christo

Didn't know you fight girls ☺

Adam

Zack doesn't understand. Three text messages, apparently all about the same thing, from friends who don't know each other. He wonders if someone's filmed him in the gym, but when was the last time he sparred with a girl? It must be more than a year ago.

But some picture of him has evidently appeared somewhere, probably on Facebook or Instagram, or some other stupid social networking site.

Zack doesn't have a Facebook account. He set one up when he was in high school, but after just two months he got sick of seeing his friends' fuzzy drunken pictures and links to funny clips on YouTube. He closed the account when he left school, and has never opened another one.

He hasn't signed up to any other sites either. He's got a few fake accounts that he uses for work, and that's enough to put him off.

His phone buzzes again. Abdula this time.

Have you seen that you've turned
into click bait?

Abdula has attached a link. Zack clicks it and finds himself looking at an article on *Aftonbladet*'s website.

POLICE OFFICER KICKS WOMAN TO GROUND NEAR FAMILIES WITH YOUNG CHILDREN

Zack scrolls down and sees a blurred picture of himself tackling Sukayana.

Shit, he thinks. Shit.

"What is it?" Deniz asks.

Two cars blow their horns almost simultaneously. Zack looks up. Green light. He accelerates hard and Deniz practically yells at him to turn left instead of right into Fleminggatan.

"Why are we going this way?"

"I've got an appointment at St. Göran's Hospital in quarter of an hour. The doctor wants to look at my neck."

"Okay."

"What were those texts about?"

"Some bastard took pictures of me when I was chasing Sukayana Prikon. And now it's up on *Aftonbladet*'s website."

"What? Let's see," Deniz says, leaning over to look at Zack's phone.

He turns into the hospital precinct and pulls up by the pavement.

Zack clicks to bring up the whole article. It's not just photographs, there's a video clip as well. A shaky sequence filmed from a distance, but still close enough for viewers to see what's going on.

Zack and Deniz read the text of the article:

It started as a pleasant family picnic. Then a policeman kicked an elderly woman to the ground—right on top of their food.

"It really was an extremely violent assault," an eyewitness tells *Aftonbladet*.

One mother had to snatch her toddler out of the way of the policeman's brutal attack in Tantolunden, on Södermalm in Stockholm.

"Everyone was screaming, it was chaos," says Sandra Johansson, 37, who was sitting nearby during Monday's dramatic events.

Other witnesses tell Aftonbladet that the fleeing woman looked terrified.

"That cop, he didn't hold back at all. He just trampled everything in his path, he was really going for it," says Joakim Pehrson, 22.

The plainclothes officer was eventually wrestled to the ground by several men, but when he showed them his police ID they let him carry on.

"A few minutes later he walked back through Tanto. By then he'd caught the woman and was holding her arm up behind her back. It looked like it was really painful," says another witness.

The police are saying little about the event.

"We can't comment on this story at present," says Torbjörn Berg of the police's public relations office.

Beneath the article there's a question addressed to the paper's readers:

Do the Swedish police use excessive force?

Seventy-three percent of readers have answered yes.

"What crap," Deniz says. "Can't they find out a few more facts before they publish this sort of stuff? That Sukayana Prikon threatened you with a knife, for instance, or that we're actually trying to catch a killer with four lives on his conscience. Maybe that would make their hysterical witnesses calm down a bit. If they even exist. I bet the reporter made up those anonymous quotes."

Zack drives up to the hospital entrance and drops Deniz off.

He sits there for a while and watches her disappear inside the building. Her body full of determination.

Where would I be without her? he thinks.

She watches out for me more than I realize.

Then he thinks about the video clip. He really didn't enjoy seeing pictures of him kicking Sukayana Prikon to the ground.

Did he have to do it like that? No, he could have handled it much better. And he could certainly have made sure it all happened somewhere other than on someone's picnic blanket.

He was slow and clumsy. Hungover, and suffering withdrawal symptoms. What happened was his fault, but Sukayana Prikon and the picnicking family were the ones who'd had to suffer for it.

Zack is just pulling away from the curb when Douglas calls.

"Have you seen the article?" he asks.

"Yes."

"The press haven't worked out that it's you yet, but they're calling pretty much every number in here to find out who it was. If they do get hold of you, just refer them to me. Tell them you can't say anything at all because of the sensitivity of an ongoing investigation. Okay?"

"Okay," Zack says.

In situations of this sort he likes his boss. Douglas always backs up his men and women when there's trouble.

He tells Douglas about Sukayana Prikon and the hospital.

Douglas says nothing for a few moments, then says:

"We're going to have to sit down and work out how much

we're going to make public. If we don't say anything at all, *Aftonbladet*—and others too, no doubt—will go on spouting articles about police brutality. But if we go public about the link to the murder investigation, they'll soon sniff out that it was Sukayana Prikon. And then all hell would break loose."

"In that case I vote for option one," Zack says, stopping at a pedestrian crossing.

"You haven't experienced a media frenzy before, Zack. It can be really bloody awful, to be blunt. Don't read what they print. And call me if you have any ideas."

"Okay."

"Did they say anything else at the hospital?"

Zack gives him a brief summary of what the doctor told him, and about the lack of witnesses. About the dog bites, and the Alsatian and Rottweiler crossbreed at the Brotherhood's clubhouse.

"That was taken off to an animal shelter, so it couldn't have harmed Sukayana Prikon," Douglas says. "But that isn't the only vicious dog they own. One of the Brotherhood's members, Danny Johansson, owns a Staffordshire bull terrier and Alsatian cross. In 2011 he was fined after the dogs attacked an elderly woman and left her with severe bite wounds on one leg. He lives in a row house in Alby."

"I'm on my way."

"Not on your own. Come in first, and we'll run through the various lines of inquiry."

18

WITHOUT HIS leather vest Sonny Järvinen looks harmless. More like an accountant than a gang leader.

But Rudolf can't see that. He listens instead. Builds up a picture of the man in front of him by registering his breathing and movements, the strength of his voice, and the changes in tone. After just five minutes he's formed an idea of an intelligent man who moves far too easily and lightly to have big, pumped-up muscles.

Rudolf likes conducting interviews down in the holding cells. On "home territory." Without a table between him and the suspect. It can foster a sense of intimacy that makes people open up.

And being underestimated is always on his side.

Sonny Järvinen is sitting in front of him, on a bunk fixed to the wall, with Rudolf's old cassette recorder next to him, and for the third time in his life he's dressed in the anonymous inmate's uniform of Kronoberg Prison. He too is trying to form an impression of his opponent, a blind old man sitting on a wooden chair he brought with him, dressed in an old-fashioned suit. Almost comically harmless. But Sonny Järvinen realizes that the man's exterior could just be camouflage, and that he needs to be on the alert.

Intelligence has nothing to do with the ability to see.

They're talking about motorbikes. Rudolf used to own a

Harley-Davidson, back in the day. A sky-blue 1959 Sportster.

"She was a real beauty," he says, then adds: "I bought her secondhand over in the States in 1968. She carried me all the way across Arizona."

Sonny Järvinen understands the old man's tactic exactly. They get close to each other, feel a sense of camaraderie in spite of their different roles, then gradually Sonny starts saying more than he meant to.

He knows all that.

But it doesn't help.

Soon he's sitting and talking lyrically about his happiest motorbike trips to Norway and Italy, and they laugh loudly as they discuss their favorite scenes in *Easy Rider*.

"Fucking hell, Jack Nicholson and Dennis Hopper. What a team!" Sonny Järvinen says.

"Listen, Sonny," Rudolf says. "I need your help."

And Sonny Järvinen can't help feeling that he'd really like to help Rudolf. He feels like dropping his guard and talking all about his life.

But his brain is resisting, telling him to get his act together.

He forces himself back to the blunt reality of the cell. Forces himself to see Rudolf in a different light.

He's a cop. He wants me to talk.

But still he says:

"With what?"

"Four women have been murdered in an apartment. They were unarmed, helpless, and they were killed in a brutal and demeaning way. The man who killed them was a weak bastard," Rudolf says. "And now a fifth woman has been mutilated. By dogs."

He leaves a slight pause, letting the words sink in. Then he says:

"Sonny, we've got a pretty good idea of what you and your members are involved in, and we know you'd never sink so low as to shoot innocent women. But you do like dogs."

"You're absolutely right there," Sonny Järvinen replies. "On both counts. But we'd never set the dogs loose on a woman."

But on others, Rudolf thinks.

"That Danny Johansson in your gang. He's got a couple of tough animals, hasn't he?"

"Danny's moved to South Africa," Sonny Järvinen says. "He had the dogs put down first. That was the only solution, because he was the only person who could handle them."

Rudolf rubs his brow.

"We think you know something about the killer," he says. "Assuming that what you're saying is true, and that you're not behind all this. We're also toying with the idea that it was him, or people close to him, that your friends on the roof were waiting for when my two colleagues showed up—leading to that unfortunate and unnecessary altercation."

Sonny Järvinen sits there in silence, but Rudolf can hear him breathing more deeply. An emotional reaction.

"Some sort of aggravated conflict has flared up between you and another organization about control of the massage parlors, hasn't it? And these murders are part of that conflict?"

"There are always idiots trying to cause trouble."

Sonny Järvinen is surprised to hear the words emerge from his own mouth. He was going to keep quiet, after all. But it's like the old man has got inside his head. As if it doesn't make any difference if he keeps quiet, because the man can read his mind anyway.

"Are you thinking of anyone in particular in relation to this specific incident?" Rudolf asks amiably.

The moment has come. Sonny Järvinen needs to make his choice, a choice that he has been lying there worrying about all morning.

Either he keeps his mouth shut and keeps his honor intact. And dies. Like several members of the gang.

His brothers.

Or he talks. Lets the cops take care of the problem and gives himself a chance to save himself and his crew.

But he isn't a snitch. And can any cop keep his word?

Maybe this old man can, despite everything. He's so damn old that he might actually still believe in a gentleman's agreement.

Sonny Järvinen looks at the bulky old tape recorder. A whirring old Panasonic with big buttons. It looks at least twenty years old. Solid. The sort of thing no one makes anymore. He guesses it's easier for someone with impaired sight to handle rather than some slim-line Dictaphone with a touch screen.

He wants to gesture toward the tape recorder so that the old man realizes he has to turn it off, but how do you express that to a blind man?

Sonny Järvinen presses the stop button. The old man doesn't react.

"If I give you a name, how can I trust that it won't end up in the transcript of this interview, or be linked to me some other way?"

"I give you my word."

"What's that worth?"

"I've been conducting interviews with people for more than thirty years, everything from pickpockets to pedophiles and sadistic killers. People with considerably more power than you have sat opposite me and given me important information on the promise of anonymity. So far I've never broken my word."

Sonny Järvinen looks at Rudolf. The old man is sitting there, perfectly calm. He finds himself wishing he'd had a grandfather like that when he was small.

"Their name is Yildizyeli," he says. "They're Turkish, fucking nasty bastards."

"I'm going to be just as open with you, even though I risk looking stupid," Rudolf says. "I've never heard of them."

"They're established here, but only just."

"Where can we find them?"

Sonny Järvinen doesn't answer at first. He's thinking about what he'd have done to any club member who'd given the police similar information.

It would have been very bloody.

Then we'd have stood in a circle and pissed on his undershirt.

"Okay," Sonny Järvinen says, and leans forward. "I'll tell you."

19

ZACK BARELY manages to open the door of the Special Crimes Unit before Douglas comes up to him.

"Sonny Järvinen has given us a name."

"What?" Zack says.

"That was my reaction as well, but it's true. The name's Ösgür Thrakya, and according to Järvinen he belongs to a Turkish gang."

"What? Are the Turks involved in this?"

"Maybe. I've just spoken to the prostitution unit. There's evidently talk among the women out on the street that the Turks have started to show up in the city. Rumor has it that they're trying to establish some sort of business involving Asian girls. It's all very vague, nothing concrete at all. But Järvinen described the Turks as the maddest of the mad."

Zack thinks back to the shootout at the Brotherhood of No Mercy's clubhouse.

Were they waiting for a gang of Turkish crooks to show up?

Are they competing for the prostitution market?

"Do we know anything else about them?"

"Very little. Sirpa's busy pulling together what we've got."

Sirpa looks up as they approach her desk.

"He seems like a really nice guy, this Thrakya," she says. "As far as his background goes, he used to be head of intelligence for some sort of Turkish militia, and there are persistent rumors that he used to boil people alive."

"That has to be made up. That sort of thing went out with the Middle Ages," Zack says.

"I'm sorry to say it still goes on. Ask people in prison in Uzbekistan. According to Amnesty, there are documented cases of prisoners being boiled alive just a few years ago," Sirpa says.

"So what else do we know about this Ösgür Thrakya?" Douglas asks.

"I'll read it out to you," Sirpa says. "He was born in 1961 in the village of Yaliköy, on the Black Sea coast in northwestern Turkey. Interpol have been looking for him since 2007, for human trafficking offenses, as well as large-scale weapons smuggling."

She scrolls down the screen.

"Today he's said to be second in command of the criminal organization Yildizyeli, which apparently means 'north wind' in Turkish. The group is believed to have several operational bases abroad, including in Germany, Britain, and in the border regions of Thailand, Laos, and Burma, the area known as the Golden Triangle. But they have no known involvement in Sweden."

Sirpa looks up at them.

"That's what I've managed to come up with so far. But I'm going to call my contact at Interpol and see if he can give us anything else."

Douglas looks like he's thinking hard. Zack guesses that he's wondering the same thing as him: What does this have to do with the murder of four women in Hallonbergen?

"Are they here to snatch a share of the prostitution market?" he says. "Could the women have belonged to the Brotherhood after all, and that's why they were killed? Or the other way round: Did the Brotherhood kill the Turks' women? To make the point that they'd crossed the wrong boundary? I mean, they were terrified when we arrived at their clubhouse. Maybe they were waiting for a revenge attack."

Douglas nods thoughtfully.

"I need to ask for more resources," he says. "This looks like it could get completely out of hand."

"Did Sonny Järvinen say where we could find Ösgür Thrakya?"

Douglas takes a notebook out of his inside pocket.

"Apparently he hangs out at a pizzeria next to Vasaparken. Some place called the Miramar. I want you to check it out, you and Deniz."

"What about those dangerous dogs in Alby?"

"Ah, yes. I haven't had a chance to tell you. According to Järvinen, the dogs are dead and their owner's in South Africa. We're sending a patrol to the address to check, but right now that line of inquiry looks pretty cold."

"In that case I'll head off to the pizzeria, then."

"Not alone. Pick Deniz up from St. Göran's first."

As Zack takes the elevator down to the garage, he thinks about Sonny Järvinen. One criminal revealing the name of another criminal after barely a day in the cells.

Things must be bad.

20

THE COFFEEMAKER in the Special Crimes Unit squirts out espresso after espresso. Tommy is bent over a table with Douglas, going through a list of known sex offenders, Niklas is fast-forwarding through recordings from a surveillance camera in the vicinity of Peter Karlson's home, and, in an office a short distance away, a woman in a blue uniform blouse is giving Rudolf a quick run-through of the latest interview with the most overweight member of the Brotherhood.

Sirpa is sitting alone at her computers, shut off from all external distractions. She's good at that. Her eyes are fixed to one of the screens as her fingers move quickly over the keyboard.

But she can't shut out the pain. She moves her hands from the keyboard to her knees and massages them. It gives scant comfort, she's been sitting down for too long again.

She has painkillers in the top drawer. Citodon and Tradolan. Strong, effective medication. But she doesn't want to take them. Doesn't want to become a pill-popping junkie like Agneta in Regional Crime, who got her elbow crushed with a baseball bat by a guy from the Firm seven years ago. Agneta loved her painkillers. She took the maximum dose for more than a year. Then she began to lie, claiming that the pain wouldn't budge. A year after that she reluctantly booked herself into a clinic, and a few weeks later she emerged as an even better liar.

Sirpa has seen her taking pills on the sly, and she's seen how distracted Agneta gets when she hasn't got any.

Sirpa would rather be in pain.

When it comes down to it, her brain is more important to her than her body, even if the two can't function separately.

She walks stiffly to the kitchen. Pours away her untouched cup of cold coffee and puts it back under the coffeemaker again. The machine bleeps as she makes her selection.

She heads back to her desk and puts the cup to one side. Tries to come up with something new to try. She managed to connect most of the anonymous email addresses in Sawatdii's customer database with real people a while back, but the last one is still causing trouble. The first step, finding a server, is child's play. Breaking into it is harder, and often against the law. Particularly when she can't even claim that the address she's trying to trace belongs to someone suspected of committing a serious crime.

Sometimes she ignores the illegality, and gets help to break through the digital walls from the hackers' network she belongs to. She never does that from the police network but from other locations and computers.

On previous occasions she's always known what she was looking for, and it's often been a race against the clock to prevent further crimes being committed.

This investigation isn't at that level.

Not yet.

But Sirpa is worried about what might happen if they don't make a breakthrough soon. She's heard about the woman with the chewed-off legs.

At least I've still got my knees, she thinks.

Her fingers tap at the keyboard for several minutes. Line after line of computer code fills the screen. She leans closer and scans the information. Where has she ended up this time? In Turkmenistan. Well, why not? A few hours ago she traced one email address to a Web server in Suriname.

She could send a request for help with the identification to the company behind the server, but she knows there's no point. People who locate their servers in dictatorships are rarely keen to share information with police authorities in the West. And even in the isolated cases when Sirpa has managed to contact helpful technicians, they often have no idea of the origins of all the traffic passing through their servers. Anonymity software distorts the signals, sending the messages via thousands of different servers, then putting the information back together somewhere else entirely.

Sirpa stares into the screen. That one address is driving her mad.

dirtysanchez@woomail.com

Dirty Sanchez. Sirpa felt sick when she found out what it meant: a man having anal sex with a woman, then smearing excrement across her upper lip, like a sort of mustache.

Disgusting, she thinks. How can there even be enough people doing that for there to be a specific phrase for it? And how could anyone want to use that expression in another context? The sort of person who would use it as an email address can't be anything but misogynist scum.

She thinks of Peter Karlson's perverse contributions to various sex forums, and of the abandoned investigation into the charge of anal rape made against him.

He could have chosen an alias of that sort when wanting to make Gustav Vasa's fantasies real.

She finds herself getting upset every time she sees the email address. These men with their warped view of women, who see women as nothing but objects to exploit as they see fit, who believe that the door is always wide open, and who don't hesitate to kick it in if that isn't the case.

Men.

She's practically ignored them since her own husband left her.

There are good men, she knows that. But it doesn't help.

She thinks of two teenage girls she saw on the way to work. Skirts that barely covered their underwear, breasts that seemed to be trying to escape from T-shirts that were too tight.

She thinks about the middle-aged men staring at the girls. But why shouldn't young girls be naïve? Why can't they have the right to affirm their femininity in whatever way they like?

They do have that right, but it's constantly being taken away from them.

Dirty Sanchez.

The implications of the address make her feel sick.

I'm damn well going to find out who the hell you are.

21

ZACK HAS driven across Barnhusbron and parked the car beside the greenery of Tegnérlunden.

He's looking at the picture attached to the email Douglas has just sent him. A picture of Ösgür Thrakya.

It's actually quite a nice portrait. Soft shadow, good light, a short depth of field. He can just see the outline of mountains in the background, but only just.

The man's face is thin, with a clear dimple in his chin. He looks like he's from the Balkans, or perhaps the Middle East. Clean-shaven, but starting to go bald, with just a hint of gray at the temples.

So why does the picture make him feel so uncomfortable?

The look in those eyes, Zack thinks. Unpleasant eyes, which seem to be staring straight through him. Cold, observant. No trace of empathy.

He thinks about what Sirpa said about the man. Maybe those rumors on the street are correct after all? That Turkish criminals are establishing themselves in Stockholm.

More drugs, more prostitution.

Just what the city needs.

But does that have anything to do with the four murdered women in Hallonbergen?

He pulls out onto the road again. Drives toward the pizzeria in Vasastan.

A gust of wind blows dust, ice-cream wrappers, and a bit of crumpled tinfoil up onto the windshield.

He thinks of what his childhood friend Ernesto Santos always used to say:

"It has to be Skultuna's oven foil. Nothing else. It's just the right thickness."

Nothing to do with cooking.

Ernesto was in the heroin business, like a number of other Chileans in Bredäng and Skärholmen. They sold their small wraps out in the suburbs, four hundred kronor for 0.2 grams, and thought they'd hit the big time just because their pockets were full of hundred-kronor notes.

"You don't want to try a 0.2?" Ernesto often used to ask. "My treat."

But Zack never tried. He found the syringes and vomiting off-putting. A lot of people vomited their guts up the first time.

He made do with occasionally taking a few of Dad's strong painkillers. Two or three Kerogan were usually enough to make the world a better place for a while.

Despite that, he used to hang out around at Ernesto's a lot. There was no risk of running into his parents: Ernesto moved out when he was sixteen.

When Zack thinks back to it now, he can't understand how he could bear being there. How he could sit there with Abdula watching *Blood In, Blood Out* for the tenth time while some forty-year-old guy sat in the kitchen smoking horse.

Ernesto used to go on about how he was going to be running the entire heroin market in Stockholm within a few years.

But he didn't live to see twenty. He weighed barely forty-five kilos in his last weeks.

THE WHITE plastic sign outside the pizzeria on Västmannagatan is broken, and the last two letters have fallen off.

What a dump, Zack thinks. The name alone: MIRAMAR.

How could you name something after a sea view when your customers are in the grayest part of Vasastan and have a view of a stone-clad 1970s building in the finest tradition of East Germany?

He drives on until he finds a free parking space between a silver BMW and a white Audi Q7. Both cars look new.

He walks back to the pizzeria. Deniz was still in the waiting room when he called her. He didn't feel like hanging around. Better to get something else ticked off the list.

He opens the Miramar's door. What greets him isn't the appetizing smell of oven-baked pizza, but something rancid, almost rotten. Like bits of old food stuck in a sink.

The décor is typical of a pizzeria with no ambition. Whitewashed walls, plain plastic chairs and tables, a cheap bowl of watery cabbage salad on a table by the wall, and a few copies of yesterday's *Metro* on the windowsill.

A grotesquely broad-shouldered man in a blue tracksuit and shiny green sneakers is sitting watching a film clip on his phone. He's got cropped hair, and his biceps would make the Hulk start taking steroids out of envy.

He looks up at Zack. One eye is cloudy, almost white.

Zack stares back.

It isn't Ösgür Thrakya.

The man puts his phone in his pocket, then tips his chair over backward, and rushes into the kitchen. Zack hears agitated voices, and the sound of baking trays hitting the floor. He runs after the man, cursing himself for never being able to learn to look away.

The kitchen smells like the garbage room out in Bredäng, and Zack shoves the back door open and catches sight of the man halfway up a rickety ladder fixed to the wall, which stretches all the way to the roof.

A Jack Russell terrier on a nearby balcony is barking at the climbing man, keen to join in the hunt.

All these fucking dogs everywhere . . .

Zack leaps up onto the rusty ladder, but slows down at once when he realizes how fragile it is.

The man he's chasing must weigh close to three hundred pounds.

Can this really hold both of us?

He looks at the fixtures, one after the other, for a fraction of a second.

Then climbs up.

The building has four floors, and the man has almost reached the roof.

Zack speeds up. Gets grit in his eyes as the bolts holding the ladder move in and out of their holes.

The dog goes on barking and barking.

As Zack reaches the black tin-covered roof, he sees the man leap onto the next one. He sets off after him across the green tarnished-copper roof, skirts a chimney the same height as him, leaps up a short ladder fixed to a steeply sloping roof, then jumps down five feet onto a black tin roof.

The man has landed heavily and Zack is gaining on him with every step.

Why are you running?

Because you murdered four women the night before last?

"Stop!" he shouts. "I'm a police officer. Stop!"

The mountain of muscle turns around and yells something incomprehensible. Then he jumps down almost seven feet onto a balcony. One foot gets caught in the railing and his knee hits the hard concrete floor and he howls with pain. He gets to his feet, clambers onto the other side of the railing, and jumps half a yard to the next balcony.

A woman in her seventies who is sitting sunbathing screams in horror as the bulky man climbs onto the railing, of her neighbor's balcony and leaps toward her. She knocks her little table over as she quickly gets to her feet.

She slams the balcony door shut a moment before the man crushes her coffee cup under his shoes.

They're thirty feet above the ground.

Zack can feel the predators' jaws from last night's nightmare trying to get him, trying to force him to fall as he makes the next jump between balconies.

But his body obeys him.

The jaws snap shut on nothing but air.

The man yells again. Zack can't even hear what language it is. He seems to be searching his pocket for something, but can't find it.

Zack crouches down, with his right hand on his Sig Sauer. He calls out:

"Stop. I just want to talk."

The man makes another jump.

His thighs must be three feet in diameter.

He lands on the last balcony on the building. No way forward from there.

A blank wall ahead of him.

No drainpipe to slide down.

No ladder.

He looks up and grabs hold of the tin roof jutting out over the balcony, climbs up onto the railing, and swings one leg up onto the roof. He tries to pull himself up, but he's heavy and ungainly, and the angle is difficult.

Zack lands on the balcony. The man makes a last desperate attempt to reach the roof. He launches himself upward, trying to pull both legs onto the roof.

But he slips.

He slips and fumbles and grunts.

Then falls, without a sound.

Just a muffled thud as his body hits the ground. The sound of something breaking.

An elderly couple walk into the courtyard. They see the man and hurry over to him.

"Get back! Get back!" Zack shouts. "I'm a police officer!"

Horrified, the pair back away a few yards but stand and stare at the lifeless body and the red pool gradually spreading out beneath its head.

Zack pulls at the balcony door and knocks on the glass. He peers inside, but the apartment is dark. He yanks the door open, rushes through the rooms, out into the stairwell, and down to the courtyard.

The man's head is lying at an unnatural angle and Zack sees immediately that he's dead.

He stands beside the body and tries to feel something.

Sympathy.

Guilt.

But instead he sees his mother in his mind's eye. Sees the old photographs of the black pool of her blood.

It's still growing. Merging with the dust and dirt.

Was this what it looked like when they found her?

22

THE SUNLIGHT forcing its way into the courtyard is blinding Douglas, and making one of his cheeks twitch in a rather odd way. Zack can't help thinking that the spasms really don't suit his boss.

A yellow tarpaulin has been draped over the dead man's body, the courtyard has been cordoned off, and forensics officers are aiming their cameras up at the balcony with its black iron railing and taking a few last pictures.

A gaggle of journalists has gathered out on the street but are being kept strictly away from the yard.

"So what happened?" Douglas asks, and Zack describes the chase to him.

Douglas listens attentively and asks a few questions to clarify some of the details.

"I believe what you say, you know that, but you also know that there's going to have to be an investigation into this."

Zack nods. He feels calm, but knows that the impending interviews will be a torment. This isn't the first time his actions out in the field have been scrutinized.

"There's a witness," Zack says. "A woman who was sitting on one of the balconies, I don't know if she saw him fall. She got scared and ran into her apartment."

"We've already started knocking on doors. They'll get her details," Douglas says.

The look in his eyes keeps alternating between hard and friendly, and Zack can't help thinking that none of the emotions Douglas is trying to convey with his eyes are what he really thinks.

"Are you okay?" Douglas asks. "Do you need debriefing? You know I have to ask."

Zack can't help smiling.

"And you know what my response will be."

Other officers can go through their entire careers without ever drawing their weapons or being involved in a dramatic chase.

Some of them are even proud of the fact. They regard it as a failure if you have to use your weapon, the same way a soccer goalkeeper can say it's a failure if he has to throw himself after the ball, because it means he was in the wrong place to start with.

Zack always wants to throw himself at things.

For him, that's the reward.

That's the only time he ever feels truly present in the moment.

That's when he feels he can do good.

Real good.

But he still wishes today's chase hadn't happened.

No one should have died today.

So damn unnecessary.

They could have done with being able to question the guy, find out what he knew. If he had anything to do with the murders.

If he was the murderer.

But debriefing? My ass.

"Do you know who he is?" Douglas asks, nodding toward the plastic sheet.

"Suliman Yel. He had a foreign driver's license in his pocket. I asked Sirpa to do a quick check. Turkish citizen. Wanted by Interpol for drug smuggling and trafficking. Just like Ösgür Thrakya."

"In other words, he had every reason to want to run," Douglas says.

"If he killed four people in Hallonbergen the night before last, he had even more reason."

"Did Sirpa manage to find any clear link between this man and Ösgür Thrakya?"

"No. But she said she'd dig a bit deeper."

Zack pulls out a folded scrap of paper.

"I found this number in Suliman Yel's inside pocket. I can't find out any details, so I'm guessing it's a pay-as-you-go cell. I was thinking of starting with that. I'm not suspended, am I?"

"No, you can carry on working, but be prepared to come in as soon as Internal Investigations call you. By the way, where's Deniz?"

"She got held up at the hospital. Didn't I say?"

Douglas gives him a weary look.

Zack turns away and calls the number.

A woman with a lively voice answers and gives her name as Rebecka Reschy. Zack introduces himself, and explains that he'd like to ask her some questions.

"Oh, what about?"

No hint of aggression in her voice. Just surprise.

"I'd rather talk face-to-face. It will only take a few minutes. Are you in Stockholm?"

"Yes, I work at the Hair Daze salon in Fredhäll. The next hour looks fairly quiet, so you can come now if that suits you."

As Zack ends the call he sees Deniz walking into the

courtyard. He can just make out a fresh white compress under her scarf.

“How did you get on?”

“The doctor says it’s healing fine. And that I should go home and get some rest.”

“So what are you doing here, then?”

“Disobeying orders. Anyway, apparently I can’t leave you alone for half an hour without you causing trouble.”

She looks at the yellow tarpaulin and turns serious.

“Zack, tell me what happened.”

“Come with me to Fredhäll. I’ll explain in the car.”

He turns around and calls out:

“Douglas, I got through to that number. We’re going to check it out.”

“Will you and Deniz have time to have a late lunch with me after that?”

“Sure.”

“The bar of the Opera House, one thirty.”

Damn it, Zack thinks. So he wants to look after us now, when we’re having a seriously bad day. Unless he has some other motive?

ZACK IS driving down Mariebergsgatan, through Rålambshovsparken. Deniz is sitting in silence, thinking about what Zack has just told her about Ösgür Thrakya, Suliman Yel, and the chase across the rooftops.

“Okay, so the Brotherhood and this Turkish mafia might have started fighting about the income from the massage parlors. But we don’t yet know which of them attacked Sawatdii and Sukayana Prikon.”

“If it was actually one of them at all. Someone else could have murdered them and tortured Sukayana, someone who knows that the criminal gangs will blame each other. Like that racist IT boss who paid for sex at Sawatdii even though he hates Asians and has no alibi for the night of the murders. Did you know he's got a medal for competitive pistol shooting as well?"

"Yes, Niklas mentioned it. Have we checked to see if he's got a dog?"

"We have. And the answer is no, he hasn't. None that shows up on any databases, anyway."

Zack rubs his eyes. The adrenaline surge from the chase has gone, replaced by a stinging tiredness.

Deniz looks at him.

"Are you sure you're okay?" she asks. "Shall we take a break?"

"No, let's get this done first. We're almost there."

The hair salon is in the ground floor of a pale yellow building from the 1960s. Leafy trees shade the quiet street and Zack guesses that the apartments on the upper floors have a view of the water.

He opens the door of the salon.

Hang on a minute.

What's this?

It can't be true.

The woman standing there with a broom in her hand next to two black leather treatment chairs, it's her, the dark-haired beauty he danced with out at the club the other night. In Heraldus's old shipyard.

The one he took cocaine with.

He remembers her bare, sweaty skin. Her lips.

Why has she popped up in this context? He considers the raid on the club again. Is all of this connected somehow? Is he going to get dragged into his own investigation?

It must be a coincidence.

A very unpleasant coincidence.

But what if she got pulled in? He had a look at the list of people who were arrested. Was there a Rebecka Reschy on there? He can't remember. The only name he was looking for was Abdula's.

What will she do if she recognizes him? Will she give him away?

"Hi, are you from the police?" she asks warmly, and smiles at Zack in recognition.

She's wearing a tight, V-necked top, and a belt containing scissors, combs, and other small tools is hanging nonchalantly from her hips.

Just as attractive as before, Zack thinks. Just rather less provocative. Beautiful, in an everyday sort of way.

He feels slightly lost and steps behind Deniz to let her take the initiative. He doesn't particularly want to show the girl his ID, even if he has to.

"Yes, that's right," Deniz says, holding up her own ID. "Deniz Akin. And my colleague Zack Herry."

Rebecka puts the brush down.

"Well, what have I done?" she asks curiously. "I've been wondering ever since you called."

"Do you know a Suliman Yel?" Deniz asks.

Rebecka gives the question some thought.

"Suliman? The big guy who's blind in one eye?"

"That's right," Zack says.

There's a large mirror behind Rebecka, and Zack can't take his eyes off her slender back and behind.

"I met him yesterday. Well, this morning, really. We were at Under the Bridge at Skanstull until five o'clock. You'll have to forgive me if I look a bit rough. I don't usually party on a

Monday. But apparently Suliman parties a lot. He was there on Sunday night as well."

"How do you know that?"

"My friend Katja said so."

"We'd like to find out how long Suliman was there then," Deniz says. "Can you call your friend for us?"

"Why do you want to know that?"

"I'm afraid we can't tell you that. Can you call her now?"

Rebecka calls her friend, explains briefly what's going on, and hands her phone to Deniz.

"Hello, Deniz Akin, Stockholm Police. I was wondering if you knew how long Suliman Yel was at Under the Bridge on the night between Sunday and Monday?"

"I got there with my friends at about two o'clock," Katja says in a loud nasal voice that both Zack and Rebecka can hear clearly. "I think he was already there with his gang then. He was drunk and happy and buying all the girls drinks. But I don't think he speaks any Swedish, and only really bad English. He mostly just stood there waving all his thousand-kronor notes around."

"How long did he stay?"

"Until they closed. I remember that because one of his friends offered to let me and my friend share a taxi with them. But we didn't want to."

"Thanks. We may need to talk to you again."

Deniz hangs up and looks at Zack. They're both thinking the same thing: another suspect to take off the list. According to Koltberg, the women were shot between half past two and half past four in the morning. Suliman Yel had an alibi for the whole of that time.

"What's happened?" Rebecka asks.

She holds Zack's gaze. He looks back. A little too long.

"How well do you know Suliman Yel?" Deniz asks.

"I've only met him twice. The first time was at Riche, I think. But that was several weeks ago."

"Who was he with last night?"

"A few guys that a friend of a friend knows."

"Do you know any of the guys he was there with?"

"No."

"Does your friend?"

"I doubt it. She might know a few of their first names, but I'm not sure. Why are you asking me about all this?"

"We can't say. But can you explain one thing to me—if you barely know this man, why does he have your phone number in his jacket pocket?"

Rebecka shrugs and replies cockily:

"How should I know? Maybe he likes the way I look and wants to ask me out. He must have got hold of my number somehow. It's not that unusual for men to want to ask me out."

Deniz realizes she's not going to get anywhere with that line of questioning.

"What do you know about an organization called Yildizyeli?" she asks instead.

"Called what?"

"Never mind. Do you know what Suliman Yel did as a job?"

"No idea. But he seemed to have plenty of money."

"Do you know an Ösgür Thrakya?"

"Never heard of him."

Deniz hands over a business card.

"Feel free to call if you think of anything that might be of interest to us. And we might have to get back to you to speak to that friend you mentioned," she says.

Rebecka turns to Zack.

"And you've got my number. Give me a call."

"I will . . ." Zack says.

He leaves a theatrical pause.

". . . when we've thought of some more questions."

On the way out of the salon he can feel his heart beating harder than he'd like.

They get into the car. Deniz glares at him.

"And what the fuck was all that about?" she says.

23

DOUGLAS IS sitting on a thronelike leather two-seater sofa at a table in one corner of the Opera Bar, surrounded by lively conversation.

Zack guesses it's his regular table.

As for him, he's never set foot in the building before. He looks around. The ceiling is exuberantly decorated and dark oak panels on the walls are so highly polished you can see your face in them. Around the tables sit advertising executives in designer suits, businessmen with graying temples, and elderly upper-class people with scarves and comb-overs.

Douglas stands up to welcome them. Once again, Zack wonders what they're doing there. Why he's invited them there today.

"You've been through a few rough days, so I thought you deserved a decent lunch in one of the most beautiful rooms in Stockholm. It's rather nice here, don't you think?" Douglas says.

"Sure," Zack replies.

"I hope you're both hungry?" he asks.

"I could probably eat for two," Zack says.

Douglas orders them the salted salmon with dill potatoes. Zack can't help being fascinated by the people at the tables around them. The way they're dressed, their gestures, haircuts.

Their air of natural superiority.

One man in his midfifties, with a white handkerchief sticking out of the breast pocket of his blue linen suit, nods to Douglas before sitting down with some men in their sixties at a table some distance away.

Zack recognizes the man. But where from?

Then he remembers.

He's the managing director of that property company, the one Sukayana snorted at when he was being interviewed on television.

The CEO is smiling and laughing with his associates. He looks considerably more relaxed among his friends than he did with the interviewer's microphone thrust into his face. A real upper-class asshole.

Hatred of rich people. Zack feels it strongly at times, but he's starting to find it harder to accept that he feels that way. His disproportionate anger is often unjustified. After all, it really isn't the fault of the rich that he grew up with a dying father in a suburb on the wrong side of town.

He ought to hate the politicians instead, the ones who set the rules of the game. And who have chosen to sit in the lap of the capitalists.

But nothing's black or white, just shades of gray defining the human desire for power.

Human greed.

And inhuman.

Zack wants to ask Douglas how he knows the CEO, but decides not to. It's none of his business, and he didn't actually see if Douglas returned the greeting. Perhaps the man was merely gesturing to the waiter who happened to be passing their table just then. The waiter who is now standing behind the bar in his white uniform, sorting glasses. Cheeks flushed red, deep lines on his face. Looks like an old alcoholic, Zack thinks. He clearly drinks too much of what he serves his customers.

A slave to desire.

Just like me.

The coffee arrives and Zack drinks it in deep gulps, even though it's so hot it burns his tongue.

Must wake up. Fight the tiredness back.

Tonight I'm going to sleep.

"How did you get on in Fredhäll?" Douglas asks.

Deniz gives him an account of their visit, without mentioning anything about Zack's relationship to the hairdresser. But Zack starts to feel uncomfortable and quickly changes the subject.

"Have you heard anything more from Södermalm Hospital?" he asks Douglas.

"No. I thought I'd call when we're finished here. But they promised to get in touch if Sukayana Prikon died, so with a bit of luck they've managed to save her life."

"Have we started looking for more crazy dog owners, the sort who've been banned from keeping animals by the local council and so on?" Deniz asks.

"Not yet," Douglas says. "But you raise a good point. It's not unreasonable to think that anyone who's trained their dogs to attack other people might have been in trouble with the authorities before, like Danny Johansson."

"What about this Ösgür Thrakya, then?" Zack says. "If he really has boiled people alive in the past, then he's pretty likely to have an assortment of other torture methods."

Zack sees Deniz purse her lips as he speaks. But Douglas picks up the subject:

"That means he'd have had to bring his man-eating dogs with him to Sweden. That sounds a bit far-fetched."

"And we mustn't let ourselves get fixated on the idea that the same perpetrator is behind both the murders and the mutilation," Deniz says. "Let's say that this Turkish mafia, Yildizyeli, are behind the murders—what happened to Sukayana Prikon could be a revenge attack for that."

"But if that's the case, why not kill her?" Zack says.

"Extreme torture can in some cases act as even more of a deterrent," Deniz says.

Zack nods.

He can clearly remember the way his own legs began to weaken when he saw Sukayana Prikon in hospital.

Douglas goes on:

"Maybe Sukayana Prikon received an offer from the Turks and decided to work with them instead. In which case her torture could be a way for the Brotherhood to warn the managers of other massage parlors involved in prostitution against following her example."

"But think about how scared they were," Zack says. "Would those same guys, just a few hours after we paid them a visit, manage to kidnap and mutilate a woman? That's hard to believe. Especially when Sonny Järvinen is still in custody."

"I'm inclined to agree with you, Zack," Douglas says. "We still know far too little. And bear in mind what Östman said, about the perpetrator probably being a loner, not part of a group. That points more in Peter Karlson's direction."

"Have we found out any more about him?"

"We've got hold of the footage from a surveillance camera in a nearby building that might be able to tell us when he got back home in his car the night before last. We might also be able to get the recording from the garage in his block. We're also going to try to obtain a search warrant for his car. Then we can use his GPS to see where he was on the night of the murders. But I'm not sure the prosecutor's going to agree to that."

"How are we going to proceed with the Turks?" Deniz asks. "Can't we find out more about Ösgür Thrakya and his organization, and what he's really doing in Sweden, if he's actually here?"

"We've got a list of five or six other massage parlors where we suspect prostitution and where there are rumors of links with the Turks. But the information's extremely vague so far. It doesn't look like anyone can say for certain whether or not the Turks have established themselves in the city. But I've got people working on the massage parlors' accounts, looking for suspicious transactions. We've got officers out in the field checking them right now. With a bit of luck that'll be one way of finding out how they recruit their staff. But it could be tricky, especially if everything's been done with fake passports. We still don't know the true identities of the murdered women. And their passports were unusually skillful fakes. Our forgery expert sounded almost impressed when he described the way they'd managed to split bonded plastic and whatever else it was."

"Are we going to put more pressure on the Brotherhood?" Zack asks. "After all, they don't seem entirely unwilling to talk to us."

"No, we're holding back with that," Douglas says.

"Why?"

"Because I say so."

They stare at each other. Zack can see how calm his boss's eyes are. The self-assurance and power possessed by truly upper-class people. The right not to have to explain themselves to their subordinates. The right not to explain everything.

The right to hide something?

A few seconds of silence pass.

Neither of them blinks. Their eyes are locked together.

Zack knows he can win this duel, but he also knows that his anger is all too visible. He looks away.

The class struggle is over.

He lost.

Deniz breaks the tense silence.

"What about the racism angle? How are Niklas and Rudolf getting on?" she asks.

"Nothing so far, apart from Peter Karlson. But he is of course interesting enough on his own, both as a racist and a crazy client."

Douglas is talking as if nothing had happened, but Zack is having trouble engaging in the conversation again. He hates that sort of power struggle, and he hates losing even more.

He looks around the room again while Deniz answers Douglas's inquiries about how she's feeling after the shooting.

Then Douglas beckons the ruddy-cheeked waiter and gets out his American Express card.

The waiter bows as he approaches the table.

"Was everything all right, Douglas?" he asks.

"As always, Sven."

Sven the waiter goes off with the card as Douglas's cell buzzes. He reads the screen quickly.

"It's Sirpa," he says. "She thinks she's managed to connect Peter Karlson with one of the email addresses in Sukayana Prikon's computer. It looks like he was trying to figure out the murdered women's work schedules."

24

GARISHLY PATTERNED fabrics hang from the orange walls. The sofa is covered with brightly colored cushions.

The woman, who looks like she's from Southeast Asia, says she's twenty-two, but looks no more than sixteen. She's standing with her arms folded, trying to look tough, but her voice trembles with fear as she looks up at the two tall, uniformed police officers who have just walked into the massage parlor on Bondegatan.

"I'm not saying anything," she repeats.

"So we heard," one of the policemen says in a voice that indicates that his patience is wearing thin. "But you're going to have to show us where you keep your accounts. I assume your paperwork is all in order?"

THERE'S A sweet scent of incense in the apartment on Skön-torpsvägen in Årsta. A worn mattress is just visible on the floor behind a half-open door, and the only light comes from a bare lightbulb, the cable of which is fixed to the ceiling with duct tape.

"Leave me alone," the woman says. "I go back to Thailand next week."

"But we just want to . . ." the police constable says.

"No. No talk. Go now."

POLICE CONSTABLE Benny Göransson kicks at an old takeout box that's lying on the living-room floor. The remnants of dried noodles skitter across the plastic rug.

The rooms are empty. The drain in the shower has dried out, and is giving off a faint smell of sewage.

He gazes out at the brick apartment blocks on the other side of Skönstaholmsvägen.

"Doesn't look like there's been anyone here for a long time," he says to his partner.

THE WOMAN who opens the door looks like she's in her forties. She's heavily built and tall, for an Asian.

They sit down in the kitchen and she opens the dark curtain that protects her from being seen from Valhallavägen.

"I want to be secret," she says. "No name, okay?"

The police officers exchange a glance and make an instant decision.

"Okay," they say.

Her Swedish is poor, but the information she provides is pure gold.

She tells them that men come each week to collect money from the business.

"Which men?"

"Big men. Nasty. They were here yesterday."

"Do they take the money you earn from providing massages?" one of the police officers says.

"Yes. And . . . the other."

"The other?"

"Not here. But other parlors. Men who buy private time with Thai woman."

She tells them the names of two massage parlors and the police write them down carefully.

Then she tells them about women who have disappeared. Young women who are supposed to have been put on the plane back to Bangkok, but who never arrive home. She tells them about relatives who wonder, but don't dare go to the authorities to raise the alarm.

"So no one know they're missing. Now say no more, no more."

The officers leave the parlor and the woman quickly packs her bag. She puts her passport in a money belt and leaves the apartment for the last time.

25

THE AFTERNOON sun burns through the window. The absurdly expensive automatic blinds have already stopped working, and Zack can feel sweat seeping out along his hairline.

Behind him he can hear Sirpa's nimble fingers on her keyboard. Just she, Deniz, and he are left there in the office. Douglas is at a management meeting, the Oracle, Rudolf, is conducting an interview with Sonny Järvinen, and Niklas has gone off to pick his daughters up from school. Tommy and Sam appear to have finished for the day.

Zack waits impatiently for his computer to connect to all of its networks. Few things make him feel as stressed within the force as this built-in sluggishness.

Or when it feels like he's treading water.

Like now.

He chased a man to his death today, yet all he can think about is how to make progress with the investigation. And how to get himself a fix.

But they're not getting anywhere. One of the members of the Brotherhood, Danny Johansson, has left the country and had his dogs put down. Several people have verified the information about Suliman Yel's presence in the nightclub, and Sirpa hasn't managed to find out anything else about the link to Peter Karlson.

Zack stares into his screen and feels the day's events settle heavily on his head and shoulders.

A fix.

He needs some sort of boost.

Anything.

He thinks about Mera, her slim, fit body.

White lines on white enamel.

It's almost five o'clock. A maximum of an hour's report writing, then he's free for the evening.

The computer finally lets him into the system. He opens the browser and brings up *Aftonbladet*'s website. The story about the police chase through Tantolunden has been deposed by a *Swedish Idol* competitor caught smoking marijuana, a cat performing tricks on a skateboard, and an article with the headline "Latvian Super-Swarm Invades Sweden."

But it's still very visible on the site, and has now attracted 178 comments from readers. Zack follows Douglas's advice and doesn't read them, and checks his email instead.

Still no questions from journalists. He wasn't expecting any either. They're going to have to put in a bit of hard work if they want to get hold of him. The film clip is very grainy, and even if someone did manage to identify him, he's not exactly an easy person to find.

His phone number is protected, and he's all but invisible on the Internet.

The biggest danger probably comes from within the building he's sitting in. The Stockholm Police is notorious for its media leaks. Ten thousand in cash for a tip-off is hard for some staff to resist.

He opens a blank report template and is about to start filling in the results of that day's interviews when Sirpa calls to him above her screens:

"Your new nickname suits you."

"Nickname?"

"The Karate Cop. Right now you're one of the most discussed Swedes on social media."

"What do you mean, 'Karate Cop'? You're kidding?"

She shakes her head.

"Come and see."

Zack goes around Sirpa's desk and leans over her shoulder. She guides him around the Net to various sites that analyze web traffic.

"That big column is you. Mirjam from *Swedish Idol* is gaining fast, but you're still king of the hill."

"Yippee," Zack says drily.

"Enjoy your fifteen minutes in the limelight. Tomorrow you'll be forgotten again," Sirpa says.

Zack sighs and turns to look at her other screen. It's showing some screen grabs from an Outlook account.

He looks at the email address: dirtysanchez@woomail.com.

"Is he the one you think is Peter Karlson?" he asks.

"It could be. Sukayana Prikon, or someone else, tried to delete a load of emails from Sawatdii's email account very recently, but I've managed to reconstruct most of them."

Zack leans closer to the screen and reads one of them.

Hello,

I received a very enjoyable treatment from Prataporn on my last visit, but because my diary is practically full I'd like to know what her work timetable is so that I can book another appointment. Or do all the masseuses work the same hours? It would be good to know.

Until next time,
A happy customer

"I agree," Zack says. "It looks like he's trying to map their movements."

"He tries again with similar questions in other emails."

"Why do you think they were sent by Peter Karlson?"

"Dirty Sanchez is a term for degrading anal sex with a defecation theme. The pseudonym Gustav Vasa likes to write about the extreme degradation of women, and Peter Karlson was himself accused of anal rape a year ago. He's also the sort of man who might well try to bring his fantasies to life."

"Were his emails the only ones that Sukayana Prikon tried to erase?"

"No, there were plenty more. But there are four or five from Dirty Sanchez among them. I just can't find out who he is, and it's really bugging me."

"What about Gustav Vasa, his favorite alias? Has he posted anything on his blog today?"

"Yes, a few hours ago. Read it for yourself. He seems a bit shaken after Rudolf and Niklas's visit yesterday evening."

She opens the blog on one screen. The latest post is visible in the left-hand column.

> Dear friends,
>
> This will be my last post for a few days. I'm taking a short break from the blog. But the struggle doesn't stop. We can all make a difference. Each and every day.

What does he mean by that? Zack wonders. That he's made a difference by murdering four foreign women?

He wants to ask Sirpa what she thinks, but she's already

moved on to something else. Her fingers are tapping at the keyboard like rain on a tin roof, and she's staring at the screen with eyes that never seem to blink.

The window of the browser looks like the screens of computers in old films from the eighties. Black background with green letters. He guesses she's in the Darknet, the hidden part of the Internet, trying to find information about prostitution or the trade in women that might help their investigation. Sirpa has shown him things before on the Darknet, things he only thought existed in horror films. Forums where children, women, and human organs are bought and sold just like any other commodity.

"Keep going for it," he says, and leaves her alone, but she doesn't even hear him.

He wonders, not for the first time, if she's ever mapped her colleagues' lives, if she knows things about him that she's never admitted.

He thinks about Rebecka in the hair salon. She could unmask him at any moment. What would he do if she tried to blackmail him?

I'm being paranoid, he thinks.

Call me.

Would I rather see her than Mera?

The person I'd most like to see is Abdula.

He makes a mental note to ask him about Rebecka when they meet later that evening, find out if he knows anything about her that he could use as a counterattack if she does try to blackmail him. Abdula always has a good idea of what's going on.

Avoiding his computer and the blank report, Zack goes over to his pigeonhole. A single brown envelope, letter size, is sticking out of it, and he picks it up. The address label was printed on a computer.

The clumsy cops in the Special Crimes Unit
Police Headquarters
106 75 Stockholm

The envelope had to find its way into his pigeonhole, of course. The caretaker is part of a gang of miserable old men who dislike Zack and think he's too young and inexperienced.

Zack opens the envelope, expecting to read some poorly spelled sentences about how useless the police are, and how they ought to try to catch proper criminals instead of trapping innocent drivers for speeding offenses.

The envelope contains a folded letter-size sheet with a single sentence.

The words make Zack's pulse race.

I'm going to kill all the fucking Thai whores in this city.

Zack turns the sheet over, looking for any clues. Nothing. He puts it down on the nearest desk, not wanting to contaminate it with any more fingerprints.

"Deniz," he calls. "Come and look at this!"

She pushes her chair back and walks over to him. Without her scarf, the compress on the side of her neck looks like a white flag against her skin.

"Read this," Zack says. "But don't touch it."

She reads.

"Who sent it?"

"Don't know. The letter and address label were printed on a computer. No sender."

"It sounds like Peter Karlson, obviously. He's getting more and more interesting."

"Koltberg will have to look at this. He might be able to find some fingerprints or fibers."

The door to the corridor opens and Östman comes in with some papers in his hand, his beige corduroy suit hanging limply on his body. They call him over.

He looks troubled, the way he always does whenever anyone asks him to do something.

"What do you think?" Zack says.

Östman throws his arms out and pulls a face as if someone just asked him to guess how much plankton there is in the Pacific Ocean.

"It could be the killer, of course, if he's an extrovert character with a streak of vanity. But it could be someone else entirely. Someone who's heard the news about the murders. Or it could just be a coincidence, some angry citizen who's decided to send us this message now. It's impossible to say."

He walks away and leaves his papers in Douglas's pigeonhole.

Zack reads the sentence again.

"Koltberg can analyze the ink," he says to Deniz. "He might even be able to find out the make of printer. But unless it's an extremely unusual model, that won't be much use."

He puts on a plastic glove and slips the letter into an evidence bag.

"Östman, can you put this in Koltberg's room?" Zack asks. "You're going past on the way out, aren't you?"

Östman looks at his watch with an exaggerated gesture.

"I didn't know it said caretaker on my visitor's card. But sure, I can take it."

He snatches the bag and leaves them.

Zack and Deniz look at each other, trying hard not to burst out laughing.

"Can you imagine him as the charmer he's supposed to have been?" Deniz whispers.

Zack shakes his head.

"It feels like he needs the longest holiday in the world."

Holiday.

What had Peter Karlson written?

I'm taking a short break from the blog.

Is he thinking of leaving the country?

"What is it?" Deniz wonders.

"Have you got any plans for the next few hours?" he asks.

"Are you thinking of asking me on a date? If you are, the answer's no."

"Don't worry, I was thinking about Peter Karlson."

"What about him?"

"Right now he's our only candidate as the author of this note, isn't he? And Sirpa's managed to find similarities between him and Dirty Sanchez, who seems to have been trying to figure out when the masseuses worked."

"Yes. So?"

"He recently wrote a post on his blog saying he was going to take a break. Maybe he's thinking of running. Do you think we should go and apply a bit of pressure?"

"What do you think Douglas would say?"

"That we should wait until we've got a bit more meat on the bones. Or until tomorrow morning at least, when everyone's here. But I have a feeling that might be too late."

"So what you're suggesting is a bit of informal questioning?" Deniz says.

"Something like that."

"Give me five minutes."

26

EARLY EVENING at the Sturehof.

Flattering light falls on the white tablecloths from lamps with lacy shades. Voices talking quietly, well-dressed groups trying to look like they're just having a relaxed meal after work or shopping, but who keep glancing around surreptitiously to make sure that they've been seen.

Like a more neurotic version of the Opera Bar, Zack thinks.

Mera likes it here, and keeps trying to get him to go for either lunch or dinner. She hasn't succeeded yet.

Zack stares at Peter Karlson's neat neckline as they follow a waiter into the large, open dining room. Presumably he feels at home here, he thinks. Safe. And that makes it more likely than he'll reveal something.

They were lucky. Karlson stepped out of the elevator in the entrance of the tower at Hötorget just as they were waiting for it.

"What do you want?" he asked. "I'm on my way to get some dinner."

"Good," Zack replied. "We're hungry too. Where were you thinking of going?"

"Sturehof. But I'm afraid I've only booked a table for one."

"I can sort that out," Deniz said.

Then she phoned and warned a maître d' that she knows.

She waves to him from a distance as the waiter leads them to a discreet table partially hidden behind a pillar.

"Why so grouchy, Peter?" Zack asks once they've sat down. "Are you starting to regret not opting for an interview room in Police Headquarters instead?"

"There's nothing wrong with the place. The company is a different matter, though," he replies.

Karlson cranes his neck and looks around. He seems worried that they might create a scene in here.

"That's just because you haven't got to know us yet," Zack says, looking at the menu. "We can be very well behaved in social situations when we set our mind to it."

"I doubt it," Karlson says. "That seems very unlikely."

Zack and Deniz both order steak. Karlson opts for the turbot, at 485 kronor, and says with a sneer:

"I assume you're paying."

When the fish arrives he sends it back, saying it's been overcooked. Says:

"Neither of you would have dared to do that, would you? That's the difference between people who make things happen, and those who are happy to make do with crumbs."

Zack feels like smashing his teeth in. Deniz's dark eyes flash almost black. Karlson notes their reactions and smiles broadly.

Zack curses himself for letting himself be provoked so easily. He sees Karlson lean back, as if he's just realized that he's too smart for these stupid cops, and has made up his mind to play with them.

Zack shakes off his anger and reminds himself why they're there.

"You have an ability to express yourself in a very concise, powerful way in writing," he says.

"Are you thinking of anything in particular?" Karlson asks.

"Yes, the letter."

"The letter?"

"The one you sent us."

Peter Karlson laughs, although it sounds more like a condescending snigger.

"I'm beginning to understand why the police's clear-up rates are so appalling. Instead of professionally and systematically gathering evidence against real criminals, you harass hardworking individuals and try to scare them with fabricated allegations."

He folds his arms on the table, leans forward, and looks first Zack in the eye, then Deniz.

"And I can guarantee that I've got considerably more interesting things to do than write letters to the police."

"Do you like dogs?" Zack asks.

"They disgust me, all that licking their own backsides."

Deniz leans over the table in the same way that Karlson just did. He is expecting a quiet, barbed remark, but instead Deniz says, loudly and clearly:

"You're going to tell us what you know, you fucking racist."

"You're also seriously perverted," Zack adds. "We know that. Reported to the police for . . ."

Zack lets the sentence die, but conversation on the nearest tables has fallen silent. The discreet sound of cutlery is the only noise. Several tables are looking at them, and Karlson looks down at the white cloth.

"I'm going now," he says. "You can't do this to me."

He stands up.

They follow him.

Deniz passes her maître d' friend on the way out.

"I'll be back soon to pay the bill," she says.

Karlson has a ten-yard lead on them when they emerge onto the pavement. He glances back with fear in his eyes. But his anxiety at losing face is greater than his fear of them, and he doesn't dare take the risk of starting to run and being pursued by two police officers. Not here, not at Sturehof. He might be seen by someone he knows.

Zack and Deniz, on the other hand, have no hesitation in running. They catch up with Peter Karlson and each take hold of one of his arms.

"You're coming with us now."

"I want to call my lawyer," he says quietly but firmly.

"What did you say?" Zack shouts back, as if he were talking to a ninety-year-old with poor hearing. "You need a lawyer?"

Several passersby turn to look at them.

"Okay, okay, just calm down," Karlson hisses back.

"Like hell we will," Deniz says.

Zack sees an open garage door a few meters farther on.

"In there," he says, steering Karlson in the right direction.

The ground slopes sharply downward. One of the fluorescent lights in the ceiling is flickering hysterically, there's a strong smell of gasoline, and the tarmac is covered with oil stains.

The metallically gleaming cars look like they belong to Sturehof's clients. Zack notes that they all seem to comply with the ridiculous trend to have an X in their name: Lexus GX, Volvo XC60, BMW X3. Then he sees an old Corvette Stingray sticking out from the crowd.

There is no one in sight. They lead Karlson into a dark, urine-stinking corner and let go of him.

The fear in his eyes is clearly visible now. Karlson is alone with two police officers in a garage, and he knows they don't wish him well. Yet he carries on spitting out his hatred at them, as if he were on a sinking ship and was desperate to have the last word.

"You pigs," he says. "Nigger-loving idiots. Why don't you just leave me alone? People like me keep this country going. I'm the one paying for those fuckers on benefits. Get out and deal with the real problems instead!"

"Are you the man behind the pseudonym Dirty Sanchez?" Zack asks. "Did you try to work out the masseuses' work schedule?"

"You're mad," Karlson says.

He's breathing quickly, small, shallow breaths, and Zack is prepared for some sort of attack. Desperate people often do desperate things.

"Explain what you were thinking when you wrote the letter," Deniz says calmly.

Karlson glares at her.

"Look, you fucking cunt, you only got your job to meet the quota, so what the fuck gives you the right to humiliate a real Swede? Why don't you go home to Rinkeby and let the state look after your eight nigger children instead, the way your sort always do when they come here."

Zack looks at Deniz. At her clenched fists and the dead look in her eyes. Her arms are hanging limply from her body.

He decides to let it happen.

Karlson doesn't realize the danger and just goes on goading her:

"And let me tell you what I think of those Thai whores. Killing them was an act of charity. A mercy killing. All the fucking Thai whores in this city ought to die."

That last sentence is what does it.

All the fucking Thai whores in this city.

Exactly the same phrase as in the letter.

Zack sees Deniz's fist fly toward Karlson's nose. He hears the sound of bone breaking, sees the blood gush from his nose as Karlson thuds into the wall and slides down onto the tarmac.

He ends up lying on his side, covering his face with his hands. He hasn't started to scream yet.

Deniz kicks him hard in the stomach.

Karlson gasps for breath. He looks up at her beseechingly, as if she could somehow help him get more air into his lungs.

Zack knows he should stop her now. This isn't what we do.

But sometimes police officers do actually do this. In the best of worlds, everything is black or white, but this world is nothing but gray, gray, gray.

He thinks of the video clip of himself in Tantolunden, which was nothing compared to this. Yet people who saw it still used words like *excessive brutality* to describe it.

If only they knew.

Karlson finally catches his breath. He's gasping for air with his mouth, groaning and spitting out blood.

Deniz crouches down beside him. She lifts his chin and looks at his face. Almost like Hamlet with the skull, Zack thinks.

Karlson evades her gaze.

"Give us something," she says. "Are you Dirty Sanchez?"

Karlson hesitates.

She flicks his broken nose hard with her forefinger.

"Do you want more, worse? You know how crazy us niggers can get."

Karlson puts his hand up to stop her.

"No, no, don't hit me again!"

Deniz stays where she is, calm now, with her left hand holding his chin.

"Well?"

Karlson says nothing, trying to buy time to think. Deniz slaps him hard across the nose.

He lets out a scream this time.

"Okay, okay! I'll talk."

He catches his breath before going on:

"There's a really crazy guy. Ingvar Stefansson. He's talked a lot about killing immigrant whores."

"How do you know him?"

"Don't ask."

"We're asking."

"He's only known to the initiated. He's really hard-core in his beliefs. Maybe a bit too much for the good of the cause. Please. Don't hit me again."

She lets go of his chin, and Karlson's head drops to the bloodstained tarmac.

Deniz looks at him for a while in silence. He doesn't dare move.

Then she tilts her head slightly and says:

"Okay, Peter. My cousins and I are going to haunt you for the rest of your life if you report this. You walked into a street lamp, okay?"

He doesn't answer.

Deniz clenches her fist and pulls it up toward her shoulder, as if measuring a punch.

"Okay?" she says.

Karlson puts his hands up in front of his face and pulls his legs up into a fetal position without answering.

They leave him and walk out of the garage. Deniz pulls

a paper handkerchief from her pocket and wipes her hands.

"*My cousins*? I didn't think you were in contact with any of your family?" Zack says.

"I'm not. But idiots like that always think immigrants have forty armed cousins they can call on when it's time to exact revenge. And who am I to crush his prejudices?"

She gets the car keys out and tosses them to Zack.

"Your turn to drive."

27

THE DOORBELL beside the lock is the old-fashioned sort, and the harsh, monotonous sound is clearly audible through the thin door of the apartment. They listen out for signs of life, but there doesn't seem to be anyone home. Through another door on the same floor they can hear the sound of a television with its volume turned up loud.

Zack looks at the time—7:43 p.m. A good time if you want to catch anyone at home.

They called Douglas on the way there. Didn't say anything about Peter Karlson. Just said they'd received an anonymous but credible tip-off about someone who might have information about the murders in Hallonbergen.

Douglas sounded dubious. Said he thought they ought to go home and get some rest.

But they insisted.

"Okay, okay. Go on, then. But be careful."

Zack rings the bell again.

The battered sign on the door says I STEFANSSON.

Leif Ingvar Stefansson. Born 1981. Taxable income: zero kronor.

That's pretty much all that's in the databases. No telephone number, no family. Just this residential address in Abrahamsberg.

They ring again. Keep the button pressed for a long while. No other sound from inside the apartment.

"Do you think Peter Karlson called to warn him?" Zack wonders.

"Not impossible. So what do we do?" Deniz says.

Zack takes out his key ring and holds up a picklock in response.

Deniz nods.

"I'll keep an eye out. And we can always say it was unlocked if we find anything," she says quietly.

Zack kneels down. Slowly inserts the pick into the old Assa lock.

He made it himself, out of a hairpin he got from Ester and a five-inch nail that he's bent at a ninety-degree angle.

He slides the nail in first. Then the curved, pointed end of the hairpin.

These old locks are easy to pick. After just fifteen seconds the tumblers give way and he is able to turn the cylinder.

The door opens with a soft creak, letting out a smell that makes him feel sick. His mind conjures up an image of a rotting corpse on a bed somewhere in there, before he quickly changes his mind. It doesn't really smell rotten. More stale: acrid and sweaty. A smell that reminds him of the old gymnastics mat that used to get rolled out for physical education lessons at primary school, when the class was being taught how to do somersaults. It always smelled of stale, ingrained sweat and urine, years of rolled-up angst.

Deniz follows him in. Turns her head away when the smell hits her.

Zack switches on the lamp in the hall and carries on into the apartment's only room.

It's like a chamber of horrors.

The first thing his eyes are drawn to are the jaws. Sharp, bone-white teeth gaping open. There are four sets hanging on the wall.

Then he sees the macabre photographs.

So many.

Enlarged pictures of mutilated Arabs. Men who have lost their legs, screaming women with dead children in their arms. Bleeding people running from smoldering buildings, men being hanged in public, their lifeless bodies swinging from nooses. Mass graves. Smashed skulls.

It's as if all the news agencies in the world had selected their very worst twentieth-century pictures of the Middle East and East Africa and arranged them as a single huge photographic collage on this living-room wall.

Around the pictures the pale-yellow wallpaper is pretty much covered by newspaper clippings with a similar content. News about bombings, reports about al-Qaida, articles about high levels of unemployment among Somali immigrants to Sweden.

On a lot of the pictures someone has scrawled words and drawn symbols in red and black felt-tip.

"Go, go, go," it says on one picture of an exploded building in a city that looks like it's in Pakistan or Afghanistan. A smiley has been drawn on a newspaper clipping about Hungarian neo-Nazis, and on a ledger-size photograph of three bloody bodies, a large thumbs-up from Facebook has been stuck on.

Zack and Deniz just stare at the wall without saying a word.

Most of it seems to cover events within the past few years, but there are older clippings here and there. A black-and-white image of naked, hanged African Americans surrounded by members of the Ku Klux Klan, with a large burning cross in the background. There's a framed photograph of Professor Vilhelm Hultkrantz from the 1920s with the caption "Founder of the Institute for Racial Biology." Beside it is an old metal sign saying WHITES ONLY.

Zack wonders if it's from South Africa or the American South.

"Damn . . . This is the sickest thing I've ever seen," Zack says eventually.

He looks more closely at the mounted sets of jaws. He'd guess they come from wolves, but they could easily be from some other predator. From another continent, even.

He runs his forefinger along the incisors and then looks at his fingertip. No dust. Cleaned recently, then.

Or hung up recently.

After ripping the flesh from Sukayana Prikon's legs?

He tears his eyes away from the wall and looks around the room. Piles of books, pamphlets, and documents everywhere. In the bookcase, on the coffee table, on the floor, among the plastic plants on the windowsill.

He reads a few of the titles: *The Turner Diaries*, *White Power*, *The Laser Man*, *March towards Ragnarök*.

Deniz picks up a blue-and-yellow book entitled *Swedish Voices: Short Stories by the Silent Majority*. She shakes her head.

"You almost can't feel angry at this. It's just sick."

Zack looks back at the wall. Trying to find something that's missing.

"He hates a lot of things, this guy. Anyone who hasn't got white skin, from the looks of it. But can you see anything to suggest that he hates women as well? Prostitutes?"

Deniz inspects the wall. Then the books and articles on the table and floor.

"No, I agree with you. If this guy did kill those Thai women, it would be because of the color of their skin, not their gender. Which is why I don't think it was him."

"You're thinking about the way they were shot?"

"Yes."

"But bear in mind what Douglas said. That could have been a red herring, an attempt to make us think the way we've just been doing."

"Yeah, but I don't know," Deniz says, leaning over to read a racist article from the Fox News website that's been pinned to the wall.

Zack goes back to studying some of the hate-filled pamphlets and books.

"He's crazy, no doubt about that, but he isn't stupid. Just listen to this title: *White Supremacy as Socio-political System. A Philosophical Perspective.* You'd need a sharp mind and excellent English to get through something like that."

"It's not too much of a surprise that he's friends with our Hötorget acquaintance. This is starting to feel like a club for racists with university degrees," Deniz says.

"Peter Karlson is easy to categorize, but I can't get a grip on Ingvar Stefansson," Zack says. "When I first noticed the smell in here I thought we were dealing with someone who's more or less mentally handicapped. But the books and macabre pictures on the wall suggest something else entirely."

Deniz shakes her head and says:

"It's almost religious, don't you think? As if we were in the home of some Nazi high priest."

"We've got to talk to him," Zack says.

"He could be anywhere."

"He was here yesterday, at least."

"How do you know that?"

"There was no mail on the hall floor, and he hasn't got a NO ADS sign on the door. That means he was here yesterday to pick up the mail, at the very latest. Surely two days wouldn't pass without a load of ads pouring in?"

Zack goes into the kitchen and opens the fridge. He has to force himself not to slam it shut instantly.

Christ, what a stink!

Breathing through his mouth, he checks the dates on the two opened cartons of milk. One has three days to go before its best-before date. The other expired a month ago.

Zack closes the fridge door and goes back to Deniz. She seems to be studying one clipping intently.

"Look at this one," she says.

She points to a large picture beside the text. It shows a screaming crowd waving red flags and holding their hands in the air.

"What about it?" Zack says.

"See what they're doing with their hands?"

"Looks like some version of the sign of the devil. A hard rock concert?"

"Don't be silly. Hard rockers stick their index and little fingers in the air like horns, but they hold their middle fingers down with their thumb. These people are sticking their middle fingers out like jaws. Wolves' jaws. That's the sign of the Grey Wolves."

"Who?"

"An extreme right-wing, ultranationalist organization from Turkey. They killed my grandfather."

She looks away from the article and stares at the jaws mounted on the wall.

"I was terrified of wolves when I was little," she says. "Everyone in the village hated them. They used to take our sheep. And there were rumors that they could take children too. Then I started to hear that the Grey Wolves came and took adults as well, but I still thought they were talking about animals. Until they took Grandfather."

She swallows hard, and Zack waits for her to go on.

"They came one night and took him and three other men in the village. Just disappeared with them. The way they took thousands more. No one knows what happened to them."

"Why did they take your grandfather?"

"He was a *peshmerga*, a freedom fighter. Fought for an independent Kurdistan. But that was before I was born. He was an old man with a crooked back who walked with the stick when they stormed in and hit him in the face with the butts of the their rifles."

"What did the police do?"

"Nothing. The Grey Wolves worked in collaboration with the police. And the military and the government and the mafia. They were prepared to sell themselves to anyone. Smuggled loads of heroin and weapons. Carried out terrorist attacks."

"Shit, and I'd never even heard of them."

"They're much weaker these days. They don't get the same protection from the authorities anymore."

"Did you ever find out what happened to your grandfather?"

"No. What do you think about this wall, is it enough to get a search warrant?"

She changes the subject so abruptly that it takes Zack a moment to catch up.

"I haven't seen any direct threats or incitement to acts of terrorism. And it isn't against the law to be racist or worship violence. What if we mention those mounted jaws, and the fact that they seem to have been hung there recently? That ought to get Douglas and the prosecutor interested."

AN HOUR later Östman is standing in front of the collection of articles and photographs.

"What do you think?" Zack asks, when Östman has been studying them for almost ten minutes.

"What can I say? This collage alone would be enough for an entire doctoral thesis in criminology. He seems to tick quite a lot of different boxes, this Stefansson."

Koltberg has unscrewed one of the sets of animal jaws and put it inside a transparent garbage bag.

"Definitely wolf," he mutters. "Just like the excrement."

"What? Have they had time to check that already?" Zack says.

"It all depends on what contacts you've got, as you know all too well."

Zack clenches his teeth and pretends not to have heard the insinuation. Koltberg goes on:

"I asked a good friend at the University of Agricultural Sciences in Uppsala to take a quick look. It was a wolf that tore Sukayana Prikon's legs off."

"A wolf. Fucking hell."

There goes any theory about the Brotherhood's dogs, Zack thinks, feeling a wave of disappointment. For every answer they get, the less they seem to know.

Douglas calls.

"I think we can rule Peter Karlson out of the investigation."

Zack turns completely cold.

We hit him.

Humiliated him.

"What's happened?"

"We've got hold of the footage from the surveillance camera in the garage below his apartment block. Peter Karlson parked there just after one o'clock on the night before last. At least an hour and a half before the women were shot. That fits with what he told us."

"He could have taken a taxi to Hallonbergen later."

"Theoretically, yes. But it's more likely that he sat down at his computer instead. At two fifteen a comment was posted by Gustav Vasa on a nationalist website, 'Free Times,' where he said he'd just been to an uplifting meeting where the atmosphere was full of refreshing Nordic values."

Deniz isn't going to want to hear this.

She's standing beside the bag containing the wolf's jaws, talking to Koltberg.

"You've heard about the excrement sample?" Zack says to Douglas.

"Yes. And I've already spoken to the animal keepers at Skansen. No one there has noticed any fresh blood on the fur of their wolves, there's been no sign that they've been disturbed, and no sign of any break-in."

"What does that mean?" Zack wonders. "That we've got man-eating wolves roaming the forests around Stockholm?"

"No. I talked to Skansen's wolf expert about that. Apparently no wild wolf has attacked a human being in Sweden in modern times, just as Sukayana Prikon's doctor said. And trying to force them to do it on command, for instance, by tying up someone who's already bleeding profusely in a forest, seems to be almost impossible. So there's probably some sort of illegal wolf enclosure around here, inside or outdoors."

"Nothing new about Yildizyeli?"

"No, no news at all."

They end the call.

Zack looks out of the window.

The evening sky is a gentle fire of pink-and-orange flames.

Wolves everywhere. From out of nowhere.

Wolf symbols here.

And somewhere out there someone is keeping wolves as pets. And feeding them live human beings. Wolves don't eat people. It's against their nature. But if they're starving, or trained to do so, wolves could presumably eat anything.

THE AIR is still mild and the outdoor serving areas full of people dressed in thin clothes when they leave Ingvar Stefansson's apartment. Deniz drops Zack off at Fridhemsplan, and he strolls down to Norr Mälarstrand instead of going home.

He tries to work out what he wants to do. Go around to Mera's? She texted him earlier. Asked if he was coming over tonight. He replied that he would be.

But he needs to see Abdula. And Abdula was going to "sort out a few things first."

Zack has learned that these things can take time.

He gets his cell out and texts Mera again.

> Might be late. Sorry.

He doesn't really feel up to seeing her now anyway. He's too restless. She's going to want to talk, ask him about everything that's happened today, everything she's heard about on the news.

But he doesn't feel like talking.

Not even after they've fucked each other's brains out and got rid off all their tensions.

He thinks about Rebecka, the hairdresser at Hair Daze.

Stupid idea. Forget it.

He stands and gazes out across Riddarfjärden for a while, looking at the reflections of the buildings and trees along the shore. Big motorboats and a couple of puttering smaller boats glide slowly across the water.

There's two of everything here.

People walking hand in hand along the footpath. On the quayside a short distance away a group of friends are laughing and drinking beer. Zack would have liked to sit there with them, dangling his legs, but he turns west instead and follows the water toward Rålambshovsparken. As he walks he turns the day's work over in his mind.

At least they've managed to shrink the investigation slightly.

Two suspects dismissed: Peter Karlson, and one member of the Brotherhood, Danny Johansson.

But they haven't really managed to find anything that's taken them any closer to the perpetrator.

It feels like everything is about the Brotherhood or Yildizyeli now.

Possibly both. One gang as murderers, the other torturers. But wolves don't fit the Brotherhood at all. And then there's Ingvar Stefansson. The lone madman they haven't yet managed to track down. But that's under way. We can start by talking to those closest to him. The others have probably already got hold of them.

A woman on Rollerblades goes past with an Alsatian on a leash, and Zack starts thinking about wolves again.

The wolves that ate Sukayana Prikon's legs.

They're dealing with something truly sick this time.

How did they, or whoever it was, get hold of the animals? By illegally hunting them with tranquilizer darts? Smuggling them into the country somehow?

Everything's moved so quickly with this investigation. None of them has had a chance to stop and think things through. And the crimes are just insane.

The smell of a barbeque reaches him from the park. And something sweeter.

Hash.

The smell wakes some old memories. But he steers clear of that sort of thing now.

He misses Abdula.

Would like to relax into the comfort of their friendship.

He's always been worried about running into him out in the field one day, on the other side of the law.

But how great is the risk of that, really? Zack wonders as he walks along by the water.

He hunts serious criminals, and Abdula is just a small-time gangster.

He gets his cell out and checks the *Aftonbladet* website. It takes him a while to scroll down to the article about the chase in Tantolunden.

It looks like the storm is passing, after all.

He puts his cell away, turns around, and increases his pace.

Now he knows where he's going.

28

DENIZ HAS left the car at Police Headquarters, and now she gets off the metro one stop early, at Västertorp. She needs air, needs to have a quiet walk in the late evening, needs space to think.

She starts walking slightly aimlessly toward the south, past the brown brick apartment blocks, trying to keep the railway bridge within sight. She passes a kebab kiosk with a line stretching back into the street.

She's never been here before, even though it's so close. She crosses a street and finds herself in a leafy area surrounding some white-gabled row houses, and turns onto a cycle path that seems to follow the line of the subway tracks.

She looks at the grazed knuckles of her left hand. What on earth did she think she was doing? She had no right to hit Peter Karlson.

There's one phrase the implications of which she really hates: abuse of authority.

It was what she was once the victim of, and was what she was going to put a stop to when she joined the police.

Yet that is precisely what she has subjected someone else to today. A person who has also turned out to be innocent of what she was accusing him of.

She curses herself. Wishes she could go back in time and stop what happened in the garage.

She behaved the way she used to when she was a teenager. She was always getting in trouble back then. Fought with anyone who provoked her, boys as well as girls. They thought they were tough and dangerous, tried to pretend they were grown up and knew a bit about life. They didn't know shit. She wasn't scared of them.

But she was scared for her little brother Sarkawt's sake. He was far too gentle and good-natured.

One snowy November day when Deniz was fifteen years old, she saw four boys force eight-year-old Sarkawt down into an ice-cold ditch. She broke one of the boys' arms and almost drowned another.

After that, Social Services decided to separate her from her little brother. "For the good of both children," as they put it.

She wasn't even told where he was living, and hasn't heard from him since then. She hasn't found out where he went. She hasn't felt strong enough to grapple with the pain of it.

The cycle path curves away to the east and Deniz follows it for a few hundred yards, parallel to the Södertälje road. She can see the cycle bridge across the expressway farther ahead, leading into Fruängen, her own anonymous little suburb.

The sun has gone down now but it's still light, and she can hear cicadas in the bushes.

She sometimes wonders if Sarkawt has moved back to their home village. If he's grown up to become the sort of man who pours gasoline over girls and sets light to them to defend the family's honor.

She wonders, like she has done so many times before, if he chose to remain in Sweden, or if he might even be dead. Why hasn't he ever got in touch with her?

What right did the authorities have to separate them?

Those men in suits and self-righteous women sitting in their meeting rooms and making decisions when they hadn't even met her and Sarkawt.

People with power. They do whatever they like. In Sweden, just like in Kurdistan.

"So do something about it then, instead of sitting here complaining," a teacher had once said to her in high school.

Lars Öhman, that was his name. Her favorite teacher.

"You're smart, and you're good at studying. Apply to go to college. Make society better. Become a politician, a judge, a police officer, a social worker. You can become anything at all, even though you seem to have trouble recognizing it."

She used to think he sounded like a dreamer.

But his words took root. The following week she knocked on his door and asked if he knew what she needed to do to get into the Police Academy.

Now she's been a police officer for over ten years. Usually a good one.

But not today.

This investigation is getting to her. Wolves, biker gangs, brutally murdered women. Plenty of lines of inquiry, but no definite direction so far.

29

DOUGLAS IS sitting on an uncomfortable chair beside Sukayana Prikon's bed.

The small hospital room is calm and peaceful, the blinds are closed, and the only light comes from a little lamp on the bedside table.

From outside the door comes the sound of footsteps passing and disappearing down the corridor. Then everything is quiet again, with the exception of the low hiss of the respirator that's keeping Sukayana Prikon alive.

Douglas holds her hand, and squeezes it tight. Her hand is small and warm, with slender fingers. He lets go of her hand for a while and just looks at her, then he takes hold of it again.

He scratches his head with the other hand and takes a deep breath that makes his whole chest swell beneath his jacket.

He looks at the empty, flat space toward the end of the bed where Sukayana's legs ought to form bumps beneath the yellow health service blanket. He puts his hand on her forehead and whispers softly:

"Enough now."

He pauses. Then he says:

"Enough now, if you feel you can't go on."

Footsteps approach the door again.

Stop.

The door opens and bright light floods the room. The

nurse is a sturdy woman roughly the same age as him, and she stops midstride when she catches slight of him. For a moment she looks horrified, then says:

"Who are you and what are you doing here? Visiting time is over."

Douglas stands up and holds out his hand. She doesn't take it.

"My name is Douglas Juste, I'm a section head with the Stockholm Police."

"Have you got ID?"

"You can always ask my colleagues sitting on guard outside."

"But I asked to see your ID."

He holds out his open wallet. She takes it and inspects his ID card carefully.

"I just wanted to look in on my way home to see if she might be in a position to answer some questions. A murderer is still on the loose, and every piece of the puzzle is crucially important to us."

The nurse returns his wallet.

"She needs rest. And if she does wake up she mustn't get upset. Even you in the police have to contact us first, actually. You can't just march in here and jeopardize a patient's health. I thought I made that clear to the officers sitting outside here the whole time."

"I was the one who ordered them to let me in. And seeing as I'm already here . . ."

"You'll have to leave now, please."

Douglas looks at Sukayana Prikon again. Her face is calm. A lamp on the control panel flashes on and off with reassuring regularity alongside her bed.

The nurse stands in the doorway with her arms folded

and an expectant look on her face. So he leaves. But he stops at the door, turns toward the bed, and says good-bye.

While he is waiting by the elevators he hears the nurse reprimand the two policemen sitting on guard outside the room.

He goes down to the lobby. Gets in his car and drives toward the city center. He parks untidily on Nybrogatan outside the blue canopy of Teatergrillen, and goes in through a door off to one side, with frosted glass and bearing the inscription MEMBERS ONLY.

The staircase leads down to a velvet-red bar. A small group of graying men are sitting and talking on dark leather armchairs. On the table between them is an array of coffee cups and cognac glasses.

At the bar sits a lone man whose rear view Douglas recognizes easily. The man turns around when he hears footsteps on the stairs.

"Douglas, it's been a while. Sit yourself down."

Douglas settles onto a bar stool. They each order a gin and tonic and talk the way they always have done. About suitable investment opportunities in the property market, and what might come up at Bukowski's auction house this autumn.

His friend smiles. Douglas looks at his face and doesn't like what he sees in his eyes.

But you have to look after your old friends, he thinks.

SIRPA IS sitting alone in the Special Crimes Unit. The clock on her screen says 9:01. She thinks about the murdered women. She has to stop joining them anymore.

Under normal circumstances she would be happy with her work so far.

She's managed to crack almost all the email addresses on Sukayana Prikon's computer, and has identified the men behind them. A few of them will probably be prosecuted for paying for sexual services.

That's good. Important.

Tomorrow Douglas can get people to check their alibis for the night of the murder, but Sirpa doesn't imagine that's going to provide anything useful. The men are just ordinary men. With wives and children. A few of them have got criminal records, for tax offenses and drunk driving. But nothing remarkable. Nothing that makes her think they've found the killer.

She clicks to open a document. Stares at the top line.

dirtysanchez@woomail.com

It now looks extremely unlikely that it's Peter Karlson. So who is it, then?

She's tried all the legal methods at her disposal to trace the identity of the sender, but it seems hopeless. She knows it isn't, though. Everyone leaves a digital trail behind them. But this individual is clever. As long as she sticks within the law he'll be able to get the better of her.

She stretches and carefully bends her legs. Her joints creak quietly. Then she takes a deep breath and lets her fingers dance across the keyboard again.

She tries to locate Ingvar Stefansson instead. She begins by drawing up a list of properties that are registered to members of the Stefansson family and his other relatives. They'll try to get hold of his closest relatives tomorrow, and question them as soon as possible.

Evening has laid its silent shadow over Police Headquarters.

She needs to come up with something.

Do good.

30

ZACK LOVES the sound of leather striking leather.

The basement on Agnegatan is actually a boxing club, but he comes here fairly often anyway. Because of the generous opening hours, but also because the people who hang out here are serious. And some of them practice martial arts, just like him.

He looks around the premises, dressed in a white T-shirt and loose black shorts. It's past nine o'clock, but there are still a dozen people there. He recognizes most of them, but not all. Not the girl with the shaved head, for instance. She's standing over in the corner, kicking the punching bag fixed to a stand on the floor. Her face is wet with sweat as she attacks it with rapid kicks. Right, left, right, left.

Two lads of eighteen or so are sparring in the ring. Zack watches them as he stretches his warmed-up leg muscles. Too much desire, too little technique. Just like him when he started.

But he was younger, only twelve years old when he reluctantly went with two older friends to a dojo in Skärholmen and took part in his first karate training session.

After just fifteen minutes he found himself in the starting position, learning the basic movements. Elbows back, fists close to the body, backs of the hands facing downward. Twist the fist on the way out. *Get your elbows in, Zack!* Alternating strokes. Left arm out when the right is on its way back. Following sensei Hiro's movements the whole time. Again and again, until his thigh muscles trembled with the exertion. He had to rest. *Zack, back in the starting position!* Shoulders back. Standing straight.

Again. And again.

He ended up becoming addicted to karate.

Six years later he became a black belt, and started to train at kickboxing and wushu.

In the end he contacted sensei Hiro again with his own ideas of how you could combine techniques from different disciplines, and maybe even introduce some modern elements.

Sensei Hiro took him on again.

ZACK GOES over to the oblong black punching bag hanging from chains in the roof. He puts his sports bag down, sits on the floor, and softens up his bandaged feet by twisting them at different angles.

Then he stands up, starts bouncing lightly on his feet, and attacks the bag. He holds back for the first few minutes, then kicks harder and harder. He uses his hips to kick.

Lets himself be swallowed up in the moment. Finds clarity in it. Expands.

Just like out at the bikers' clubhouse, or when he was chasing Suliman Yel.

He died because of me.

He kicks with all his strength. Feels the sweat running down his temples and back.

He made his choice.

I was only doing my job.

The large bag sways with the kicks and starts to swing violently. He meets it as it comes toward him with even harder kicks.

He switches to waiting for the bag to swing back, then dodges it at the very last moment. A quick swerve of the hips to the right, then a rapid ura mawashi geri. The chains rattle as he swings his left leg around the bag and hits it hard with his heel high up on the opposite side.

All the pent-up energy from the working day finds its way out in his kicks. His thighs are burning with exhaustion, and he's enjoying the physical challenge. He carries on dispensing kicks until he can barely lift his legs anymore.

He takes a break. Goes over to the stainless-steel water cooler and drinks straight from the jet of water.

A wiry man with the skipping rope comes toward him.

Zack goes back to the punching bag. He takes two batons out of his sports bag and clicks to extend them, and starts whirling them around his hands like drumsticks. He bounces around the bag on his toes, then attacks it with the batons in what looks almost like a dance.

The young men and the woman with the shaved head stop to watch him, wide-eyed, almost as if he were from a different planet.

Zack whirls the batons over his head, behind his back, in large, sweeping arcs in front of his body.

He shoulder still aches slightly from breaking down that door, but he ignores it.

He spins around, dispensing blows, slipping out of the way of the bag, attacking it with both batons at the same time. Twists around. Strikes again. The batons make a whistling sound in the air, and the blows sound like whip cracks.

A quarter of an hour later he feels he's done enough for

the evening. He sits down on the floor and unwraps his feet. Checks his iPhone. He's received a message from Abdula.

AS HE heads west along Fleminggatan he thinks about Ester. He wonders if she's been sitting outside his door this evening waiting for him.

Others might have reported her situation to Social Services, but Zack doubts that any good would come of that. There's no question that she has a wretched life, but the alternatives are hardly any better: being shuffled between different foster homes where, at worst, sadists and men with a taste for young girls might be waiting to get their claws in her.

At least Veronica is kind toward Ester, even if there's no way she could be described as a functional mother.

Outside Stockholm Kebab at Fridhemsplan subway station, four loud mouthed men in their twenties are stuffing their faces with doner kebabs. One of them is swaying noticeably, and white kebab sauce is dribbling down his shirt collar.

Zack takes a look inside, sees seven people at the white tables, but no Abdula. He decides to wait outside, and stands and watches the anonymous faces of people entering or exiting the subway.

One of them could be the murderer, he thinks. Anyone. We know so little about him.

Someone shoves him in the back. He slips to the side instinctively and raises his arms in front of him.

It's the drunk from the gang of young men. He glares at Zack and says angrily:

"What the fuck, watch where you're going."

The drunk is standing far too close. Stupidly cocky and

provocative from the alcohol. One of his friends comes over and tries to pull him away.

"Perra, come on. We're going."

Perra waves him away and carries on glaring at Zack.

"I'm just wondering why this fucker was shoving me."

That voice. He sounds like Seb.

The same threatening tone when Seb came up to Zack on the football pitch a few weeks after he'd seen him down on the tracks with the boy.

Zack can still remember how frightened he was. Remembers the heavy, cold rain. Remembers the way Adam, Ernesto, Alex, and Nabila ran off and left him alone when Seb and his two friends came walking across the pitch. And then Seb's hate-filled voice:

"It was you who snitched, wasn't it, you little bastard?"

The drunk waves his kebab in front of Zack's face. Some of the sauce lands on his face.

Like Seb's saliva.

"Watch yourself, you bastard."

Those words.

Zack looks at the drunk's friends. Anger is bubbling inside him far too quickly now.

"Are you going to get him away from me, or do I have to do it myself?"

They see the look in Zack's eyes and are sober enough to realize that they need to leave.

They lead their protesting friend away. Off toward the subway.

Zack massages his temples.

Shuts his eyes.

He's back on that rainy football field

"Okay, you little bastard. Not so tough now, are you?"

Seb was wearing a red Champion sweater and Buffalo shoes. He was at least a head taller than Zack, and a good fifty pounds heavier. And he had his two friends with him. The guy with the trucker's cap and the one with the buzz cut.

Zack could probably have run away from them. He *wanted* to run away from them, but a different part of him made him stay.

If he ran, he'd have to run again tomorrow.

But he'd never been in a fight with anyone, except for fun. And there were three of them. Older than him. Bigger.

They were standing in a ring around him and started shoving him.

One of them spat at him, hitting him on the cheek, and someone kicked him in the shin.

They shoved him some more. Zack was expecting one of them to hit him, so he could start hitting back.

But Seb pulled out a butterfly knife.

"What have you got to say now, you little shit?"

Then there was a muffled sound and the boy with the cap was on the ground.

"Ooow!" he yelled, clutching his cheek.

He looked at his hand, saw the blood, and his face contorted with fear.

"What the fuck's going on?" Seb shouted, and Zack noticed the stones on the ground.

Someone was on his side.

The rain was pouring down, and Seb yelped when a stone hit him hard in the back.

"Come on, then, you bastard! Come out and I'll cut you!"

And he did come out. It was the dark-haired boy Seb had been dangling over the railway track a few weeks earlier.

He looked completely crazy as he ran toward Seb with a metal rod in his hands.

The metal pole hit him hard in the shoulder, then the hand holding the knife. Seb ran off.

The boy with the buzz cut looked terrified. He started to run, but Zack knocked him to the ground without really thinking about it. He sat on his back and pressed his head down into the cold, wet grit.

It didn't feel like him doing it.

But it felt good.

He didn't want to stop.

He rubbed the boy's face on the ground hard, until he shouted, with a sob in his voice, that he gave up. Only then did Zack release his grip and let him go.

"Come on," the boy with the metal rod said.

And they ran into a doorway and sat down at the bottom of a staircase.

"My name's Abdula," the boy said.

"My name's Zack."

"Thanks for helping me down by the tunnel."

"Thanks for helping me today."

"Seb's mental. Properly, I mean. I think he's got something wrong with his brain. Do you want to come upstairs?"

Now Zack can see Abdula coming up the escalator, wearing a tight black T-shirt and a blue hooded top. He's standing one step below two teenage girls, but he's still taller than them. And probably heavier than the pair of them put together.

He sees Zack and they embrace.

"Sorry I'm late. The was some sort of holdup at Skanstull."

"No problem," Zack says. "I just got here."

They go into the kebab shop and each orders a doner kebab to go.

"Where do you want to go?" Abdula asks.

"How about AG?"

"You can't quite tear yourself away from familiar territory, can you?"

"Don't think we'll find anything better around here."

"Okay. There were lots of nice things to look at there last time."

They head off in silence, eating as they go. The air is still mild, and the last pinkish light in the sky hasn't yet given way to darkness.

"Any more drug raids coming up?" Abdula asks between mouthfuls.

"Not that I know of. But you've seen how little I know these days. I almost got caught myself during that last raid."

"They got one of my mates before he had time to flush everything away. Pocketful of crank. Started babbling to the cops that it was for his ADHD."

Zack laughs.

"Seriously, man," Abdula says, "I'm kind of worried about him. The stuff he had on him came from a new lab in Lund, and even if he's a decent guy, I'm not sure he's the sort who'll be able to keep his mouth shut when your friends start putting pressure on him."

Zack says nothing for a while, struck by the absurdity of the conversation. His best friend has just told him about a new Swedish lab producing methamphetamine, and what does he do? Ask to hear more? Put him under pressure? No, he laughs and carries on walking, as if they were talking about some funny television program or something.

"Have you found out any more about the raid?" Zack asks after a while.

"Like what?"

"I don't know. I thought you might have talked to some of the people who were questioned."

"I've only heard a few things indirectly. It sounds like your friends weren't after anyone particular; they just received a tip-off that loads of drugs were being taken at the club. And they were right about that, of course."

Zack nods.

"I'll try to have lunch with some of the guys in the drug squad sometime soon. If I hear anything about what they're planning, I'll let you know, okay?"

Abdula holds out a clenched fist. Zack bumps his knuckles against Abdula's.

"Right now we're checking out a possible flare-up between the bikers in the Brotherhood and a Turkish organization called Yildizyeli," Zack says. "Could be connected to the murders of those four women in Hallonbergen. Yildizyeli are said to be involved in prostitution and trafficking, among other things. Have you ever heard of them?"

"No, not my area at all, but I can check."

"Anything you could find out about the organization and someone called Ösgür Thrakya would be very interesting."

"Okay."

The bouncer outside the AG restaurant looks askance at Abdula, but lets them in.

The décor seems to have been inspired by a sophisticated slaughterhouse. The walls are covered with white tiles, and chunks of meat have been hung up on general display behind the glass doors of the fridge. The music is loud, as is the level of chatter from the clientele. They order two very expensive beers and check out the smart middle-class crowd.

"Look at them," Abdula says, shaking his head. "They think they're so cool. That they've found a style of their own.

But if some fashion magazine told them the top they're wearing is passé, they'd chuck it away the next day."

Zack nods.

"It's tragic," Abdula goes on. "Look around, Zack. It's like that kids' game, what's it called . . . ? Follow the leader. This is like a fucking macro version of follow the leader. Everyone here obeys the slightest nod given by the interior design magazines and fashion designers. They're just too stupid to realize it."

"But it was the same when we were growing up. Don't you remember being thirteen? If you didn't have a pair of Fila shoes, you hardly dared go out."

"True," Abdula says. "But that's the point. We were thirteen. These people are adults."

The beers arrive and they raise their glasses in a toast.

"Speaking of Fila," Abdula goes on, "do you remember Nabila, that skinny guy from Pakistan? That time we forced him to put firecrackers through the headmaster's mailbox and he got his hand stuck?"

Zack laughs.

"Don't! I still have nightmares about what happened to his fingers."

They go on relating anecdotes from the past, and order more beer from a young waitress with fair hair cut in a short, unkempt style.

"Here you go, gentlemen," she says, giving Zack a barely perceptible wink before moving on to the next customer.

They both watch her as she walks away and gets a bottle of Laphroaig down from the shelf. Then they look at each other and shake their heads. Raise their glasses in another toast.

"It was always good having you around," Abdula says. "A

white guy who looked nice and harmless. They never suspected anything—before it was too late. Like that time with the kiosk in Tyresö."

"Tyresö—I'd almost forgotten that!"

"Your performance there was worth an Oscar, the way you lured him away to help you with your bike."

"While you stole as many sweets as you could get your hands on."

"Forty-four pounds. I remember us weighing it."

"I was sick that might. Dad couldn't figure out why the vomit was so brightly colored."

Abdula laughs.

They fall silent for a moment.

"Actually, it was fucking awful really," Abdula says. "And do you remember how jealous all the others were, specially Abbe? He couldn't believe that you and I had so much freedom."

"While all we wanted was what he had. A normal Swedish life. I still remember what it was like around his house. Nice and tidy. And it always smelled of baking."

"I was so fucking impressed when you sometimes did the cooking when the three of us were around at yours," Abdula says. "And that you used to clear up and wash the dishes while your dad was asleep."

"A bit different to the way Abbe grew up."

"He had everything going for him. But he was too weak," Abdula says.

"How long has it been now, ten years?"

"Something like that. I was there when they found him. The syringe was still in his arm. That was when I decided. Needles weren't for me."

Abdula's mobile buzzes.

"I need to get going."

"A deal?"

"The less you know about what I do, the better."

Their hands meet in the air.

Then Abdula heads out into the Stockholm night.

31

THE GLASS of beer in Zack's hand is still half full, and he lingers in the bar. It's half past eleven and AG is full of drunk people.

He looks around. Can't see any solitary single women, they're all in groups. And that pretty, short-haired waitress has finished for the evening.

He gets his cell out and brings up the number of the beautiful brunette hairdresser they saw earlier in the day.

Rebecka.

Should he call her?

He hesitates.

Stop it.

Go home to Mera. Now. At once. That's the right thing to do.

He walks as far away from the speakers as he can and dials Rebecka's number.

Two rings.

Maybe she's asleep.

Three.

"Hello?"

Her voice doesn't sound sleepy.

"Hi, it's Zack."

A short pause. Then:

"Dance partner or policeman?"

She's quick.

"Which would you prefer?"

He takes a taxi to Tegnérlunden. Taps in the door code she gave him, opens the heavy wooden door, and walks up the stairs to the fourth floor.

The stairwell is very smart, elaborately decorated. He wonders how a hairdresser can afford to live here.

Maybe she inherited money, like him.

Or perhaps she's been doing business with Suliman Yel and his friends?

In which case, what are you doing here, you moron?

She opens the door dressed in a white undershirt and gray jogging pants.

He hesitates, unsure of what to say.

"Hello, you," Rebecka says with a smile. "Come in."

There's something about the way she looks that makes Zack feel like a thirteen-year-old on his first date without his parents.

The living room is illuminated by just three large candles on a silver dish, set on a low, square table in front of a bulging red sofa. An old-fashioned table lamp stands like a statue in the window. Zack sits down among a mass of subtly colored cushions and Rebecka sits down right next to him, facing him.

"I've made up my mind," she says.

"About what?"

"About who I want you to be. I don't want the policeman, I want the guy at the club."

Zack laughs.

"Sure. Whatever you want."

"Good, so you're not a policeman now?"

"No."

"So if there's any coke in the apartment and someone offered you some, you wouldn't arrest them?"

"You don't get arrested in Sweden. You get taken into custody," Zack says. "But, no, I wouldn't take that person into custody."

"Well, then."

She stands up and goes into the bedroom. Zack watches her, checking out her firm body beneath her saggy trousers.

He hears her open a drawer and rifle through it. When she comes back she's got a small bag of white powder in one hand, and a silver case in the other.

She sits down on the sofa and opens the case. It contains a mirror, a razor blade, and a small chrome tube. She tips the powder onto the mirror, chops it up, and divides it into six lines.

"Peruvian," she says. "The purest you can get right now."

She hands the tube to Zack.

"Guests first."

Zack leans over the table and snorts one line. Then another, in his other nostril. The effects kick in and he leans back in the sofa, takes some deep breaths, and feels a combination of calm and clarity spread through his body.

Any trace of tiredness vanishes.

He hears Rebecka snort one of the lines. Then she leans toward him and puts her feet up on the table.

"Do a lot of police officers take drugs?" she asks.

Not judgmental, just curious. But Zack feels his stomach clench, in spite of the cocaine.

"I don't actually know," he says. "I don't think so. But plenty are hard drinkers."

"Are they?"

"You should see our staff parties."

He looks at her, and sees the way she's studying him, as if she was looking for an answer.

"What?" he asks.

"I've been thinking about something since you came to the salon and I realized you were a police officer. When we met at the club, were you the one who tipped off your colleagues later that night?"

"No, of course not. Did you really think it was?"

"I honestly don't know. I don't know you. All I know is that you're a police officer who takes coke at illegal clubs, and that now you're sitting here doing it again with a girl you questioned about some secret criminal investigation earlier today."

He laughs quietly, but it just sounds brittle and fake.

There's a floor-length mirror on the other side of the room, but he avoids looking at his own face.

He ought to get up off the sofa and go home, but the cocaine is making him feel wonderfully fluid, and right now it doesn't seem to matter. He stares out into the room and nods to himself.

"Detective Double Standard," he says.

She gently takes hold of his chin and turns his face toward her.

"But you are very handsome," she says.

Her lips move closer. She presses them to his and he wants her never to take them away. She kisses him for a long time, and then she sits astride him and pulls his T-shirt off. He tugs off her undershirt and she kisses him again and is gentle with him in a way he discovers that he's been missing.

He lays her down on her back and removes the rest of her clothes, and as he throws her trousers away they hear a hissing sound followed by a small thud, and see that one of the candles has fallen onto the rug. It starts to smolder and Zack leaps off her and stifles the fire with her trousers.

She giggles, and he becomes aware that he's sitting on her floor naked with a pair of charred jogging pants in his hand. She stands up and takes his free hand and they go into the bedroom and get into bed.

They make love gently, and when Zack pulls her hands up and holds them tight above her head, out of habit, she whispers in his ear, telling him to take it easy, and he lets go and she puts her arms around him, showing him the way.

Afterward they lie side by side in silence. The cocaine rush has faded. She lights a cigarette and he gets up from the bed and goes over to the sofa and gets dressed. Then he goes back into the bedroom and kisses her on the forehead.

She doesn't ask him to stay.

OUT IN the street it's dark. Or as dark as it gets in June at almost one o'clock at night.

He hails a taxi.

"Kungsholms Strand."

When the driver pulls up at his door he asks the driver to wait. Five minutes later he gets into the backseat again. His hair is wet from the shower, he's wearing a fresh T-shirt, and has swapped the Rick Owens jacket for a sweater. He doesn't want Mera to see the bullet holes.

"Where now?" the taxi driver says.

"Floragatan, Östermalm."

Mera is angry when she opens the door.

"I thought you were going to be here much earlier."

"I had to meet an important source."

"Your hair's wet."

"Then I went to the gym."

"Time for more exercise now."

In the bedroom she gets out the handcuffs.

"Tie me up."

Her eyes flash as Zack takes control. When he makes her beg and plead.

She screams out loud when she orgasms, almost a scream of pain, and Zack can hear his mother in that scream and wonders why he's thinking about her again when he's having sex with Mera. And he wonders if she screamed when she realized that everything was coming to an end, far, far too early.

Did she scream because she didn't want to leave me?

Afterward they lie naked on a soft, striped Missoni blanket in front of the fire in the huge living room. The blanket feels like ten thousand dollars against Zack's skin, and he wonders how long he'd need to save up to afford the furniture, paintings, and interior design items in Mera's living room.

"I read about the latest murder," Mera says. "The man who was pushed off a balcony. They said it had something to do with your case."

"He wasn't pushed. He was being chased, and he fell."

"Was he the murderer?"

"We don't think so. But we don't know enough yet."

He pauses.

"Anywhere near enough."

"I heard there's a journalist at *Expressen* who's been looking into the involvement of criminal gangs in Thai massage parlors, apparently he's working on some sort of scoop," Mera says. "His name's Fredrik Bylund."

"I know who that is," Zack says.

"He's pretty go-ahead."

"That's putting it mildly. But he's okay to talk to. I'll try to arrange a meeting and find out what he's got."

He reaches for his phone and looks at the time. Quarter past two.

"Have you got his number?"

"You're going to call now?"

"No, I'll text him. Evening tabloid reporters are always up late. And if he doesn't want to be disturbed he'll have his phone switched off."

Mera fetches her own cell and sends Zack the number. He taps out a quick suggestion of a meeting over breakfast.

"He's bound to want something in return," Mera says.

"I can feed him an unimportant side line for him to get excited about."

"The way his colleagues at *Aftonbladet* got excited about you?"

"You could tell it was me?"

"Of course I could. Who were you chasing?"

"The owner of a massage parlor. The four women who were killed worked for her. She thought I was the murderer and panicked when we turned up to talk to her."

Mera moves closer to him. Strokes his ribs with her stiff nipples.

"I got a bit excited when I saw the film."

She moves her arm toward his groin and takes hold of him in her hand.

Then her mouth.

She decides she wants to be taken from behind, and Zack is aggressive and in the heat of the fire sweat runs down their bodies.

"Zack, wait," she says.

He stops moving, but stays inside her warm dampness. She turns her face toward him. Looks him in the eye.

"Can't you . . . I'd really like it if you used one of those lumps of wood and . . . burned me with it. Just a little bit."

"What the fuck, Mera . . . ? No, I'm not doing that. That's not on."

"I just want to know what it feels like."

She looks beseechingly at him.

"You can feel this instead."

He grabs her arms and pulls then back hard, so she falls forward onto her stomach on the blanket, then he twists them up behind her back and pushes them higher. She's screaming with pain now and squirming beneath him, but she can't move at all, and he uses his body weight to push her down and then thrusts into her, hard and fast.

She screams and screams.

He thinks of Rebecka and her softness, and pushes still harder into Mera, unable to stop himself thinking about right and wrong, and what it is she actually wants from this.

Mera falls asleep on the blanket with a smile on her face. Zack grabs a poker and pushes the wood toward the back of the fire, beating out any sparks nearest the grate. Then he fetches her duvet from the bedroom and lays it down beside her so she can pull it over her when the heat of the fire dies down.

His cell buzzes just as he closes her front door and is on his way down the stairs. A text from Fredrik Bylund.

> Working late, I see. Sure, happy to
> meet. Hotel Diplomat, 9.00 a.m.? It's
> on you.

Zack replies, "OK," and shoves the door open. The pavement is wet and the damp air smells pleasantly of summer rain.

He thinks about Ester, and finds himself hoping that

she'll be sitting waiting for him on the stairs. But it's half past three in the morning. She should have been in bed asleep for the past seven hours.

He hopes her dreams take her to a world that's better than this, and hopes that she has the strength to get through yet another day when she wakes up.

He reflects that she might be the only thing in his life that is wholly good.

32

DOUGLAS IS lying in his big, handcrafted bed, sleeping fitfully. His outfit for the next day is hanging on the valet: a blue Egyptian cotton shirt with a matching blue tie and a dark gray suit, tailor-made by Anderson & Sheppard in London.

He twists uneasily between the silk sheets, muttering indistinctly and breathing quickly and shallowly.

He wakes, sits up, and stares out into the large room. The clock radio is showing 03:40.

He doesn't want to think about the investigation. Or about the rumors he keeps hearing about Zack's drug use. He needs him now, and Zack is still easy to direct where Douglas wants him.

How the hell am I going to pull this off? he thinks. It's complicated, so very complicated.

He shuts his eyes. Thinks of the loneliness hiding in every corner of the apartment. He loves being alone, contrary to what everyone believes. He would always be alone if he could.

He drinks a glass of water and tries to get back to sleep. Hopeless. He doesn't even feel sleepy now.

SIRPA IS sitting in bed with her MacBook on her lap. The pain in her knees woke her up when she'd only been asleep for three hours. A large cup of steaming hot chai tea is standing on the bedside table, and she's reading what the online editions of the newspapers are saying about their case. Some newsrooms have chosen to focus on gang rivalries, others are speculating about a lone sexual predator.

She tries to find information about Ingvar Stefansson, but can't find anything useful. Nothing to help move them forward. They're going to have to rely on his relatives knowing where he is.

Beside her on the bed lies Zeus, her Rhodesian ridgeback, snoring with his head on his front paws. He always sleeps on her bed. It's her way of salving her guilty conscience for leaving him alone so much.

He twitches in his sleep and she strokes his back reassuringly.

"There now, Zeus. There's nothing to worry about."

She finds herself thinking about men again. How tricky they are. How little they see in her. Zeus is the only male she needs. Even if right now she would prefer a different sort of warmth.

The dog sits up with a start. Holds his head quite still and listens to the night.

Sirpa quickly sits up. Listens as well.

But she can't hear anything. It must have been a mouse, or a bird. Zeus rolls onto his side and goes back to sleep.

Sirpa closes the laptop and puts it down on the floor. Then she curls up and lays her head on Zeus's body, close to his heart. Its rhythmic beating resonates through her and she falls asleep again.

DENIZ IS lying with her arms stretched out above her head in bed in her apartment in Fruängen.

A lamp on the bookcase is spreading a soft red glow, and she feels the tongue moving in her groin, loves it being there.

She reaches down with her hand and feels the mass of blond hair. She squeezes the soft shoulders and can feel herself getting close.

It's like being given another body, another world, for a short while. But she wants to wait a bit longer.

And then a bit more.

She grabs hold of the hair again, pulls the head up toward her own face.

Skin against skin. Breasts against breasts. She looks into the green eyes. Thinks: you're incredibly beautiful, Cornelia.

She kisses her. Tastes herself.

IT'S ONLY just gone half past three on this night between Tuesday and Wednesday, but Rudolf is already up. Since losing his sight he goes to bed early and wakes up early, and he hasn't had to set his alarm clock for years.

He can hear the patter of the rain on the roof tiles, and in his mind's eye sees the dry earth soften at last, and thinks back to when he was a young boy, watching his grandfather dance with joy at the rain after a difficult period of drought that had left the fields yellow.

He refills his coffee cup and sits down at the kitchen table. He spills some on his fingers and pulls his hand away in surprise. It's a long time since he scalded himself with coffee.

He reaches for some paper towel and remembers how badly he used to burn himself in the early days following his stroke. Time used to feel like it was passing incredibly slowly, and he doubted he could bear to live out all those days the doctors said he had ahead of him.

A difficult time.

But even then he knew it was down to him. It was a fairly straightforward choice: grit his teeth and start again from scratch, or succumb to self-loathing.

He takes a sip of coffee.

It tastes of more now than it used to when he could see it.

33

THE HEAVY rain clouds are obscuring the light of dawn. Large raindrops hit the ground, releasing a smell of dirt and wet tarmac in the center of Stockholm.

A Thai flag hangs like a damp rag outside a metal door on Klara Norra Kyrkogata, and the pink neon sign in the window reflects faintly in the growing puddle where the road and pavement meet.

CITY THAI MASSAGE.

A weak night-light glows in the neat little massage room beyond the lobby. On the floor two women lie fast asleep on thin mattresses. They don't hear the splash of a shoe stepping right into the puddle outside. They don't hear the door opening, or the cautious footsteps creeping toward their room.

The muffled sound of a whip crack makes one of the women start. She begins to move uneasily in her sleep, but then the sound echoes again and she is still.

A stream of blood is running out onto the pillow, and then the silenced pistol fires again and again, and blood starts to pour onto the mattress between her legs as well.

The man stands still, breathing hard. Feeling the power, smelling the intoxicating scent of blood, but something else too. Something that worries him. He thinks of Thai superstitions, and begins to wonder if there are angry spirits drifting about the room, out to get him.

He puts the pistol in his jacket pocket and rushes out of the massage parlor.

The rain is pouring down.

He likes that.

It's as if the gods want to help him erase any evidence.

THEY WAKE up early.

Because of the cold and damp.

And something else.

A sound. Muted at first, then louder.

A car approaching through the forest.

The three girls huddle together, with Sanda Moe in the middle. She's fifteen, the eldest. She acts as the younger girls' mother. But she could do with a mother of her own.

The car gets closer. Stops. The engine is turned off, doors open and close.

The fear is paralyzing.

They've taken Sanpai.

They've taken Tin Khaing.

Whose turn is it now?

Someone is pushed in, so scarred and bleeding that at first they don't see who it is.

The door slams. The bolt slides shut again.

The girl curls up in a corner.

Tin Khaing.

She's wearing nothing but underpants and a T-shirt that's far too big for her. Someone else's T-shirt. An old man's.

She lies down with her back to the wall, and stares in front of her with the only eye she can open.

Sanda Moe goes over to her. Tears some sheets from the roll of toilet paper, scrunches them up, and moistens them with water from the bucket. Then she begins gently wiping the dried blood from Tin Khaing's cracked lips.

Than Than Oo and Law Eh are sitting hunched up, looking on in horror. Incapable of comprehending the evil that has struck their friend.

Law Eh wipes her hand on her filthy striped undershirt, then lays it on Than Than Oo's bulging stomach, as if to seek comfort from what is inside.

She feels something move beneath the warm, taut skin.

34

THE RAIN isn't letting up. Quite the reverse.

Zack runs from the inadequate shelter of the tree he's been standing under outside Mera's building to wave down a vacant taxi. He feels the rain penetrate his top as he gets into the backseat and leans back.

Trickles of water form strange patterns on the side window. It's already light out, but the streets are strangely deserted.

The driver heads west along Kungsgatan and Zack watches ghostly images of Hötorget and Drottninggatan pass by outside the car.

The taxi brakes as a man in dark clothes, a cap, and sneakers dashes across Kungsgatan from Klara Norra Kyrkogata, but Zack takes little notice as he yawns and rubs his eyes. They're stinging with tiredness and pleading for rest behind his closed eyelids.

But his body is restless. He can't sleep yet. He needs more.

Shit.

It's a few minutes before four in the morning. He would just have enough time.

No, stop thinking like that. You need to go home and get some sleep.

As they're crossing the bridge to Kungsholmen he says to the driver:

"Can you head out to Sundbyberg instead?"

"Sure. What address?"

"I'm not entirely sure. I'll give you directions when we get closer."

The taxi swings right into Sankt Eriksgatan and then turns north onto Torsgatan, which becomes Solnavägen as they cross the E4. As they approach the center of Sundbyberg, Zack guides the driver into an industrial zone west of the railway line. He asks him to pull up outside a large warehouse with graffiti-covered walls that shine wetly in the early morning light. The heavy thud of bass music can be felt inside the car.

Zack pays cash and goes inside the building.

It's much smaller than the old Heraldus dockyard where he was on Sunday night, but the ceiling is extremely high. Fifty or so sweaty people are dancing through the early morning, as sunlight shines through the dusty windows up by the roof onto rusting steel pillars and concrete walls covered in graffiti.

The pressure from the sound system makes his heart contract in his chest. Zack recognizes the track, a new one by Avicii or one of the other stadium DJs.

He tosses his sweatshirt onto a chair and heads out onto the dance floor in jeans and T-shirt. Most of the others look like they're a few years younger than him. Many of them are shut off from their surroundings, others high on more than just the music.

He needs to be here.

Wants to disappear into dance. Forget who he is and what he's done tonight.

And all the other nights.

He looks around, trying to get some idea of who might

be selling. They aren't usually difficult to pick out. Always more in control than everyone else. Careful to keep an eye on what's going on around them, alert to discreet signals from potential buyers. Businessmen with the dance floor as their sales area.

He feels a gentle touch against the top of his arm. Dark hair with the shimmer of a black diamond sweeps past his eyes and he sees beads of sweat on a suntanned neck before she turns toward him and he disappears into a pair of eyes that have a soft yet radiant blue color. Her cheekbones look like they've been chiseled by a master craftsman, they seem to reflect all the beauty of the world. Her nose is straight and her lips are a perfect brushstroke—the two halves meet in a heart shape below her nose.

She smiles at him, a barely perceptible smile through closed lips.

He recognizes her now.

She turns her back on him, but goes on dancing close to him. Beneath her sparkling green sleeveless top he can see her bare waist, and beneath that a thin, ankle-length summer skirt in an Oriental pattern. The fabric hugs her figure, and she moves in a way that makes Zack believe that gravity can be defied.

She dances a few steps farther away from him, then turns and looks him in the eye.

He remembers seeing her in a picture in a newspaper not all that long ago. She's the heir to some sort of fortune. But he can't remember which family.

Those eyes.

For a brief moment he thinks he's staring into himself, as if she already knows more about him than he himself will ever know.

He dances closer. Their bodies touch. Hip meets hip. He looks into her eyes for a long time, and she doesn't look away.

The look goes on and on and on.

I'm not going to look away first.

But in the end he does.

He feels like holding out his hand to touch her cheek, her hair, her movements, and hearing the voice he's never heard.

He stands still.

Shuts his eyes.

When he turns around again she's gone. He looks around the room but can't see her anywhere.

Unobtainable.

He feels a firm hand on his shoulder. He knows whom it belongs to before even turning round.

Abdula.

Their hands meet in the air.

In a nondescript toilet cubicle they snort cocaine through pink straws. Open the door and go out and feel the heavy club music receive them with open arms.

35

THE HOTEL Diplomat on Strandvägen, just before nine o'clock on Wednesday morning. Cell phone conversations in English, the *Financial Times* and iPad minis next to coffee cups on the breakfast tables. Flour dust from freshly baked bread. Muted conversations between suited colleagues sitting on armchairs, and an atmosphere of self-proclaimed importance over the whole place.

Zack is fresh from the shower. He's changed into a clean pair of jeans and a black T-shirt with a low-cut neck. He hasn't slept a wink since his visit to the club in Sundbyberg. The cocaine is keeping him awake, but he feels sick, the world has shrunk to a narrow tunnel in front of his eyes, and a headache has settled like a band of lead around his head.

He's a few minutes early. The maître d', a neatly made-up woman in her midthirties, looks askance at him. He wonders if she can see any traces of the night in his face, or if she just doesn't like the way he's dressed.

She shows him to a table in a distant corner, passing a mirror on one of the wall pillars—Zack doesn't think he looks too bad. He's had worse days.

The smart businesswomen make him think of the woman he was dancing with a few hours earlier; she probably dresses like that during the day, the way she was in the newspaper article he saw her in. What was it she had inherited? Or was she just the heir apparent? He tries once again to place her, but gives up.

He slumps into the soft armchair and sees her before him. Her face, her body.

Her black, diamond-shimmering hair.

Those eyes, which could have been his own. He can't quite make sense of the feelings she arouses in him. Surprise, confusion, the beginnings of infatuation? Like the poet Petrarch, who saw his Laura once and spent the rest of his life writing about her.

Then he sees Mera's face.

What am I doing?

Who do I think I am?

He starts to feel distinctly uncomfortable, and rather nauseous.

Someone laughs at a nearby table. He turns and sees a middle-aged man cast a quick glance at him as he says something inaudible to the red-haired woman opposite him. She giggles quietly and tries to turn her head discreetly in his direction without him noticing. But it's not just them. Zack looks around at the other tables. All of the smart clientele are sneaking glances at him. He's the one they're all whispering about. He's the one they're laughing and shaking their heads at.

The laughter and chatter are getting louder and louder. He can't bear it any longer, he has to get out of there. Just as he's getting up from his chair he sees Fredrik Bylund walk into the hotel in jeans, a creased shirt, and jacket. Classic reporter's uniform.

Bylund catches sight of him and Zack forces himself to raise his hand in greeting.

Too late. Damn it.

He sits down heavily in his chair again.

Pull yourself together now. Focus.

Bylund makes his way through the breakfast room without waiting for a member of staff to show him the way.

"Zack! Okay?"

His handshake is firm, his voice bright. But his face is etched in small wrinkles, as if he were considerably older than his twenty-seven years. He's got big bags under his alert eyes, and he's skinny, with sunken cheeks and sharp shoulders. He looks as if he neglects himself the way that plenty of men and women who work long hours do.

Or does he lead the same sort of life as me?

Bylund goes off and gets some breakfast before sitting down opposite Zack.

"Mmh, good coffee," he says, and stuffs half a croissant in his mouth, with all the hunger of a starving animal.

Zack couldn't keep anything down. He feels even more sick from watching Bylund stuff his face.

Bylund's cell buzzes. He sticks his hand in his pocket and pulls it out in a fraction of a second. Zack tries to swallow his nausea and notices an unusually large birthmark on the back of Bylund's hand as he quickly reads the screen.

"A new exclusive?" Zack asks.

"Hardly."

Zack empties his cup of coffee in several gulps, and wonders whether journalists might actually be even more cynical than police officers. Bylund drains his own coffee at similar speed. They beckon over a nearby waiter with a chrome coffeepot in his hand.

"Looks like we share an addiction," Bylund says.

Zack's headache eases slightly and he feels that he rather likes this journalist. There's something solid, honest about him, even if he does spin his stories a bit too much sometimes.

"Seriously, though, how are you getting on?" Bylund asks once they've both had more coffee.

"You know that as well as I do. After all, you write several articles each day about the hunt for the killer and all our mistakes. So what have you got going on?" Zack asks.

"This and that. Nothing I can share right now."

He sounds wary now.

"Maybe we could swap some information," Zack suggests.

Bylund straightens up.

"What did you have in mind?"

Zack detects a caution in the reporter that feels out of place. Fear, almost. As if he were sitting there with dynamite in his lap, afraid it might explode with the slightest movement.

"You know something," Zack says.

"I can't let you have it. Sorry."

"Is it anything to do with the Turkish mafia?"

Bylund raises his eyebrows.

"No," he replies.

A little too quickly.

"What? Tell me more," he adds.

Zack tries to think. What can he say, and what can't he? And how much does Bylund actually know? Never underestimate an experienced journalist.

He sits back heavily, suddenly exhausted. He can almost feel the last of the cocaine leaving his system, as if it were the last drops of fuel in a stuttering engine.

He tries to drink more coffee, but its bitterness catches in his throat.

"That's just a sideline. I can't say more than that."

"Seems like we're both a bit too cagey today for this to be particularly worthwhile."

Bylund stands up.

"I need to get going."

Zack looks at the time.

"Me too."

Bylund stands where he is for a few moments, looking down at Zack.

"Maybe the two of us could help each other. Soon. Very soon. But for God's sake, make sure you get some sleep. You look like you've snorted a whole mountain of coke just to get yourself here."

36

PAW HTOO'S wrists ache from the previous day's twelve-hour shift. She rubbed Tiger Balm into them before she went to bed, but it hasn't helped. Every muscle aches, but her foot is the worst.

She takes the escalator up to Sergels Torg, limping as she crosses Klarabergsgatan and heads west. She see the perfume in the window of Åhléns, then the handbags and clothes. She's nineteen years old and there are so many things she would like to buy. But her money goes to her family in Mae La. To Mom, Dad, Grandma, and all the brothers and sisters who never know if there's going to be food on the table the next day or not.

She lives with a number of other women in an apartment in Husby, ten of them in a small three-room flat.

She's been here just over a year now, and is going to be allowed home in October, so they say.

Almost three months. An eternity. But she has to find the energy from somewhere. Has to bear it.

For her family's sake.

It's a little easier now. Sometimes she manages to take herself mentally to a different place while it's going on, and the new mama-san who has taken over the running of the parlor isn't as untrustworthy as the last one. Paw Htoo is allowed to keep half of what she earns from the extra services, and thirty percent for massages. And every third massage is off the books, which means that she gets more money.

A Romanian woman is sitting cross-legged on the pavement, rattling a paper cup. She reaches out a beseeching hand to Paw Htoo, who feels a pang of guilt for having just dreamed of buying luxury products.

In this woman's eyes I'm well off, she thinks. But back home I could be the one sitting there begging, being spat at by others.

She turns into Klara Norra Kyrkogata, crosses Mäster Samuelsgatan, and sees the Thai flag wave gently in the breeze outside the door. The flag is heavy from the night's rain, and looks heavy, almost sorrowful.

She pushes the door handle down.

Unlocked.

They're very quiet.

"Hello?"

They were probably partying last night, she thinks.

They do that sometimes, when the homesickness gets too much and they need help relaxing after their long shifts. Dreaming themselves back home again, away from all the kneading of fat backs, and the tugging on stiff, smelly penises.

Paw Htoo has an idea. She's going to creep up to the door, yank it open, and shout at them with a deep voice, pretending to be Mama-san.

That will get them moving.

She smiles to herself as she tiptoes silently across the floor.

She takes hold of the handle, pushes the door open, and screams.

Not because she wants to.

But because of the sight that greets her.

PART III

About how a friend is always a friend,

A doomed king's vain prayers,

And the women's journey toward eternal light.

37

THE DARK clouds have moved away to the west and the morning sun is busy clearing away the last traces of the night's rain.

But Klara Norra Kyrkogata is still in shadow. There are puddles on the ground, and the water splashes as yet another police car turns into the narrow street. The driver blows his horn to make the crowd of curious onlookers move, then pulls up immediately in front of the cordon.

"Almost identical to the murders in Hallonbergen," Douglas tells Deniz. "The only difference is that these two seem to have been taken by surprise in their sleep, thank God."

Koltberg is standing outside an open door, a white coat over his navy blue suit. He is gesticulating wildly at a cop, calling him a useless incompetent. The cop stands there rather forlornly with two evidence bags in one hand. One contains a crumpled red-and-white cigarette packet, the other a used condom wrapper.

Zack looks at him over Douglas's shoulder. He wonders if Koltberg is actually capable of seeing people as anything but objects for examination.

Zack is still breathing hard as a result of the sight he has just seen inside the massage parlor. One of his hands is shaking, but Koltberg not only seems unconcerned, but also appears unable to understand that other people might be upset by the sight.

Today of all days Zack wishes he could see those bodies through Koltberg's eyes. When he walked into the room they were lying in, he couldn't summon up any defense against the brutality, and now the images are coursing through his mind.

The blood.

The smells.

The fleshy hole where an eye should have been.

He looks through the window of a police car parked close to the door. A young Asian woman with straight dark hair is sitting in the backseat with an older female police officer. She was the one who found the dead women. She can't speak any Swedish, and barely any English either. But she managed to say the words "police" and "help," and that was enough for a passing teenage girl to sound the alarm.

Her face is swollen and she's sitting there staring ahead of her with red, puffy eyes.

Her face blurs, and Zack realizes that he's having trouble focusing on anything for more than a few seconds. He shuts his eyes and rubs his face with the palms of his hands. Deniz looks at him and shakes her head. Douglas notes her reaction, seems to be weighing something up, then turns to look at the door again.

"I don't think this is going to end here," he says.

The first journalists have arrived on the other side of the cordon. Large telephoto lenses focus on the doorway, and one reporter tries in vain to get a uniformed officer to say something.

Koltberg walks over to Douglas, Deniz, and Zack. He greets them with a barely perceptible nod, then directs his attention to Douglas alone.

"Same caliber weapon, same modus operandi. I'd say

with ninety-nine percent certainty that these murders are connected to those in Hallonbergen. We'll see if we can find any fingerprints to compare as well."

He goes back inside the massage parlor.

Douglas is about to say something to Deniz when a howl rings out somewhere nearby. They turn around, but can't work out the source of the noise at first.

"There, from the car," Zack says.

The young woman who only minutes ago had seemed apathetic now seems to be having some kind of fit. The police officer in the car is trying to calm her down, but her whole body is shaking, and she carries on screaming, her head turned toward the roof of the car. She manages to open the door and practically falls out of the car.

The journalists' cameras start to click. The volume increases immediately, and the scream really does sound like a howl. A howl full of pain that seems to transmit itself to everyone who hears it, a pain that can only be expressed by someone who no longer feels that there is any good in humanity.

The woman gets to her feet and runs a few steps, but she seems to be having trouble putting any weight on one of her feet. She stumbles and collapses onto the tarmac, and then falls completely silent. Zack rushes over and picks her up in his arms.

She doesn't even seem to notice his presence. She just stares up at the cloud-free sky, as if her body decided to numb her out of sheer mercy.

"Who is she?" one reporter calls out.

"Does she know the murder victims?"

Zack turns his back on them and carries her to the patrol car and carefully sits her in the backseat once more. The female officer helps strap her in.

She looks at him as if she's expecting a reprimand. But Zack merely says:

"It's good that you're with her if she comes around."

Douglas comes over to the car. He leans in and asks:

"What's your name?"

"Karin Åkerstig."

"Is your partner nearby?"

"Yes, he's standing over there. His name's Karl Skog."

"Good. Then can you and Karl take this woman to the acute psychiatric department at St. Göran's Hospital? She needs proper medical treatment."

She nods.

"Karin, I want the two of you to stay at the hospital and guard her room. It's of the utmost importance that she isn't left unprotected."

Karin Åkerstig looks surprised, but nods and calls her partner over.

Douglas turns to Zack.

"We'll just have to hope she's in a state to be questioned later. Can you and Deniz take care of that?"

Zack mutters a weary yes and tries in vain to stifle a yawn. It feels like someone's thrown a handful of grit in his eyes. He shuts his eyes and massages his eyelids in an attempt to wake them up.

Outside the cordon all of the national media has fallen into line. *Expressen, Aftonbladet, Dagens Nyheter, Svenska Dagbladet,* TV4, Swedish Television. The atmosphere is feverish and the reporters are trying in vain to attract the attention of any of the police officers inside the cordon.

"Come on, you've got to give us something!"

"Is it true that they've been shot?"

"Are there more than two?"

"Have you got a suspect?"

Zack can understand their eagerness. Six women shot and killed in three days. Nothing like this has happened in Sweden in the past twenty years, not since that madman in Falun shot seven people in the course of one night.

The cameramen are jostling for the best angles. One television cameraman stumbles forward with such force that the cordon tape almost breaks.

"Okay, you all need to calm down now," one of the two uniforms charged with keeping people out says.

Zack tries to identify Fredrik Bylund, but he can't see him. Maybe all that coffee left him with an upset stomach?

But that wouldn't have stopped him being here, he could have stood there with a sick bag in one hand and his cell in the other, Zack thinks, then hears a cry:

"Zack?"

"ZACK!"

Douglas's voice in his ear. Zack turns around and finds himself looking into his boss's irritated face.

"I was just saying, we'll have a quick meeting in the command vehicle."

Zack follows Deniz and Douglas into the sparklingly clean van. He sits down beside Deniz and hopes she can't see how out of it he is.

"Okay, what are we dealing with here?" Douglas says, to kick-start the discussion.

"This feels more and more like gang war," Deniz says. "What do we know about this massage parlor?"

"Nothing yet. It's not on the list of parlors that were checked yesterday. But obviously we need to look into it at once. I'll put someone onto that."

"They were shot the same way as the others, weren't they?

So we could be dealing with a racist, misogynist mass murderer," Zack says. "What was Peter Karlson doing last night?"

"Naturally we need to look into that," Douglas says. "But could we really be looking at something as straightforward as racism? Or misogyny?"

"And where does Sukayana fit into the picture? Why would a mass murderer want to leave one of his victims alive?" Deniz asks, turning to Douglas. "Have you heard anything more about her condition?"

"She's still sedated. I called the hospital this morning. She's got an unknown and extremely aggressive bacterial infection that the doctors are having trouble controlling. It probably came from the wolf bites, but seeing as neither we nor they know where the wolves come from, they're having to work on trial and error."

They sit in silence for a moment. Realize that they haven't made much progress with the investigation.

"Nothing new about Ingvar Stefansson?" Deniz asks.

Douglas shakes his head and says:

"We're still trying to track down his family. We're also talking to his neighbors. The ones we can get hold of, that is."

"Could we be looking at more than one killer?" Zack says, mainly to show that he's actually trying to think.

The other two look at him in surprise.

"But what about that text from one of the women, 'He kill all'? That suggests we're dealing with a single killer," Deniz says.

"It could be a copycat," Zack says tentatively. "Someone who's heard about the first murders and is doing the same thing. That sort of thing has happened before, and it wouldn't be unthinkable in this case, at least not if we're dealing with people goading each other on to commit hate crimes."

"That feels like a long shot," Deniz says. "I think the murderer is one person who's got some experience of the prostitution that's been going on. Who else would go to a massage parlor in the middle of the night on the off chance that the employees are sleeping at work? That's hardly particularly common in Sweden. The door wasn't even broken in. That could mean the killer had a key to the parlor."

"So we could be dealing with an insider?" Zack wonders.

"I don't know," Deniz says. "We need to start looking into that angle as well."

Douglas nods. Zack can see how stressed and focused he is, and understands all too well that they've got to hurry now if they don't want to find themselves being called out to yet another massage parlor tomorrow morning.

He tries desperately to pull himself together. He wants to wake up, he wants to solve the murders, and give these women some sort of justice. He wants their children, parents, and relatives to know that the murderer who took their loved ones from them has been punished. He wants them to be able to sleep at night, even if he can't give them peace.

"What if these women aren't the only ones?" Deniz says.

"How do you mean?" Douglas asks.

"You read that report on the interviews we've conducted at different massage parlors, haven't you? One of the women said that a number of women have disappeared without a trace. They think they're going home to Thailand, but never get there. What if those women have been murdered as well, without us knowing anything about it?"

"We've been trying to get hold of the woman you're referring to, to question her again, but she seems to have vanished into thin air," Douglas says. "We're still looking. Let's just hope nothing's happened to her."

Zack's brain feels like it's boiling.

"Fucking hell, we don't know a thing," he says, far too loudly.

"We don't know much yet," Douglas says calmly, "but if we're going to solve this, we all need to take our responsibilities seriously and make sure we're working to the very best of our abilities. And make sure that we're capable of doing that."

He looks at Zack, and Zack looks down at the floor.

Douglas's phone rings.

"Hang on, I'll put it on speaker," he says once he's answered. "Zack and Deniz need to hear this."

It's Sirpa.

"Good morning. I've spoken to my contact at Interpol, and I've got a bit more information about Yildizyeli. He doesn't know anything about them moving into Sweden, but he did have a few other interesting things to say, concerning right-wing extremism, torture, and wolves."

Deniz and Zack lean over the phone to hear better. Don't want to miss a single word.

"This Ösgür Thrakya seems to be one of the founding members," Sirpa says. "He used to be in Bozkurtlar, an ultranationalist Turkish organization that's evidently claimed thousands of lives. The name means 'the grey wolves.'"

Deniz and Zack look at each other. They're both thinking the same thing: the newspaper clippings in Ingvar Stefansson's apartment.

Is he their lone madman? With some sort of connection to the mafia?

"Ösgür Thrakya made a name for himself in his twenties as an effective interrogator during the Grey Wolves' brutal raids against Kurds, Armenians, and left-wing sympathizers in both Turkey and other countries. To put it bluntly, that means he's horribly good at torturing people. According to Interpol, he was in Chechnya around the turn of the millennium, fighting with the separatists against the Russians. When he returned to Turkey he broke away from the Grey Wolves along with some of his closest followers and formed a criminal organization of his own, Yildizyeli."

Which he's now trying to establish in Sweden, Zack thinks as Sirpa and Douglas end their conversation.

Wolves, right-wing extremism. Links to a lone madman.

"I'll get a warrant issued for Stefansson," Douglas says. "It's time for that now."

Suddenly it feels like a number of pieces of the puzzle are falling into place.

"We've got to get hold of him," Zack says. "Right away."

38

AS THEY'RE on their way to St. Göran's Hospital to question Paw Htoo, Deniz turns into Kronobergsgatan from Fleminggatan without any warning.

"What are you doing?" Zack asks.

"You need to sleep."

"No, I'm fine. I just had a bit of an odd night."

"I'm not going to ask what you're on," Deniz says. "But if you're going to work with me, you need to get some sleep."

"We haven't got time. We've got to talk to Paw Htoo. And we need to go on looking for Stefansson."

"You can't have more than an hour's sleep. Then we go to the hospital."

She turns onto Kungsholms Strand, parks outside Zack's building, and they go inside.

Zack unlocks the door, kicks off his shoes, and lies down on the unmade bed. He's asleep before Deniz has even hung up her jacket.

She stands beside the bed and looks at him. He's lying on his front, slightly to one side, breathing heavily.

He looks so young. Young and exhausted. Like a twenty-seven-year-old who's just got home from a week in Ibiza. She gets a blanket from the sofa and tucks it around him, then strokes his curly blond hair.

She's eight years older than Zack, but she doesn't usually

think about the age gap. She may have been through a lot, but so has he. He understands her better than anyone else in Police Headquarters, and he's a good friend.

He always backs her up when older, prejudiced colleagues try to patronize her, because she's a woman, a lesbian, or an immigrant. Or all three.

She thinks of an incident several years ago, when a superintendent slapped her on the backside when she passed his table in the dining room. Zack dropped his tray on the floor with a crash, and as the shards of porcelain flew through the air, he pushed the superintendent's face into his mashed potatoes.

Or the time when, for some unfathomable reason, she found herself suffering from unbearable homesickness for the village she grew up in. She slept badly for weeks, and was worried that she was heading into severe depression.

Zack organized a surprise party for her in Empati, the Kurdish restaurant, and invited friends she had no idea how he'd found. She'd never forget that evening. She danced half the night away, and when she woke up the next morning she finally felt a bit better.

She looks at his face. It's as if his features have been chiseled by some powerful force of nature, she thinks, and feels very grateful she doesn't find men attractive. It would have been very hard to work with Zack if that had been the case.

She knows he's broken plenty of hearts over the years, and can't help thinking that he's probably going to break Mera's before too much longer.

She suspects he's being unfaithful to Mera. She thinks of the way Zack and that hairdresser looked at each other, and the time last winter when she was supposed to pick him up from his apartment one morning, and he called at the last minute and asked if they could meet in Gröndal instead.

Deniz doesn't understand how people can do it, how they can look their partners in the eye after they've been with someone else. It must show, surely?

She'd never betray Cornelia like that. But perhaps she lets her down in other ways. Cornelia wants them to move in together. She's wanted that for a long time, but Deniz keeps putting off the decision. She can't imagine how she'd cope with having to tell someone else what she's planning to do, or when she's going to be home. Or having to get someone else's agreement before repainting the hall or hanging a new picture on the wall.

Zack stirs in his sleep. She stokes his hair again.

She trusts him, and he trusts her, even when things look like they're getting out of hand.

But he's impulsive.

Takes too many risks.

Sometimes crosses the line into foolhardiness.

Sometimes Deniz can't help wondering if he does it on purpose, as a way of testing himself.

Or because he doesn't care if he dies?

That thought has struck her more frequently recently. Zack isn't like other people. He can do great things. But he keeps on putting himself in harm's way. More and more.

She wonders how many drugs he's actually taking, and how often, and worries about losing him. Worries that he's pushing himself toward the edge of the cliff.

To shake herself out of her thoughts she walks around the small apartment. She picks up the framed photograph of Zack's parents.

Roy and Anna. They've got their arms around each other

and are smiling. She estimates that they must have been about twenty-five when the picture was taken. Zack has his mother's fair hair, but his father's face.

Roy was a handsome man. Dark-haired, with symmetrical features. He looks healthy and fit in the photograph.

Before the illness.

Zack's told her about Roy's work as a bodyguard. How he was discreet and professional and therefore popular with celebrities and people "with far too much money," as Zack put it. People like the Heraldus billionaire, Olympia Karlsson.

Until he finally messed up because of his lupus, the illness that he didn't know he was suffering from at the time. It affected his joints, his breathing, and could make him incredibly tired.

According to Zack, Roy had fallen asleep on duty when he was working for a foreign pop diva while she was visiting Sweden. While he was asleep someone broke into her hotel room and stole her valuables, including some diamond jewelry.

People started to talk in the industry. Didn't he look like he was drinking too much? Red cheeks. Clumsy. He had been spotted dropping a walkie-talkie in the middle of a crowd, and on another occasion he tripped over a step and fell on top of the businessman he was supposed to be protecting.

Work soon dried up, and by the time Anna died he was not only unemployed, but also visibly marked by illness.

Deniz puts the photograph back again. Poor Roy, she thinks.

And poor Zack too.

She asked him once if he had any memories of his father

while he was healthy, and she could still remember the sadness in his eyes when he said he didn't.

There's a thick, black leather folder on the bureau next to the photograph. She saw it once before on his desk back at the station, and recognizes it even before she reads his mother's name on the front.

Are the contents of this folder what's tormenting you, Zack? she wonders. Is this where your demons come from, all the things you have to resort to chemicals to deal with?

She's tempted to look inside, but she leaves it where it is. If he wants to show her, he will.

She goes into the tiny kitchen, manages to find the coffee, and switches the machine on. Then she calls and requests a Thai interpreter for their interview at the acute psychiatric department at St. Göran's Hospital.

She pours herself a cup of coffee and sits down on the sofa to read the news on her cell. The article about "Karate Cop" has disappeared from the main page of *Aftonbladet*'s website, and it doesn't look like any of the other papers have picked up the story.

She takes out her notebook and writes down a few questions they need to ask Paw Htoo. Then she leans back and shuts her eyes. Thinks about the way life always seems to come full circle. The Grey Wolves took Grandfather, and now they've turned up here in another guise. She thinks about her brother, and wonders where he might be. After fifteen minutes she wakes Zack up by splashing cold water on his face and offering him a fresh cup of strong coffee.

He sits up slowly and scratches his messy hair. Then he staggers into the kitchen, turns on the cold tap, and dunks his head under it. He stands there so long that Deniz thinks he's fallen asleep again. Eventually he turns the tap off, attempts to dry his hair on a dish towel, then drinks the coffee.

Five minutes later they're in the car, on their way to the hospital.

PAW HTOO is in a single room in the acute psychiatric unit. Karin Åkerstig and her partner are sitting on guard outside the door.

A gray-haired doctor with hexagonal glasses leads Zack, Deniz, and their interpreter, Erica Sörensson, to the room.

"I must warn you that the patient is currently strapped to the bed. To anyone not used to it, it can look unpleasant."

"Why is she strapped down?" Zack asks.

"She had a fit when she arrived, screaming and scratching at the eyes of my staff. She's been given a sedative now."

"Can we talk to her?"

"You can try. Do you want me to be there?"

"No, I think it's best if we're on our own."

"As you like. Press the red button by the bed if you need us."

Zack and Deniz say hello to their colleagues, then go into the room, followed by Erica Sörensson. They sit down on chairs on either side of the bed. The narrow tunnel of Zack's reality has expanded again, thanks to the nap and coffee. His eyes have stopped aching, his brain is engaged, and his heartbeat has resumed its usual rhythm.

Paw Htoo looks at them through half-open eyes. Her face doesn't show the slightest trace of emotion. They explain who they are, and show her their ID. Erica Sörensson translates into Thai, but Paw Htoo just looks at her as if she doesn't understand a single word.

Erica Sörensson tries again, but Paw Htoo looks equally uncomprehending. In the end she does say something back, and Erica Sörensson turns to Zack and Deniz.

"What did you have in mind here?"

"How do you mean?" Zack says.

"This woman doesn't speak Thai. It sounds more like Burmese to me."

Burma, Zack thinks. The Golden Triangle. Wasn't that where Ösgür Thrakya's organization had one of its outposts?

Heroin isn't the only thing that comes from there.

Women do too.

What was it Sonny Järvinen had said about the Sawatdii massage parlor? *They can't even be bothered to provide the real thing.*

That was why the murdered women in Hallonbergen had fake passports. Because they weren't from Thailand. They were from Burma.

And that was why the members of the Brotherhood had their fingers on the trigger when we arrived. They were expecting a visit from the Turkish mafia, led by a battle-hardened torturer.

He looks at Deniz. She certainly looks Turkish.

"We're very sorry," he says to the interpreter. "We thought she was from Thailand."

Erica Sörensson ignores him and says:

"I'll be invoicing for two hours. That's my minimum."

"Of course, by all means. Do you happen to know of an interpreter who speaks Burmese?"

She stands up and adjusts her blouse.

"No—you might have trouble finding one."

"So what do we do now?" Zack says once she's left the room.

Deniz has already pulled out her cell and is searching Google.

"There are a few amateurs, at least—people who organize

tours and lectures about Burma," she says, scrolling through the results. "Here's one in Stockholm. I'll give him a call."

Zack looks at Paw Htoo. She's twisting in bed, trying half-heartedly to get free.

Imagine being strapped to a bed in a hospital room in a strange country, unable to make yourself understood. How would he react to that?

He desperately wants to explain to her why she's lying there, but he can't, and when she looks at him with her big, pleading eyes, all he can do is hope she sees goodwill in his own.

"Is that Svante Stahre? Hello, my name's Deniz Akin, I'm calling from Stockholm Police," he hears Deniz say over the phone. "We've got something of an urgent problem . . ."

A BIT of luck, at last.

Twenty-five minutes later a man with an Einstein haircut, a full, bushy beard, and a Hawaiian shirt is sitting on a stool next to Paw Htoo's bed, talking quietly to her in Burmese.

Svante Stahre and Paw Htoo speak for a long time before he finally turns to Zack and Deniz.

"She's a member of the Karen tribe, if you're aware of them?"

Zack and Deniz both shake their heads.

"They're an ethnic minority who have been persecuted by the ruling military junta for years. Their villages have been burned down, women raped, men assaulted and murdered. Several thousand of them have fled to vast refugee camps in the border region between Burma and northern Thailand. One of the biggest is called Mae La, and that's where Paw Htoo has spent almost all her life. I'm having a bit of trouble understanding everything she says, because Burmese is only her second language, and she speaks it rather unclearly, possibly because she's sedated, but she says that one day some well-dressed foreigners came to the camp and promised her a job with a good salary abroad. That was how she ended up here. Sadly her fate isn't all that unusual. A lot of the women and girls in brothels in Thailand come from Burma. And evidently that trade has now reached here as well."

Zack turns to Paw Htoo.

"My name is Zack Herry, I'm a police officer. I was the man who helped you up when you fell earlier."

Svante Stahre translates.

"I didn't fall," she says.

"Do you remember what happened when you arrived at work this morning?"

"I worked. I give massages."

She's suppressing the memory of what happened, Zack thinks. Perhaps that's the only way for her to bear it.

"Can you tell in a little more detail about how you came to Sweden?" Deniz asks, and Zack realizes that she's trying to approach that morning's events from another direction.

More words in Burmese. Sad eyes, revealing that this woman will never trust anyone ever again.

"The men who came to Mae La were foreign businessmen. They looked European, but they weren't blond, and they looked like they had a lot of money. They spoke a little Burmese. They said they worked in both Burma and Europe, and that they were looking for workers on behalf of different businesses."

Slowly but surely a tragic story unfolds, with all the typical ingredients. The men showed her a beautiful brochure full of colorful pictures of Stockholm, and told her how the Swedes love Burmese massage, and how easy it was for hardworking women to get jobs as masseuses at fancy hotels and health spas. They promised to pay for her flight, and would make sure she was trained in massage in Sweden, and told her about the high wages in Sweden and helped her to work out how much money she would be able to send home to her impoverished family each month.

She ended up having to borrow the money for her flight, and she never received any training. That wasn't the sort of massage she was expected to give. She never saw the men again. Others took over in Sweden.

"I refused to give that sort of massage. Then the big man hit me. Over and over again. Hard."

Paw Htoo tries to raise her hands, and looks surprised when she can't, as if she were only now realizing that she was strapped down.

Zack takes out his cell and shows her a picture of Ingvar Stefansson.

"Is this what he looked like?"

"No. I've never seen that man before."

She tugs at the straps a few times. Still with a look of surprise on her face.

"Who's the big man? Do you know his name?" Deniz asks, to distract her from the straps and keep her mind on her story.

"No, they have strange names."

"They? There are more of them?"

"Different men pick up the money from the massage parlor. But there's only one who hits us."

"What does he look like?"

"He's really big. Dark hair. With one eye that looks all milky. He comes in several times a week."

Suliman Yel, Zack thinks.

"Did he hit you inside the massage parlor?"

Paw Htoo nods.

"In front of clients?"

"No, but in front of the others. Not in the face, because then the clients wouldn't want you. In the stomach. Hard, so I couldn't breathe. But I still refused. And then . . ."

She starts to cry, but when she goes to wipe her tears the straps stop her. Deniz takes out a tissue and wipes her cheeks.

"They held me down," she says. "Then they put a big pan of boiling water on the floor. And they forced me to put my foot in it."

She cries again, harder this time, but it feels like she has to finish the story.

"I screamed and screamed, and they asked if I was going to be nice to the clients, and I promised and then they took my foot out at last. And they said that next time they'd put my whole body in, the way they did with other disobedient girls. In boiling water."

That was why she limped, why she fell, Zack thinks.

Because they practically boiled her foot.

He'd like to take her sock off, look at her foot. But he doesn't, because he realizes she doesn't want anyone to see her injuries. Perhaps she thinks they're a mark of shame.

Svante Stahre turns toward Zack. He looks like he's about to faint.

"Look, I don't know if I can handle any more of this."

"Try," Zack says. "What she's telling us might very well help us to catch these bastards."

Svante Stahre nods and swallows hard.

"Okay. But promise to let me know when you get them."

Deniz puts her hand on Paw Htoo's shoulder.

"You've been very strong," Deniz says. "You put up more of a fight than most other people would."

Paw Htoo smiles at them, and her eyes look clearer. Zack wonders if the sedative is starting to wear off.

The smile fades, and she asks them:

"They promised I be allowed to go home soon. How am I going to get home now?"

"We can help you contact the right people. But first we need you to help us," Deniz says. "Where do you live?"

"In Husby."

"In an apartment?"

"Yes, with other girls from Burma."

"Did you live with the women you worked with? The ones you found dead?"

Paw Htoo shuts her eyes, as if to block out the image of the bodies in front of her. Tears begin to trickle from her closed eyelids again.

"Have you lived there the whole time?"

"No, not to start with. They drove us out into the forest, and . . ."

She falls silent and turns her head away.

"Paw Htoo," Deniz says. "What happened in the forest?"

But she just shakes her head and presses her lips together.

"You've got to tell us. We want to stop the people who hurt you."

Paw Htoo's whole body is shaking. Deniz strokes her shoulder.

"Paw Htoo, where did you live to start with?"

She's shaking more and more violently, and the metal bed frame starts to creak.

Deniz tries to get eye contact with her, but Paw Htoo stares straight through her with bulging eyes.

"In a house. In the forest. There are still little girls out there."

"Where is the house?"

"We couldn't get out. And the dogs. The mad dogs. No, no!"

Her body tenses and arches up, straining against the straps as she screams at the top of her voice. Her eyes swivel up into her head and her body starts to shake again, it looks like she's trying to escape from herself, from the world.

Zack presses the alarm button.

Thirty seconds later the doctor and a nurse come in and give her an injection. Her body relaxes instantly and Paw Htoo falls asleep.

The doctor looks at them.

"I'm afraid I'm going to have to ask you to leave. She needs to rest."

THE SHARP sunlight hits them as they walk back to the car. Zack's headache is starting to come back, and he curses himself for not having his sunglasses with him.

"Are you thinking the same thing as me, about that house she was talking about?" Deniz asks.

"Yes," Zack says. "And I've got a horrible feeling that we need to work out where it is as soon as possible."

He pauses. Hears the sound of Deniz breathing.

"And maybe that's where Stefansson is," he adds.

39

THE CONFERENCE room is as warm as the inside of a car that's been standing in the hot summer sun.

Zack wonders if Douglas has switched off the air-conditioning on purpose, to make the meeting short and effective. No one will want to stay here and talk for a minute longer than necessary. Which is just as well. It's already a quarter past four.

He wants to get out of there. Go home. A cold shower, then close the blinds and go to bed.

"God, it's hot," Niklas says, taking off his jacket.

Zack looks at the sweat rings under the sleeves of Niklas's shirt. His own T-shirt is sticking to his back, and his skin feels greasy.

Deniz is wearing just her undershirt, Sirpa is fanning herself with a sheet of paper, and Rudolf has loosened his tie and rolled his shirtsleeves up. Douglas, who is still wearing his jacket, is the only one who seems untroubled. Zack guesses that he's wearing a specially designed cooling suit that cost a fortune.

The head of the unit clears his throat.

"The identities of the two women found murdered in the massage parlor on Klara Norra Kyrkogata remain a mystery," he says. "In all likelihood their passports are fake, and after the interview with . . . what's her name . . . ?"

"Paw Htoo," Zack says.

"That's it . . . After the interview with her, we can assume for the time being that they too come from Burma. Getting their identities confirmed will be difficult. I've just spoken to our contact in Bangkok, and he says we shouldn't pin our hopes on the willingness of the Burmese police to help us track down people belonging to a minority that they've been persecuting for decades. Besides, the Burmese authorities are deeply involved in heroin production, and probably have business dealings with mafia organizations like Yildizyeli. We'll have to try going through various aid organizations and see if there are any registers of people living in the refugee camps."

"Fucking hell," Deniz says through gritted teeth. "First they have to flee their own country because of rape and murder and having their villages burned down. Then they end up in the hands of human traffickers from Europe, are forced into prostitution, and then shot. It makes you want to cry."

"Our examination of the accounts from Sawatdii is complete," Douglas goes on. "There isn't a single invoice from Recruitment Solutions Ltd in the files, or anything else that suggests the two businesses had anything to do with each other. Either she was lying about their collaboration, or it was being kept off the books."

"I think she was lying," Deniz says. "She seemed terrified for her own safety, yet she still told us about Recruitment Solutions without us exerting any great pressure on her. She could have done that to make us focus out efforts elsewhere, away from Yildizyeli."

"In which case she was helping them," Niklas says. "So why would they set the wolves on her?"

"Maybe they thought the fact that she was talking to the police and letting us look at her accounts was enough of a reason?" Deniz says.

"Maybe Sukayana was actually trying to help both us and Ösgür Thrakya by directing us toward the Brotherhood?" Zack says. "If all the murdered women were from Burma, we can probably assume that they were brought here with the help of Ösgür Thrakya's gang. Which means that the Brotherhood would have had a motive to carry out the murders. Perhaps to torture Sukayana Prikon as well. Why would the Turks ruin one of their own sources of income?"

"We don't know if the murdered women in Hallonbergen were Burmese, do we?" Niklas says. "Just because they had fake passports doesn't mean they weren't from Thailand. Which means we might be dealing with two different murderers. First one who kills the Brotherhood's women, then one taking revenge on Yildizyeli by shooting two of theirs."

"In theory, yes. But we've found two emails in Turkish on Sukayana Prikon's computer. I'm afraid I've only been able to trace them to an Internet café in Bangkok," Sirpa says.

"So she speaks Turkish?" Niklas wonders.

"Either her or someone else with access to the massage parlor's email account."

Douglas takes over:

"We've had the emails translated, but they don't contain any names or useful leads, just rather cryptic information about the delivery of something, and that the 'dirty washing' would be picked up according to their arrangement. As long as Sukayana Prikon is sedated, we won't be able to make any progress there."

"Deniz, you know Turkish, don't you?" Niklas says. "Couldn't you take another look at those emails?"

“I only know Kurmanji, and I’m not even very good at that.”

“I thought that was the same thing?”

“What, like Swedish and Sámi, you mean? How much Sámi do you know?”

Douglas clears his throat and turns toward Zack and Deniz.

“We need more names. As far as Ösgür Thrakya is concerned, we haven’t even managed to confirm that he’s in the country, even if his organization seems to be here. And we’re not going to be able to find out much more about Suliman Yel, I’m afraid.”

“What have we got from the latest round of interviews?” Rudolf asks.

“The people at the Miramar pizzeria aren’t saying a word. They say they’d never seen Suliman Yel before, and have never heard the name Ösgür Thrakya. And that hairdresser’s friend claims she only knew him superficially.”

“What about Koltberg? Hasn’t he managed to find out anything about Yel?”

“Nothing that links him to the murder scene in Hallonbergen.”

“Who owns the massage parlor in the city center, then?” Zack asks.

“A homeless man whose only contact is a post office box,” Douglas says. “Presumably a front. I’ve got people looking for him. We don’t even know who was running the business. It could have been one of the two women who were murdered.”

“If we understood Paw Htoo correctly, different people kept showing up at the parlor to pick up the money,” Deniz says. “It looks like they changed fairly regularly.”

"They're probably exploiting the three-month rule on temporary residency. But people can apply to the Immigration Office for permission to stay longer. I'll check the databases to see if any Turkish citizens have applied recently."

"Good idea," Douglas says. "But they wouldn't have wanted to end up on any official databases."

"The most important thing right now has to be finding out more about that house Paw Htoo mentioned. We've got to find the girls she said were still there," Zack says.

"Yes, but a house in the forest isn't much to go on," Douglas reasons.

"I think that house could be the key to everything," Zack says. "If you're going to keep wolves, you're going to want to live well away from anyone else. In which case Paw Htoo's house could well be the place where Sukayana Prikon was set upon by wolves. If we find that house, we find Yildizyeli."

"I share my younger colleague's view," Rudolf says.

"And where were you thinking of looking?" Douglas says.

Why's he being so resistant? Zack wonders, convinced that they need to hurry.

There are women to rescue, children. They can't afford to hold back now.

"We could contact the Stockholm branch of the Hunting Association," Rudolf suggests, in his usual measured tone. "Someone might have noticed something, or had a dog that reacted when it was close to the house. And I think we should make another attempt to talk to Paw Htoo as soon as possible. She may well be able to give us more to go on. Was the drive leading to the house gravel or Tarmac? Is there a lake nearby? Things like that. I can contact the Hunting Association as soon as we're finished here."

"Do that," Douglas says drily. "At the same time, we need

to bear in mind that these murders may not have anything to do with organized crime. White racial hatred is still a live line of inquiry. But we can forget all about Peter Karlson. We've had confirmation that he left for Spain yesterday evening. Which leaves us with Ingvar Stefansson, who may be linked to the Turks, although that's by no means certain. Koltberg has produced a fresh report about the examination of his apartment, but he can't say much yet about whether the jaws we found in Ingvar Stefansson's apartment are from the wolves that attacked Sukayana Prikon."

"What about Stefansson himself, then?" Deniz says.

"We still haven't managed to find him. None of his neighbors knows anything about him. They say they've never even seen him."

"He doesn't seem to be very active online either," Sirpa says. "I've tried various ways of finding him, but I haven't managed to link him to any interesting sites or forums."

Zack feels a drop of water hit his hand, and realizes that it's sweat from his own forehead.

He wipes his face with a paper handkerchief.

Shuts his eyes.

Opens them again. The white tabletop is moving in front of him. Like it is floating in water.

He tries to focus, but it's impossible.

Must take something. Now.

He manages to pull himself together.

Think, for God's sake. Think.

But he can't seem to pull everything together to form a whole.

"I've finally managed to talk to Stefansson's brother and mother over the phone, and they were both equally unpleasant, and more or less slammed the phone down on me. I think we should bring them in for questioning," Niklas says. "They're his closest relatives."

"Good," Douglas says. "Sort that out, Niklas, and make it the first thing you do tomorrow."

He concludes the meeting and everyone stands up quickly to get out of the room as fast as possible.

Zack and Rudolf are the last ones to leave.

"Thanks for backing me up," Zack says when the others are out of sight.

"Sometimes the blind have to lead the blind," Rudolf says with a smile.

ZACK IS doing his best to concentrate, but the letters on the screen stubbornly persist in blurring together.

This particular job is killing him.

Searching databases.

He can't understand how Sirpa can spend days on end just doing this.

They've spent the last half an hour together, trying to find any Turkish citizens who own or lease property in sparsely populated areas of forest around Stockholm.

It's so damn important, but he's so tired.

That short nap in his apartment hasn't done much good in the long run.

The flashing of the cursor is hypnotic.

The sound of the fan soporific.

He feels Sirpa's finger in his side and realizes that he's been asleep with his eyes open.

"Okay, go home and get some sleep," she says. "I'll finish the rest on my own."

He can't even summon up the energy to protest.

40

THE WALK from Police Headquarters to Kungsholms Strand feels endless, and when Zack is finally standing in front of the door of his apartment he can barely get the key in the lock. He's so tired that it physically hurts, and his brain is responding to the lack of sleep by giving him the motor skills of a longtime alcoholic.

He leans forward and takes aim carefully. The key slides off and scratches the door for a third time.

Oh, for God's sake . . .

He takes a deep breath and tries again.

"Shall I help you?"

He looks up.

Sees Ester sitting on the bottom step.

He forces a smile.

"Please."

He holds the key out to her.

She opens the door. Gives him his key back and waits.

He knows she wants to come in, but he can't, not now.

"I'm tired," he says.

"So I see."

He goes inside the flat, turns, and sees her standing there in her white summer dress, watching him, her strawberry-blond hair tickling her thin shoulders.

"Another day," he says, and closes the door behind him.

Silence.

Calm.

He lies down on the sofa and switches the television on. Suppresses the image of the light in her eyes going out as he spoke.

It's six o'clock and the early evening news has just started. The murders at the massage parlor on Klara Norra Kyrkogata lead the bulletin. First a few establishing shots of Åhléns department store and the scene of the murders. Zack sees himself standing in the street talking to Deniz. Then the camera creeps closer. Karin Åkerstig is shown talking on her phone in close-up, a yellow body bag is carried out to an ambulance, then Douglas appears. He is surrounded by outstretched microphones and smartphones, explaining with professional vagueness how the police are ruling nothing out, and that it's too early to say if there's any connection to the previous murders. Then a television reporter appears on-screen and concludes the item with the words:

"So the police don't yet have any clear leads on what could be the worst mass murderer in Stockholm in modern times."

Great, Zack thinks. More than enough to terrify the viewers. As if ordinary people risked being shot the moment they opened their front doors.

But at least they didn't show any footage of Paw Htoo. They do have a bit of heart after all.

He switches the television off. Lack of sleep has left his eyes feeling dry, but he still can't settle.

He feels like going up to see Ester, to apologize and ask her to come downstairs for a while.

But he stays where he is.

An image of Rebecka pops into his mind, but he brushes it aside.

He calls Mera. She answers after two rings.

"Hi," she says. "I just saw you on the news. Where are you?"

"At home. Are you busy?"

"No, I just got in. I've been to the gym with Camilla."

"I miss you."

"So come over, then."

THEY'RE SITTING curled up on Mera's white Vitra sofa. Zack is lying back against the huge cushions, with Mera's head on his chest. Gentle piano music is playing on the built-in speakers, she's poured them both some wine, and Zack doesn't want to be anywhere else.

At last.

"Where did you get to last night?"

"I couldn't sleep, so I went home and carried on working on the case."

"So you didn't go anywhere else?"

"No, I went home, I just said."

He can hear how unnecessarily sharp he sounds. Like a liar. She's got all the reason in the world to be suspicious, and he knows that sooner or later he's going to be found out.

When he and Mera first started seeing each other seriously, they agreed to give each other a lot of freedom. Neither of them would demand full access to the other's life. But that freedom probably didn't cover either drugs or sex with other people.

Mera once asked him straight out if he used drugs. He said he'd tried cocaine a few times, and since then she hasn't asked.

Zack assumes she's tried it herself, at parties. He knows there's cocaine in pretty much every jacket pocket and handbag at most of the parties she goes to. No one even bothers to pretend otherwise.

"Sorry," he says, and strokes her dark, glistening hair. "I can see why you'd ask. I'm just exhausted. Somewhere out there there's a man who's murdered six women and possibly mutilated a seventh, and we still haven't got any good leads to go on. It feels like we're fumbling in the dark."

He kisses the top of her head.

"I swear, once we've caught him, I'm going to sleep for twenty-four hours."

"The women he shot, did they have children?"

"We haven't been able to identify them properly yet. But we found some profile pictures on Skype, and one of them had some photographs in her purse of a little boy."

"Oh dear . . ."

Mera curls up closer to him, and he hugs her.

They've never talked about having children. Once Mera mentioned in passing that she wanted to wait a few years. Until her career was in a more stable phase. Her PR agency is making its way into smart society, and has been commissioned by Volvo and Ikea. She can't stop now, she needs to get to a point where she won't risk being overtaken. She needs to expand, take on more staff. Maybe get bought out.

"Shall we go to bed?" she whispers.

"Yes."

Mera creeps beneath the covers of the big double bed naked, the same as Zack.

"Hold me," he says.

And she holds him.

They lie there close together and he can feel her soft, warm skin against his.

They lie there in silence for a while. Her caresses, which

seemed full of desire at first, become calmer. She strokes his back. Slow, delicate movements between his shoulder blades.

He drifts off.

And finally falls asleep.

41

MARTIN STEFANSSON has a large number of dried-in gray stains on his white overalls. He's sitting in the interview room with his bulky arms folded, and is very obviously annoyed at being brought in for questioning just before the breakfast break at the building site. They've got a lot to do before the end of the day, and the whole job's supposed to be finished by the weekend.

"I haven't got a fucking clue who he hangs out with. I've already said, I don't have any contact with my brother anymore."

"Is that anything to do with his political views?" Niklas asks from the other side of the table, where he's sitting next to Rudolf.

"Political views? I don't even know who he votes for."

"I was thinking more of his views about dark-skinned people and Arabs. He doesn't seem to like them very much."

"No, but who the hell does?"

"Would you say your brother has a violent nature?"

"We used to fight when we were kids, like all brothers. But I've got no idea if he still fights. I'd be surprised, though. He's not the type."

"We've been trying to find him at his home. Do you know where he could be?"

Martin Stefansson grins at them, and leans over the table.

He leaves a long pause, then takes a deep breath, as if he's about to reveal something important.

ZACK SITS up as straight as he can on his chair, as if to put as much distance as possible between himself and Ingela Stefansson. Her breath is a mixture of hangover and decaying teeth.

She's in her sixties, more or less the same age his own mother would have been if she'd lived, but she looks older. Her unwashed hair is gray and matted, and rolls of fat make doughy patterns beneath her ill-fitting, washed-out blouse. Zack tries to retain the memory of Mera's body beside him, but it's fading away rapidly now.

"I'm not talking to the authorities, I've already told you that. You've never helped me, so why should I help you? You're just sticking your noses into things that are none of your business."

"Right now, we're trying to solve a number of murders," Zack says. "And for that reason it's extremely important that we talk to your son."

"Crap," Ingela Stefansson says, waving her hand dismissively. "My son's no murderer."

"We haven't said he is," Deniz says. "But he might be able to give us information that could help us make some progress."

"Have you been to his apartment?"

"Yes, but he wasn't there."

"Did you go inside?"

"Yes."

"So you've seen . . . ?"

Ingela Stefansson's bottom lip starts to tremble, then her face contorts into a grimace and she starts to cry.

"I haven't had it easy," she says, pulling a tissue from her battered, fake-leather handbag. "You haven't got any idea," she says, with anger in her voice.

Zack takes a deep breath. He hasn't got the patience for this sort of crap today. He leans his head back and shuts his eyes, but the room starts to spin at once and he straightens up again.

It doesn't help.

The floor seems to be slowly revolving, his vision seems blurred, and it isn't Ingela Stefansson sitting there now.

Mom.

Her soft cheeks, even softer hair.

You're saying something, Mom. A soft whisper at first, as if you want to comfort me, but then you get angry, almost like a different person, and you stand up and threaten to hit me.

Don't hit me, Mom.

Don't hit me.

Zack hears a sharp noise and feels the sting of a slap, and puts his hands to his face, and when he removes them again he sees that Ingela Stefansson is standing up, and that her chair has fallen over behind her.

She must have hit me.

Mom.

Ingela Stefansson.

Her fat frame wobbles as she shouts angrily at Deniz:

"What do you think it was like? Trying to raise two boys in those circumstances?"

Zack looks at the angry woman.

Tries to work out what's going on.

Not bothered by the slap.

Where did that image of his mother come from? She never did anything like that to him, did she? But he can't help feeling troubled, and tries to suppress the memories by concentrating on the hysterical woman whose voice has just switched to falsetto on the other side of the table.

"Let me tell you," she says in a voice shaking with emotion, wagging her finger at Deniz, "if only us Swedes got as much as you people get when you come to our country demanding a load of benefits even though you haven't done a thing to deserve them."

Zack sees red. He loses control, hits the table hard with his fists, and stands up, yelling at Stefansson's mother:

"Now you're going to cut the fucking crap and tell us where your son is!"

WHEN MARTIN Stefansson finally speaks, what he says isn't the important information Rudolf and Niklas were hoping for.

"I don't like my brother," he says. "But if you think I'd give him up to you, you're seriously fucking mistaken."

He folds his arms again.

"And I'm not saying anything else without a lawyer."

All these phrases from American cop shows, Rudolf thinks. People seem to believe that's what happens in real life.

"As I said earlier, you're not under suspicion of anything. You're being questioned to see if you can help us. So you don't have to say anything, but you also don't have the right to have a lawyer present."

"In that case this conversation is over. Can I go now?"

"You can go," Niklas says.

INGELA STEFANSSON is taking short, shallow breaths, and looks as if she doesn't dare move as she stands there in front of her overturned chair.

Zack slowly sits down again, still with his eyes fixed on her.

Deniz is looking at Zack with eyes full of questions, but she quickly turns back to Ingela Stefansson to make the most of the moment.

"Six women are dead. Women like you and me. Brutally shot in cold blood. We believe that the man who did it will do it again. If you agree to help us, we can stop that happening."

Something changes in Ingela Stefansson. She tugs her blouse slightly, then says quietly:

"I sublet an allotment cottage in Tantolunden. Ingvar was there with me a few times, he knows where the key is. He might be there. That's the only place I can think of."

Zack and Deniz get the address and hurry out of the room.

"Tantolunden," Deniz says. "Close to Sawatdii."

Out in the corridor they hear Ingela Stefansson's thin voice behind them.

"You'll treat him right, won't you? Promise me that!"

"She did hit me in there, didn't she?" Zack asks. "When I had my eyes shut?"

"What are you talking about?"

Zack looks at Deniz.

"I was just kidding. Of course she didn't hit me."

42

DOUGLAS WATCHES Sirpa from a distance as the coffeemaker prepares his double espresso.

She was still working when he left last night, and she was here when he arrived this morning. Even though he got here at half past seven. How many hours is she actually working?

It's eleven o'clock now, and he hears a door open at the far end of the open-plan office and sees Zack and Deniz disappear.

They're going after Stefansson.

Finally, it looks like we're going to get hold of the bastard.

Please, just let us have a bit of luck for once, he thinks. We need it.

He takes his mug and goes over to Sirpa's desk. He puts his hand on her shoulder and says:

"How are you doing?"

"I think I'm making good progress mapping this," she says, without taking her eyes from the screen, then pushes her chair back and pretends to read something on a printout to get his hand to move from her shoulder.

"I didn't mean like that," Douglas says. "I'm asking how you are. You've been working extremely hard recently."

Sirpa spins her chair around and looks up at her boss.

"Do I look that bad?" she says, thinking that if that is the case, then Douglas is her exact opposite.

The red handkerchief in the breast pocket of his dark gray suit matches the narrow red stripes on his tie, his eyes are clear, and his blond hair is combed in its usual neat waves.

Douglas laughs.

"No, Sirpa. You don't look that bad, but I'm worried about the hours you're putting in. This group needs you, and I can't let you run yourself into the ground."

She nods.

"Maybe I have put in a lot of hours in the past few days, but once this is all over I promise to behave. Okay?"

"It's about time you started to come to grips with that mountain of vacation pay."

"Do you want to know how I'm getting on with this or not?"

He smiles at her.

"Yes, I do."

"I've had some help putting together a register of the Sawatdii's customers. A lot of them were women, so she did run a regular massage business as well. And presumably most of the men who pay for sex do their best not to end up on any customer databases or pay by card. But we've managed to track down another two men we suspect of paying for sex among the emails we've been able to recover. And another one who sent text messages to Sukayana Prikon's cell asking about sexual services. To be honest, they don't seem all that exciting, but I'll let you have an outline of all three in a little while. Then there are the seven we'd already identified, but we're already on top of that, aren't we?"

"Yes, all but two have already been questioned. One of them has been in Crete all week, and the other evidently got home last night from a fishing trip to Norrland. We've got confirmation that neither of them was in Stockholm at the times of the murders."

"What are we going to do with them now? The men who paid for sex, I mean."

"The prostitution team are already involved. The human trafficking group as well, because they want to look at it from the other end. It does look like several of the women had been tricked into coming here on false pretenses. I daresay they'll be getting in touch with you sometime today."

Sirpa nods.

"We're going to start looking through the computer files and email accounts of the second massage parlor soon, but there's still one email address among Sukayana Prikon's customer contacts that I haven't been able to trace."

She points to it on the screen.

dirtysanchez@woomail.com

"I can't get at that address using legal methods. The server's in China, which means there's no chance . . ."

She leaves a long pause before finishing her sentence:

". . . unless we hack it."

Douglas says nothing, and Sirpa is unable to read his silence. Does that mean yes or no?

"I know it's important. We need to know the identity of the man behind this account," she says.

"How can you know that?"

"Call it intuition."

She regrets saying the word as soon as it's out of her mouth. Douglas is analytical, not the sort of person who relies on intuition to take decisions. Which is just as well, she thinks. But she's convinced she's right. She can feel it. And sometimes you have to trust your feelings.

"Just take it easy," Douglas says, and walks away from her desk.

Sirpa watches him go with a quizzical look on her face. *Take it easy*. What does that mean? What sort of fucking answer is that?

Take it easy.

Does that mean that she has permission to make her way behind the locked door, as long as she's careful?

She decides that must be what he meant.

43

THE FRONT door of the little allotment cottage has been painted a bright yellow that clashes badly with the pale green walls. Beige curtains are drawn across the kitchen window, and on the other side of the door three stone hearts hang on thick brown ropes from rusty nails. Spindly roses in various colors are fighting for space in the flowerbeds, and the worn handles of some garden tools stick up from a broken bucket.

The recent rain has made the plants and flowers put on extra growth, and the large leaves sticking through the rotting planks of the fence look sharp enough to cut yourself on.

A lawn mower and children's laughter can be heard at a distance, and in several of the surrounding allotments people are spending their holidays sweating as they weed their small gardens.

Zack and Deniz keep the yellow door under observation from their vantage point behind a tree and some bushes a short distance away among the allotments of Tantolunden. The bushes smell of ammonia from last night's parties, and an empty bottle of Explorer vodka and two disposable barbeques have been kicked into the bushes where they're standing.

The morning sun makes the black leather of his Rick Owens jacket burn his skin, but Zack keeps it on to conceal his holster. He looks enviously at the others, Deniz hiding her equipment under a thin, airy cotton cardigan, and the four cops in their short-sleeved uniform shirts.

Six people. Zack thinks that should be enough to bring in someone like Ingvar Stefansson.

If he's involved in holding women or children captive, this is hardly where he'd keep them. *A house in the forest*, Paw Htoo said. Not even the most hard-boiled child of the concrete jungle could mean somewhere like this.

After the interviews with Stefansson's brother and mother, Zack and Deniz had a short discussion with Douglas about whether to call in the rapid response unit for this operation, but they all agreed that it was unnecessary. Ingvar Stefansson isn't a formal suspect yet, for either the murders or torture, and he has no prior convictions for violent offenses. His only clear link to Yildizyeli is a newspaper clipping about an extreme right-wing organization that Ösgür Thrakya was once a member of.

Those wolf jaws could be the connection they need, to tie Stefansson to the mutilation of Sukayana Prikon, at least. But they don't know that yet. He could just as easily have bought them from an illegal hunter, or off the Internet.

"Doesn't look like there's anyone home," Deniz says.

"No, and considering how overgrown the garden is, there doesn't seem to have been anyone here for a while," Zack says.

He looks off toward the park by the water, and thinks back to chasing Sukayana Prikon between the picnic blankets. That was only three days ago, but it feels like weeks. He can't stop thinking about his decision not to take her into custody, and wonders if a different decision would also have saved the lives of the two Burmese women on Klara Norra

Kyrkogata. Maybe Sukayana Prikon would have said more if they'd brought her in and put her under more pressure, maybe she might have said something that would have led them to keep the other massage parlor under observation. He's convinced that she knows far more that she made out.

Zack stretches and tries to focus. He woke up in bed with Mera after just four hours' sleep, and couldn't doze off again. He knows why: remnants of cocaine being released by the cells of his body, setting him going again.

He would have liked to get up later and make breakfast with Mera, but he couldn't relax. He lay awake for almost an hour, holding her. Then he walked home, even though all he wanted to do was stay.

Now he's standing behind some bushes that stink of urine, staring at an ugly allotment cottage, and trying to understand his choice. Right now there's nothing he'd rather do than curl up on Mera's big, soft bed and pull her billowing covers over him.

In the car on the way here he fell asleep, and dreamed of amphetamines. He woke up with a start and for a moment believed that he'd actually taken some pills in front of his colleagues.

First being slapped, now taking drugs.

Constructs of his overheated brain.

The thought of taking drugs in front of his colleagues brought him out in a cold sweat. The car felt horribly claustrophobic, and he felt like opening the door and jumping out while it was still moving.

Then he thought about sensei Hiro, and the times they sat and meditated together.

Empty your head of thoughts, Zack. Let them pass by like the wind.

He shut his eyes in the passenger seat and meditated for a few minutes. It didn't work as well as it used to in the dojo, but he did manage to stop thinking about his headache and withdrawal symptoms, and become more present in the moment.

But not entirely. He still feels rather distracted, and is glad Deniz is leading the operation rather than him. Douglas picked her without giving him so much as a glance. Zack guesses he doesn't want to take any risks after seeing the state he was in yesterday.

Or else he knows more about me than I think.

Deniz turns to the four cops. They've been called in for this operation from the City Police, and they all look expectant. Being picked to help the Special Crimes Unit looks good on their CVs.

Three of them, two women and a man, look like they're in their thirties. The fourth is maybe ten years older. Zack was struck straightaway by his relatively advanced age and lowly rank, but the older officer introduced himself as Theodor Larsson, and explained that he used to be a teacher and only recently joined the police.

Then he asked Zack if he had children.

"No," Zack replied, rather taken aback by the question. "I need to do a bit more growing up myself first."

"I just thought you looked like you weren't getting much sleep, that's all."

"Really? No, I've just been working a bit too hard lately."

"I hope I didn't speak out of turn. I've recently become a dad for the third time, so I know what a lack of sleep feels like."

"How's little Oscar getting on?" Maria asked, and Theodor whipped out his cell to show her the latest pictures.

"Can I see?" Deniz said, and gazed at the pictures with a maternal look in her eyes.

"Oh, he's so cute!"

Zack couldn't even be bothered to pretend to be interested. He's never found it particularly interesting to be told things about strangers' children, or partners he's never met.

But he can understand why other people find it interesting. Gossip can help you feel like part of the gang, a member of the collective.

He looks back toward the allotment cottage again.

So which gang do you belong to, Ingvar Stefansson?

"You two stay here," Deniz says to Theodor and one of the women, "while you two go around the back so you can keep an eye on the rear of the cottage. There could well be another door there. Zack and I will wait until you're in position, then we'll creep up and take a look."

Something crashes into the tree and all six police officers crouch down instinctively and put their hands to their holsters. A black-and-white football bounces to the ground in front of the them, then rolls off onto the path.

They look at each other and laugh.

"God, that scared the life out of me," Theodor says.

A boy of about ten, with curly brown hair, runs up to fetch the ball. He stops when he sees the four uniformed officers and two other grown-ups slowly getting to their feet behind the bushes.

"Oh," he says. "Sorry. I didn't mean it. Did it hit you?"

"No, it's fine," Deniz says. "But we'd appreciate it if you could stay a bit farther away for a while. Okay?"

"Sure," the boy says, and runs off with the ball.

A minute later Zack and Deniz are creeping toward the cottage under cover of the surrounding vegetation.

“Are you okay?” Deniz asks as they crouch behind a rhododendron. “I mean, really?”

“What do you mean, really?” he replies.

“I didn’t like what I saw during our interview with Ingela Stefansson. It may have got good results, but if everything kicks off I need to know you won’t flip out. *Did she hit me*? What the hell was that about?”

Zack wonders if he should explain what happened, that he saw his mom before him, and felt her hit him, but decides against it. Deniz would only think he was hallucinating.

Because that’s exactly what I was doing, isn’t it?

“It’s fine, I promise,” he says.

She looks him in the eye. He meets her gaze, and holds it until eventually she looks away.

“Okay. I’m going into the garden to take a look around. You wait here,” she says quietly.

She has stood up to walk toward the gate when they both see one of the curtains flutter. A quick movement, a shadow moving away from the window.

A man? It must be a man.

Ingvar Stefansson.

Deniz turns and gestures to the officers behind them to be ready. They nod back.

“I’m coming with you,” Zack tells Deniz.

“Okay.”

They walk toward the little cottage. Talking in a normal conversational tone, they point at various plants.

There shouldn’t be any danger. Maybe Stefansson doesn’t even know they’re looking for him.

But maybe he does.

Zack pulls his Sig Sauer from its holster, but Deniz pulls a face at him and shakes her head.

A woman in her sixties, wearing a straw hat and huge red-framed sunglasses, walks past, and Zack tucks his pistol back in its holster under his leather jacket again.

Deniz has reached the fence now. Zack is right behind her. She carefully lifts the catch on the gate and pushes it open.

The gunshot pierces the summer idyll.

Zack and Deniz throw themselves to the ground and snake off along the fence until they're hidden from the cottage by a large lilac bush.

The woman in the straw hat screams and starts running away on stiff legs.

Zack draws his pistol.

The grass is still damp with dew in the shade, and he can feel it seep through his jeans as he crawls forward to find a gap in the dense foliage. There, a glimpse of the door. Still closed. But the window is ajar. He detects rapid movement behind the glass. A flash of metal.

He aims and fires, but realizes what a fool he is as the glass shatters. There could be anyone inside the cottage. A child, a woman. He has no idea of whom he might have hit, or where he might have hit them. A shot at that height could easily cause fatal injuries.

Someone grunts something unintelligible nearby, doors slam, and an unsteady old man two cottages away trips over his patio table and falls to the ground as he tries to take cover.

"Police! Come out with your hands above your head!" Deniz shouts.

No response.

Zack turns to see if he can get eye contact with one of the cops, but from his prone position he can't see them through the bushes.

A young woman with headphones on is jogging along the path toward Zack and Deniz. Zack waves his hand to get her to turn back, but she's staring at the ground and carries on running.

Something comes flying through the air at high speed, over the fence. Something black and white.

It hits the yellow door with a thud and immediately two more shots go off. Someone screams, and Zack looks up and sees that the jogger with the headphones has fallen. She's lying completely exposed outside the open gate, clutching one arm and slowly rocking back and forth.

Zack rushes up to her, takes hold of her good arm, and pulls her with him.

She yelps with pain, and another shot goes off, and he hears another scream, farther away this time.

"He's hit. He's been hit!"

One of the female officers shouting.

Who's been hit? Theodor? The boy with the football?

Zack tugs the young woman's arm harder. Her headphones have fallen out, and are dragging on the ground behind her. Zack hears the chorus of an old Nirvana song as he pulls her behind a thorny hedge. He kneels down beside her and examines her arm, while yelling as loudly as he can:

"Maria, are you and Theodor okay?"

No answer.

He looks up and tries to get eye contact with Deniz. She's on her knees behind the lilac hedge, with her pistol aimed at the cottage. She's got her coms radio in the other hand, and he can see her talking into it. Good, he thinks. Getting a fix on the situation.

Zack tucks his pistol into his waistband and turns the woman's bleeding arm over. Another hole there.

"What's your name?"

"Linnea."

"Okay, Linnea. The bullet's gone right through. You're going to be fine. Are you hurt anywhere else?"

Sobbing, she shakes her head.

Zack tears off a large piece off his own T-shirt and ties it tightly around her arm.

Linnea groans with pain, and Zack can hear Deniz's voice from over by the hedge.

"I've called for backup and an ambulance. Are you okay, Zack?"

"Yes, but I don't know how the others are doing."

He looks back at Linnea again.

"We need to move, get you away from danger. Can you walk?"

"I think so."

He runs another ten yards with her, then he leaves her behind a large tree.

"Just stay here, and try to keep your arm up. An ambulance is on its way."

He runs back toward the cottage at a crouch. When he gets close to the fence he stops behind a hedge and calls to the female officer again:

"How are you doing?"

Her voice is weak when she finally answers:

"Theodor's dead. He's not breathing."

Zack's field of vision contracts.

Here and now are the only things that matter.

His whole body is action now, muscles moving toward a single goal, set free from all thought.

"Deniz, cover me!" he shouts and leaps over the fence. He hears a whining sound close to his ear while he's in the air, and as he lands and rolls, over his shoulder he hears Deniz fire back several times. He reaches the wall of the cottage and stands up with his pistol drawn. More shots are fired through the window and Zack yanks the door open and fires two low shots toward where the shooter must be.

A man screams.

The floor rocks when he collapses. Something bounces across the wooden floorboards.

Metal?

A hand grenade?

Zack takes a chance that it's the pistol and rushes into the single room of the cottage. A man in a short-sleeved check shirt and dark green shorts is lying curled up on the filthy wooden floor with his hands over his crotch.

No grenade.

The man's pistol has slid under the kitchen table.

Zack ducks beneath the window and reaches under the table to pick up the gun. Then he stands up against the wall, as close to the window as he dares, and yells:

"Cease fire! Cease fire!"

And finally everything goes quiet.

The man on the floor looks up at him, but says nothing. He just lies there, taking deep, rattling breaths.

It's Ingvar Stefansson. Skinny, short hair. Considerably less hair that on his passport photograph, but it's definitely him.

Zack looks around the room. A kitchen sofa, a table covered with a stained, pale blue cloth, and two simple chairs. A few shelves on the walls. An embroidered picture in a frame. That's all. There's no second door, no large piece of furniture to hide behind.

"Are you alone here?" Zack asks.

The man nods, still pressing his hands to his groin.

A dark stain is slowly spreading across his shorts, and Zack wonders if he managed to shoot him in his familly jewels.

"Put your hands behind your head!" Zack says. "I need to look at your injury."

Stefansson reluctantly lets go, and only then does Zack see the blood pumping out of his thigh.

The large aorta. He's dying.

He hears footsteps behind him and turns to see Deniz in the doorway.

"He needs urgent medical attention. Can you call the ambulance and tell them he's been hit in the aorta on the left side of his groin?"

She nods.

Zack puts the pistol down out of reach, then kneels beside Stefansson. The pool of blood is starting to spread across the floor and his breathing is getting weaker.

Zack pulls off the thin tablecloth, rolls it into a ball, and presses it hard against Stefansson's groin. It turns dark red almost instantly.

"I've got nothing to do with the murders," Ingvar Stefansson says.

So he knows, Zack says. Peter Karlson must have warned him.

"So why were you shooting at us?"

Ingvar Stefansson smiles weakly. A friendly smile.

"You have to make a stand. I'm the thin red line."

His breathing is even weaker now. His face is pale, his eyes are becoming dull, and Zack can see the life slowly running out of him. But he goes on talking:

"There's a war going on in this country. A race war. Haven't you noticed?"

Stefansson takes one arm from his head and fumbles for Zack's hands as they press the cloth to his crotch. He feels across the back of Zack's right hand with his fingers, and Zack lets go of the bloody rag and lets him hold his hand.

No one should have to die alone.

Stefansson looks at Zack, and there's a strange conviction in his eyes. The look of someone who thinks he's found the answer.

He takes one last breath, then peace settles across his unshaven face.

44

POLICE VEHICLES and ambulances are squeezed into the narrow footpaths around the allotments. Dense crowds have gathered behind the cordons, and up in the trees curious bystanders are perched next to professional photographers with huge telephoto lenses. *Aftonbladet* and *Expressen* are both broadcasting live on their websites.

"The idyllic setting of the allotment cottages of Tantolunden today became the scene of a blood-soaked tragedy when two people were shot by a man armed with a pistol," *Aftonbladet*'s reporter is saying, with ill-concealed excitement in his voice. "At least two people were killed in the exchange of fire, and another injured. According to *Aftonbladet*'s sources, those who died are a policeman and the man who is suspected of shooting and killing six people in the past few days. The hunt for Stockholm's worst mass murderer in modern times may well be over."

Within the cordon that atmosphere is considerably more subdued. The raw jokes and noisy laughter that often characterize crime scenes, even where the most brutal crimes have been committed, are here replaced by quiet voices.

Zack looks around his colleagues. Somber expressions, anger, and sorrow in their gestures.

Was this what it was like when Mom was killed?

He's never been involved when a fellow officer has been

killed before. But he knows that the feelings in the air are about more than a desire for revenge and a democratic society's need to strike back hard at anyone who attacks the upholders of the law.

It's about the awareness that each of them feels at times like this.

The sense of staring at your own mortality.

No one can bear to go around the whole time thinking that life could end at any moment. But when a colleague gets killed on active duty that awareness comes back with a vengeance. The awareness that it could end anytime. Even when you're only on a routine job.

Like Theodor, Zack thinks, looking at the yellow body bag.

And now he's dead. A father with young kids. For no good reason. Hit in the forehead by a stray bullet from an idiot who was aiming at something else. An idiot who didn't even know that Theodor Larsson existed.

Blood.

Grass.

The scent of summer blossom.

A dead man in the midst of all this greenery.

Zack's legs go weak and he sits down on the ground. He rests his head on his knees and he can hear his own breathing clearly, just like he did that night so long ago. The night when he looked straight up at the stars and didn't dare look away. The night when he wished he could drift off into space and forget everything.

And then footsteps. Getting closer.

Shoes on grass.

Closer and closer.

A hand on his shoulder.

"Zack, how are you doing?"

He lifts his head quickly and stares at Douglas, trying to work out what's real and what isn't.

Douglas crouches down.

"Do you feel up to talking?"

"Sure," Zack says, coming back to the present as he slowly stands up. "Here, or what?"

"No, let's go to the back of the cottage. It's quieter there."

They walk into the garden, past the broken bucket full of garden tools, and see an inquisitive old man stick his head up above his hedge as he pretends to rake the grass.

Douglas turns his back on the man and looks at Zack.

"I thought you might want to know what's likely to happen."

"That I'm going to be suspended."

"Probably, yes. At least temporarily. You have, directly or indirectly, been the cause of three deaths in three days. That's probably some sort of record in the history of the Swedish police."

Douglas's tone of voice hardens.

"You're going to be thoroughly investigated. And with every justification. If we weren't in the middle of a murder investigation, I'd personally see to it that you ended up filing reports for six months."

Douglas takes a step closer and practically hisses:

"Whatever it is you've been getting up to in your free time, you need to put a stop to it. You're barely holding it together, and I'm starting to have serious doubts about your judgment. I need you in the group, but there are limits. The bodies are piling up around you and you're exposing yourself and—even worse—your colleagues to danger."

Douglas stares at Zack, and Zack looks down at the ground.

Part of him wants to shout back that it wasn't his fault if people fell off roofs or got hit by stray bullets, but he keeps his mouth shut.

Douglas is right.

He's far too close to some sort of ultimate boundary, and maybe he would have taken different decisions if he'd been himself. Decisions that could have saved lives.

The drugs are turning me into what I'm supposed to be fighting, he thinks briefly, but drops the thought at once.

"We need you," Douglas goes on. "But we need you in decent condition. This is just getting worse and worse."

Zack nods but doesn't meet his gaze.

"Can you handle a quick run-through?"

"Yes."

"Good. Come with me."

They leave the little garden and Douglas waves Deniz over from where she's talking to Johan and Jennie, the two cops she positioned at the rear of the cottage before the shooting started.

"Come on," he says. "Let's go and sit in the command vehicle."

They open the van's sliding door and are met by a smell of tannic acid and summer sweat. They sit there in silence for a while, just breathing. None of them really feels like talking.

"We could have called in the rapid response unit," Deniz finally says. "We even talked about it. Why didn't we make sure we were prepared for every eventuality?"

"There was no good reason to call them in. You were going to bring in someone with no criminal record for questioning. Deniz, listen to me: no one could have predicted this. No one," Douglas says.

Deniz is staring at the seat in front of her, and Zack can

see that she's trying to deal with the worst moment of her career so far. She has just led an operation in which a fellow officer was killed, along with one other person.

"I can get hold of some psychologists. You need debriefing."

"We need to solve this case," Deniz says.

"Don't mention psychologists again," Zack says irritably.

Douglas meets their replies with a dubious look, but drops the subject.

"Well, today Ingvar Stefansson gave us the clearest possible evidence that he was capable of killing other people," he goes on instead. "That probably came as a surprise to all of us. Do you believe he was the man who killed the masseuses?"

"He told me he didn't do it," Zack says. "Why would he lie when he knew he was dying?"

"To protect someone else. Maybe he knew the murderer and wanted us to stop looking for him," Douglas says.

"In which case surely he would have confessed to the killings himself?" Zack counters.

"Maybe he wasn't involved at all," Deniz says. "Maybe the whole of this line of inquiry is a dead end. Which means . . ."

She swallows hard before going on:

". . . that Theodor's death was totally fucking pointless."

There's a knock on the door of the van. Douglas opens it.

Koltberg, looking as smug as ever. He's wearing an almost unbelievably crisply pressed blue linen suit.

He holds up a plastic bag containing Ingvar Stefansson's pistol.

"An old Luger," he says. "There's no similarity at all between this relic and the Beretta that the women were shot with. There were no other weapons in the cottage, but we have found a Samsung cell and a laptop. They'll be going straight off to Forensics."

"Good work," Douglas says.

Koltberg nods. A sort of *yes, I know* nod.

He looks at Deniz and Zack with what looks almost like sympathy.

"Just solve this, for God's sake," he says. "There are so many bodies it's starting to look like a Greek tragedy."

He leaves the door open as he walks off, and Zack looks out at their surroundings.

So many journalists. They're everywhere. Their newsrooms must all be deserted, he thinks. But no Bylund in sight so far. What could he be working on that's more important than this?

A helicopter circles the welding-arc blue sky. Zack leans out and looks up. Presumably one of the media companies trying to get some good aerial shots of the scene of the drama.

"Let's suppose Stefansson didn't shoot those six women," Douglas says. "Where do we go from here?"

"I've got something I want to look into," Zack says. "Just a short conversation."

"Who with?" Deniz asks.

"I can't say."

"Do you really think this is the time for secrets?"

"Calm down," Douglas says. "I'm sure Zack has his reasons. You and I can work out our main priorities in the meantime."

Zack gets out of the van. Out into the chaos. He steps over the fence into the allotment and finds a quiet corner by one wall of the cottage.

Bylund answers after the first ring.

"Are you on holiday, or at death's door?" Zack asks.

"What do you mean?"

"Four new deaths in two days, and no sign of you."

"We've got other people there."

"As if that would stop you."

Silence on the line. Then Bylund says, very carefully, as though he were weighing his words:

"I've got other things to do."

"Come on. What sort of information are you sitting on? How many more people have to die?"

Zack can hear Bylund's breathing down the phone. Then he says:

"I haven't got anything."

"Tell me. I'm asking you seriously. There's a risk that more people will be murdered, and that has to be more important that a few juicy headlines in *Expressen*, for fuck's sake."

Silence.

"How many more people have to die?" Zack repeats. "You know something, and your silence is making you complicit in what's going on."

Zack can almost hear Bylund wrestling with his conscience on the other end of the line. Then he says:

"You're out on very thin ice, Zack. Be careful."

"Maybe you're the one who should be careful," Zack says, and ends the call.

45

DOUGLAS IS writing something on a pad when Zack climbs into the van again.

Deniz looks at him as he sits down.

"Well?"

He shakes his head.

"It was a long shot. Which didn't pay off."

Douglas stands up.

"I need to organize the ongoing work out here, and try to sort out some sort of improvised press conference. Start thinking about which lines of inquiry you want to delve deeper into."

He leaves the van as two overweight police officers in suits make their way under the cordon. Åke Blixt and Gunilla Sundin, both in their sixties. They've seen and heard everything. Internal investigators. As popular as cholera.

They catch sight of Douglas and set off toward him at once.

"How are you, Douglas?" Blixt says.

"We are where we are. We don't believe the man in the allotment cottage was responsible for shooting the six women."

"No?"

"No, but I haven't got time to go through all the details right now."

“I understand. Look, we need to talk to Zack Herry and Deniz Akin.”

“I know. But you can’t right now.”

Blixt and Sundin look surprised.

“We bent the rules the other day, when that Turkish man fell off the roof,” Blixt says. “But this time we can’t let it pass.”

“Of course not. You’ve got to do your job, just not right now. There’s a murderer on the loose, and we need Zack to help us catch him.”

“Maybe Zack’s the one who ought to be taken off the streets,” Gunilla Sundin says.

Douglas stares at her.

“I’ll do you a big favor and pretend I didn’t hear that. There are three other officers who were part of this operation. Start with them, and I promise you’ll get all the time you need with Zack and Deniz later.”

He walks away before they have time to reply.

DENIZ AND Zack are still sitting in the van.

They’re discussing how to find out more about Ösgür Thrakya and his organization. They’ve already talked to the drugs division, and the Border Control Agency. And the prostitution unit. They’ve contacted the Turkish police, and approached both Europol and Interpol. No one seems to know anything. The guy seems to live a entirely analog life.

“As long as Sukayana Prikon remains unconscious, he’s the only name we’ve got to go on,” Zack says. “And we really need to make some progress. We can assume that those young girls in the forest really do exist.”

“They do. We’ve got to hope Paw Htoo can tell us more about that house. Niklas and Rudolf were going to St. Göran’s to make another attempt with her today," Deniz says, just as Zack's cell starts to ring.

Sirpa.

"I've checked to see who owns the buildings housing any massage parlors we suspect are being run by the Turks."

Zack wonders how she finds time to do everything.

"The buildings are all owned by a company called Merkantus, which is part of the Heraldus conglomerate," Sirpa goes on. "I've got hold of the contracts for the buildings. Sukayana Prikon's name is on one of them, but the funny thing is that the CEO of the company is listed as the other party, on all the contracts. It would be more usual for someone lower down the hierarchy to do that. Especially in a business with over three thousand employees. It might not mean anything, I just got a bad feeling about it."

"What's the CEO's name?"

"Sten Westberg."

They hang up and Zack tells Deniz what he's just heard.

"That name sounds familiar," Deniz says. "But I don't know why."

But Zack does.

He remembers the discreet nod from the well-dressed man in the Opera Bar.

"He was the one on the television news when we were questioning Sukayana Prikon, the one she snorted at. Sirpa's right. There's something going on here."

Deniz nods.

"I just keep wondering how the hell it all fits together."

She gestures to the scene outside the van.

"I don't know what you think, but my feeling is that Ingvar Stefansson wasn't part of this, even if he was clearly mad."

"We've got to tell Douglas about Sirpa's latest discoveries," Zack says.

Douglas is on his way back to them when they step out of the van. He points to the two internal investigators, who are standing outside the gate to the allotment.

"They're going to want to talk to you later. But I've managed to fend them off for the time being."

"Thanks," Zack says. "Listen to this. We've just had some good information from Sirpa."

He relates the telephone conversation, expecting some show of interest from Douglas, but he dismisses it as if it were nothing.

"We can't start investigating a CEO just because his name is on a few contracts. We've got enough to go on already, and priority number one is to find Ösgür Thrakya, or anyone else who can be linked to Yildizyeli. It looks like the Brotherhood didn't have anything to do with the murders, seeing as everything seems to point in a different direction."

Douglas is about to leave, but Zack blocks his path.

"Let us look into this. It won't take long. And we haven't got any good leads on Thrakya at the moment anyway."

Douglas responds with the same look and tone of voice he used when he reprimanded Zack behind the cottage earlier.

"Find Ösgür Thrakya," he says. "See you back in the office later. I've got to deal with these journalists now."

Zack swears quietly to himself.

His private cell buzzes in his pocket. A text message from Abdula:

> Meet me at the Kaknäs Tower in half
> an hour.

46

"LOOK AT all that water, dear! What a city. So beautiful."

"Marvelous! And look at those kites!"

The loud-voiced American retirees in the café of the Kaknäs Tower are having trouble tearing themselves away from the view.

Zack can see why. This is Stockholm at its best. Gärdet, Djurgården, Gamla Stan, Östermalm. An impossible range of different greens, even more shades of blue. Treetops and water. All made more beautiful by sunlight that seems utterly unaffected by the terrible things that are going on in the city.

Zack finds Abdula sitting on his own at a window table. He's rocking on his chair with a Coke in his hand. At the table in front of him is a family with three children, and behind him there are four Japanese tourists with a large spread-out map of Stockholm.

Zack didn't tell Deniz whom he was going to meet when he left Tantolunden. He just said that it could be important, and she accepted that.

He orders a large coffee and can feel his hand shake as he carries it over to Abdula's table.

"Why did you want to meet here, of all places?"

"I've never been up the Kaknäs Tower before. Thought it was about time."

Zack shakes his head.

"And it's anonymous. There's hardly any risk of running into anyone you know up here."

Zack laughs and the pressure he has felt in his head since the events of Tantolunden eases slightly.

"Have you seen the view?" Abdula goes on. "I had no idea the city was this green. It's like we're living in a jungle."

Zack looks out of the window.

He can't help but agree. It's almost hard to believe that there's so much woodland in the city. When you're moving about at street level it mostly just looks gray.

A number of large kites, all different shapes, are floating in the air above the parkland. Green, yellow, red.

People are sunbathing and eating picnic lunches. Zack feels like going and lying down there as well. Listen to the hubbub of strangers' voices and just doze off in the sun.

But not in the grass.

Never in the grass.

"You look tired," Abdula says.

"Don't ask."

"Okay."

"Oh, to hell with it. Okay, this is what's happened." Zack leans over the table, and says in a low voice: "I killed someone today."

"Did you shoot the guy who killed all those women?" Abdula whispers back.

"No, we don't think he did it. But he'd just shot and killed one of my colleagues. Not that he meant to. It was just extremely bad luck. And I didn't mean to kill him either. I was aiming for his legs, but hit him too high up, in his groin. He died of blood loss."

"Shit. So if he wasn't the murderer, why was he shooting at you, then?"

"It's complicated. It feels like everything's totally fucked up right now. We don't even know who the victims were, or where they came from. We thought they were from Thailand, but now it looks like they were Burmese."

Abdula looks at him.

"You look like a fucking ghost, Zack. Are you pushing yourself a bit too hard at night, or what?"

"No, last night was fine. I was around at Mera's, that's all. Had some wine, talked. Really good. But I can't sleep properly these days. I wake up in the middle of the night, and just have to get up."

"Do you need something to help you chill?"

Yes, I really fucking do!

"No, no more chemicals. I don't want to get addicted. But enough of that. What have you got?"

"On the Turks? Nothing new, really. There's talk of drug smuggling, of course. Heroin, a bit of opium too. Apparently they're working with the 'Ndrangheta, which gives them access to the huge, mafia-run harbor at Gioia Tauro in the south of Italy."

"Nothing about trafficking women?"

"Not that I've heard."

"And Ösgür Thrakya?"

"No one I've talked to has seen him. No one seems to know anything at all. Just a load of rumors. A lot of people don't even believe he's in Sweden. His nickname is evidently Gölge. It means 'shadow' in Turkish, which seems pretty appropriate. He's like some sort of fucking shadow."

"You haven't heard anything about a house in the forest outside the city? Somewhere they keep wolves? And women and young girls."

"No, but someone did say something about wolves. That

Ösgür Thrakya is supposed to have kept wolves as pets on some farm up in the mountains in Turkey. I thought that sort of thing only went on in Texas. I saw a documentary about it. People with lions and tigers and all sorts in their gardens."

The young family get up to leave. The father runs after a laughing toddler who's heading in the wrong direction.

Zack lowers his voice further.

"You must have found something, or you wouldn't have dragged me out to this tourist trap."

Abdula takes a sip of Coke.

"There's a guy called Mehmet Drakan. He's supposed to be one of Ösgür Thrakya's lieutenants, and he's in Sweden."

"Where do I find him?"

Abdula holds out a handwritten note.

"Here's the address of a garage out in Farsta where he messes about with old cars. I don't know any more than that."

Abdula checks his cell.

"I've got to get going. Look, take care of yourself. These guys you're after really aren't very nice."

Zack stays at the table with his coffee, watching Abdula as he disappears into the elevator.

On his way to another meeting, no doubt, to do deals with the sort of people Zack's supposed to be catching.

Sooner or later we're going to run into each other out there, he thinks. Me as a police officer and you as a criminal.

And then what do I do?

SIRPA IS sitting at the kitchen table at home in her apartment. What she's about to do isn't something she can do from the network at Police Headquarters.

Zeus is sitting next to her, wagging his tail whenever it looks like she might turn in his direction.

"Go and lie down," she says sternly. "I'm busy."

Disappointed, he lumbers away.

She types a short email in English, using the sort of clumsy language she guesses that Ösgür Thrakya's associates would use.

Please take a look at next delivery of Burmese girls that will come to Stockholm soon. I can promise they will give you and other customers good satisfaction.

And then the link.

The infected link.

She sends the email. It doesn't look like it comes from her, but from one of the Turkish email addresses she found in Sukayana's computer.

Now all she can do is wait.

And hope.

If Dirty Sanchez clicks the link, a Trojan will infiltrate his computer, enabling Sirpa to gain access to the whole of his hard drive without him being aware of it.

She guesses he'll take the bait. Dirty old men usually have trouble resisting that sort of link.

She gets up from her chair. Zeus goes almost mad with delight.

"Okay, okay, just a short walk, then," she says. "Then I've got to get back to work."

She leaves her laptop on the kitchen table.

The screen is black, apart from a flashing cursor and some discreet characters in the top left corner.

Waiting for connection.

47

EARLY AFTERNOON. The shadows are still short, the sun's rays intense.

Zack pulls the door open. Welcomes the coolness of the stairwell. Unlocks the door of his apartment, shuts it behind him, and stands still.

Closes his eyes.

Sees his mother's face. Sees Theodor's, and Ingvar Stefansson's.

The boy's face in the tall grass of the meadow.

The incarcerated girls' faces. The ones he's never seen. The ones hidden in shadow.

It feels like he's drifting through a confused, unmapped landscape where past and present run into each other like watercolors.

And he wishes he were somewhere else.

In a different life.

But he's got to cling onto what he's got. Not fade away.

At last he's got a new name to look for, and from a reliable source as well.

He goes into the living room and opens the secret compartment in the floor. Moments later he has the thin plastic bag in his hand. Ten pills left. And the little bag of sticky, pale yellow powder. Tulip whizz. Its intense, instant effect is incredibly enticing. Just a tiny bit of powder in a piece of toilet paper. Swallow. Boom! The kick of all kicks.

But he can't take anything like that now. Not when he's got to work. He opens the bag and takes out two white pills instead.

He gulps them down with some tepid tap water in the kitchen, then sinks onto the sofa and waits.

Longing for the first tickling effect.

But all he can feel is a black substance seeping into his lungs, making it impossible to breathe. And he curses himself.

How the hell could he be taking drugs now? In the middle of the day? In work time?

Should he run into the toilet and stick his fingers down his throat? He'll have time if does it now.

He has to do it.

So get up, then.

But he doesn't move.

How could he have let it go this far? He started off being in control, after all. Just took a bit when he wanted to. Like having sweets on a Saturday, just to clear his thoughts. But always clean during the week. Never taking it simply to pick himself up.

Unless it's impossible to be in control?

He always thought he was.

Until the dreams came back.

The dreams that tear his soul apart every night.

Dragging him deeper and deeper into the abyss.

But not now.

It's going to be all right.

He opens his eyes. The light is back, and a gentle summer

breeze soothes his face. And then they come, at last. The first faint shivers. Like a woman with long nails scratching the back of his neck, then running her fingers down his body.

Tiredness drains away from him, sounds become sharper, colors clearer.

He's going to solve this case now, once and for all. This is the time for it to happen. He can feel it.

And then the dark clouds will disperse for good.

He leans his head back, relaxes, and lets the amphetamine kick spread out into every cell of his body.

Then he goes out into the hall and pulls on his leather jacket. The twenty-thousand-kronor jacket peppered with bullet holes.

He leaves the apartment, locks the door behind him, and takes the elevator down to the garage where his Suzuki Hayabusa is waiting for him. He imagines the bike practically jumping with joy when it sees him. Like a Doberman that hasn't been walked, bursting with pent-up energy.

There, there. You'll soon get the chance to run off some steam.

Not bothering to put on his helmet, he roars out of the garage. He lies low into the ninety-degree corners, enjoying the wind that makes his hair blow about as he accelerates hard between each red light. He pushes hard through the Söderleden tunnel, until the engine sounds like ten million angry bees as the noise bounces off the walls.

Out on the Nynäshamn road he slows down. The traffic is heavy and Zack realizes that he's attracting enough attention just by riding a bike without a helmet. He checks the side mirrors to make sure there's no patrol car heading in the same direction.

He sees a light blue Audi A6 pull out into the fast lane three cars behind and overtake a Nissan pickup.

Fuck, he thinks. It's after me.

Shit, it really is after me.

He looks again. Imagines he can see the Audi pull out of the file of vehicles repeatedly, as if to keep an eye on him.

Shit, who are they?

The internal investigators, Åke Blixt and Gunilla Sundin?

Or the Turks?

They want to get him. He can feel it very clearly. They're out for his scalp.

He checks the side mirrors again, taking care not to let the wind catch his head. The Audi pulls out to overtake again, but Zack has had enough. He accelerates to 125 miles an hour in no time. Racing past everything, looking so intently in his mirrors that he almost misses the turning to Farsta. He swerves sharply across the right-hand lane, starts to wobble badly, and almost drives into the side of a timber truck that flashes its lights and blows its horn at him.

Once he's on the slip road he decelerates and tries to calm down. He checks the mirrors again. No Audi.

He's shaken them off.

It's crazy to ride so fast, really. But it can't be helped. No one can handle a speeding bike better than him. It's as if he's more aware than other people, has quicker reflexes. And, in the middle of an adrenaline rush, you don't think about the consequences of a crash.

As Zack approaches the center of Farsta he turns left after the railway bridge. He can see the map clearly in his head: first left, first right, second left.

He parks the bike outside a large brick apartment block. The worn sign above to the black double doors says ANDERS-

SON'S GARAGE, but Zack guesses it's been a while since anyone of that name ran the business.

One of the doors is open. Zack creeps up and looks inside. There's a smell of oil and old metal in the gloom. He can hear a faint banging sound, like stone against metal, and see two legs clad in overalls sticking out from beneath an old Chevrolet that looks like it's going to need a lot of love if it's to regain its former glory.

Zack assumes that the man working on the car is Mehmet Drakan. He takes a few cautious steps across the concrete floor, but accidentally kicks a small steel spring that rolls off and hits a white metal panel leaning against the wall.

The knocking stops.

The man under the car calls out "Hello?" and Zack responds by grabbing hold of his legs and pulling him out from beneath the car.

It turns out to be unexpectedly easy. The man is lying on a wheeled trolley, and Zack's hard tug means that he shoots out at speed and hits his feet on the metal panel.

Mehmet Drakan is sinewy and muscular, and dressed in dirty green overalls.

He yelps in a language that must be Turkish, and slips partway off the trolley as the metal panel falls on his legs. He kicks at it angrily and makes a move to stand up and go on the attack with the heavy wrench in his hand.

Then he sees the pistol pointing at him.

He puts the wrench down and holds his hands up in front of him.

He looks like his passport photograph, Zack concludes.

Shaved head, with a large tattoo covering half his neck and part of his left cheek. A skillful but unpleasant image of a rearing horse with predator's teeth.

Zack shows his police ID and Drakan looks relieved, as if the police were the least dangerous of the possible alternatives.

"Lie still, you bastard," Zack tries to say, but his jaw muscles won't obey him and the sounds that emerge are strangely twisted, as if certain letters have been removed.

The amphetamines.

"I don't speak Swedish. English?" Drakan says, and starts to sit up.

"Stay where you are," Zack says, having to make a real effort to control his jaw muscles.

Drakan lies back on the uncomfortable trolley, and Zack starts to question him in English.

"Tell me about Ösgür Thrakya."

"Who?"

"I know you know him. Tell me."

"I don't know anyone of that name."

"We know you're involved in the murders in Hallonbergen and on Klara Norra Kyrkogata."

"What murders? I haven't murdered anyone."

Really?

Zack ponders various ways to get the Turk to talk, and finds himself thinking of the scene in *Reservoir Dogs* in which Mr. Blonde cuts off a policeman's ear.

Or should he slowly lower one of the Chevrolet's wheels down onto Drakan's legs?

An eye for an eye, a leg for a leg.

Zack is suddenly struck by how easily such violent thoughts come into his mind. Without any emotion at all. As if they came from the very deepest part of his being. He knows other people don't react that way. That most people have emotional boundaries different from his.

He wonders if Mehmet Drakan was there when they kidnapped Sukayana Prikon. And stood and watched as her legs were torn apart.

"Where are the wolves, Mehmet? And the girls?"

The Turk starts.

"I don't know what you're talking about."

"The girls, for fuck's sake."

"What girls?"

"You don't know much. So you might as well shut the fuck up."

He doesn't recognize his own voice. The words sound wrong as he says them, and his jaw is so tense that he could chew through wire.

Christ, he's thirsty.

He imagines he sees movement from the corner of his eye and spins around.

No one there.

Or is there? Is there someone there somewhere? Someone he can't see. Has that Audi pulled up outside?

Stop it, Zack. You're being paranoid, and you know why.

But he can't shake the feeling. He takes a few steps away from Drakan, without letting him out of sight, and looks around the garage once more.

At the back there's a small office. He looks inside. No one there.

"Everything's a real mess here, Mehmet. Maybe I should help you tidy up."

He gets his handcuffs out and fastens Drakan's right hand to the left front wheel of the Chevrolet.

Then he starts searching the garage with all the finesse of a steamroller. He needs to give his muscles something to do, get rid of all that energy. He empties boxes, clears shelves with a sweep of his pistol, tips the contents of various wooden crates on the floor, and kicks though the resulting mess.

"Like I said, Mehmet, it really is a fucking mess in here."

It seems to him that he's given Drakan the chance to talk, to cooperate. But given that he's chosen not to . . . well, Zack's just going to have to underline the point.

In the office he discovers a dirty fridge with a bulky old television on top of it. He opens the fridge, finds a can of Coca-Cola, opens it, and downs it in a few short seconds.

He crumples the can and throws it hard against the wall. He sees some papers on the desk. A dreary vehicle service history. He leafs through the pile, but is unable to concentrate properly.

He sweeps all the papers onto the floor and starts tugging at the doors of the cupboard on which the desk is perched.

Locked. Shit.

I'm going to smash this fucking cupboard apart.

He goes back out into the garage to find a suitable tool. Sees a crowbar leaning against the wall next to a shelf of tools. He grabs it with both hands, liking the weight and the coolness of the metal in the palms of his hands. Then he returns to the office and smashes the crowbar against the cupboard, over and over again. He strains and pulls until sweat is trickling down his temples and the doors are lying in pieces on the floor.

The cupboard contains a few folders and a small black sports bag. He pulls it out and opens the zipper.

The bag is full of cash. Thick bundles of used notes, held together by brown elastic bands. On top is a page torn from a spiral-bound pad.

"Dirty money for Dirty Sanchez."

Zack stops. Tries to calm down.

Dirty Sanchez.

The alias that Sirpa hasn't been able to crack.

He takes the bag out to Drakan and shows him the contents.

"I assume you've declared all this for tax purposes?"

For the first time, Drakan looks scared.

"It's not my money. I didn't even know what was in the bag. I'm just looking after it for a friend."

"Of course you are," Zack says. "Who's Dirty Sanchez?"

The words are still coming out strangely.

"Don't know."

Zack leans over and pushes his pistol hard against one of Drakan's nostrils.

"Wrong answer," he snarls. "Seriously fucking wrong. I'll ask again: Who. Is. Dirty. Sanchez?"

Zack twists the barrel, trying to stick it up into Drakan's nostril, but it's too big. Drakan grimaces with pain, but says nothing.

"Okay. You need to listen to me seriously fucking carefully now," Zack begins, but falls silent when he sees a shadow on the floor.

Zack and Drakan are hidden by the Chevrolet and the new arrival hasn't seen them yet.

"Mehmet?" a male voice calls out.

Zack peers over the hood of the car to see who the man is. He's expecting some guy from the suburbs in a hoodie, but instead sees a well-dressed man with graying hair in a dark gray suit. The man turns in Zack's direction, and suddenly he recognizes him:

Sten Westberg, CEO of the large property company Merkantus.

48

WHEN WESTBERG catches sight of Zack he turns and runs out of the garage, while Zack remains rooted to the spot.

What's Westberg doing here? And why is he running away?

He hears Sukayana Prikon's voice in his head:

In my homeland they're all like him: corrupt.

It wasn't just a passing remark.

She knows him.

Doesn't she?

Zack doesn't want to leave Drakan alone in the garage, but he needs to get hold of Westberg.

He quickly kicks any tools out of Drakan's reach, then runs out into the road.

He can see Westberg barely fifty yards away, and sets off after him. Westberg isn't used to trying to shake someone. Instead of dodging in among the buildings he carries on running straight, in full view of his pursuer.

Zack feels like a wolf hunting a rabbit, a terrified little wretch that's missed its last chance to jump into a hole and hide.

Zack the wolf is young and fast.

Westberg is over fifty, dressed in a suit and smart shoes, and is running like a man who's used to doing no more than walking.

Zack is gaining on him with every meter.

Westberg tries to shake him off by running into a parking lot where some sort of local market is taking place, zigzagging between the tables and stalls. When he turns and sees that Zack is still gaining on him, he manages to overturn a table full of glass ornaments, which crash to the ground.

People start screaming and shouting.

Zack takes a different route, behind the tables, and sees Westberg set off toward a large patch of trees on a hill beyond the parking lot.

The path through the trees slopes steeply upward, and the CEO can't get any grip with his hard, flat soles. Zack is right behind him now, but he lets Westberg run a bit farther until they're both out of sight of the parking lot. Then he kicks one of his legs out from beneath him, sending him tumbling over some twisting tree roots before he has time to break his fall. Zack forces him onto his back, sits on his stomach, and locks his skinny arms down with his knees. He clenches his right fist and pulls his arm back, and all he wants to do is punch him, and keep on punching. But the amphetamine rush isn't as intense now, and when he sees Westberg's wide-open eyes, he manages to redirect the downward momentum of his fist, and punches the ground next to the man's ear instead.

A thin cloud of dust swirls up.

Westberg shuts his eyes and turns his head away.

"Who are you? And what do you want with me?" he asks.

Zack pulls his ID from his inside pocket and holds it up in front of his face.

"Zack Herry, detective inspector with the Stockholm Police."

At first Westberg doesn't seem to understand.

He blinks the last of the dust from his eyes and looks up at Zack, and a thought slowly seems to take shape inside him.

He practically grins.

“Why did you run?” Zack asks.

“I thought I’d stumbled into some sort of gang dispute. What the hell do you think it looked like? Mehmet Drakan’s a tough guy.”

“What were you doing there in the first place?”

“I was going to pay the bill for repairing my car.”

Zack sucks his lips in, then spits out:

“Would a man like you leave his car to be repaired by a Turkish professional criminal with a garage in Farsta?”

“What do you mean, a man like me?”

Zack opens his mouth to say that he knows who he is, but changes his mind.

“You look pretty upper class. The sort who gets his chauffeur to take his car to a garage in Östermalm.”

“This place was recommended to me. Rumor has it that there aren’t many mechanics who understand old cars like Mehmet Drakan.”

He’s breathing hard with Zack’s weight on his chest.

“I’ve got an old Chevrolet Impala from 1974. There aren’t many mechanics who know how to look after it these days. Can you get off me now? It’s a bit hard to breathe with you sitting on me.”

Zack ignores the request.

“So you weren’t actually there to pick up a small bag?”

“What sort of small bag?”

“Payment for your dealings with the Turks. The Turks who rent a number of your properties.”

“I have tenants of many different nationalities, among them Turks, I assume. So?”

"Why is your own name on the tenancy agreement for the Sawatdii massage parlor at Hornstull? And on the contracts covering the leases on other massage parlors controlled by the Turks?"

Zack imagines he's forced the CEO into a corner, but Westberg looks at him scornfully.

"You really don't seem to like Turks."

"I asked you why you personally signed the rental agreements for the massage parlors."

"My name is on a lot of contracts. That's standard practice, especially if they're needed in a hurry, or people are on holiday. It means I can sign them straightaway, without having to sort out power of attorney for people lower down the organization. I'm a very hands-on person."

"What do you know about Yildizyeli?"

"This is getting ridiculous."

"Mehmet Drakan is mixed up in all this, and so are you."

"I want you to move, so I can get up and go. Unless you've got any more conspiracy theories you'd like to get off your chest first?"

Zack hesitates.

He's trying desperately to think of something smart to say, something that would make Westberg reveal his hand. But he can't think of anything. So he stands up and moves aside.

Westberg gets to his feet and starts to brush off the earth and pine needles. Some red ants are crawling across the back of his jacket, and Zack can't help hoping they manage to find their way under his shirt collar. Without another word, and without looking at Zack, Westberg walks away, out of the woodland.

Zack stands among the trees for a while.

Westberg is lying, he's sure of that. Maybe that Chevrolet isn't even his. He'll have to check.

If only I'd got to the garage quarter of an hour later, he thinks. Then I could have caught Stenberg with the bag of money in his hand, and that would have been more than enough to take him in.

Now I haven't got anything at all.

His arms are itching. And his chest. A vague sense of unease is creeping up on him, and he knows this is only the start.

He has to go back to Mehmet Drakan and the bag. He runs back to the garage and finds the door still open.

Two teenage boys cycle past on mountain bikes. He waits until they're out of the way, then draws his pistol and peers inside.

Empty.

One part of the cuffs is still attached to the wheel. There's an angle grinder on the floor.

How did he get hold of that?

His cell, you moron. He called for help. Why didn't you take his cell off him?

He'll show up again. Probably when I least expect it.

He looks for the bag, but of course there's no sign of it.

He curses himself. Now the Turks know that they've been detected, and have presumably already begun to cover their tracks.

All he's got is the link between the money and that email address in Sukayana Prikon's computer.

Dirty Sanchez.

An alias. But whom does it belong to? The connection to Peter Karlson turned out to be too weak, after all.

It could just as easily be Sten Westberg. Or Ösgür Thrakya.

Or someone else entirely.

You know nothing, Zack. Nothing.

You had your chance, and you blew it.

Will more women die as a result?

And what about the girls?

Where are they?

49

ZACK IS sitting on the visitor's chair in Douglas's office, shivering. The rush has been replaced with withdrawal.

He really did do it.

Took drugs in work time.

He's taken benzos a few times in the past, but only small doses to stop himself feeling anxious. This is different. This is definitely crossing a boundary.

He looks at the time: ten to six. It's been about three hours since he took the pills. The worst of it is about to start.

All he was thinking of doing was dropping his pistol in at headquarters; he can't afford a third warning in such a short space of time. Then he was going to go home and call Sirpa and Deniz to tell them about the note in the bag, and the money, and Sten Westberg's unlikely appearance at a garage he had received a tip-off about.

But in the lobby he bumped into Douglas, who was walking through in the company of a superintendent from National Crime.

Douglas turned to him and said:

"Zack, my room in five minutes."

He went completely cold.

Saw the blue Audi in his mind's eye.

He knows amphetamines usually make him paranoid, but maybe he really was being followed this time. Maybe they were filming him as he rode far too fast, without a helmet.

He shivers again and wonders how long Douglas is going to keep him. Quarter of an hour, maybe, half an hour at most.

Thirty minutes. Can he hold it together that long? He'll have to.

Fuck, it's cold.

But Douglas has taken his jacket off. He's even loosened his tie.

He must have noticed something when they met down in the lobby. Zack wonders if his pupils are starting to go back to normal, or if they're still covering almost the whole of his irises. Probably. That's why Douglas has taken his jacket off. To demonstrate his power. So he can roll his sleeves up, fold his arms, and tell Zack he's a disgrace to the force, and that Douglas therefore has no choice but to fire him.

Zack wonders what happens when a police officer is fired, if it's like in American cop shows, where the dismissed officer has to leave his badge and service weapon on his boss's desk before leaving the room with his head bowed.

His heart is pounding like a hammer.

Pull yourself together, Zack, for God's sake.

Zack looks at the picture on the wall behind Douglas's desk to have something to concentrate on. It's a small painting in various shades of ochre, of books in an evidence bag. Zack's never noticed it before.

"It's a Carl Hammoud," Douglas says, noting what Zack's looking at. "I like him. He always seems to be searching for some kind of truth, just like us."

Zack nods. Keen to show agreement. Keen to keep Douglas in a good mood.

He guesses he could buy thousands of books for the price of that picture. Or another motorcycle.

But now he won't be able to afford anything, now that he's going to be dismissed. He squeezes the armrests of the chair so tightly that his knuckles turn white, and tries to focus on looking normal.

"The woman who was shot in the arm is going to make a full recovery," Douglas says. "Theodor probably never had time to realize what was happening. But he leaves a wife and three children. I believe the youngest boy is only a month or two old."

The pictures on his cell.

His children.

Good thing I didn't look at them.

He could have prevented their dad's death. He was the one who shot back at the window without thinking, thereby provoking Ingvar Stefansson into firing more shots.

Why?

Because you live the way you do, you fucking idiot. Because you take so many drugs that you aren't in control of anything anymore.

"Have we got someone looking after his family?" Zack asks.

"They've got access to the best help available."

They sit in silence for a moment.

Zack feels like sliding off his chair and lying on the floor. Crawling out of his own skin.

Douglas looks at him.

"Now tell me about Farsta," he says.

His tone is neutral. Commanding, but not accusatory.

How can Douglas already know that I was there? Zack thinks.

Was he actually being followed?

Sten Westberg. Westberg must have called Douglas and told him to control his young subordinate. They acknowledged each other in the Opera Bar. They definitely did.

Zack thinks back to Westberg's grin when he showed his police ID and told him his name. He must have known that Zack worked for Douglas, and that he could exploit that fact.

Zack does his best to appear untroubled. He just needs to find the right thread. How the hell did he end up in Farsta?

Ah, yes. Abdula. The Kaknäs Tower.

"I was given a name by a source, and I thought I'd check it out," he begins.

He talks about the garage he went out to look at, about Mehmet Drakan's reluctance to talk, and about the CEO of Merkantus suddenly showing up, claiming to be paying a car-repair bill.

Sitting on the chair is easier now he's got something to concentrate on.

"You have to admit that it's a bit odd. First his name appears on the lease agreements for several of the massage parlors we're investigating, and then he turns up in a garage owned by a Turk with a criminal record, where there coincidentally also happens to be a bag full of cash. It's obvious that he's mixed up in all this."

"I agree that it's certainly an unusual coincidence. But sometimes that's all it is: a coincidence. Is the car registered in his name?"

"Yes."

Zack checked the car's registration as soon as he bumped into Douglas down in the lobby. He had been hoping that the car belonged to someone else, someone who had no logical place among Westberg's acquaintances. But that wasn't the case. The Chevrolet had had four owners, but had been registered in Sten Westberg's name for the past seven months.

"Well, from now on we're dropping that and working with what we've already got," Douglas goes on. "Forensics have started to go through Stefansson's laptop and cell, and I'm expecting a preliminary report on what they've found shortly. We've got a number of massage parlors under observation, and we're trying to identify which ones use staff from Burma. We've also received an anonymous tip-off about a small, ultrareligious sect that has resorted to extreme violence in the past to protest against sexual promiscuity. Apparently two leading members have been seen in Stockholm during the past week. I thought you could take a look at that."

Zack is no longer listening. He's wondering why Douglas doesn't want to talk about Sten Westberg.

Because all the men in fancy suits protect each other.

But what's the difference between their loyalty and mine and Abdula's? Those of us who come from the sewers protect each other too.

"Here, Zack," Douglas says, holding out a piece of paper with some names and ID numbers on it. Zack glances at the note and leaves the office.

He's still got a job, but he's being given crap to work on.

Has Douglas worked it out after all? Is this his way of punishing Zack?

DOUGLAS IS still sitting at his desk. He waits until Zack is out of sight.

Then he picks up his phone and dials a number.

50

HOME AGAIN.

Welcomed by nothing but countless dust balls.

No Ester in the stairwell.

He would have liked her to be there. Today he could cope.

But today she wasn't there.

He's alone with his dirt. Internal and external.

And he can't even summon up the energy to deal with the external sort.

Zack hasn't even got a proper vacuum cleaner, just a small one he sometimes uses to clean the table, or to suck up piles of dust he's swept up with the broom. But even that was a long while ago now.

He often hears people say how nice it will be to get home again when they've been somewhere, but he's never felt like that. Never ever.

Even when he and his dad were moving their furniture into the three-room apartment in Bredäng, he knew he would be leaving one day, and he never let go of that thought for as long as he lived there.

It's the same with this apartment. He's lived here for four years now, but it still doesn't feel like home.

I ought to have a home, he thinks. Everyone should.

The way Abdula does. He says he could never leave Bredäng.

"Isn't it about time you thought of moving into the city?" Zack asked him the last time he paid him a visit.

The old apartment block looked worse than ever. Graffiti-covered walls, stinking bags of garbage outside the door, and boarded-up windows in the basement where the glass had been kicked in.

But Abdula simply shook his head.

"This is my patch. You can't just leave that behind."

Zack knows what it's about.

Identity.

A sense of belonging.

He's seen it in plenty of guys from the suburbs. Maybe Sweden doesn't feel like home. Nor does their parents' homeland. But no one can take the place they grew up in away from them. It's where they have their roots.

He thinks of Said, one of his childhood friends, who came from Skärholmen. He tattooed his postcode, 127 31, on his arm. That gave him a certain status, even with people who didn't know him very well. The tattoo acted as a sort of mark of quality.

One hundred percent Skärholmen. No additives.

Even so, he can't help getting fed up with all the suburban guys who feel obliged to sing the praises of their shitty little patches of territory. Who talk of concrete with love in their voices.

It's all bullshit.

Zack isn't sure he'll ever find somewhere he can call home.

He pulls the blind down and shuts out the summer evening. Gets a Coke from the fridge. Downs it. Puts the empty can in the garbage, along with all the others.

He thinks about the garage in Farsta. How he threw that

crushed can at the wall, how he swept through and wrecked the office.

He sits down on the sofa, but gets up almost immediately and starts walking around the living room.

He shouldn't be a police officer. He's no better than the people he tries to catch. Koltberg is right. He's a fraud, who's taken shortcuts through the hierarchy thanks to his mom.

He checked out the names on the note Douglas gave him. Obviously they turned out to be a dead loss. Just as he'd known they would. Not that it makes the blindest bit of difference now. It's over. He's failed.

He didn't get fired today, but he will be soon. He's not suited to be a police officer.

He's known that all along, really. He felt it very strongly on his first day, when he walked through the doors of Police Headquarters to work his first shift after graduation.

He had enjoyed the training and had become good friends with several of the others on the course. But when he found himself walking through the entrance that he'd scrawled graffiti on just a few years before, to become a *proper* police officer, he felt nothing but unease.

It was as if he had was going inside the building against his wishes. As some sort of punishment for past misdeeds.

He can clearly remember his thoughts at the time:

I don't belong here. This isn't the right place for me. What do I have to do to get out of here?

I have to solve Mom's murder.

But there had been something else as well. Things that needed doing, but which he didn't yet know about.

Truths to be uncovered.

Truths that were far bigger than him.

———

HE WALKS back and forth in the dusty apartment.

Knows there are pills hidden away that could bring him down in just a couple of minutes.

But he resists.

Enough already.

I can't resist.

Then there's a knock at the door. Three hesitant little knocks.

You've come after all.

You're saving me. It ought to be the other way round.

"Hello."

Her smile seems to fill her whole face, and she's got her folder and a brown pencil case in her arms.

"Hello. Do you want to come in?"

"Yes, please."

They sit down on the sofa and Ester puts the folder on the table.

"More homework? Isn't that summer course over soon?" Zack asks.

"There's one week left."

"So what have you got to do for tomorrow, then?"

"Just some math. We've started to do area."

"Is it hard?"

"No, it's just multiplication, really. First you measure the two sides, then you multiply the number. And that gives you the answer. If it's a rectangle, that is. If it isn't, it gets a bit more complicated."

"Why don't you show me how to do it?"

She takes her math book out of the folder and opens her pencil case. She sharpens the pencil carefully in a little green pencil sharpener, then gets out a white eraser and a transparent ruler.

Everything in perfect condition. No teeth marks on the pencil, no bent corners on the book.

Zack remembers his own schoolbooks. Battered, covered with scribbles, their corners bent over. He always found the work easy, but he was ridiculously careless. He often left his books and other schoolwork at home. Or would turn up for school trips without a packed lunch and change of clothes.

His dad didn't really have the energy to get involved.

He would have liked to, but couldn't.

Like Ester's mother.

But Ester probably doesn't forget that sort of thing anyway.

Zack looks at her as she carefully measures the sides of a five-sided shape, then writes down the numbers on the lines beneath it.

As long as you can get through these years, he thinks. As long as you don't end up with the wrong crowd.

Or get kidnapped and sold by criminals.

Locked away in a house in the forest.

With wolves.

"There," she says a short while later. "I'm done now."

"You made that look really easy," Zack says.

She looks at him quizzically.

"Not that I'm surprised. Have you got any more homework?"

"No, I did the rest at school."

"Do you want to watch a film?"

She gets out her cell, an old Nokia 5310, and looks at the time.

"No, I've got to go back up and make tea and sandwiches for us both. Mom's probably awake now."

She gives Zack a long hug on the sofa, and he hugs her back.

Then she picks up her folder and pencil case and leaves. Zack hears her footsteps in the stairwell and hopes that Veronica has woken up and feels up to spending some time with her daughter.

Then he gets a text from Fredrik Bylund.

> Meet me at the Grand Hotel at
> 9:00 a.m. tomorrow morning.

Zack wonders why Bylund always wants to meet at such fancy places, and replies:

> Sure. You're paying.

He gets a smiley with devil's horns in response.

Zack would rather have met up with him straightaway. He knows the newspapers sometimes receive tip-offs from people who for various reasons are reluctant to contact the authorities, and hopes that Bylund has something for him that can finally point them in the right direction.

But he doesn't want to put pressure on the reporter. Better to let him establish the rules of the game.

Anyway, Zack needs to get some sleep.

He wishes Ester could have stayed. Then he'd almost certainly have fallen asleep on the sofa. He looks across at his hiding place. But, no, no more chemicals now. He doesn't want to rinse the crap away with more crap.

He opts for a different method instead, one which is painful, but he knows he'll feel better as a result when he wakes up.

He takes his jeans off and starts doing push-ups on the living-room floor. He keeps up a fast pace, his chest touching the floor each time he dips down.

After fifty push-ups he rolls onto his back and does some sit-ups. He tortures himself to do almost one hundred. Then he runs out of energy.

He brushes his teeth, pulls down the blind, and gets into bed.

Shuts his eyes.

And falls asleep instantly.

But, once again, sleep is no safe refuge. His dreams are full of snapping jaws in dark corridors, wolves howling, women's legs torn apart, bullets penetrating skulls, and two boys at night in a summer meadow that smells of blood.

WHEN HE wakes up he doesn't know where he is at first.

He reaches for his cell, which he's left to charge: 1:17.

Friday now. But this crazy week is probably far from over.

It's as if time has been compressed. So much has happened, his brain hasn't managed to keep up.

He goes over to the window and opens the blind. The summer night is dark blue, and white pinpricks are shining faintly in the sky. He tries to find a constellation he hasn't seen in a long time. It's big, but indistinct, almost impossible to see with the naked eye. Especially in the city.

But he looks anyway. Searching for the four stars that form a shape that looks a bit like the Plow, then for the smaller stars that stick out like arms and legs.

Hercules.

A memory comes back to him. He's somewhere in the countryside with his dad, who's still healthy. It's late August, and they're standing outside in the dark, looking at all the stars.

Crickets are chirruping in the mild night, and his dad is

crouching beside Zack, and has just pointed out Hercules to him.

"But why is he running, Dad? Is he frightened?"

"No, Hercules is brave. This constellation can be depicted in different ways, and some people see it the way you do, with two running legs. But Hercules is actually on his knees, raising his club, ready to tackle ever more dangerous creatures."

Zack looks at the constellation for a long time. Then at all the other stars. It's almost impossible to believe there are so many.

"Do you know how the stars were created?" his dad asks a little while later.

"No."

"Well, when Hercules was a baby he was placed next to the goddess Hera to suckle while she was asleep, but she woke up and pushed him away, and the milk that spurted out formed the Milky Way."

Zack looks at him.

"Not really, though?"

His dad smiles at him.

"Everyone's free to believe whatever they like."

Zack looks up at the stars again. His dad but his arm around him, and Zack wishes they never had to go back indoors again.

IN A forest some distance northwest of Stockholm, the stars are shining considerably brighter than in the city. The dark outline of a large barn sticks up among the fir trees and undergrowth. Beside it stands a smaller farmhouse, its lights still on.

Some men are walking toward the barn from the house.

The glow of a cigarette is clearly visible in the darkness, and the animals begin to bark as they hear the voices.

Fredrik Bylund hears the old door open, hears the stairs creak beneath the men's weight, and then sees three faces staring down at him from some sort of loft. The men talk to each other in low voices, and one of them laughs.

Bylund tries to move, but his chained wrists and ankles are already scraped and bleeding, and he has no energy left.

He can't even summon up the strength to cry for help anymore.

One of the men goes off. He hears footsteps on the stairs again, then a scraping sound, and Bylund sees a large hatch in the wall slowly open.

The animals' growling and barking becomes more intense.

What's going on? What the fuck is going on?

The hole in the wall gets bigger, the wolves rush into the room, and he screams louder than he ever has in his life.

THE SCREAMING.

There it is again.

Far away. Yet close at the same time.

Sanda Moe starts to sing in a trembling voice, so Than Than Oo won't hear the faint sound reaching them through the damp walls of the cellar. She strokes her cheeks and lets her hand linger intentionally for a few seconds over her ear.

Than Than Oo's forehead is wet with sweat. She's lying on a dirty mattress on the floor, trying to breathe through the pain of the cramps. They're coming close together now.

Twelve-year-old Tin Khaing is crouched between her spread legs, ready to help the baby out.

Sanda Moe speaks softly to Than Than Oo. "It's going to be fine. You're strong."

She knows no one is going to rescue them.

They were doomed even when they were in Burma.

Maybe even in the camp on the other side of the border.

Than Than Oo screams out loud when the first real contraction starts.

That's good, Sanda Moe thinks. Let the scream of life drown out the scream of death.

Maybe someone will save us.

In spite of everything.

ZACK WAKES up on the sofa at quarter past five in the morning. His back is sore from having slept in such an awkward position.

But he feels rested.

He must have fallen back to sleep when he was lying there looking at the stars, and he quickly calculates that he's slept for a total of nine hours since the previous evening. It's been a very long time since he slept that long in one night.

He goes out into the kitchen and switches the coffeemaker on. Then he gets out the black leather folder and spreads the pictures of his mom out on the floor.

He turns them the wrong way up to make himself see them in a new way. Goes through the investigation in his head. Tries to identify mistakes in his own reasoning and conclusions.

What is it that I'm not seeing?

51

COME ON, answer.

Sirpa has the phone clasped between her cheek and shoulder. Her fingers are dancing across the keyboard as she hunts for more information about Dirty Sanchez.

She feels exultant. Almost giddy with excitement she gazes out across the open-plan office of the Special Crimes Unit.

We've got him now.

An hour ago she was in her kitchen putting coffee in the French press when the laptop in her bedroom bleeped.

Ignoring the pain in her legs, she hurried in to look at the screen.

It now longer said: "Waiting for connection."

It said: "Connected."

Dirty Sanchez had walked into the trap.

She immediately went into his hard disk, found his real name, and yelped out loud in delight.

Zeus jumped up onto the bed, wagging his tail and barking like an idiot, but she barely noticed him.

So *he*, of all people, was Dirty Sanchez. Not Ösgür Thrakya, not Peter Karlson, not Ingvar Stefansson. *Him.*

Poor Zeus only got a brief minute outside. A quick pee, then back in again. Then Sirpa set off for work.

Answer, for God's sake.

After eight rings she gives up and calls Deniz instead. She picks up at once.

"Hi, it's Sirpa. I can't get hold of Zack. Is he with you?"

"No, I've just been to the Miramar. We got a tip that Ösgür Thrakya had been seen there, but it was shut up, no lights on anywhere. I've been trying to call Zack as well, but he's not answering. He seems to have gone off on some one-man mission."

"Sten Westberg, that businessman Zack bumped into at Mehmet Drakan's garage, is Dirty Sanchez. He must have been there to pick up that bag full of money. Just as Zack thought."

"What did you just say? How do you know that?"

Sirpa gives a brief summary of what she's been doing.

"Last night he opened the email and clicked the link, so now I've managed to download loads of files from his computer."

"Wow. Is that legal?"

"No, it's a massive invasion of privacy. But we've got a mass murderer on the loose out there, haven't we?"

"We have."

"I've only had time to go through a few of the files so far," Sirpa goes on. "But it's enough to confirm that he's a real perv. I'm going to carry on going through his emails, Word documents, and all sorts of other stuff now, but I wanted to let you know right away. I can keep trying to get hold of Zack if you like."

"Good. I'm on my way in."

Sirpa hangs up and dials Zack's number again. She's getting impatient now.

She stares at the passport photograph on the screen. Sten Westberg, CEO of the property company Merkantus, ranked seventy-sixth on the list of Sweden's highest earners.

But also the man behind the email address dirtysanchez@woomail.com.

She scrolls quickly through some of the emails she managed to download when Westberg was online earlier that morning.

He doesn't appear to send many emails from that address, and she is able to look back through his history fairly quickly. A few mails from Sawatdii that she recognizes from Sukayana Prikon's computer, one concerning registration with a new porn site, *www.barelylegal.com*, two emails in English containing inquiries about the cost of different hotels in the Philippines.

She assumes he's planning some sort of sleazy sex holiday, and moves on to another email.

What's this?

She reads the first lines, holding her breath.

Then sees the photograph.

Fucking hell . . .

The motive for murder.

Here it is.

Pay us 100,000 kronor, or we tell what you done with us.

Money transfer through Western Union by June 13 at the latest.

She stops short when she sees the date. *June 13*. Last Monday. That was when the first women were found murdered.

The rest of the email contains instructions of how he should transfer the money, and what number to call when it's all done. The international dialing code is +95.

She quickly googles to find out which country that is.

Burma.

She looks at the picture again.

The picture that was supposed to get him to pay up.

And who wouldn't pay?

Westberg is standing with the trousers of his suit pulled down, in front of a naked woman on her knees, her face turned away from the camera.

Sirpa guesses the woman herself set up a remote-control camera somewhere in the room.

Smart.

And courageous.

Then she realizes that the woman in the picture could be one of the murder victims. Was this the last thing she did when she was alive? Give a blow job to a bastard in an expensive suit?

The email was signed by eight people. Maybe they thought there was strength in numbers, that he wouldn't dare attack them if there were so many of them.

Six of the names match the names in the fake passports of the murdered women. She can't find any trace of the other two, no matter how hard she tries. They don't occur in any official Swedish databases, and seem to be invisible on the Internet. She can't even find them on any sex websites.

She clicks to open another email, a long exchange of mail between dirtysanchez@woomail.com and a Turkish email address that she traces back to a server in Italy. From the exchange it is clear that Westberg has helped the Turks to acquire cheap premises, in exchange for backhanders in cash.

"My position as CEO in the company will serve as a guarantee against unwanted inquiries," he writes in one of his early emails.

Such a high salary, Sirpa thinks, yet he still wants more. She's seen it countless times before. And presumably money wasn't the only form of payment.

Zack still isn't answering.

She'll give him another try in a while.

52

ZACK GETS his cell out of his pocket and calls Fredrik Bylund for the fourth time. Sirpa and Deniz have both called him several times, but he doesn't want to take their calls in case Bylund tries to call at the same time. They can manage without him for an hour, even if he has an idea that Deniz is annoyed with him for disappearing without telling her.

No answer this time either.

He's at the Grand Hotel, and has just moved from the lobby to the Cadier Bar. The dark paneling is decorated with gold, but the service is clumsier than at the considerably simpler cafés he usually frequents. He had to wait ages before anyone took his order, and then had to wait even longer for his espresso, which was lukewarm when it arrived.

But it's all fine. He feels better than he has all week.

Properly rested, and temporarily free from both angst and cravings.

But it doesn't look like Bylund is going to show up.

Zack calls *Expressen*'s newsroom and is told that Bylund isn't there at the moment because he was working late yesterday evening but might be in later.

There are some newspapers on the table in front of Zack. *Dagens Nyheter*, *Svenska Dagbladet*, *Dagens Industri*. No copy of *Expressen*.

He spots the name Merkantus on a headline in the front of the business paper, and pulls it out of the pile.

Sten Westberg's company.

Zack leafs through until he reaches the article.

CRISIS AT MERKANTUS

Merkantus's management team is in trouble. After a long period of dissatisfaction, the company's owners at Heraldus are planning to make sweeping changes.

After the recent collapse of two proposed deals, confidence in the management of property company Merkantus is at rock bottom. *Dagens Industri* has learned that the company's proprietors at Heraldus are planning a comprehensive restructuring of the entire company.

Heraldus today declined to comment on this.

"We'll be issuing a statement when we're ready to do so," Harald Sundborn, Heraldus's head of information, said.

Heraldus, one of Sweden's so-called "big five," has long been renowned for its almost ruthless attitude toward management teams that have failed to live up to expectations.

HERALDUS.

That's what she's going to inherit, that woman in the club out in Sundbyberg.

The one with the deep blue eyes and glossy dark hair.

But what's her name? He can't think of it.

Her eyes, her mouth.

He looks up from the newspaper and notices a commotion at the other end of the room.

Camera flashes. Agitated voices. At the center of attention a slim woman in a long, black dress who has sat down at a round table.

Noomi Rapace.

Lisbeth Salander.

She's being interviewed by a suited man with thinning hair while a young photographer in a crumpled shirt and three days of stubble darts about taking pictures of her from every possible angle.

Around the table stand two men and a woman who look like they've been plucked from a commercilal set in an office. PR people, Zack guesses. There to make sure the reporter asks the right questions, and that the star gives the right answers.

The smart side of society. The one so many people are striving to join.

Luxury, attention, and endless ingratiating smiles.

So unlike his own world.

He realizes that he's sitting there staring at Noomi Rapace, and she glances in his direction, smiles, and raises one eyebrow slightly.

Zack wonders about setting her a test. Seeing how long she dare hold his gaze.

Then he pulls himself up. Come on, you've got a killer to catch.

Focus.

Someone's phone buzzes nearby, and it takes him a moment to realize that it's his. He snatches his jacket from the seat opposite him and grabs his phone from the inside pocket. At last, Fredrik Bylund is getting back to him.

Then he sees the name on the screen.

Sirpa again.

Fucking hell.

Just as well to take the call. After all, something might be going on.

"Hi," he says.

"Zack, Sten Westberg is Dirty Sanchez."

Two minutes later he puts his phone back in his pocket, all thoughts of meeting Fredrik Bylund forgotten.

He can smell victory.

They're close now.

He beckons a waiter over, having to make exaggerated gestures to get noticed. As he holds out his credit card he thinks about what Sirpa has just told him of the attempt by the eight women to blackmail Westberg.

His motive is crystal clear. They could have wrecked his entire career.

One businessman's honor versus six Burmese women's lives.

Apparently not a difficult choice.

We need to get hold of him at once. We may still have a chance to save the last two women.

And maybe also the girls in the forest.

"There you go. Thanks."

The waiter hands his card back along with a receipt.

Eighty kronor. That's what he normally pays for lunch.

But no doubt Westberg doesn't.

There's a logic to the fact that his name was on those contracts, Zack thinks. It's one way of ensuring a bit of quick extra money now that his position as CEO is looking uncertain.

He thinks of the bag in the garage. The scrap of paper on top of the bundles of notes.

Dirty money for Dirty Sanchez.

But a wealthy and apparently functional business leader as a mass murderer? Has there ever been a similar case?

And why the excessive brutality? Zack doesn't understand.

An attempt to focus attention elsewhere, perhaps. Or because he hates women, or because of his violent desire for them, as Östman suggested.

But he doesn't fit the profile. Westberg isn't a lone wolf. Zack himself saw him having lunch in the Opera Bar with some other suits, men he seemed to know well. And he has a sociable job that involves meeting new people all the time.

What else had Östman said?

A man used to moving in criminal circles. . . . Probably not someone who belongs to any organized group.

That fits fairly well, on the other hand. Westberg has a business arrangement with Yildizyeli, but doesn't belong to it.

He could have got hold of the murder weapon from the Turks. Or anywhere. It's easier to get hold of a gun than mashed potatoes made from real potatoes these days, as Zack's older colleagues often put it.

But there's more that doesn't quite make sense. Why would the Turks tolerate Sten Westberg destroying their property? It can't be that hard to get hold of business premises illegally in Stockholm. So why haven't they stopped him?

If he really is the murderer.

Where does Sukayana Prikon fit into the picture? She wasn't involved in the blackmail, after all, at least not according to that email.

So her mutilation must be the result of someone else's work. Yildizyeli's.

Is that actually connected to the murders at all?

Zack runs his hands through his hair.

Tries to think logically.

Suppose Westberg *is* the murderer. If that is the case, then he probably didn't get the Turks' approval for the murders. But he went ahead and killed the women anyway. Why? To prevent his life being ruined by the women blackmailing him. If that hidden-camera picture of him with the Burmese woman had found its way into the media, his lovely office would have been replaced by a prison cell.

So why not just make the payment through Western Union? After all, the amount is peanuts to someone like him.

Zack thinks of his own encounter with Westberg. Of the derision he saw in his eyes. His scornful sense of superiority. And he realizes what this is all about.

Power.

Sten Westberg hates those women because they were trying to strip him of the power to which he believes he is entitled. He hates them because he is a successful white man and they're just insignificant Asian prostitutes who don't know their place.

He simply *can't* do as they demand. That would destroy his whole self-image. He would be allowing himself to be led by the nose.

Under normal circumstance he probably wouldn't take such a massive risk. But his power was already under serious threat.

Westberg is about to lose his job. And with it his title, his power, and his financial security.

And then who is he?

What does that make him?

Desperate.

And desperate people are dangerous people. They do crazy things.

Like committing murder. Like challenging ruthless criminals.

His business dealings with the Turks also act as his defense.

They don't suspect anything.

Do they?

Zack feels a chill run through him.

The garage in Farsta.

Zack showed Mehmet Drakan his police ID.

Drakan may have remembered his name, may have checked out which department he works in. May have seen on the television news that the Special Crimes Unit has been brought in to investigate the murders at the massage parlors, and he may now be wondering why one of the unit's detectives was chasing Westberg.

They know.

Just like we do.

We've got to get hold of the killer before they do. Force him to lead us to the house in the forest.

An image comes into Zack's head: Sten Westberg being torn apart by wolves in some isolated shack somewhere.

He calls Deniz on her cell as he runs out of the hotel.

53

ZACK RUNS north along Grevgränd, turns left into Arsenalsgatan, then carries on running north along the side of Kungsträdgården.

His breathing is easy, and he feels he could run forever at this speed.

On the other side of the street the Japanese cherry trees line up in perfect rows. In an hour or two the park will be full of locals and tourists eating ice cream, but there aren't many people about at the moment.

Zack reaches the junction with Hamngatan and stops outside Max's hamburger bar on the corner as one of the Djurgården trams glides past.

It was his suggestion to meet here rather than at the hotel. Now they won't have to weave through the backstreets, which will save them precious minutes.

He sees her approaching from the west in the Special Crimes Unit's Volvo V50. She pulls over, with two wheels on the pavement, and Zack jumps into the passenger seat before the car has even stopped moving.

"Head for Engelbrektsgatan."

"Engelbrektsgatan?"

"Merkantus, the property company, has its headquarters there. It's time to bring in our beloved CEO."

"For murder?"

"For anything. What matters right now is getting hold of him. And stopping him. Preferably before the Turks get him—I think they're looking for him as well now."

"But Sirpa tracked him down illegally. The prosecutor will never accept that."

"We'll have to come up with something else. We could have got an anonymous tip-off from a public-spirited hacker, something like that. We'll think of something."

"Has Douglas given the go-ahead for this?"

"I haven't asked. I get the impression that he's trying to protect Westberg."

"Why would he want to do that?"

"He goes on the defensive whenever we mention Sten Westberg. Maybe they belong to the same golf club. And I think Westberg called Douglas yesterday to complain about me getting his suit dirty out in Farsta."

"Yes, speaking of your adventures in Farsta . . ." Deniz says.

"I know," Zack says. "I've got loads I need to explain. I'll do it when this is over, okay?"

Deniz says nothing for a few moments. They drive past the trees of Berzelii Park. Some of the branches hang out across the street, shading it with their leaves.

"Okay, we'll take that up later."

She does a sharp left turn in front of the Royal Dramatic Theatre and heads up Birger Jarlsgatan. She swears when she realizes she can't turn right past Humlegården because Engelbrektsgatan is a one-way street.

She carries on and takes the next right, into the narrow Eriksbergsgatan, then turns right into Engelbrektsgatan from the other direction.

"There it is," Zack says, pointing at a flashy building overlooking Humlegården.

Deniz looks up at the turn-of-the-century building.

"Douglas really isn't going to be happy with us bringing in Sten Westberg without telling him first."

"I'll say I thought Sirpa had informed him. It'll be fine."

Deniz looks at him and smiles.

"What?" Zack says.

"Nothing. You just seem on the ball today."

"Hmm," he murmurs.

THE RECEPTION area of the property company has white paneled walls and framed black-and-white photographs of old building sites and construction workers in white T-shirts, smoking. Zack guesses they depict the early history of Merkantus.

The reception desk is staffed by a smiling woman in late middle age, dressed in a white blouse and dark blue jacket with outsized shoulder pads.

"Good morning, how can I help you?" she says in a pronounced Östermalm accent, her gaze focused on Zack.

"Good morning, we're here to see Sten Westberg."

"I'm afraid he isn't in the office."

"Do you know where he is?"

"No, I saw him leave in a hurry about fifteen minutes ago, but he hasn't logged out," the receptionist says. "That's odd, he usually does. Can I give him a message?"

Zack shows her his police ID.

"It's extremely important that we get hold of him as soon as possible. Can you put us through to his secretary?"

"By all means," the woman says, trying in vain to hide her curiosity. "Hold on a moment."

She dials an internal number.

"Hello, Jeanette, this is Agneta. I've got a police officer

down here who'd like to speak to Sten. Can you talk to him? Thanks. Here he is."

She passes the phone to Zack.

"I'm sorry," Jeanette says in answer to Zack's questions. "I don't know when he'll be back. He didn't say where he was going. The only thing on the calendar for today is a meeting with representatives of a foreign client. He's supposed to be showing them some premises at noon, but I don't know what he's got planned until then. I've just tried to get hold of him myself, but his cell is switched off."

"Okay, thanks for your help."

A foreign client, Zack thinks as they leave the building. From Turkey? Another massage parlor, perhaps.

He's about to open the car door when Sirpa calls again.

"I've just found them, the last two women. Their names are Nang Mon and Ah Noh. They sound pretty Burmese to me. Sten Westberg mentions their names in one of the Dirty Sanchez emails. He wrote to ask when they were going to be working."

"Where do they work?"

"At Eastern Massage in Skärholmen, and guess what? It's on the list of massage parlors with suspected links to Yildizyeli."

"Sirpa, you're the best."

"There's something else it could be useful to know. When the human trafficking unit visited that parlor, it was closed and the women weren't there. That was the day after the murders at City Thai Massage. But I've just called, and a woman with a strong Asian accent said they'd been open for the past hour or so."

Zack feels a chill run through his body.

"Sirpa, can you get some backup out there? I think Sten Westberg's on his way there now."

Deniz sets off at speed and pulls out onto Birger Jarlsgatan, but gets stuck almost at once behind a courier van in a traffic jam.

Zack gets the revolving light out of the pocket in the door, winds the window down, and sticks it into the magnetized socket on the roof.

"Get the siren on, that'll shift them," he says.

She does as he says and the road ahead clears.

"Do you really think he's planning to shoot them now, in full daylight?" she asks.

"He's desperate. I just read an article about how badly his company is doing, and how precarious the position of its managers is. And after Farsta he knows we're onto him, and he may have worked out that the Turks are starting to get suspicious. I think he's planning to get rid of the last of the blackmailers, then leave the country."

"But why wouldn't he have killed the women earlier, last night, for instance?"

"Sirpa said the parlor has been closed, and that there was no sign of the women. If our colleagues couldn't find them, maybe Sten Westberg couldn't either. He's probably been calling to check several times a day. Sirpa said they only opened up again an hour or so ago. If he was lucky, he might have called as soon as they were open."

Zack looks at the time.

Fuck!

If Westberg set off for the massage parlor more than quarter of an hour ago, then he's got quite a head start on them. They aren't going to get there in time.

He tries to contact the duty officer to see if they've managed to send a patrol car, but Rakel, the police radio system, is completely dead.

Useless damned system. It was supposed to be idiot proof, but it's caused nothing but problems.

He calls the duty officer's phone instead.

Engaged.

He calls Abdula. He lives at the south end of Bredäng, just a few minutes' drive from the massage parlor.

No answer. Zack sends a text:

> Eastern Massage on Äspholmsvägen. Man in suit on his way to take out two masseuses. Must be stopped. I'll be there in 12 mins.

STEN WESTBERG parks his Mercedes CL600 outside the massage parlor in Skärholmen, and looks up at the seven-story building. The pale yellow façade is peeling, and the balconies have been covered with dark blue panels in a vain attempt to make the place look more appealing.

The pistol hangs heavy in his suit pocket.

At first it scared him, but now he knows what it can do. And he likes it. The way it puts those fucking whores in their place.

Who do those cunts think they are?

When he got the first message from them he almost felt pleased that they had the ingenuity to try something like that.

He knows you have to help yourself if you're going to get where you want to go. But not everyone has it in them. The necessary ruthlessness. Only a small number of people have the strength required.

I'm one of them, and I'm going to make sure that carries on being the case.

I could have turned Merkantus around, he thinks, I could have been a hero to Olympia Karlsson and the whole of the Heraldus empire. And then she'd have made me a seriously wealthy man.

But those ungrateful whores got in the way. I've made a lot of money from the Turks. But now everything's gone to hell.

And it's all the fault of those fucking whores.

I'll put a stop to them. They deserve no better. I'm going to wipe them out.

By this time tomorrow I'll be leaning back and gazing out at a completely different view. Palm trees on a Filipino island. A twenty-two-hour flight, a bit of money stashed away in various pockets, and I'm gone for good.

Cunts.

There are plenty of those in the Philippines. Fresh ones too.

He fingers the Beretta. Feels a tingle in his crotch as his hand touches the metal.

One last time. Then order will be restored.

He still can't understand how those ungrateful whores could be so stupid. He's been good to them, after all. Helped their employers find premises, made sure they had the chance to make a bit of extra money. Let them have sex with him. Hell, he even paid them, even though they liked it and the Turks had promised to let him have free access to the meat.

Then they complained that he was a bit rough with them.

Crybabies.

It wasn't that bad, surely? A bit of light whipping, a couple of slaps. The occasional fist when things got a bit too exciting.

Right up inside them.

All the way in.

They screamed with pleasure, and then claimed they were screaming in pain.

So what? Life must be a hell of a lot worse in the brothels of Bangkok. Or in Doha, where Asian whores have to take twenty Arab cocks at the same time.

They should have stayed at home, if things were so fucking great in the refugee camps. They shouldn't have come over here to tempt people. Who can resist a tight Asian cunt? Tighter than any Western cunt could ever be.

If they hadn't come here, they'd still be stuck over there. That's all there is to it.

He feels his stomach clench. How could they treat him like this? When it comes down to it, he's always been kind, has always meant them well. But if you show them a bit of love, they let you down. I always end up getting betrayed, he thinks.

And now the Turks seem to have worked out that I'm the man behind the murders. Presumably because of that fucking little bastard out in Farsta.

They called Jeanette yesterday morning and asked to postpone yesterday's meeting until noon today.

He guesses the call came from Tuncay Çelik. It's usually him.

But he never postpones meetings. And he's never called his secretary before.

That means they're after me.

With their wolves.

Like that Thai bitch at Hornstull.

He can see Ösgür Thrakya's back framed in his mind's eye.

He's never seen his face, but he's heard his voice. Strangely thin and squeaky, but full of latent violence.

"If you let us down," he once said, "I'll boil you alive."

Westberg tries to stop his hands shaking.

He squeezes the pistol in his pocket, feels his hands become steadier.

He gets out of the car and adjusts his suit.

Whores.

If anyone's been made to suffer in all this, it's him.

54

OUT ONTO the E20. Sticking in the outside lane.

Deniz is driving fast but steadily. Not getting carried away.

The various districts of the city pass by quickly. Concrete rises up on either side of them. Stockholm gets more ugly with each mile they drive farther south.

"Feeling homesick?" Deniz says as she sees Zack gaze out at the looming gray skyline of Bredäng.

"Not much."

He'd like to explain how he feels. That *home* for him is more a state of mind. And, ideally, a state of motion.

Like now. Sitting in a car with Deniz. That's home.

But he's not sure she'd understand.

That anyone could understand.

And it doesn't matter.

"Is there a shortcut if I turn off here?" Deniz asks as she pulls into the right-hand lane.

"No, take the next one. It's quicker."

She pulls back into the outside lane and overtakes a truck and two cars.

Zack looks at the clock on the dashboard, and imagines he can hear it ticking. *Tick-tock, tick-tock*. Far too fast.

He tries calling Abdula again. Still no answer. And no reply to the text he sent.

Deniz turns off toward Skärholmen.

They've stopped talking now. Sinking into themselves, aware that what happens next could be crucial.

They circle the center of Skärholmen, drive up a small slope, and turn in among the seven-story apartment blocks.

A police car is parked outside the massage parlor and Zack feels relief spread through his chest. A patrol from Årsta, he guesses. Good.

They jump out of the car and run across the street toward Eastern Massage. A graphite-gray Mercedes CL600 is parked beyond the patrol car. Sten Westberg's? Zack curses himself for not finding out what other vehicles were registered in his name when he was checking the ownership of the Chevrolet.

A gust of wind blows down the street, and Zack looks up to see dark clouds building in the sky to the east.

More rain on its way.

He pulls the door to the massage parlor. Locked.

Through a gap between two curtains across the window in the door he can see a flashing light from some neon-colored LED lights. He peers in and stops breathing.

There's a female police officer with dark hair and open eyes lying on the floor. In front of her lies another officer. It looks like a man, but Zack can only see legs and a pair of boots. As the lighting switches from pink to yellow, the bodies seem to glow, and the blood looks green.

Blood seeping from the policewoman's head and neck.

A lake of blood.

Maybe I should be feeling scared, Zack thinks. But the blood makes him calm, almost alarmingly focused. How can I be like this? he thinks fleetingly, then swats such thoughts aside.

He quickly pulls back from the door and gestures to Deniz to do the same.

"There are two officers shot in there."

"Shit. I'll call for backup."

Zack quickly runs through the options in his head. The killer could still be on the premises. So should they be cautious and wait for reinforcements? No, the women could still be alive, and if they are, they need help. And they need it now.

Deniz ends the call, and Zack says:

"We're going in."

She nods and draws her pistol.

Zack quickly examines the door. It looks just as flimsy as the one he forced at Sukayana Prikon's parlor. He kicks it with a hard sokuto kick just below the handle.

Splinters fly through the air.

The door hits the wall with a crash.

Zack throws himself to the side, expecting a hail of bullets to come through the doorway.

But nothing happens.

Absolutely nothing.

He glances inside quickly, then turns to Deniz.

"It looks empty."

Holding his Sig Sauer in front of him, he darts inside the premises.

White wallpaper with a red floral pattern. A huge poster of a golden Buddha. A worn pine reception desk. A closed door.

Deniz comes in behind him and they check for signs of life in the police officers on the floor.

Deniz puts her fingers to the woman's neck.

"No pulse," she says.

"Same here," Zack says, kneeling by the other officer, an almost bald man with a red beard and bushy eyebrows. He has a hole in one breast pocket, and around the hole a large stain is spreading out.

Zack averts his eyes from the woman.

From her neck.

A faint sound, footsteps, perhaps, from the other side of the closed door.

Zack and Deniz get up cautiously and stand on either side of it.

Another sound. Sobbing?

Are they lying on the floor wounded?

Zack pushes the handle down and shoves the door open, then snatches his hand back. His temples are pounding and the butt of his pistol is wet with sweat.

The sobbing is louder now. And someone's heavy breathing.

Zack tries to slow his own heartbeat. He takes a few deep, silent breaths, and peers quickly inside the room.

Sten Westberg.

Dressed in a dark blue sweater and jeans, with a black baseball cap on his head. With a pistol in one hand and the other arm around the neck of a young Burmese woman in a silk kimono. Where's the other woman? Already dead, perhaps?

Zack has gestured to let Deniz know what he's seen, when Westberg says:

"Drop your gun, or the bitch dies."

Has he seen Deniz, or can I go in on my own?

Zack looks at the time. They can't count on backup arriving for several more minutes.

"Throw your guns in, then come out where I can see you both. With your hands above your heads."

Shit.

Zack and Deniz look at each other, trying to work out what to do.

They're both good shots, but from their respective positions there's no way they can rush in and shoot Westberg without running the risk of harming the woman he's holding. Or getting shot themselves.

Try to persuade him to surrender? Out of the question. Westberg has come here to kill. He knows it's all over if he leaves anyone alive.

"I'm going to count to three," he calls out. "One . . ."

Damn. Why haven't I got two pistols?

Deniz holds her arms out, as if to say: we've got to do as he says. What else can we do?

"Two . . ."

"Okay, okay," Zack shouts. "We'll do as you say."

He puts the safety catch back on the Sig Sauer, crouches down, and carefully slides it in through the doorway.

"That was a fucking pathetic little throw," Westberg says.

Then Deniz tosses her own pistol in, slightly farther than Zack's.

"Now come out with your hands up," Westberg repeats.

Zack puts his hands behind his head and steps into the doorway.

He's expecting to be shot in the face, and has to fight an instinct to close his eyes.

But nothing happens. He takes a step into the room, and sees Westberg aiming a nine-millimeter Beretta at him.

"Now you too," Westberg says, waving his pistol toward Deniz, who's standing right behind Zack.

Deniz takes a couple of steps and stands beside Zack. She too has her hands behind her head.

“That’s better,” Westberg says, and smiles at them.

Only now does Zack notice the second woman.

She’s sitting on a massage table to the left of the door. Her round face is framed by a short bob, tears are streaming down it, and she’s dressed in the same sort of shimmering kimono as her colleague.

So young. No more than a teenager.

She looks at Zack.

Save me, her eyes are screaming.

I’m going to save you, he thinks. Don’t worry. I’m going to take care of this.

He looks at Westberg again. His eyes are glinting with excitement. It’s as if he knows everything is over, but has decided to enjoy it. Then something else crosses his eyes.

A bitterness behind his hatred, the feeling that might perhaps be the cause of it.

A loneliness that can only be sated by misdirected desire.

He keeps moving the pistol between Zack and Deniz.

“I’m not going alone,” he says, as if in response to Zack’s thoughts. “Today I’m going to take all the fucking pigs with me.”

55

FOR SOME reason Zack finds himself thinking of chess. A deadly game where he's one of five remaining pieces on the board.

You have to dare to be provocative, but without taking too great a risk. One wrong move and it can all be over.

He glances quickly around the room. A few shelves holding massage oils and neatly folded towels. A cane chair. A small table with some gossip magazines on it.

Nothing he can use.

His eyes settle on a red curtain behind Westberg. He wonders what it's hiding. The entrance to another room? Or a corridor, like in Sukayana Prikon's massage parlor at Hornstull?

The woman who's got Westberg's arm around her neck starts shouting loudly in Burmese. It sounds like, "I don't want to die, I don't want to die," and Westberg tightens his grip of her neck and yells:

"Shut up, bitch!"

She falls silent and her brown eyes open wide as she struggles for air.

The other woman makes to get off the massage table to help her, but Westberg points the pistol toward her:

"Sit down, whore!"

She sits back down.

She starts hyperventilating, and Zack can also hear a

strained hiss as the woman in Westberg's grip finally manages to breathe some air through her constricted windpipe.

"Sten, it's over now," Zack says calmly. "Reinforcements are on their way, if they aren't already here."

But it's as if he isn't listening.

He's still pointing the pistol at them.

"Pigs, pigs, pigs. I'm not going to let you stand in my way."

"Let them go, Sten," Zack says. "My partner and I are the pigs, not them."

Westberg is breathing hard, his mouth open. Every sinew in his body is tense, to the point of bursting, and the woman he's got in a stranglehold is gasping for each breath.

"Everyone in here is going to die, pigs and whores alike," he screams.

His outstretched right hand is trembling and the barrel of the Beretta is bobbing up and down in the air with quick, jerky movements.

Zack wishes he could send him flying into the wall with a kick or a blow of his baton, but they're almost ten feet apart. He can't get to him quickly enough.

Westberg would shoot him. Or the woman. Or both of them.

He aims the pistol at her head again. Presses it hard against her temple. She shuts her eyes and starts to shake and cry.

"Let's get started then," Westberg says.

"Sten . . ." Zack says, but he just smiles and pulls the trigger.

The noise makes Zack put his hands in front of his face, but Westberg just laughs, and when Zack looks up again he sees that the woman is still alive. Westberg fired the pistol next to her head.

"That scared you, pigs!" he says.

He presses the pistol even harder against her temple and she grimaces, her face twitching.

Zack detects a slight movement behind Westberg.

The curtain.

There's someone there.

A hand at the edge of the fabric. An eye peering out. The curtain is pulled slowly and silently aside.

Zack tries not to look, he doesn't want Westberg to notice where he's looking. He focuses on the woman on the massage table instead. She's still staring at Westberg and her colleague, and doesn't seem to have noticed what's happening behind them.

"Well, that's enough messing about," Westberg says. "It's high time we put an end to this business."

A black-clad arm and shoulder become visible behind the curtain. A leg. Someone slipping into the room sideways.

Abdula.

Westberg's finger is on the trigger. As if in slow motion, Zack watches it slowly squeeze tighter. Soon the critical point will be reached.

Abdula is fully visible now.

It's too late, Zack thinks. Far too late.

Abdula's clenched fist strikes Westberg on the temple with immense force. He screams with pain and surprise and lets go of the woman as he stumbles to the side, waving his arms to keep his balance. But he's still holding the pistol, and spins around as Abdula throws himself at him from one side, while Zack moves in on the other.

A shot goes off and Abdula's body jerks in the air. He falls just as Zack's kick hits Westberg's hand.

The pistol flies into the wall and bounces onto the floor right in front of Westberg.

Zack can hear his own breathing and his pulse ringing in his ears.

Time seems to slow down again, and from the corner of his eye he sees the two Burmese women hugging each other as they sink to their knees, screaming out all their pent-up mortal dread, he sees Deniz finally realize she can take her hands down from behind her head, he sees Abdula lying far too still, and he sees Westberg bend down toward his own weapon.

Zack leaps forward to shove him aside, but realizes he isn't going to make it in time.

Two more shots, but with a different sound.

A Sig Sauer.

Time speeds up again.

Blood splatters across Westberg's chest. He falls to his knees, a look of total shock on his face.

Zack turns around and sees his boss in the doorway next to Deniz.

Douglas Juste.

In a suit.

With his service pistol in his hand.

He fires again.

And again.

Westberg's body jerks with each shot. He falls sideways and lies motionless. His eyes stare up at them sightlessly.

The women stop screaming, but they go on hugging each other and gasping for breath as they stare at the suited man in the doorway.

A good person?

Or another sadist?

Zack crouches down beside Abdula. In the weak light he can't see any blood on his long-sleeved black T-shirt.

Where was he hit? Is he alive?

"He wasn't armed," Deniz yells somewhere behind him. "He wasn't armed!"

"Of course he was," Douglas says calmly, pulling on a plastic glove. Then he picks the pistol up off the floor, goes over to Westberg, and presses it into his hand.

Zack turns toward Douglas.

What's he doing?

He sees Deniz slowly shaking her head, as if she can't believe her eyes, but then he hears Abdula cough and turns his attention to him again. Abdula is clutching the left side of his stomach, and when Zack pulls his hand away and pulls his top up he sees blood gushing out of his gut.

Fuck, fuck, fuck.

Zack quickly snatches up a scrap of cloth from the floor, screws it into a ball, and presses it against the wound as he takes out his phone and dials Control.

"Äspholmsvagen, Skärholmen. Several people shot. Some fatalities. At least one seriously injured. Shot in the gut. Ambulance required IMMEDIATELY!"

He hangs up.

His other hand is already wet with Abdula's warm blood.

Deniz checks Westberg's pulse. His face has already set in a grimace, and it looks almost as if he's smirking, as if he's happy with the devastation he's caused. Zack feels like cutting that smirk off with a blunt knife.

Then everything happens all at once. A powerful blast, the violent shaking of the floor and walls, windowpanes shattering, a rain of glass flying through the air and falling on the two dead police officers in the lobby.

What the hell . . . ?

Zack hears screaming out in the street and realizes that there's been an explosion.

Have Yildizyeli gone on the attack?

Deniz runs out, her pistol drawn.

Zack lets go of the scrap of fabric and puts Abdula's hand on top of the wound instead.

"Keep pressing," he says, but by the time Abdula groans something inaudible in reply, Zack has already left the room and run out into the street, pistol at the ready.

Black smoke is billowing from Westberg's Mercedes, or rather what's left of it. The entire roof has blown off and is lying in the road several yards away. All the windows have been blown out, and the inside of the car is ablaze with hot orange flames.

An elderly couple are sitting on the pavement on the other side of the street, blood dripping from their hands and faces.

Deniz runs over to them, but Zack remains where he is, staring at the car and trying to understand what's happened.

He can hear ambulance sirens in the distance as the thick smoke makes him cough.

The Turks, he thinks. I was right.

But why has the bomb only just gone off?

Because it was on a timer.

Zack checks the time. 11:53. The bomb must have gone off at about 11:50. What had Westberg's secretary at Merkantus said? Something about a meeting with a foreign client?

He was going to meet the Turks.

And their plan was for him to be blown up on the way there.

Then Westberg changed his plans.

But even if Sirpa hadn't managed to track him down, he would probably still have been sitting in his car at the time, on his way to Arlanda Airport after two more murders. Then he'd have been blown up on his way to Terminal 5 instead.

His number was up today, one way or the other.

Two bright yellow ambulances swing into the street, sirens blaring, and Zack runs back in to Abdula.

IN THE intensive care unit of Södermalm Hospital a monitor begins to bleep.

A doctor with a goatee looks from the screen on the monitor to the patient's face, back and forth, as if he were watching a tennis match.

He sees her move her head slightly. Blink cautiously a few times, and twitch.

Then Sukayana Prikon opens her eyes.

56

THE SMOKE from the fire has made its way into the massage room. Abdula is coughing from deep in his lungs, his face contorting in pain. A thin trickle of blood is seeping from his mouth.

Zack turns toward the door, wants to shout at someone to get the paramedics to hurry up. But there's no one there.

He wipes the blood from the corner of his friend's mouth. Abdula is staring up at the ceiling, and seems to be trying to stay in the room, and he looks improbably small lying there on the floor.

As if he were shrinking as the life runs out of him.

"Hang on, my friend," Zack whispers. "Just hang on. They'll be here any minute."

He wants to scream, cry, but that will have to wait.

He needs to focus on saving Abdula now.

Then he'll have his revenge.

Take down the bastards who are responsible for this.

Abdula is breathing more calmly again after his fit of coughing, but the smoke is still billowing in, a scratchy smoke that smells of burned plastic, and Zack is worried Abdula is going to start coughing again.

Two paramedics in green-and-yellow outfits come into the room. They close the door behind them and Zack stands up.

"He's been shot in the gut. I've put a makeshift compress on the wound, but he's coughing up blood."

The paramedics lean over Abdula. One gently lifts the compress and inspects the wound.

"You've done a good job," he says to Zack. "But he needs to get to a hospital at once."

OUT IN the street the fire brigade have just arrived, but the car is still burning and black smoke is pluming up from the wreck. The heat hits Zack's face.

A crowd of curious onlookers has gathered outside the police cordon. People holding handkerchiefs over their mouths, young people filming the fire on their cells. Agitated voices in a number of different languages. Women in niqabs, short men in shabby suits. Children staring and pointing, at the fire, at the flashing blue lights, the police officers, and the fire brigade.

Zack holds the door open as they wheel out the gurney with Abdula on it. He looks out at the street, at the burning car, and thinks that it looks more like Aleppo in Syria than a Swedish suburb.

A short way along the street Douglas is talking on his cell, and giving out orders to three uniformed police officers.

How could he have got here so quickly?

Douglas ends his call. He seems to see straight into Zack's head and comes over to him.

"I know what you're thinking. Westberg was an old acquaintance from my days at boarding school in Sigtuna. We met up occasionally. Had a drink or two. He called me after you chased him out at that garage. Wondered what the hell we were playing at. Wanted me to see to it that he was left in peace. He's always been a tough bastard, but last time we met I got a feeling that he was crossing the line. You have to believe me, Zack. I knew nothing about his sadistic side, or how perverted and desperate he was."

"You got here quickly."

"Sirpa told me what she'd found out, and that you'd set off after Westberg."

Zack looks at his boss. At his face, which is showing not the slightest sign of sorrow or regret. He's just shot an old schoolmate and seems to feel nothing.

"I had to shoot him," Douglas says. "I thought he was armed. It was kill or be killed."

Then Zack realizes that Abdula's gurney is about to be rolled into the ambulance and runs after it, calling to the paramedics to wait.

They stop at once and Zack reaches the gurney. He leans over Abdula and strokes his forehead, but Abdula's eyes are closed. He can't see him.

But maybe he can sense that I'm here.

You've got to make it, he thinks. You've got to.

Then they push the gurney inside, the doors close, and the ambulance sets off.

Zack sits down on the pavement, resting his arms on his knees, and leans his head on his hands.

He shuts his eyes and listens to the sounds and voices around him. Water spraying from hoses, people shouting, excited voices in several languages.

He barely notices the woman who sits down next to him and puts an arm around his shoulders.

She holds him tight, and he leans his head against her chest and recognizes the faint smell of perfume.

Deniz.

He keeps his eyes closed and stays in her embrace. Takes

several deep breaths and realizes that it isn't over yet. They still don't know who mutilated Sukayana Prikon, and they have no idea where the house in the forest is.

Where are Ösgür Thrakya and his men hiding? And where's Fredrik Bylund?

Zack was expecting the find the journalist here. Possibly dead. But now more police patrols have checked the area, and there's no sign of another body. So what's happened to him?

Have the Turks got him? That almost has to be the explanation.

"Was it Abdula you were trying to contact when we were on our way here?" Deniz asks.

Deniz has met Abdula before, albeit very briefly. She recognizes a criminal when she sees one, and Zack knows she has trouble understanding his choice of friends. But he also knows that she understand the value of friendship.

"Yes. He lives around here. I just thought he might be able to take a look and let us know the situation."

"Don't you want to go to the hospital?"

"I'll go a bit later. It feels like we aren't done here yet."

"Do you feel up to coming with me to question the women from the massage parlor?"

"Yes."

She stands up, then helps him to his feet. He can't help thinking how exhausted she looks, and feels like giving her a hug, to show her he cares about how she's feeling.

But there's no time for that now.

The Burmese women are sitting in the back of a patrol car. Not the best place to conduct an interview, Zack thinks as he opens the driver's door and sinks onto the seat.

Deniz gets in the passenger seat. She turns around and

tries to smile at the women. One has long, glossy hair tied up in a ponytail that hangs over one shoulder. She seems to be in her twenties, and still has red marks on her neck from where Westberg was holding her.

The younger woman is holding her friend's hand, and looks up at Deniz and Zack with frightened eyes.

"How are you?" Deniz asks.

They shrug their shoulders.

"Do you understand Swedish?"

"English is better," the woman with the ponytail says.

"What are your names?" Deniz asks in English.

"My name is Nang Mon, and this is Ah Noh," she says.

Zack recognizes the names from his conversation with Sirpa. Two of the eight women who tried to blackmail Westberg.

The only two who've survived.

"We'll make sure you get away from here shortly, and we'll help you to contact your families, but first we need to ask you some questions. Is that okay?"

"Yes," Nang Mon says.

"Are you from Burma?"

"Yes. But we lived as refugees on the Thai side of the border after our village was burned down. We belong to the Kachin tribe, we've been persecuted by the military for many years."

Yet another persecuted minority, Zack thinks. How many can there be?

"Tell us about Sten Westberg," Deniz says. "The man who was holding you when we arrived."

"He is a bad man."

"In what way?"

Nang Mon turns her face away and looks out through the side window.

"Do you know that six women from Burma have been murdered in Stockholm in the past week? They all worked in massage parlors, just like you," Zack says.

He purposefully doesn't mention any names, doesn't want the women to get scared and clam up.

Nang Mon and Ah Noh stare at him as if they misheard him.

"We believe Sten Westberg may have killed them," Zack goes on, "but we're not sure. The more you can tell us about him, the easier it will be for us to solve this."

Nang Mon runs her hand down her ponytail and seems to be thinking. Then she says:

"If I tell you, will you have to tell my family?"

"No," Deniz says. "But the newspapers will probably write about the case, and we have no control over that information."

Nang Mon looks at Ah Noh, and they seem to communicate wordlessly about what to do.

Then Nang Mon turns back to Deniz, nods, and says:

"Okay, I'll tell you. Mr. Westberg wasn't like other clients. He liked to beat us too. Spit in our faces. And then . . ."

She falls silent and takes a deep breath before going on:

". . . then he would use shit, and tell us we were his filthy whores. That he was going to fill us with shit. He smeared it on my lips. Refused to pay. Said he owned me . . ."

The words catch in her throat.

She wipes a tear from her cheek and Deniz reaches backward and puts a hand on her knee.

"You don't have to say any more about that. That's enough."

Deniz turns to Zack with a black look in her eyes, and he can see how hard she's having to try not to throw the door open and go and stamp on Westberg's dead body.

Nang Mon continues:

"No other client was allowed to hit us. It was forbidden. But he was allowed to. He paid Tuncay for it."

"Who's Tuncay?" Zack asks.

"One of the men who came to pick up the money. He has a big scar on his face," she says, running one finger down her cheek, past the corner of her mouth to her neck.

Someone else we don't know about, Zack thinks.

Ah Noh whispers something in Nang Mon's ear.

"She wants me to tell you what happened when we refused."

"What happened?" Deniz asks.

"Tuncay got out a laptop computer and made us watch a recording someone had filmed in a barn on their cell. We could see Tuncay and some other men.

"And then we saw Sanpai, a girl who came to Sweden at the same time as us. She was so young, just twelve or thirteen. They held her down and she cried and screamed."

Ah Noh starts sobbing helplessly. She hides her face in her hands to stifle the weeping, but she can't stop shaking.

"I'm sorry," she says. "I'm sorry."

"It's okay," Deniz says, and turns to Nang Mon. "Go on."

"There was a hole in the floor, and they dragged her over to the edge and pushed her in, and then we saw . . ."

Nang Mon can't go on.

She puts her hands to her mouth as if to stop herself throwing up, and starts to rock back and forth, whimpering.

"Nang Mon," Deniz says. "What did you see? You have to help us."

Nang Mon takes long, wheezing breaths as she looks at Deniz.

"We saw . . . we saw the wolves eat her. They tore her apart while she was still alive. They were mad with hunger, and trained to eat human flesh."

Utter silence descends inside the car.

Zack and Deniz can't think of anything else to ask.

It's as if they've just caught a fleeting glimpse of pure evil. As if everything that could be said has been said.

But Nang Mon isn't finished.

"Then Tuncay shut the laptop and said: 'That girl also refused.' "

Zack can barely remain in the car. He wants to find this Tuncay and tear him to pieces with his bare hands.

They threw a twelve-year-old to the wolves.

What if someone had shown him a film showing grown men throwing Ester to starving wolves?

He can't even imagine how that would feel, or what he would do to someone like that.

"Is Tuncay the only one who comes to pick up the money, or are there others?" Deniz says, once she's composed herself.

"There's one more, but I don't know his name," Nang Mon says. "I just remember his eyes. You get scared when he looks at you. He came with Tuncay a few times, always wearing a black suit, but he stays in the background and never says anything. He's death. He devours spirits."

Ösgür Thrakya, Zack thinks.

"Is there anything else you think you should tell us?"

Zack realizes that Deniz means the attempt to blackmail Sten Westberg.

The young women sit in silence.

Zack and Deniz wait.

“One of the other women from Burma we’ve talked to mentioned a house in the forest outside Stockholm. Was that where Sanpai was? Have you been there?”

Ah Noh hides her face in her hands again.

“We were taken to the house in the forest when we first arrived in Sweden,” Nang Mon says.

“Do you know where it is?”

“No, but it seemed to take a long time to get there.”

“How long?”

“An hour, perhaps. First on a big road. Then winding roads in the forest. In the end it was just a rough track.”

“What did the house look like?”

“It was red. Two stories. That was where we met Sanpai. There were other girls there. Very young, just children.”

“How many?”

“Five, I think. Or six.”

“And how many men?”

“Three, from what I remember. They had guns, and they locked us up in a dark storeroom at night. That was when I realized something was wrong.”

“Do you remember anything else? What did the countryside around the house look like?”

“There was an old barn nearby. I think that’s where they kept the wolves. The house and barn were both painted red. And there were lots of strange, tall trees all around. I don’t know what they’re called. The branches went all the way to the ground, and they were covered with tiny green needles.”

“I think you mean pine trees. Anything else?”

“I can’t really remember. We were only there for one day. Then we were driven here and had to start . . . working.”

"The girls you mentioned, the children, what do they do with them?"

"They get sold to men. Then they get driven back out into the forest again. They don't all come back."

"Do you think there are still girls there now?"

"Yes, the ones who aren't dead."

57

THE NUMBER of heartbeats appears as blips in a regular green line on the monitor. Sixty-two beats per minute. Occasionally sixty-three. Zack stares at the screen, hoping to see a change, some sign of consciousness. But nothing.

He's sitting alone by Sukayana Prikon's bed, on the same pale brown visitor's chair as before. From the other side of the door he heard the low voices of the two police officers who are sitting on guard outside the intensive care room. One of them asked to come in, but Zack said no. He wants to be alone here.

He's holding Sukayana's hand in his, massaging it gently with his thumb. She's lying with her face toward him, and looks paler than he remembered. The doctor said she'd regained consciousness, but Zack can't help thinking she looks a very long way away.

In spite of the tube leading into her mouth, she looks peaceful.

Zack doesn't like it.

It's as if she knows she's going to die, and has reconciled herself to it.

Zack feels like finding that bearded doctor and asking about her condition, but resists. He already knows that Sukayana's body is fighting a battle of life and death against alien bacteria.

A violent fight on a bloody battlefield. Yet so calm on the surface.

He leans closer and whispers in her ear:

"You've got to help me, Sukayana. Where are they? Where are the girls?"

He wonders if any part of her brain registers his words. He once read about a Belgian man who lay in a coma for twenty-three years, then woke up and said he had heard everything that had been going on around him.

"We can't find the house, Sukayana," he says. "And the barn with the wolves. We know there are girls there, and we've got to try and rescue them. Please wake up. Tell me where the house is."

The monitor starts to bleep and Sukayana opens her eyes.

Slowly comes around.

She looks at him.

"Do you remember who I am?" he asks.

She nods, but the tube is in the way when she tries to talk.

"I need to ask you a few questions. Can you write, if I give you a pen and paper?"

She nods again.

He digs out a spiral-bound notepad and ballpoint pen from his inside pocket and puts them in her hands. She raises the pad and starts writing before he has time to ask a question.

The letters take shape slowly and unevenly, and he can see that the pulse monitor clipped to her index finger is getting in her way.

Zack leans over and reads.

A pole.

"What sort of pole?"

She goes on writing.

Spinning at the top. Like a sun.

Is she hallucinating? Zack wonders, or is she remembering something from her childhood?

In his mind's eye he can see a bucket of children's windmills, the sort they used to sell at markets when he was little. They were on short sticks, and when you blew them they spun around and made colorful patterns.

She puts her hands down on the covers again and he sees her eyelids close. He gently takes hold of her shoulder to try to keep her awake.

The monitor carries on bleeping. The door swings open and the bearded doctor hurries over to Sukayana.

"She was awake a few moments ago," Zack says.

The doctor studies the graphs and numbers on the monitor and pulse oximeter.

"She's still weak," he says. "Very weak. You can have a little while longer with her, five minutes maximum, no more. Then she needs to rest. Okay? I'm afraid it looks as if the infection is getting the better of her."

Sukayana opens her eyes again, picks up the pad, and carries on writing.

Incredibly slowly now.

It's close to the house.

"You mean the house in the forest?" Zack asks. "What's close to the house?"

She looks at Zack and he can detect a weak smile at one corner of her mouth. She looks down at the pad again. The monitor is still bleeping. Zack feels like smashing it.

Tricked them. Was awake in the car afterward.

Saw it through window.

Don't remember more.

She puts the pad down and looks like she's gathering her

strength. The doctor is standing on the other side of the bed. He looks impatient and Zack is worried he's going to break off the interview at any moment.

She picks up the pad again. Her hand is trembling with the effort.

It was tall, you'll be able to see it.

"What will I be able to see?"

Five mins from house.

I think.

He tries to understand. Something spinning on a pole that she saw from the car. Is that what she means? But she was lying down in the car, so must have been looking up. So it must have been very tall. Something tall. A pole, she wrote. A flagpole? No, nothing ever spins at the top of a flagpole.

Then an image appears in his mind, a scene from a black-and-white Western movie.

"Do you mean a wind-powered water pump? Sixty-five feet high, maybe, with a load of windmill blades at the top?"

He thinks he can see a trace of a nod, but he's not sure.

The pen falls to the floor. Zack picks it up and tries to put it back in her hand, but she hasn't got the strength to hold it.

Her eyes are closed again. She's lying completely still.

Zack wants to ask so much more, but she's no longer with him.

The bleeping changes pitch. It cuts through Zack's ears.

"Damm it," the doctor says. "Out of the way!"

Zack gets up.

He looks at the monitor.

The line on Sukayana's EKG is flat.

58

ZACK RUNS into the Special Crimes Unit and sees that Deniz has moved her chair to Sirpa's desk and has her laptop in front of her. Behind them stand Niklas and Douglas, staring at one of Sirpa's screens.

Deniz waves him over.

"Look at this. I think we've found it."

She looks extremely focused. It's as if the events in the massage parlor just a few hours before never happened.

Zack hurries over. Tries to forget about Sukayana Prikon and the fact that he has just seen her die.

On the screen is an article from a daily paper.

Above the headline "New Hope for Old Technology" is a large picture that could have been a hundred years old if the colors weren't so sharp.

There it is. Exactly like he imagined.

The water pump consists of a wooden tower made up of four legs, getting narrower toward the top, held together by a number of diagonal crossbeams. At the top twenty small rotor blades are fixed to a large wheel, and out of the back sticks a tail that makes sure the rotor blades are always facing the wind.

Zack didn't even know there were such things in Sweden.

"The article was published in *Sala Allehanda* in September 2007," Sirpa says. "Now we just need to locate it on the map."

On a different screen Deniz is looking at Google Earth. She's zoomed in on Vittinge, a small village between Sala and Uppsala, where the article says the water pump is located. She zooms closer in an attempt to find it.

"What the hell," she says. "Why couldn't the reporter have been a bit more specific about the location? *North of Vittinge*, that could be anywhere."

"Isn't that a bit too far from Stockholm?" Zack asks.

Deniz types Kungsholmen and Vittinge into Google Earth to get a route description.

"No," Deniz says. "It takes about an hour and a quarter from here, so something like fifty minutes from Arlanda. That fits fairly well with what Nang Mon and Ah Noh said about how long they were in the car after arriving in Sweden. Anyway, there doesn't seem to be another pump like this closer to Stockholm."

"Look at this," Sirpa says. "I've found a better map."

Zack and Deniz lean in front of the screen. It's an article about the water pump, published on the Forestry and Agriculture website.

"Can you enlarge the map?" Deniz says, as she adjusts her own search on Google Earth.

Sirpa clicks and the map fills the screen, and in less than a minute Deniz has found what she's looking for.

"Look, it must be the thing sticking up from this meadow. That matches the picture in *Sala Allehanda* as well, doesn't it? Fields and meadows in the foreground, forest, and those two buildings in the background."

Zack examines the satellite image on Deniz's screen. If Yildizyeli wanted a base where they would be left undisturbed, they'd certainly found it. There aren't many houses in the border district between Västmanland and Uppland.

The farm with the water pump is relatively close to a main road. A series of four smaller roads lead from there to the house, probably narrow gravel tracks. The drive ought to take between five and ten minutes, matching what Sukayana Prikon said. One of the roads carries on quite some distance, but the other three all seem to stop at separate little cottages in the forest.

Zack thinks he's seen something, and points at the screen.

"Can you zoom in where that road ends?"

That makes it easier to see the house. And, even better, the barn next to it.

"It must be that one. A farmhouse and a barn. Just like Ah Noh and Nang Mon said."

There's no time to lose.

The Turks must know that Westberg's car exploded in Skärholmen, and not on the way to their meeting. They might also be aware of what happened at Eastern Massage, and that the police will have spoken to the Burmese women.

So what would they do then?

"Sirpa, have you got a list of the phone numbers of the massage parlors controlled by Yildizyeli?" he asks.

She points to a sheet of paper on the desk.

"I want each of us to dial one of the numbers, right now. Okay?"

He allocates numbers to Deniz, Sirpa, Niklas, and Douglas.

Douglas says nothing. Just nods and follows orders as if he were at the bottom of the hierarchy.

He killed his own friend.

If anyone ever needed debriefing, he does.

But Zack hasn't got time to think about that now. There are more lives at risk.

"Isn't Rudolf here?" Zack says.

"Right behind you, lad," Rudolf says, heading toward them with a mug of coffee in his hand.

"Great. Rudolf, can you call this number?"

He reels off seven digits.

"What do you want us to find out?" Deniz asks.

"If any of them are open."

They each call a number. Total silence descends on the office as they wait for the calls to be answered.

"Mine's gone straight to the answering machine," Deniz says.

"Same here," Niklas says.

Douglas, Zack, Rudolf, and Sirpa are still holding their phones to their ears. Five rings. Ten. They hang up.

"Let's check the last three numbers as well," Zack says.

Two more answering machines, and no answer from the third.

"They're shutting down," Zack says. "No doubt about it."

The others look at him quizzically.

"Yildizyeli. They're shutting down their operation in Sweden. Getting rid of the evidence and leaving. What do you think they'll do with the girls in the forest?"

He looks at the map on Sirpa's screen.

"Sirpa, can you print that out, please?"

He walks over to the printer and waits. Deniz goes with him.

"We're going to need backup," Deniz says. "And this time there's no question of the rapid response unit not coming."

The color printout emerges. Zack picks it up and examines it carefully.

"You're right," he says, giving the map to Deniz. "I just need to check that I've got enough extra clips."

He feels the leather pockets on his holster.

"Fuck!"

"What?"

"My Sig Sauer. I left it at the hospital."

"You're kidding? Why did you put it down there?"

"The magazine's been sticking for the past couple of days, and I was sitting there trying to clean it while I waited for Sukayana to wake up. Then her doctor came in, so I hid it quickly under the cushion of the chair. I didn't want him to see me sitting in Intensive Care with a pistol. Later I just picked up my jacket and left, without even looking at the chair. I was badly shaken up by Sukayana's death."

Deniz shakes her head and looks at him with concern.

"You've really got to get your act together."

"I'll go back to the hospital and get it. Can you sort out the operation in the meantime? I'll be back within half an hour."

"Come down to the garage when you get back. We should be ready to set off by then."

Zack closes the door of the Special Crimes Unit behind him and heads toward the elevators. He looks back to make sure no one's watching, then stands on tiptoe and carefully pushes up one of the ceiling panels. He sticks one hand into the gap, grabs his pistol, and tucks it inside his jeans. He pulls his T-shirt down over it, and presses the elevator button.

59

TWO MEN leave the house, following a well-worn path into the pine forest.

One is wearing a black T-shirt and has an Uzi slung over his shoulder. A livid red scar runs down one cheek to his neck.

"Did you bring the ropes, Hakan?" he says to the other man, with cropped hair in camouflage clothing.

"Yes, I've got them here," Hakan says, holding up the coils in his hand.

The air is buzzing with midges.

"Fucking hell," the man with the scar says, scraping the remains of a bloody midge from the back of his neck. "They're almost worse than back home. I lay awake half the night scratching."

"You've turned into a real wimp, Tuncay, an urban sissy," Hakan says. "I'll have to ask Thrakya to put you to work up the mountains, to make a man of you again."

"Like hell you will."

Hakan holds out a pack of Maltepe. "Here, have a cigarette. The smoke keeps them away."

As they approach the dug-out cellar Tuncay pulls off his Uzi and aims it at the door. Hakan takes a jangling set of keys from his jeans pocket and looks through them to find the right one.

Then he pulls a pistol from the waistband of his trousers, a silver Zigana M16, and holds it in his hand as he undoes the padlock.

Inside the dark cellar the girls huddle together as they hear the men's voices, then the sound of the padlock being removed and the bolt slid back.

A newborn baby is lying in the arms of one of the girls, Than Than Oo. A little boy with black hair, curly from the damp air of the cellar.

He's lying in his mother's arms, sleeping soundly. Than Than Oo holds him tightly to her chest and whispers that everything is going to be all right.

60

ZACK PULLS on his helmet and turns the ignition of the Hayabusa, and it roars into life.

Deniz is going to kill me, he thinks. But time's running out. If he waits until the operational team is assembled, it could be too late.

The Turks are shutting down.

And they're unlikely to go to the effort of taking the girls out of the country.

Alone against five, ten, maybe twenty armed members of the Turkish mafia. What a great idea. How exactly were you thinking of sorting this out on you own?

He knows it's crazy, but he has to make sure that real justice is achieved.

There are young girls out there.

Children, like Ester.

He has to do it, for her sake.

For Sukayana's.

And for the murdered women. The ones who were forced to come here and were treated like meat by men like Sten Westberg.

And for Mom's.

The clock on the instrument panel says 5:36. He should be able to get there before half past six if he tries.

He flies along the E18 at ninety miles an hour, and is

fifteen miles from Enköping when he hears the police siren behind him.

Not now.

He checks the rearview mirror. A patrol car. Probably a traffic unit from Enköping or Uppsala.

There's no way he's thinking of stopping.

The wind tears at his jeans and thin leather jacket as he accelerates to 120 miles an hour, and watches the patrol disappear from view behind him.

A few minutes later he reaches Enköping, slows down sharply, and leaves the freeway without encountering another patrol. He carries on heading north on minor roads, passing villages with names like Äs, Brunnsta, and Larsbo, houses with traditional rust-red façades and white paintwork, until he eventually reaches Highway 72, where he turns left toward Vittinge. When he reaches the village he turns off again, following a winding road lined with dense forest, before taking another left turn and heading due north along a poorly maintained gravel track, surrounded by even thicker forest.

Clouds of insects hit the visor of his helmet, and the trees are the height of three-story buildings. He imagines he can see wolves in the darkness between the trees, and wonders if he's getting as crazy as the people he's hunting.

Then the landscape opens out. Large yellow fields spread out, and off to the left he sees what he's been looking for: the water pump.

It stands on the boundary between field and forest, and Zack can't help feeling that he's been transported back a hundred years in time.

He slows down to take a better look. It's nowhere near as tall as he was expecting. Perhaps fifty feet at most. At the base of the wooden tower is a small round pond, but Zack can't see if there's any water in it.

The treetops are swaying gently in the light breeze, but the rotor of the wind pump isn't moving. Zack wonders why anyone would choose to build it there, of all places, in a field surrounded by tall forest. The island of Öland or the southern province of Skåne feel like they would have been more suitable locations.

Perhaps someone thought it was attractive, or just wanted to have a unique landmark. They certainly achieved that.

Zack checks the GPS on his cell. About two miles to go. He rides a bit farther along the gravel road, keeping an eye out for the even smaller track that ought to lead off to the left anytime now.

It appears immediately after a sharp bend, and even though Zack is driving slowly he only sees it at the last moment. The opening is almost covered by leafy branches.

The track is more of a wide path than a road. It's made of compacted soil and roots, and so narrow that the branches must scratch the paint of any vehicle that tries to drive down it. Zack can barely manage twelve miles an hour, and has to weave constantly between the biggest roots and rocks to avoid damaging the Hayabusa.

After half a mile he stops and checks the GPS again. He's about half a mile from the house now, and he doesn't want the Turks to hear the sound of the motorcycle and get suspicious.

He looks for a suitable place to hide the bike, and discovers two rough tire tracks made by a heavy-duty piece of forestry machinery leading off into the pine trees to his right.

He follows one of the tire tracks until he's out of sight from the main path. He leaves the bike there leaning against a tree. He's shivering after the cold ride, and the midges start to attack him at once. He swats them away, jogs back to the track, and runs the last stretch toward the house. Every sense is alert, he slows down at the slightest sound, ready to throw himself into the forest at any moment.

A ramshackle little cottage with large holes in its roof appears on his left. Zack can't recall having seen it on the satellite picture of the area. Huge pine trees reach up into the sky on either side of the shack, and Zack guesses that their branches hide the roof from above.

A hundred yards farther on, Zack can just make out a large barn through the trees, and he darts quickly into the forest. The ground is covered with soft moss, and he moves silently and carefully.

Soon he can see the whole of the faded red side of the barn. He crouches down behind a large, moss-covered rock, looking for any sign of movement. There's no one in sight.

The silence is broken by the sound of an old door opening. Then he hears the screaming of frightened girls.

And barking and growling.

Fuck. What's going on? Are they throwing more people to the wolves?

He pulls out his Sig Sauer and runs toward the barn.

DOUGLAS COMES rushing out of his office.

"Where's Zack?"

"On his way here, I hope," Deniz says.

She's just put on her thin white summer jacket, and is on her way down to the garage for a last run-through with the rapid response unit.

"So why have I just been told that he was seen a short while away racing away from a patrol car on the E18 outside Enköping?"

Deniz freezes midstride.

"Zack, you bastard," she mutters to herself.

He tricked her. He tricked them all. He didn't go to Södermalm Hospital to pick up his pistol. He headed straight off to Vittinge.

He's thinking of tackling the mafia guys on his own.

She looks at Douglas and can see in his eyes that he too has worked out what's going on.

He grabs his jacket so roughly that the hanger falls to the floor, and says as they're hurrying for the door:

"Now it really is urgent."

Deniz follows him out.

Why, Zack? What are you trying to prove? she thinks. Do you think you can save your mother by rescuing those women in the forest?

In that case you're more damaged than I realized.

But also braver.

Braver than anyone should be.

HIS SIG Sauer feels cold in his hand as Zack creeps along the back of the barn.

Crooked planks, red paint peeling off.

He's trying to find a door, but can't see one, and follows the wall until he reaches the corner. He crouches down.

Dare I look around the corner?

Is someone standing there with a pistol, ready to shoot me?

Sweat on his forehead.

Racing heartbeat.

More screaming from inside the barn.

He hasn't got a choice. He peers cautiously around the corner.

Thirty yards away is a small red farmhouse, tucked next

to the edge of the forest. A black Toyota van is parked on the grass beside it. An out-of-place warm glow is coming from the kitchen window, but he can't see any movement.

Tall, wide doors in the middle of the barn wall.

Closed. He can't go in that way, or he'll run straight into Yildizyeli.

But beyond the doors is a sturdy flight of wooden steps that must lead up to a hayloft.

The shutters of the loft are wide open, and that's where the screaming is coming from.

And the growling.

Zack looks out at the idyllic scenery. The greenery, the wind rustling the trees. Then comes another scream, and he thinks of what Nang Mon said in the police car out in Skärholmen.

They pushed her over the edge.

The wolves tore her to pieces.

In here is where it happens.

Then there's a gruff male voice, a baby starts crying, followed by a woman's voice:

"No, no. Please, no!"

Zack can hear the terror in her voice. Clutching his Sig Sauer, he runs for the flight of steps.

He's expecting to be shot at any moment, by someone in the house or hidden among the trees.

But he doesn't hesitate, as if bullets can't hurt him now. As if he has some sort of invisible protection that other people lack.

He practically flies up the steps with his pistol raised in front of him.

The screams.

Forcing their way into him for good. Pitch-black screams, as if from a world bereft of light.

Zack doesn't hesitate.

He rushes out into the loft.

Piles of old hay to his left. A pitchfork and a rusty shovel leaning against a wooden crate.

Farther in, a muscular man with an Uzi in his hands, and an ugly scar covering half his face.

Tuncay.

Next to Tuncay, three girls, skinny and dirty. One of them has a naked baby in her arms.

In the gloom he sees what he came to put a stop to.

Another girl, far too close to the edge of the loft. A pumped-up man with cropped hair and wearing a camouflage jacket is holding her tightly in his thick arms.

The girl's hands have been tied behind her back, and she falls silent when she sees Zack, staring at him in surprise, and the look in her eyes pleads: *Save me!*

Keep me in this world.

When the man catches sight of Zack he picks her up and swings her over the edge.

Let's go.

The girl screams again as she falls. A scream beyond the bounds of humanity.

A different sort of scream from the mouth of the baby.

The girls are looking at Zack.

Tuncay. The other man.

Everyone is looking at him.

There are wolves growling below the loft, and then that scream which can't be human but is.

Tuncay raises the Uzi and aims it at Zack, who throws

himself to one side as he fires off three shots in quick succession.

Bullets spray out of the Uzi. Hit the space where Zack was standing, and as he tumbles onto the rough wooden floor of the loft he sees blood seep through Tuncay's shirt. He drops the Uzi and falls heavily.

Zack hears jaws closing on flesh, a throat crushed by a carnivore's teeth, and then the baby is screaming alone.

The man in the camouflage jacket has pulled out a pistol.

From his position on the floor Zack fires his Sig Sauer again. He misses, but the man's fear of being hit makes him take a step in the wrong direction.

He stumbles over the edge of the loft.

Flails with his arms.

Grabs one of the three remaining girls by the arm and pulls her down with him.

Zack throws himself forward.

Grabs her other arm by the wrist and braces one shoe against a protruding piece of wood. He stops her falling, but the man hanging from her other arm is pulling her down.

She screams. Out of fear, pain.

Zack is close to the edge now, looks down, and sees a creature with a gray-white pelt tearing lumps of flesh from the body of the girl who fell.

The straw is turning red.

So much blood.

The girl's arm slides through his grasp. He struggles to get a better grip and she looks up, begging with her eyes.

A snarling wolf jumps up and sinks its teeth into the calf of the man in the camouflage jacket.

He roars with pain.

Kicks at the air, and Zack can no longer hold on with just

one hand. He lets go of the pistol and takes hold of the girl's wrist with both hands, and tries to find somewhere firm to brace his other foot, and then the wolf lets go of the man's leg and Zack finally manages to get a better foothold.

He pulls.

Then the wolf takes another leap and bites the man in the crotch.

And clings on.

The look in the man's eyes changes, becomes nothing but pain, and his hand finally lets go of the girl's arm.

Zack pulls her up as he sees the wolves descend upon their new prey.

She curls up silently on the floor of the loft.

Zack gets to his knees and tries to find his pistol.

There.

It's balanced on the edge of the loft, its barrel sticking out, and he's about to reach for it when he looks up and sees a skinny man in a black suit holding Tuncay's Uzi in his hands.

The narrow face.

The dimple in his chin.

The dead look in his eyes.

Ösgür Thrakya.

The shadow.

He smiles, and his greenish-yellow eyes flash like a wolf's.

Zack looks into the barrel of the Uzi pointing at him and is filled with shame.

You let them down.

He looks at the girl who's still lying beside him, not daring to move. The young mother has taken a few steps forward and is halfheartedly trying to soothe her child. The slightly older girl standing beside her in a torn red undershirt is shaking.

The mother stares at him, a pleading look in her eyes.

Ösgür Thrakya smiles and shakes his head slightly.

Go on then, do it.

You're enjoying this, aren't you? Looking at me before you kill me.

"You're going to die now," he says in heavily accented English.

"Go to hell."

"So much effort for a few whores."

Ösgür Thrakya's voice is thin but full of poison.

"Kill me, then. But why do you have to kill the girls and the baby?"

Ösgür Thrakya smiles again.

"They're no use to us anymore. You know how it is, stock that isn't being used is just a waste of money."

"And the baby?"

"The wolves will probably have room for that too."

Tuncay is writhing in agony next to Ösgür Thrakya. He looks up at his boss and says something, and Ösgür Thrakya nods and turns back toward Zack.

"I was thinking of letting the wolves have you, but Tuncay says he wants to shoot you."

Tuncay manages to sit up. Without moving the Uzi away from Zack, Ösgür Thrakya reaches out a hand to help him up.

Then it happens.

The girl in the red undershirt makes her move.

Every muscle in her body tenses, and she throws herself at Ösgür Thrakya with a howl. She grabs his narrow waist in an attempt to knock him off balance and bring him to the floor.

For a moment, no more than two seconds, the barrel of the Uzi is pointing up in the air.

That's long enough.

Zack kicks Ösgür Thrakya in the face and hears his nose crunch.

The Uzi fires off a hail of bullets, hitting a wooden beam in the roof and showering the loft with splinters.

Another kick, and Ösgür Thrakya falls, with the girl still clinging onto him. The Uzi slips from his grasp and Zack grabs it just as Thrakya manages to shove the girl aside. He gets to his feet, shakily, with blood running from his nose and mouth.

Zack takes a deep breath, relieved at having the situation under control at last.

The girl with the baby smiles, as does the girl in the red undershirt, but then their smiles fade as Zack is forced down by an immense weight on his back and shoulders.

Tuncay. How the hell could I forget him?

Somehow he manages to stay on his feet, and keep hold of the Uzi.

He uses the momentum of Tuncay's body and leans forward, crouches down, then pushes up with his legs. They turn a somersault together and Tuncay ends up on his back with Zack on top of him, just three feet from the edge of the loft.

Ösgür Thrakya has pulled a knife and is coming toward them.

The long curved blade shimmers faintly, but Zack still has the Uzi in his hands and fires a hail of bullets that tears off Ösgür Thrakya's entire left arm.

The skinny man stops.

Stares at the blood pumping from the stump.

Zack tries to get to his feet, but Tuncay's strong arms are holding him tight and he is slowly being dragged toward the edge. Then he hears a sharp metallic clang and feels Tuncay's body go limp.

Zack looks up and sees the girl in the red undershirt holding the rusty shovel in her hands.

Tuncay is lying motionless on the floor.

Ösgür Thrakya staggers toward Zack with the knife.

Zack has been longing for this moment.

He could disarm Ösgür Thrakya and then hold him until backup arrives, but he's not going to do that.

He has no intention of listening to his lies in an interview room.

He's not going to let him fly in a team of expensive lawyers who will make sure his sentence gets reduced.

The judicial system doesn't apply here.

Divine justice will be served.

Here and now.

Ösgür Thrakya stabs at him several times with the knife, but Zack is ready for him. He kicks him on his bleeding stump and Thrakya's legs give way in agony, and Zack follows through with another kick, this time to the arm holding the knife.

The knife falls down toward the wolves.

Zack twists the stump of Ösgür Thrakya's arm behind his back.

He knows the pain must be unbearable, but the man doesn't scream.

Zack leads him toward the edge of the loft.

You're going to die now.

"You'd never do it. You're a Swedish policeman. I know how you work," Ösgür Thrakya gasps.

Zack looks down into the wolf pit.

Body parts and entrails are strewn about the floor.

A sea of blood.

Four wolves chewing on human flesh.

"I'm doing it now."

Zack gives Ösgür Thrakya a shove in the back and watches him land on the remains of the man in the camouflage jacket.

Two of the wolves look up from their lumps of meat and growl, their jaws dripping with blood.

Ösgür Thrakya is on his feet, limping toward the wall, reaching his remaining arm up toward Zack.

At last he looks scared.

"Please, help me up. I'll give you all the money you want."

Money.

He was going to throw a baby to the wolves.

He was going to throw the girls down there.

Girls the same age as Ester.

"Please. I'm begging you."

The open hand.

But Zack turns and walks away from the edge.

Then comes the howl.

Tuncay is lying motionless on the floor. The girl in the red undershirt is still standing over him with the shovel, and the others are huddled behind her. The baby is still crying.

Zack turns Tuncay over, sits on top of him, gets out his cuffs, and fastens his hands behind his back. He looks up at the girl with the shovel.

"What's your name?"

She looks at him uncomprehendingly. He repeats the question in English.

"Sanda Moe," she says.

"Are there any more men in the house, Sanda Moe?"

Zack searches Tuncay methodically, and he groans weakly.

"I don't know. We've never been there, only in the dark place."

Zack finds nothing but a pack of cigarettes.

"The dark place?" he asks.

"It's like a small hole, dug in the forest."

"How long have you been in Sweden?"

She thinks.

"Three weeks."

"Have you been here in the forest all that time?"

She doesn't answer.

Zack can see the girls shivering in the cool night air of the loft and decides to take them to the house.

"Sanda Moe, can you handle a pistol?"

"No, but Tin Khaing can."

She points to the girl in the large T-shirt, the one Zack saved from the wolves. Her lips are covered in sores and she has a livid black eye.

Then Sanda points to the girl with the baby.

"And that's Than Than Oo and her son. He's only one day old and doesn't have a name yet."

The little boy's crying has stopped, but Zack's ears are still ringing.

"Well, his lungs certainly work," he says, attempting a smile, but it just feels stiff and unnatural.

Zack hands the Sig Sauer to Tin Khaing.

"In case anyone else shows up," he says.

"Okay," she says.

Tuncay lifts his head and looks around in confusion. Zack drags him to his feet, presses the barrel of the Uzi hard in his back, and leads him away toward the steps.

Sanda puts the shovel back against the wooden crate and follows them.

The crate.

Zack stops and stares at it.

It's almost as big as a coffin. Fully covered by a lid, with two holes in one of the ends.

He turns to Tuncay.

"Lie down on your stomach!"

Tuncay doesn't move.

Zack sighs and kicks his legs out from under him.

Tuncay lands heavily on his front and the breath goes out of him.

"Tin Khaing, shoot him if he moves."

He goes over to the wooden crate and lifts the lid. At one end, around the two holes, are patches of dried blood.

At the other end is a colorful scrap of fabric. He picks it up.

A plaited wristband.

The sort Sukayana Prikon was wearing when we questioned her, he thinks.

They must have shut her in the crate, with her legs sticking out of the holes.

And then lowered her down to the wolves.

How could anyone do that?

He goes back to the girls. Tin Khaing is pointing the pistol at Tuncay's head.

Zack pulls him up onto his feet again and says to them:

"Come on. We're leaving."

Out into the light summer evening. The midges are buzzing, and a smell of pine forest replaces the animal excrement and blood.

The kitchen window is still lit up, but there's no sign of life.

"Sanda Moe, is it far to that dark place you mentioned?"

"No, it's just over there."

"Show me. I was thinking we could put Tuncay in there for a while."

For the first time Zack sees her smile.

"Fine by me."

Zack knows he ought to question Tuncay about Yildizyeli, about Sten Westberg, and how many women in total they've smuggled into the country. But he hasn't got the energy. Not right now. Someone else can do it.

But he does have one question that can't wait.

"Mehmet Drakan. Where's he?"

The man in the garage out in Farsta, the one with the tattoo on his neck. He ought to be here.

"Mehmet . . . I don't know a Mehmet." Tuncay smirks in response.

Zack shoves him into the cellar and locks the door. Then he creeps into the house and checks that it really is empty before beckoning the others inside.

THEY'RE SITTING around the kitchen table, drinking steaming hot cups of tea. Zack has found some blankets that he's draped around their shoulders, and Than Than Oo is nursing her son.

Tin Khaing is sitting on the kitchen sofa with Sanda Moe, sobbing in her arms. Zack assumes they're mourning the loss of their friend. The one he didn't arrive in time to save.

He doesn't even know her name.

Sanda Moe strokes Tin's cheek and looks at Zack.

"You're a good person," she says.

Am I? Zack wonders. I fight and kill without reflection. I have no respect for my own life. Can a man like that be a good person? I may well have rescued you for my own sake.

He looks out through the kitchen window. He wonders how long it took Deniz to see through his bluff, and he considers what to say to her when she arrives.

And to Douglas.

The baby finishes nursing. Than Than Oo stands up and goes over to Zack. She holds the boy out to him.

Zack takes him.

So small, so light.

He holds the baby stiffly, cautiously, as if he were made of the most fragile glass. Looks at the tiny hands, feels the warm little body against his. Smiles at the child's happy burbling.

Than Than Oo looks at Zack.

"What's your name?" she asks. "I'm going to name him after you."

61

Aftonbladet, June 18:

Here, in a ramshackle barn in the forest, wolves were fed with human flesh.

"The victims included children," a police source has told *Aftonbladet*.

The truth behind one of the most shocking waves of murders in modern history is gradually becoming clearer.

A criminal network with links to Turkey and Burma has been smuggling women into Sweden for prostitution. The police now suspect that several of the women were murdered and thrown to the wolves, which were kept locked in a barn in the forests outside Vittinge, west of Uppsala.

A number of people fell victim to the wolves, and *Aftonbladet* can today reveal that . . .

Svenska Dagbladet, June 19:

The remains of another victim have been found in the so-called "wolf barn" outside Vittinge.

A total of six people are now feared to have died.

"But that number could rise. Our forensics officers are still busy at the scene, and we have sent bones and other remains to the National Forensics Laboratory for analysis," says Torbjörn Berg of the Stockholm Police's Information Department.

The discovery of the wolf barn is the result of intense detective work led by the Special Crimes Unit, the department of Stockholm Police that focuses on particularly complex crimes.

Zack Herry, a detective inspector with the unit, is being praised as a hero by the survivors.

"He was the one who found us and rescued us. Otherwise we would have been thrown to the wolves as well," says Sanda Moe, one of the Burmese girls who were being held captive in the forest.

An extensive trafficking network which brought Asian women into Sweden to work as prostitutes has been broken up.

A 37-year-old Turkish citizen has been remanded in custody on suspicion of involvement in the network. He was arrested by Zack Herry at the barn.

Several other members of the group are believed to be at large.

"We can't rule out the possibility that they may have left the country," says Douglas Juste, operational head of the Special Crimes Unit.

The four wolves, believed to be an alpha pair and their adult offspring, have been taken to the wildlife park at Kolmården. Their origins are as yet unknown, and tests will be taken in an attempt to determine if they were captured illegally or smuggled into the country.

The wolves' fate has not yet been decided.

Expressen, June 19:

Expressen's crime reporter, Fredrik Bylund, was among the victims of the Wolf Gang.

His remains have been identified in the torture barn outside Vittinge.

"This is an extremely tragic day for *Expressen*, but our thoughts are primarily with his family," says the paper's editor-in-chief, Thomas Mattsson.

Bylund, crime reporter for *Expressen*, had devoted days of hard work to investigating the convoluted wave of murders being committed in Stockholm.

He left the newsroom late on Thursday evening, and was never seen again.

"We were supposed to meet at nine o'clock the following morning, but he never showed up," says an anonymous source.

The police suspect that Bylund was kidnapped sometime that night, in all likelihood because he knew too much.

"Fredrik Bylund was an extremely dedicated reporter, he never backed down until . . ."

Avpixlat, nationalist website, June 22:

Ingvar Stefansson, the Swedish patriot who was murdered by the Swedish police on Thursday, was innocent.

While the police devoted a vast amount of resources to hunting him down, a gang of Turkish criminals was able to continue committing appalling crimes on Swedish soil.

Stefansson was a knowledgeable and popular contributor, who wrote incisively about new research into migration and ethnology—important information which the established media persist in ignoring.

Stefansson was wrongly accused of involvement in a crime which had nothing to do with him, and was shot and killed by police officer Zack Herry, a man who, according to information received by *Avpixlat*, had his ideas of right and wrong shaped by growing up in a suburb with a high immigrant population.

Ingvar Stefansson died a warrior's death, murdered by the Swedish authorities because of his beliefs.

We shall never forget him.

62

ANOTHER AREA of high pressure has swept in, and the twenty-five-year-old laborer is sweating in his blue T-shirt as he kneels down to screw a new lock onto the door of a massage parlor in Vasastan.

The lobby smells of cleaning products, and in among the massage tables two men in leather vests are talking to three young women in identical turquoise T-shirts.

"No, nothing's going to change," one of them says, a slim, intelligent-looking man. "The only difference is that we'll be organizing things instead of the Turks. Okay?"

A short-haired woman in a tight top and gray tracksuit bottoms says:

"We're happy to go on working here and give massages, but there were other things we had to do before, and we don't want to do those anymore."

The man's smile vanishes.

"Like I said, nothing's going to change. You're going to carry on offering clients exactly the same services you offered them before."

63

ZACK IS standing next to the hospital bed, looking at Abdula's face. His eyes are closed, and there's a plastic tube sticking out of his neck.

He's just spoken to one of the doctors in the intensive care unit. Abdula can't breathe on his own, and he's not responding to pain or light. It's unclear if he's ever going to regain consciousness, or what state he'll be in if he does.

Zack stands by the bed for a long time. Listening to the rhythmic hiss of the respirator.

"Sorry," he whispers. "I'm sorry."

He sees Abdula come running with the metal rod in his hands. Sees him dancing through the night in the flashing light of the stroboscope.

Their hands meeting high in the air, over and over again, through the months and years, throughout the whole of their lives.

Is all that over now?

It can't be over. The thought makes him utterly black inside.

He squeezes his friend's hand.

Then he walks out into the bright sunlight, over to the parking lot where he left his motorbike.

He weaves his way out through the Karolinska University Hospital's maze of buildings and temporary cabins and heads south.

From death's waiting room to death's final stop.

A journey of a quarter of an hour.

He turns off the Nynäshamn road at Tallskogen and rides into the lush greenery of the Woodland Cemetery. He parks on Minneslundsvägen, drapes his leather jacket over his shoulder, and heads down the gravel paths to his mother's grave.

Doesn't look back over his shoulder,

Doesn't see the car pulling up behind him, or the man who gets out.

The green grass looks radiant in the hot sun, and in his mind's eye he sees his colleagues' blood in the neon light of the massage parlor in Skärholmen.

He can smell it, as well as the scent of the flowers.

A mixture of the two.

And then he's back in that meadow again.

Isn't it ever going to end?

The grit on the path crunches beneath the soles of his shoes as he wanders through the neatly kept cemetery toward the grave. There are fresh flowers in front of many of the gravestones. Three roses, a colorful summer bouquet, a teddy bear, and some drooping bluebells in a child's mug with big yellow ears for handles.

There are no flowers on Anna Herry's grave. The headstone is partly covered by a thin layer of green moss, and the lettering has lost its luster.

Zack stops in front of it, puts his hands in his jeans pockets, but takes them out again.

Anna Herry.

The name is carved in ornate, gilded lettering at the top of the stone. The plan was that there would be space for Dad's name underneath, but Zack didn't want that. He wanted to be able to visit them separately.

Sometimes he regrets his decision. Now he has two graves that he doesn't look after instead of one.

Anna Herry.

What happened to you, Mom?

Who were you?

He conjures up an image of himself sitting in her lap.

He can still feel her soft knitted sweater against his cheek. Hear her soothing voice as she patiently replies to his questions, feel her breathing through the sweater. But he can't see her face in front of him anymore.

He tries to get the five-year-old boy to look up at his mother's face, but doesn't succeed.

All he sees are the police photographs of her after the murder. Her pale skin. The slash across her neck.

He doesn't want to think of that now. He wants to think about how soft that knitted sweater felt against his skin. But he feels sweaty and dirty and far too hot. And his mom isn't smiling when he does finally see her face. She looks angry. She's shouting at him. He doesn't understand what he's done wrong, but she's furious.

Lashes out.

Burning pain in his cheek. He puts his hand to it. His cheek is hot from the sun.

He leaves the grave and walks into the shade of a large oak. Sits down on the grass. Then lies back.

No one else in sight.

He's alone.

Or am I?

Something feels wrong, and he sits up.

Is someone watching him?

Not here. Not in this place.

He lies back down again.

Shuts his eyes.

Completely alone in a green sea of the dead.

Then he hears something approaching across the grass. A body, a man, and before he has time to sit up again he feels a sharp pain in his forehead.

He looks up, unsure of what's happening.

He can see a face getting closer, a large tattoo, a rearing horse with sharp teeth.

Mehmet Drakan.

Another blow. This time to his chest.

Zack rolls away, trying to catch his breath.

Searing pain in his lungs. Several of his ribs must be broken.

He parries Drakan's next blow, sees the brass knuckles on his fingers, but doesn't manage to roll out of the way. Drakan is on top of him now. His hands are clutching at Zack's neck, and he feels his consciousness begin to drift off into blackness. The first blow clearly hit him hard. And Zack kicks, scratches, twists his body, and tries to push upward.

Feels the smell of the grass.

Wishes he had some sort of weapon.

But he hasn't.

And Drakan pants as he squeezes Zack's throat tighter.

Blackness. Darkness.

Not now. Not yet. Not here. Not like this.

And Zack summons up all the strength in his body and directs it upward. He feels the weight on top of him ease, the grip around his neck loosen.

He gets up into a crouch.

Mehmet Drakan on the grass beside him. Starting to stand up.

Never.

Zack hurls himself at him. His own hands around a neck now.

He stares into Drakan's bulging eyes. Changes his grip.

And twists.

Hears the crunch of vertebrae snapping.

Zack rolls off him and lies back, flat out on the grass again.

No smell of blood now. Just grass and death.

He closes his eyes. Pretends it's night, and that he's surrounded by dark sky.

He feels his body being pressed down into the ground, as if the Earth were accelerating.

He's tired, beyond the bounds of tiredness.

He wishes he were a boy again. A boy who still bears the hope that the stars might come and carry him off into space.

Out into the vastness of forgetting.